W0028027

Dedication: Sherwin Rodrigues

I would like to take this opportunity to thank you for all your help. You believed in my writing ability from the very onset and gently pushed me to pursue my life's dream and follow it through. You have worked tirelessly reading and editing the manuscript in order to give it the finishing touches that it needed. I truly value your friendship and honesty. You have always been there for me. Thank you for being you and may God bless you.

Reader's Note

After any traumatic episode it is always important that you share your experiences with someone that you feel close to; someone who will keep your confidences and stand by you as you struggle to get your life back together; someone to help you deal with the resentment, anger and pain; a true friend who will not judge but will be there for you to help pick up the pieces of your shattered life and help you find solace. Although the names and places in this novel are fictional some of the events that transpired are based on actual occurrences. Due to my love for writing I made a death-bed promise to a dear friend. It was her wish that I share the events that she had lived through to let others know that no matter what a person experienced in life if one had the support, love and understanding of family and friends they could make it through anything and become a stronger person because of that…

Chapter 1

I sat quietly on a rock by the water's edge. I looked out over the water and watched the waves as they caressed the shore; with every wave lapping the sand, leaving it fresh and untouched. How I wished that the water would do the same thing for my mind…help me forget all those painful memories of the past. In time you will forget…that is what I keep telling myself but as time passes the painful memories seem to be finding their way much closer to the surface. I console myself…One day you will awaken and be free of the memories and flashbacks forever. The tears begin unnoticed, slowly sliding down my cheeks. If only I could understand 'why'. Did it really mean nothing to him? What was to be gained? Would I ever be able to face the future without him? Could I ever really trust another man? He loved me, he told me so many times over the years. The promise…our promise to each other. Were they only empty words to him? I still held these words in my heart. Maybe if I could get past the hurt, the memories would go away? But how does one erase all that has happened? All these questions repeatedly flooded my mind…

The screech of the seagulls brought me back to reality. My body shivered from the cold and my mind was numb. I slowly stood and walked along the water's edge. Forget…that was the important thing. Push the memories deep inside and do not think about them any more. One day I would finally come to understand. Somehow I would eventually get to know the answers that I so desperately sought.

It was late by the time I returned home. I was still shivering from the cold. A nice warm bath would help me relax and perhaps see things differently. When I got out of the car I could smell the lilacs and roses that were in bloom in the back yard. The house was a small single-floor two-acred ranch. I had purchased it shortly after I had graduated from college. It had been built the year before and I fell in love with it as soon as I walked in the door. As soon as I saw the deck overlooking the backyard, I envisioned the landscaping that I would do. I would put in flower gardens leading to the pond. From the first day I moved in that was my sanctuary and I spent most of my time either working in the flowerbeds or sitting on the porch swing because it was so peaceful and serene. It was located on the edge of town and it gave me the privacy I desired but also it was close to town and work, making it convenient for me.

I put the tea kettle on to heat some water. As I ran my bath I lit the candles around the tub. The soft, sweet fragrance of the candles filled my nostrils and cleared my mind. The whistling of the tea kettle startled me. I quickly ran to take it off the burner to stop the noise. My head was pounding. I made a cup of tea to take to the bath so that I could relax in the warm water, slowly sip my tea and forget about everything else. As I stepped into the hot water my muscles began to relax and I leaned back pushing all thoughts from my mind. It felt good to be in the hot water. Complete silence and tranquility. For the first time all day…no thoughts…just the smell of the candles and their light dancing on the walls and the ceiling. If only things could remain this peaceful and serene. No worries, thoughts or memories. If only…

The ringing of the phone jolted me back to reality. The quiet was now gone. *Let the machine take down the message* I told myself. *Just relax and do not think about anything.*

"Hello, I know you are there. Come on, pick up the phone. I will come over if you don't pick it up." There was giggling at the other end. "Did you think about what we talked about? I know it would help if you would just go."

"Do you still have his card?" inquired the female voice.

"Come on, pick up the phone. Okay, I will try again later. I will not stop until you answer the phone." There was more giggling at the other end.

It was Carol, a friend of mine, calling again to see if I was going to call the doctor—a therapist friend of hers. *How could I talk to a stranger about all that had happened to me? I would not know where to begin. Carol knew him well and knew that he could help bring me out of my shell, but why bring it all up again? What difference would it make now? The damage was done and there was no turning back. Maybe someday when I was ready I would give him a call.*

I got out of the bath and dried myself off...warm and relaxed but exhausted from the day's events. I finished the last of the tea and decided to go to bed. I needed a good night's sleep. I walked by the phone and pushed the button to erase the message. I looked down on the table and there was the card. I picked it up and looked at it. 'Dr. Shawn Goodson' it read. "Well, Dr. Goodson, do you think you can help me remember? Should I give you a call and see what kind of magic you could really perform? Do you have all the answers to my questions?" I asked aloud. I studied the card for a few minutes and then set it down. *Maybe when I am ready then I will give you a call, Dr. Goodson. But for now I am not ready to face the demons of my past.*

As I climbed into bed the thoughts began to surface again. *Why? If only I knew 'why'* I was fairly certain that I would not be troubled in this manner. *Could I not have just one night without the memories, flashbacks and nightmares? Maybe I should call Dr. Goodson? No, I was not ready to relive the past. I would rather just leave it alone. I will learn to get by and I will learn to be stronger and will just continue to fight it by myself. I know I will feel better in the morning. Things are always clearer in the morning light.* I felt uneasy but could not attribute any reason behind it. As I lay there thinking, I could feel myself drifting off to sleep...

Sleep came quickly but it was not the sound restful sleep that I had hoped for. As I tossed and turned on the bed, I could hear the thunder in the distance. I drifted back to sleep but soon the dreams surfaced again. As always it starts out with me being driven in a car. Headlights blind me. I cannot see where I am going. Never-ending brightness hurting my eyes. *No, please not again! Let me awaken…I do not want to experience it again!* The ride seems to last forever. *Why am I begging not to go? Why am I so afraid? Once again we are going by the lake. Please stop…let's just sit and enjoy the water. Don't take me any further. Please stop now!* Desperation in my voice. Jumbled memories flashing through my mind. *When is it going to stop?* Being taken from the car to a house. *Where am I? I do not know this place…nothing is familiar to me. Why am I here?* Fear and terror…those are the only things I can feel right now. *Please make it stop!* A flash of lightning bolts across the sky and the thunder rumbles menacingly. *Go, you must go now! Get out!* I am petrified for an instant in sheer terror and unable to move. Then my body reflexes respond and I run. *Run…go now before they get you! But who is going to get me? Why are they after me? My dream-like state is playing tricks with my mind…or is this real?* Terror fills my body. I am running now. Running for my life! Down into the woods but the path has gone. I am lost and do not know which way to go. The rain begins pouring down on me…Lightning flashes across the whole sky and the thunder resounds through the woods. *Run, don't stop now…run! Is it the storm or is it only my mind playing games with me? Each time the sky lights up it gives me the eerie illusion that the trees have come to life…mocking me, trying to grab me with their branches…holding me back so that I cannot run. The ferns and briar bushes seem to grow in front of my eyes…grabbing at my legs and ankles, slowing me down. Run, don't stop!* My own scream awakens me and I jump from my bed drenched in perspiration while tears stream down my face. My heart is pounding so hard it feels as though it is going to explode in my chest. My lungs are exhausted from breathing so hard from running. My arms and legs are burning from the skin being ripped off them by the thorns and briars. My bare feet bleed from the cuts caused by the tree roots and thorns. I look down at them and there are no scratches and no blood…only profound and vivid pieces of memories from deep within me. I pace the bedroom floor like a caged animal looking for a way to escape. *Why? Will I ever remember what happened that night or will I only be forced to live it out in my dreams? If only I knew 'why'.*

The room starts to close in on me. I go to the kitchen to make some tea. Tea always seemed to relax me. I sat at the table trying to figure out what I should do next and my eyes fall over the card once again. I pick it up and look at it. "Well, Dr. Goodson. Do you think you can help me? Can you tell me what these nightmares mean when I can't seem to remember?" A slow smile comes over my lips. *How could I talk to you Doctor Goodson when I could not seem to talk to anyone else about it? If only you could really help me. But was the pain too much for me to remember?* Eight years is a long time to be burdened with these painful memories. Bits and pieces were all I could seem to remember and it did not make any sense to me. I set the card back down. *Maybe one day I would have the strength I needed to walk into your office and open up my memories, mind and nightmares to you? Maybe you could figure out what they meant and why I could not seem to force them out of my mind?* As I sat there thinking, the sun started to rise in the sky…a glorious red sunrise. *If only my life could be as uncomplicated and beautiful as the sight before me. One day maybe…I could only hope…*

Chapter 2

The ringing of the phone broke the silence. I got up from the deck to answer it.

"Hello," I answered.

"Hi honey. Where are you?" queried Mom on the phone.

Laughing, I said, "Mom, I am standing in the kitchen talking to you on the phone."

She giggled and said, "You know what I mean. They are here setting up for the auction and you are supposed to be here to help."

"I'm sorry," I replied. "I got busy and lost track of time. I am going to take a quick shower, get dressed and will be right over."

"Okay, I will see you then. Bye for now," replied Mom.

"Bye, Mom," I replied cheerily.

After a quick shower I jumped in the car and was on my way. It was a bright sunny day for the auction. This was the second annual hospital benefit auction. This year they were having it out at my parent's farm. It was an 800 acre beef and horse ranch that had been handed down through the generations of our family. My great-great grand parents had purchased it in the early 1920's and it had been given to my parents when my grandmother passed away. When my parents got the house they made some renovations and made the necessary updates but they used as many of the original antiques that they could. Partly for the memories they held but mostly because Mom wanted to hold on to the past and the nostalgia that everything in the house held. Nothing was thrown out and she kept everything down to the last trinket that was in the house when they moved in. The house was built on a knoll. It overlooked the valley that led down to a pond that Dad had put in which was always full of wild birds and animals that would stop by to drink. It was a huge two-storey farmhouse with six bedrooms on the top floor. The main floor had a living room, parlour, bathroom, sitting room, dining room and the kitchen. There was also a smaller room off the kitchen where the servants used to eat. Most of the rooms were no longer used but Mom kept them cleaned and ready because she always maintained, "You never know if you are going to have unexpected guests and would need them." Over the last couple of years the cattle had been sold off keeping only a few cows along with the horses, goats, pigs and chickens that Mom just didn't want to part with. There was plenty of room and it would be easier to set up all the tables for the auction. Moreover, the ponies were there for the kids to ride. All the days' events were planned and if all went as scheduled there was still about an hour left to finish setting up.

As I pulled alongside the drive I could see all the commotion. Hank was setting up the harness ring to hook up the ponies. They had already dumped the sawdust for the money search. The tables were set up for the kids' party. Even the clown was dressed and ready to go, in case we had early arrivals. The stage was finalized and the banners were already in place. The band was doing a sound check so that they would be ready when the guests started to arrive. I rushed up to the house to see where I was needed the most. As I ran up the flight of stairs to the house my Dad opened the door for me. He was fifty-six years old with graying hair. His eyes were dark brown. He was a tall man with a very muscular build from all the work he had done through the years on the ranch.

"And just where have you been young lady?" he reprimanded in mock anger. "You were supposed to be here two hours ago." He did his best to look angry but I knew better.

"Oh Dad, you know me. Once I get started on something I hate to quit. I am here now and I am ready to help," I offered.

He smiled at me and I went up and gave him a hug and kiss. "You really need to work on your angry face," I said. "It's not working." I laughed and was quickly out the door to look for Mom who would be giving orders somewhere. She had turned fifty-six this year but looked very young for her age. Her hair was auburn and she had hazel eyes. She was as tall as dad but had a thin figure. She tended to worry too much about everything and was a very expressive person often using her hands when she spoke. She frequently put her hands on her hips to emphasize what she was trying to convey.

I stood on the porch and scanned the grounds looking for her. She was trying to convey what she wanted to a man whom I did not know. I could see the troubled look on his face, so I ran to his rescue.

"Hi, Mom. What do you need help with?" I inquired.

"It is about time you got here, Missy. I am trying to have the podium set just right and I can't seem to find the best place to put it. I don't want the announcer in the hot sun but the sun will be moving. I am just not sure where to put it," she explained with her hands perched firmly on her hips.

I looked around and came up with the best answer that I could think of: "I know Mom. Place one microphone here at this podium and we can get the other one from the hospital to use at the stage. That way you won't have to worry about the sun and we won't have to keep moving the podium around," I reasoned. "I can call Carol and have her pick it up on her way out," I offered helpfully.

"Great! With that done everything else is all set. Why don't you run down to see if you can help Hank bring up the ponies and get them up here? We won't hook them up just yet but we don't want to bring them up with all the children running around," Mom stated looking around with that worried look in her eyes.

As I ran to the barn I felt like a child again with all the excitement going on around the house. I ran into the first barn and almost knocked Hank over.

"What exactly is your rush Katie, dear?" asked Hank.

"I'm sorry, Hank. I wanted to see Lacey before I helped you bring up the ponies. I didn't know you were in here," I explained apologetically.

"Well, slow down before someone gets hurt." His mocking, angry voice made me giggle as I ran past him to Lacey's stall. Lacey was a beautiful raven-black Arabian horse with a white diamond on her forehead. She whinnied when she heard my voice. I took out the carrots that I had brought for Lacey and spoke softly to her as I fed her. "I am spending the night, Lacey, so when everyone leaves we can go riding. It has been a long time since we have taken a night walk and it will be exciting," I whispered to Lacey confidentially.

"Are you going to help me or not?" Hank yelled as I stroked Lacey's neck.

"I'll be right there, Hank." A quick kiss on Lacey's nose and I was off to saddle up the ponies. "How many ponies are you going to be taking up, Hank?" I asked, as I finally caught up with him.

He replied, "We will start with ten and can take the older horses for the teens to ride. We can put them in the corral so they won't go running off on them."

"Which ones do you want me to start with?" I asked as I brushed the hair away from my face. The wind was blowing lightly and people were already starting to arrive.

"I'll grab the ponies that I have saddled and you can start putting the rest of the saddles on and bring them up when you are done," he replied. "We will wait until we know if we need the other horses. It doesn't take long to get them ready if we need them.

I watched as Hank slowly led the ponies out to the staging ring. He was fifty-five years old and could still work harder than the younger farm hands. He was just under six feet tall with broad shoulders and a narrow waist. His eyes were sky blue but you could see the sadness that lay within them. When his wife was alive I used to go over and help her with the canning each fall. We used to sit and talk for hours. They had wanted children of their own but after a year of trying to conceive she went to the doctor for tests and found out that she had cancer. The treatments worked for a while but soon spread rapidly throughout her body. She had passed away two years ago and Hank missed her dearly. I was glad that he had decided to continue working on the farm instead of leaving everything behind and traveling with the rodeo. I had known him all my life and he lived in the small cabin, right next to our farm. He was like a father to me. He watched out for me and was always giving me good advice. It was he that I usually went to when I needed someone to talk to.

I finished saddling the rest of the ponies. Hank had returned by then to take up four more ponies. I grabbed the reins and brought up the remaining two. Hank thanked me for my help as we finished hooking them up into the harness rings. He was going back down to the barn. I told him that I had to go help with the chairs but I made him promise me that he would come up later to join in the festivities. He placed his hand over his heart and promised. I told him I would come and get him if he did not show up.

I headed back up to the house and I saw Carol drive up. Carol and I had gone all through school together and to the same college. Later we had ended up getting jobs at the same place. She was just five feet tall with long flowing blonde hair. She had dark blue eyes and flirted with every man she saw. She did not have a perfect figure but she got noticed wherever she went. She was quick to anger and was not shy about speaking her mind when she had something to say. I went over to help her get the podium out of the car.

Scott arrived at the same time. Scott had gone to school with Carol and me. He had brown hair and blue eyes. He was short and stood just a few inches taller than Carol. He was wiry and thin and didn't have much of a personality. He acted like those around him owed him and most of the time he was rude and disrespectful. He always showed up at every function but it was mainly just to watch and see what he could get. He grabbed the podium and carried it over and placed it under the shade of the tree and hooked up the microphone. Now everything was ready for the auction. This year's proceeds were going to help build a new wing on the hospital for disabled children so that they could come in for physical therapy treatments.

During the previous year Carol and I had gone to every business in town. No matter how small, we stopped in to see if we could get their support and let them know about the benefit auction. Today we would find out just how many people we could count on for the project. Paul was our poster child for the benefit. He was a five-year old little boy with muscular dystrophy—a little blonde angel with beautiful blue eyes. I met him for the first time a few days after he was born. He was fine at first and then when he was three years old the disease took over his little body. He would be coming today and I was looking forward to spending time with him.

As people started arriving Carol and I would take the children to the circus spot that was set up just for them. We had the pony rides and had brought up a cow, lamb, goat and pig for the children to feed and pet. We had trained trick dogs to entertain them. Even Clyde the clown had decided to stop in to help out and make some animal balloons for the children. We had the CD player and CDs all set for the dancing too. As the children were gathered around the table we had them write their names on the name tags sitting on the table. Carol got out the paints and brushes and let the children color pictures for the auction. I looked up just as Shirley was pushing Paul's wheelchair towards us. I stopped what I was doing and went up to meet them.

"Hi, Paulie!" I yelled. "How are you doing today? Are you ready to have lots of fun? I hope so because we have a lot of things planned and I don't want you to miss a thing."

"Do you want me to stay and help you," Shirley asked.

"No," I replied. "I have everything under control. You go up to the house and enjoy yourself. I will take good care of Paul and will make sure that he enjoys today." I pushed him over to the table and sat in a chair next to him as I asked him to pick out a name tag.

"What color would you like to write your name in sweetie?" I asked.

He looked over all the markers and said, "Katie, I would like blue. Blue is my favorite color in the whole wide world." I picked up the blue marker and handed it to him. When he was done I took the name tag and placed it on his shirt.

"There. You are now officially at the party!" I giggled as I watched him.

We started out with the money search. They had made three different piles of sawdust and had put change in so that the children could find the money and buy something at the auction. I asked Paul if he was ready.

"I can't do that," he said frowningly as he looked around.

Why not?" I asked.

"I can't reach the money in my chair," he replied.

"I will help you. I have an idea and I know it will work," I told him as though I had just come up with the biggest plan that could ever be imagined.

"Here let me unbuckle your belt for you. I am going to pick you up and we will sit on the ground and together we will find all kinds of money."

"You will really help me, Katie?" his eyes became as big as saucers as he looked at me.

"I will help you any time you want me to," I whispered into his ear.

He looked around as though he was afraid everyone had heard our well-thought-out plan. He quickly unbuckled his safety belt. I picked him up and waited for the 'one...two...three...go' signal. Carol counted it out and I quickly sat him on the sawdust, sitting behind him to help support him as he searched for the money. We had a jar next to us so that he could fill it. The other kids had gone to the first two piles thinking there was more money in them. There were only five of us in our pile. Paul giggled as he found the first few coins and he placed them in the jar. For the next ten minutes we searched and threw sawdust at each other. His jar was almost filled when the whistle blew to signal the end. We looked at each other and laughed because we didn't know what had more sawdust, the pile or us. I picked Paul up and put him back in his wheelchair and brushed myself off. The auction was beginning because I could hear the auctioneer commence his speech to the waiting crowd. I asked Paul what he would like to do next. His eyes looked around and grew very large when he saw the ponies.

"Do you think I could pet one of the ponies?" he asked in a voice just above a whisper.

"You can do more than that. Come on I will show you," I volunteered.

I pushed him over to the ponies and I had Hank hold the pony while I picked him up and placed him on the pony's back. He looked at me with fear in his eyes.

"Don't worry, Paul," I said as I placed him in the saddle. "I am right here and I am not going to let anything hurt you. I will walk with the pony. Hold on firmly to the reins and you will be able to ride."

At first he was very tense but as I slowly walked beside him holding him in the saddle he gradually relaxed and enjoyed his first pony ride. The ringing of the bell signaled that it was time to eat and the kids ran over to the tables to pick a chair to sit in. I slowly picked Paul up from the saddle and put him back into his chair. I pushed him over to the table and asked him where he wanted to sit. I suggested that he sit on the end table because there were a lot of empty seats and I could sit and have lunch with him.

"That would be great!" He giggled as I pushed him along the other table.

I got him all set up and then went to fix our plates. He sat there so proudly because he got to participate in the fun instead of having to sit and watch from his chair. After we had eaten and cleared the table, we set up the CD player and put in a CD. Carol announced to have all the kids make a big circle.

I asked Paul if he was going to dance and with tear-filled eyes he said, "I can't dance, Katie.

"I am supposed to be in the middle of this circle and tell the kids what they are supposed to do. I can help you dance if you let me. Would you like to dance with me, Paul?" I asked.

"But I can't dance," he replied dejectedly as he looked around at the other kids.

"Do you trust me, Paulie?" I asked him.

"Yes, Katie I do," he responded.

"Okay, let me pick you up and you can dance with me. I will show you how," I told him.

I picked him up and carried him to the center of the circle and as Carol put on the music we began the 'Hokey Pokey'. I told Paul what we needed to do and he yelled out each step. As he called it out I had him do the moves.

"You sit on my hip and I will do the leg part and you do the rest of the parts and you will be dancing," I whispered into his ear.

Next we did the 'Bunny Hop' followed by the 'Chicken Dance'. After the songs were over I put Paul back into his chair and told him that I had to go up to the stage and help with the auction but that I would be back soon.

"Thank you, Katie," he said gratefully. "I have never danced before and it was really fun."

"You are the best dancer I have ever danced with, Paul, and I am honored that you let me be your first dance partner." I leaned over and kissed him on top of his head and turned to go.

I walked over to the table and stood next to it. Small items were being put together to be auctioned off by the auctioneer.

"You are a hard person to keep track of," laughed Dad.

"You knew where I would be Dad," I smiled as I looked at him.

"You should get married and have children of your own," he said.

"I am not ready to settle down yet, Dad. I will know when I am ready and I don't want to rush into anything," I replied.

Carol came up to me and asked if I had finished playing and was ready to get to work. I laughed and told her that I enjoyed playing with the kids much better.

"Scott has been looking for you," she said. "He really likes you and would like to ask you out."

"Carol I am not interested and I am not ready to settle down. You sound like Dad now," I protested.

"Okay, then have you thought any more about calling Dr. Goodson and going in to talk to him?" Carol pressed on knowing how I felt about it.

"I thought about it," I answered, irritated by her nagging.

"But you haven't called, right?" she asked, looking at me. "Katie, he can help you. He can stop your nightmares. All you have to do is call him and go in and see him."

"He is the magical cure for me, right?" I snapped. "Just call him and he can snap his fingers and I will be over and done with my past?...Carol how can I talk to him? I don't know him and I don't think I can tell him when I can't seem to remember what happened to me," I replied glaring at her.

"Just give him a call and go to see him. What can it hurt?" Carol persisted.

Just then Scott came up and asked if we could help get the stage ready for the band.

"Thank you, Scott. You just rescued me from another of Carol's lectures." I laughed and winked at Carol as we turned and walked over to the band.

"I have been looking for you," Scott said as we were walking.

"I am not that hard to find. I have been busy helping with the children and now I am ready to finish up with the band," I replied.

"There is a group of us getting together next weekend for a BBQ and canoeing. Would you like to go with me?" he asked.

"I would but I have other plans right now. Sorry," I politely excused myself.

"You know, Katie, I will not stop asking you. One day you will go with me and I am not going to stop until you do," he said confidently.

The band was setting up and was almost ready to begin playing when we reached the stage.

"I am going to make the announcements and then the final speaker is going to make his last plea for money from the crowd. After that the speaker will announce the first dance which will be a dedication dance," I informed the band leader.

"Okay. Just let me know when they are ready and we will begin," he replied me with a smile on his face.

The auction was over and night was beginning to fall. The lights were lit on the stage and the people began to mingle near the stage. I stood up and announced into the microphone for everyone to gather around because Mr. Sweeny had a few words that he would like to say to all. Everyone clapped as Mr. Sweeny walked across to the stage. I handed him the microphone and left the stage as I took a seat in the audience. As he spoke I looked at the crowd wondering if his words would help…wondering if the people would really reach deep into their pockets to give as much as they could to help the children with the new wing. He spoke for what seemed an eternity. He finally concluded his speech to the applause of the crowd. He then went on to thank everyone who organized and help put together the auction and arranged for all the games and prizes for the kids. "We would like to have those people begin tonight's first dance," he requested. "As your name is called out please grab a partner and come up to the dance floor."

He started calling out the names. I looked around the group trying to decide who I wanted to take to the dance floor with me. They called my name and as I stood up I could see Scott setting his drink down and puffing out his chest. He figured I would take him. I looked at him and he smiled back at me. I continued looking and noticed that Paul had been pushed up to the chairs and was looking at me to see who I would choose. I looked at Paul and smiled and he shook his head—as in a tacit 'yes'. I slowly walked over to Paul as Mr. Sweeny announced the next name. He already had his seatbelt unfastened. I entwined my fingers together as I picked him up and held him to my chest. I placed his legs around me holding them up with my elbows and walked up on the stage. Scott looked at me with a smirk on his face, downed his drink and ordered another one. I could tell he was upset by the expression on his face.

As he walked past me he said, "Nice pick…enjoy your dance, doll."

I replied by saying, "He was the best man here."

Angry I walked to the middle of the stage and turned and waited for the music to begin. As the last couple came up on stage the music began. I had already requested a slow dance and as the couples began to dance Paulie told me he had made me something and reached into his pocket and pulled out a piece of red paper that was all folded up. I asked him to open it for me. As he started to unfold the paper I could see that he had made a big red heart for me. He had written my name across the middle of the heart.

"That is the most beautiful heart I have ever seen in my life and you made that just for me?" I asked him.

"I did it all by myself just for you, Katie" he said and his eyes showed the pride he felt in himself.

I could see that he was very tired and I told him that because it was a slow dance that he had to put his head on my shoulder. As we danced around the dance floor his eyes closed and he fell asleep. As the music stopped I walked off the stage and his father walked up to me to take him. "I can put him in his chair if you like. That way he won't awaken," I whispered as he got closer.

"We are going, so if you want you can put him in the car and I will take his wheelchair," he replied.

As we walked to the car he thanked me for giving Paul such a wonderful day to remember. "He told me that you had taken him for a pony ride and that you taught him to dance and how to make balloon figures," he said gratefully.

"He is a wonderful child and I don't know who had more fun today, he or I?" I replied as I laid him on the back seat of the car. Paul was still holding the heart that he had made for me. He woke up as I laid him down and handed me my heart. I leaned over and kissed him on the forehead and told him that I would see him soon. He fell asleep again. He looked like an angel lying there. They thanked me again and got in the car and drove off.

"How touching!" Momentarily startled, I turned to see Scott standing there. "You prefer dancing with a child when you could have been dancing in my arms?" he sneered.

"Yes, as a matter of fact I did. You have been drinking and I wish not to talk to you now," I said to him as I turned to go back to the stage.

"You can't fight me off forever you know," he said menacingly in slurred words. "I always get what I want one way or another," he went on.

"I don't plan to, Scott. I don't ever remember telling you that I wanted to be with you or anywhere around you for that matter," I retorted. "Now if you would like I can have someone drive you home because you are drunk or you can sleep it off in the car, I really don't care. I have other things I need to take care of," I told him as I walked past him and didn't bother to look back.

"One day you will feel differently, Katie Lynne. I am just not sure if I will be waiting for you," he mocked.

"Don't bother," I replied as I looked over my shoulder. "I have other plans and they don't include YOU."

All the guests had left and the cleaning crew was busy cleaning up the last of the trash. I ran up the stairs into the house. Dad had gone off to bed and Mom was in the kitchen.

"Nice turn out," I said. "I hope the donations are enough."

"We have already met last year's total and they aren't done counting yet," she said. "It will be wonderful to get the new wing completed."

"Yes it will," I told her.

"Are you hungry or would you like some tea?" Mom asked.

"No, Mom. I am fine," I replied. "You look exhausted, Mom," I observed.

"Yes, I am. It has been a very long day for all of us," she sighed.

"Why don't you go on up to bed now?" I asked her and continued: "The cleanup is done now and everyone has gone."

"I guess you are right, Katie. No sense in sitting here. I might just as well go on up to bed," she replied.

"I am tired and going up to bed too. Good night, Mom. See you in the morning. I love you." I gave her a hug and kiss as I walked by.

"Good night, dear. I am glad you are spending the night and I will see you in the morning and I love you too," Mom replied.

I went up the stairway to my old room. As I was walking up the stairs fear began to fill me. *Why was I afraid? What do I have to fear here? I have lived here with my parents for years. I have nothing to be afraid of.* With each step I took the stronger the feeling got. I stopped when I was almost at the top. My heart was pounding in my chest. *Turn, run…quick before they get you! Why do these thoughts keep haunting my mind? What had happened? Why can't I remember?* I took a deep breath and finished climbing the stairs. I went into my room and closed the door. The room started to close in on me. I could hardly breathe. *Run* my mind kept telling me. *Run NOW, run FAST.* I quickly removed my clothes and put on my sweats. Mom had gone up to bed and the house was quiet. I slowly opened my door and ran down the stairs to the door. I quietly opened the door and closed it. *Run, run FAST. Go, don't stop! Run!* Fear was driving me now. I ran down to the barn. I didn't stop until I got to the door. There was still a light on in the office. I walked inside and Hank was sitting at the desk.

"Just where do you think you are going this late at night, Katie Lynne?" Hank inquired.

I looked at him and felt uneasy.

"Are you okay? You look frightened," he said as he scrutinized me.

"I am fine. I just wanted to see Lacey before I went to bed," I lied to him and hoped that he wouldn't see through my lie.

I turned on the barn light and Lacey was already out of her stall. I turned to look at Hank and he had a big smile on his face.

"You didn't really think that I thought you were just going to check on Lacey, did you?" Hank said with a twinkle in his eye. "I have known you too long for that. She is ready but please don't stay out too late," he cautioned.

"Thank you, Hank!" I exclaimed.

"It has been a long time since you went riding and after tonight I thought you might try to sneak out again," he explained.

"Oh, Hank. You know me better than anyone else seems to know me," I laughed.

"Come on, I will help you up on her back," he offered.

I liked to ride bare-backed and Hank knew that already. He walked over to Lacey, turned and intertwined his fingers and I put my foot on his hands and he lifted me up on to Lacey's back.

"Here, take this. I know what you are going to do," he said as he shook his head and handed me the duffle bag.

I looked at him and laughed. "Please don't tell on me, Hank.' I begged.

He replied, "Have I ever told on you about your late night rides? Just be very careful. I don't want to have to come looking for you," he stated.

I turned Lacey around and we headed out the door. I took in a deep breath as we cleared the barn. The air was fresh and the sky was full of stars. The moon was full and high in the sky and there were no clouds visible as far as I could see.

"Let's go, Lacey. You know the way." She whinnied and started off for the woods.

Lacey started walking slowly at first. Then she began to trot. She was anxious so it did not take her long until she was at a full run. I squeezed my legs tighter around her back and could feel her strong muscles moving underneath me. I thought to myself, *Run, Lacey run. Don't stop! Run, Lacey before they get us!* She knew exactly where I wanted to go and it wasn't long before we reached the pond. Unlike the pond by the house this one was three miles from the house and was hidden by the trees. I slid off her back and opened the bag that Hank had given me. Sugar cubes and carrots for Lacey and a towel for me, lay inside. I laughed when I saw it. Yes, he did know me very well.

I gave Lacey a sugar cube and carrots and she started grazing on the grass. I slipped out of my clothes and walked into the pond. The water was cool against my warm skin. It felt good. I could finally relax. The auction was over and we could get the final total in the morning. There was nothing left to do except enjoy the water and relax. I went down into the water submerging myself completely. I tilted my head back as I came up and it pulled my hair straight back. I stayed in the water awhile, letting it relieve the day's tension. I watched the stars twinkling in the sky trying not to think of anything else. I was enjoying the quiet of the night. After about an hour I got out of the water, grabbed the towel and dried myself off. My only thoughts then were for some sleep. I quickly got dressed and calling Lacey over I used the tree stump to get back up on her.

"Ok, Lacey, let's go home now," I said and I could hear the exhaustion in my voice.

Once again she began trotting but soon was at a full run. The wind was blowing my hair back and drying it as she ran. She slowed as we got closer to the barn. *Did she sense my hesitation? Could she feel that I did not want to climb those stairs again?* Very slowly she began to walk. When we reached the barn Hank was still waiting up for us.

"You should have gone to bed, Hank." I yelled at him.

"You know I can't sleep when you are out at the pond. Now let me help you down and you go quietly into the house before we both get into trouble," he said jokingly as he took Lacey's reins.

"Thank you, Hank," I told him as I gave him a hug and kiss.

"Thanks again, Hank. I love you," I said.

"I love you too, Katie dear. Now off with you before we both get into trouble. You know your Mom's temper," he laughed. "Go on up to bed, Katie. I will take care of Lacey. It is good to have you home even if it is only for one night," he smiled as he said it.

He took the reins and walked Lacey into her stall and I turned and walked slowly up to the house.

I slowly opened the door. I am not going up the stairs again I thought to myself.

"I would have thought you have outgrown your mischievous ways young lady," Mom reprimanded as I was closing the door.

Startled, I turned on the light. Mom sat there in her robe waiting for me.

"Did Hank tell you I was out?" I asked her.

"No, just like every other time he never said a word," Mom explained.

"What is bothering you, Katie? Are you having the nightmares again?" she asked in a concerned tone.

"No, Mom. I just wanted to go for a quick swim in the pond. I have done that for years," I reasoned.

"I know you have but I did not know you would sneak out at night to go," she sounded concerned as she spoke.

"I am sorry if I woke you. I couldn't sleep and I knew if I went swimming in the pond I would be better able to," I explained apologetically. I tried my level best to sound convincing.

"I have something I want to give you, Katie," Mom said as she handed me a card.

"What's this?" I asked as I took the card and looked at it. *Dr. Shawn Goodson* the card read. "Where did you get this Mom?" I said as I felt my temper rising.

"Carol gave it to me and told me she has been trying to get you to call and go in and see him. Have you called him?" she queried.

"No" I said "and I don't plan on calling him."

"Katie, don't you want the nightmares to stop? Don't you want to find out what happened? Maybe Dr. Goodson can help bring back your memory?" she pleaded.

I took the card from her and told her that I would think about calling him. "I am really tired Mom. I am just going to go home so that I can sleep in, tomorrow morning," I told her as I turned to walk out the door.

"Katie, I know you are going because you don't want to climb those stairs again. Please, honey, call him," she pleaded.

"I will think about it, Mom. I will talk to you tomorrow. I love you." I turned and went to my car.

As I drove home I thought maybe Mom was right. *Maybe I should call him and see what he could do for me? Carol said he could help me. She knew him and had worked with him and maybe he could help me. But what if he could not?* I went into the house and locked the door behind me. I slipped off my clothes and climbed into bed. The exhaustion from the day had finally caught up with me and I fell into a deep sleep…

Chapter 3

As I slept the dreams slowly worked their way back into my sleep. Running...I am running through the woods again but it is different this time. A bright light is blinding me and I cannot see where I am going. Run! Fear and terror fill me. I am back at that house again. I do not know where I am and I am very frightened. The light is gone...I am panting and can hardly breathe. I quickly look around me trying to figure out where I am at. The blinding light returns obscuring my view. Why? Why am I here? Who is trying to hurt me? Run...run, leave! Escape is all I can think about but I remain transfixed, unable to see or think. Help me please, I need to get away! I am running again...Splash and I am in water. I am fighting my way to the surface. Where am I? I am gasping for air trying to breathe.

I sit upright in bed panting as I try to get air back into my choking lungs. My arms clutch the air as I begin sinking in deep water. Frantically I look around trying to figure out where I am. My body finally relaxes as I realize that I am in my room and not fighting for my life in deep endless water. Overwhelming relief sweeps over me as I realize that it was only another nightmare. I sit on the edge of the bed as my breathing gradually returns to normal. I had not noticed the tears that had slowly begun to flow.

Am I ever going to remember what had happened? Why do these dreams and nightmares continue to haunt me? I asked myself. They seem to be getting worse instead of better. *If I cannot remember what happened, why do these nightmares return and seem so real?* I do not want to remember. I want to forget, to push the memories at the back of my mind. After all this time I thought that the nightmares would have stopped. Instead they return more often and last longer. *Am I going crazy? What does it all mean? Is it time for me to remember? Is that why I could not sleep any more without reliving bits and pieces of a past that I had fought so hard to forget? Why did my mind not let me remember what happened? What could have been so horrible that my mind has indelibly erased it from my memory except for the nightmares with nebulous bits and pieces that I cannot piece together?*

The nightmares are now more frequent and the last few have added new images that had never been there before. The fear and terror are so very real and stay with me long after I wake from the nightmare. Fear that penetrates to the very core of my being. *Maybe memories of my elusive past are ready to surface? Maybe the nightmares will continue to give me more flashbacks that I will be able to recognize?* This way I might get to know where I was and who was trying to hurt me. *On the other hand, were the nightmares real or are were they simply figments of my imagination? Maybe there was really nothing for me to be afraid of? Maybe it was simply just a vivid imagination?* Nobody seemed to talk about it. *If I had indeed gone through a horrible ordeal would not have Mom, Dad or even Hank said something to me about it?* None of them had mentioned anything except Mom who could always tell when the nightmares were back just by looking at me. It all seemed so confusing to me. Even Carol had never mentioned anything to me about an ordeal from the past and we have known each other since grade school. *Maybe nothing had ever happened? Maybe I was reading more into my nightmares than there really was? Maybe one day everything would finally make sense to me?* Until that day I would have to deal with it as best I could.

I get up from my bed as I did not wish to sleep any longer. It seemed that each time I slept the flashbacks kept returning to haunt me. They mocked me showing me fragments of a past that I did not want to remember. Only tiny little bits and pieces…nothing that I could put full memories to. Just once if I could see a face or if I could place the house that I was so afraid of. *Why did I have a fierce need to run? Who was I running from? Why did they want to hurt me so? At this point I was not sure which was worse…the nightmares or waking up after those and trying to puzzle out what had happened and why?* The nightmares always scared me so I was afraid to find out the real truth behind them. *Will any of it ever make sense to me?*

All my nightmares appear in slow motion to me. They seem very real at the time. Such is their intensity that even after awakening from a nightmare my muscles feel taut and I am panting as though from the furious effort of running. I am trying to figure out the new portion of the nightmare. I have never been afraid of the water and have always enjoyed going to the lake. It was so peaceful there. *Why did it turn into a place of terror in my nightmares?* The only place that I had felt very secure in now seemed to become a part of the nightmare.

I slowly walked to the kitchen to boil water for some tea. As I waited for the water to boil I happened to glance at the card on the kitchen table. I read the words on the card slowly. *Call Dr. Shawn Goodson for emergencies* it read at the top. I laughed as I read the number. *Now would this be considered an emergency? Should I call to see if he could help me? What would I tell him? How could he help me when I myself did not know what had happened? I was not even sure if anything ever really did happen? If I could not remember how could he help me?* A part of me urged me to pick up the phone and give it a try but another part of me cautioned that it would only be wasting the doctor's time. *Maybe he could give me something to help me sleep to get me through a few nights without the nightmares? Maybe I was just so tired that my imagination was conjuring up all the different images that flooded my mind?* It all seemed so confusing.

The tea kettle began to scream and I walked over to the stove to take it off. I walked out onto the deck and sat on the swing watching the birds come to the feeder and grab seeds; then fly to the trees for cover so that they could eat only to return for more. I watched as the clouds began to form in the sky. Beautiful, white, fluffy clouds. As I looked I could pick out shapes and forms. The sight was so serene and peaceful. A soft, warm breeze caressed my face and gently blew the hair back from it. If only my sleep could be so serene I reminisced…

I did not know how long I sat staring into nothingness. Time seemed to stand still and I did not seem to care. The smell of the roses, lilac and honeysuckle relaxed me as I breathed in, closing my eyes and letting the fragrance fill my nostrils. Not wanting the moment to end, I sat a few minutes longer. I looked at my watch and decided to make a move if I was going to get anything done that day. I wanted to go out to the farm to pick up the rest of the paperwork from the auction and take back the donation jars. I slowly got up and walked back through the kitchen to the bathroom. I would take a quick shower before setting off. It was still early morning. As long as I was at the farm I would take the time to go down to the barn and brush out Lacey and perhaps go for a ride too. Riding always made me feel better.

A short while later I pulled up the drive. I could see Mom outside working with her flowers. She had Dad helping her and he looked like one of the farm hands with his bib overalls and huge straw hat bouncing in the breeze. I chuckled as I looked at them. What a sight! They both waved as I pulled up.

"I have an extra shovel and rake ready for you Katie. You got here just in time to help plant all the new flowers your Mom just brought home." Dad waved his hand over the flats of flowers lying on the ground by his feet. With dirt all over her face and looking like a child, Mom looked up and reminded him that he was the one that needed the exercise. Mom got to her feet and brushed the dirt off herself. She suggested we all go in for some lemonade to cool down.

"That sounds wonderful," Dad said. "I have been working very hard and I need something cool to drink."

"Oh, listen to you! Katie he has only been standing here for about ten minutes," Mom said as we all laughed and headed for the house.

"Would you like something to eat, Katie?" asked Dad.

"No thanks, Dad. I just need to pick up the auction papers but I think I will run down to the barn and spend some time with Lacey while I have nothing else planned. Maybe later after I am done…but thanks," I replied.

Motioning with a finger to his lips to indicate to me to be very quiet, he quietly turned and left the room before Mom could give him something else to do. After Mom turned off the water and was drying her hands she turned and looked around the room and seeing that Dad had sneaked out she glanced at me and smiled.

"Katie, that man can disappear faster than a schoolboy when the school bell rings," she laughed.

Mom poured some lemonade for us and we sat at the table. It was just the two of us so I thought I would take the opportunity to ask her if she knew of any reason behind the nightmares.

"Mom, I was wondering if you could tell me something?" Before giving her a chance to respond I went on.

"I have been having the nightmares again and I need to ask you some questions about them." She rose from her seat and walked away from the table and stood looking out the window avoiding eye contact with me.

"Katie, have you given any more thought about calling Dr. Goodson?" she inquired. "Carol said that he is a wonderful doctor and he could probably tell you more about your nightmares than I could darling. Why don't you give him a call? I have his card, if you need to get the number. He might have an opening and you could get in to see him today," she continued.

"Mom, why does everybody keep pushing a doctor at me?" I replied frowning. "Can't you tell me anything? I am beginning to wonder if there was really anything that had happened to me or if the nightmares are just meaningless dreams that come to me?" I snapped back sharper than I had meant to speak.

She remained silent, so I continued.

"Mom was there something horrible that happened to me or did somebody hurt me in some way?" I was getting very frustrated because of her silence. "I can't seem to remember and the nightmares only give me bits and pieces and I can't make any sense out of them," I explained.

Still she did not say a word. I calmed down a little and went on, "I can't very well go to the doctor if I can't remember anything. I will really feel silly if nothing had ever happened and they are just nightmares," I said, tired of trying to get the response I was hoping for.

"Katie, we have not talked about this before and I am not sure that I really want to or if I should get into it," she said. "It is not that I don't want to help you, dear. I would do anything I can to help you but…" at that she stopped and turned around to face me. She slowly walked across the room and sat at the table with me.

"I really think you should call the doctor, Katie. If there is something that you are not remembering he is the one that would be able to help with it," she tried to convince me.

"Just give him a call and see what happens," she added after a long uneasy pause.

"Mom, the only thing that I would like to know is if anything really happened to me?" I inquired slowly. "Can't you just tell me that?" I asked, knowing instinctively she was not going to do so.

Silence…

I went on, "The nightmares had stopped for a while but recently I have been unable to sleep without having them creep back frighteningly." I was almost pleading with her but I could tell that she did not want to discuss the matter any more.

"Okay, if you won't talk to me about it, can you just tell me if something happened to me?" "At least that way I will know that I am not going crazy." I could feel myself getting impatient with her.

"Katie, in time you will understand everything but for now you need to just let your memory work." Mom spoke very low and very quietly as though she thought someone might be listening to us speak.

"I was hoping that you could jog my memory a little and give me some idea of what it could have been," I said as I felt the tears well up in my eyes. "I am going to go down and brush Lacey and go for a ride. Maybe I can come up with a reason about you not wanting to talk to me about it," I said as I got up and put my glass in the sink.

She did not reply but looked at me as I turned and walked out the door as the tears rolled down my cheeks. I sighed as I walked down the steps.

I saw Hank reading over the paper as I walked into the barn. I just walked by without saying a word to him. He did not seem to notice me and I did not feel like talking to anyone at the time. I opened the stall door and led Lacey out of the stall. I walked her down to the hose and went to pick up the brush. As I turned Hank was standing right beside me. My breath caught in my throat because he had startled me. My mind was deep in thought and I had not heard him come up behind me.

"You startled me, Hank. I didn't hear you come up," I said a little shakily.

"You were deep in thought. I said 'Hi' as I came up but you didn't hear me," he said as he frowned and looked at me.

"What is wrong, Katie?" he asked with concern written all over his face. "You never just walk in and go to Lacey without stopping first to talk or at least say 'Hi' to me. Something is troubling you." His look told me that he was more concerned than he was letting on.

"Oh, Hank, it is the nightmares! They are back and I tried talking to Mom about them but she does not seem to want to share any information about my past that might help me. I don't understand why she can't give me a few simple answers. I guess she just doesn't care," I said despondently.

"Katie Lynne. How can you say such a thing? You know how much your Mother loves you and that she would do anything she could to help you." Hank was very agitated by the words that I had spoken.

"Then why, Hank?" I asked. "Why won't she talk to me and help me figure out the things I don't remember?"

"Give it time, Katie. You will remember if anything happened to you," Hank began. "But in the meantime don't you ever think that your Mom or Dad for that matter, don't care about you or your past."

His voice was strained now as he spoke. "If you need me I will be in the office," he said as he turned and walked away from me.

I finished brushing Lacey out and decided to wash her after I got back. We would be running so washing her would do more good after the run. I took the reins in my hand and stepping on the upturned bucket I climbed on Lacey's back.

"Come on, Lacey. Let's go. Maybe I can get you to talk to me," I said mockingly.

Lacey slowly walked through the coral as if she wasn't sure what I wanted her to do. At that point I wasn't sure where I wanted to go either. I just knew I wanted answers but nobody seemed anxious to provide them.

I did not pay attention to where Lacey was going. She picked up the pace and I knew that she was ready to run. She had been in the barn for a week now and she was ready to get out and run.

"Go ahead, Lacey. Run like the wind girl," I laughed as I said it, wanting to run and escape as much as she did. She gave a soft whinny and began to trot. It was as though she was trying to get my attention.

"Let's go, Lacey!" I yelled.

With that she began to run. It felt good. I became one with her, giving her the choice on where we went. I tightened my legs against her sides and let her run free. Across the pasture and through the field she ran. Long strides…running as though she was being chased. She ran past the pond where I had initially thought she was going. I began to think that I should slow her down or even stop her and turn around but Lacey seemed to have a purpose. *I will let her run a little longer…then I will slow her down and go back.* Lacey began to slow down and started to walk again shortly. Suddenly she stopped dead in her tracks. I looked around. We were on the edge of the woods. She pawed the ground below her as if impatient for me to do something. I held the reins tight in my fingers and tried to make her turn. She would not move from the spot.

"Come on, Lacey! Let's go." I could feel the uneasiness in my voice as I spoke. Still no movement from her…Lacey had never acted this way before so I was unsure what she wanted.

"Let's go, Lacey," I spoke very sternly.

This time I pulled on the reins moving her head back but once again Lacey refused to move. She pawed at the ground and shook her head. I looked around again paying more attention to the surroundings. Very slowly I looked at the woods seeing for the first time the same image that appeared to me in my nightmares. I could feel terror envelop me. I sat staring at the woods for sometime not quite understanding what I was seeing. I knew it had something to do with my past but I wasn't exactly sure what it was. I had a sudden uneasy feeling and wanted to leave at once.

"Come on, Lacey, let's go," I begged as I heard fear creeping into my voice. This time I used my heels and kicked her sides to get her to move. I pulled on the reins and her head turned but she walked straight for the woods. I pulled harder on the reins. "Lacey, stop!" I screamed.

She refused to listen and kept walking towards the woods. I pulled back on the reins as hard as I could.

"WHOA!!" I screamed in panic.

Lacey took a couple of steps more and then stopped abruptly. She must have sensed my fear and known that if she took another step towards the woods I would have jumped off her back. She remained standing very still. For some reason Lacey had brought me here. She had never disobeyed when given an order. I sat very still on her back and once again looked all around me. The clouds in the sky had turned from white and fluffy to dark and menacing. Once could hear the thunder rumble in the distance. It wasn't close and we had time to get back to the barn. My mind was reeling from the sight of the woods before me. These were the same trees that were in my nightmare. This was the same place that I was running through trying to get away from whatever it was that was chasing me. *How could Lacey have known?* I was not riding her that night. *I was in a car with blinding lights or was I? Why couldn't I remember?*

"Please go to the barn, Lacey," my voice was barley audible.

My throat felt constricted as though I had been screaming for hours. This time she did not hesitate and turned. Lacey did not wait for the command to run. She walked a few steps and went into a full run. I felt numb and just wanted to get back to the house where I was safe. She must have known my need to get home because she did not stop at the pond like we always did when we went out riding. Lacey ran hard and fast straight for the barn and to safety. She did not stop running until we got to the coral. Hank was standing in the doorway of the barn and came running out when he saw how fast we were coming in. Lacey stopped and Hank grabbed the reins.

"Are you alright, Katie?" he asked with panic in his voice. "Did something spook, Lacey?" he asked worriedly. "You two never come in that fast," he noted.

He reached up and pulled me down from Lacey's back.

"Talk to me, Katie," he held me as he spoke softly. "Please say something!" he said, still speaking very softly.

I just looked at him unable to speak.

"Come on, Lacey," Hank said.

Lacey followed us into the barn. She went into her stall and turned around as I watched. Hank took me in the office and set me down on a chair. He took out a cup and filled it with water and handed it to me.

"I'll be right back," he said.

He went and closed the door on Lacey's stall. A short while later he returned.

"Please Katie, tell me what happened out there," the concern was back in his voice. "Are you alright?" he asked.

I just looked at him blankly at first. Then I whispered, "The woods."

I was shaking and the tears began to fall. "Katie, was there anyone out there in the woods?" Hank asked barely above a whisper.

"No, Hank. Nobody was out there but it was the woods from my nightmares. The woods I am running through…trying to get away from someone," my voice began to quiver. "Someone that wants to hurt me," I continued.

As he looked at me with concern written all over his face I asked, "Hank, do you know what happened to me? Do you know the answers to the questions that I need to know?"

"Oh, Katie, I can't tell you," he answered quietly.

He stood up and picked me up from the chair. After sitting down himself he sat me on his lap and held me as I cried. Slowly he began to talk to me.

"Katie, something did happen to you," he started.

After a pause…"You don't remember anything?" he asked again.

I shook my head in the negative and rested my head on his shoulder as I began to sob.

"Can't you tell me anything, Hank?" I spoke, barely audible through my sobs. "Why doesn't anyone want to talk to me or tell me anything about what happened to me?" I wailed. "These nightmares are going to drive me crazy and everyone keeps quiet," I burst out in complete frustration.

My body shook as I cried on Hank's shoulder. He held and rocked me gently as I cried.

"Let me tell you this, Katie," Hank began very slowly.

I knew that he was going to tell me as much as he could. I knew he wanted to tell me but for some reason he always stopped.

"Yes, something did happen to you," he began cautiously. "The doctor told us not to say anything…that your memory would come back to you one day. Until that happened we would only make things worse and confuse you by telling you things," he said. "The doctor said that it could push you into an unresponsive shell if we forced you to remember events too quickly," he explained.

"That is why your Mother can't say anything," he went on. "She wants to help you more than anyone else but she also knows that by telling you she runs the risk of bringing the memories back too soon and that would cause more damage than you remembering on your own," he explained. "In time you will remember everything."

Hank paused for a minute before going on: "Until that day comes we can only stand by you and be there for you when you do remember," he said. "Katie, I love you like my own child and I would never do anything to hurt or harm you but I can't tell you what happened for your own sake." As he spoke I could hear the love and compassion he had in his heart. "Please believe me when I tell you this because one day you will remember and you will know and understand everything that happened." He stopped speaking and continued rocking me.

"Hank, how did Lacey know about the woods?" I asked. "She took me there on her own," I spoke with disbelief in my voice. "She wanted to run and like I usually do I let her run free. She ran without stopping until we got to the edge of the woods." I slowly continued: "She stopped there and refused to move even when I kicked her sides. Instead she pawed the ground and did not leave until I had looked into the woods," I said as my voice began to quiver again.

"How could she know, Hank?" I asked. "Was I riding her when this happened?"

Hank rocked me back and forth in the chair as one would a child. "No, Katie. I was riding her that night I came looking for you," Hank replied. "She knows that that is the place where I found you." He continued cautiously: "I never thought that she would take you there on her own," he said. "You are safe now, Katie," he said. "Don't think about it. Just sit here quietly and relax," he advised gently.

I felt safe in Hank's arms and I knew how frightened he was when he saw us riding up to the barn so fast. I just wanted to get home. I stood up and told Hank that I was going up to the house to pick up the papers and go home.

"Thank you Hank for telling me what you did," I told him. "I will not tell anyone about our talk and please don't worry," I said. "If you don't mind I will come back and talk to you if I have any more nightmares," I said, looking at him. "Not to ask questions but to let you know what the nightmares are," I explained.

"Thank you, Katie. Always remember that I am here whenever you need me. If I am not here I will be at the house. Just come on over," he said. After a brief pause Hank continued, "I am going to give Lacey her food and water and then will walk up to the house with you. I will brush her out after I get back."

"Sounds good. I will just wait here for you to come back," I said as he went off to take care of Lacey.

I stood gazing through the windows. The lightning was fast approaching and the sky was very dark. The rumbling of the thunder made my body shiver. I could hear Hank shutting the back barn doors and locking them to prevent the wind from blowing them open and letting the rain pour in. A great bolt of lightning flashed across the sky, striking a rock in the field...just missing the big apple tree by a few meters. The resounding thunder that followed shook the barn. I could feel the room closing in on me. The room began to spin. Run, run now...Get out while you can! My mind was racing frantically as fear gripped me. I turned to run and ran straight into Hank. He grabbed me so that I did not fall. Everything went black. Hank picked me up in his arms and gently carried me out of the office and through the barn door. He was carrying me up to the house. My eyes opened suddenly and I looked in dread at the face of the man carrying me. It was not the face that I had expected to see. He looked down at me feeling me stir in his arms.

Hank spoke very reassuringly to me: "Katie, you passed out honey. I am taking you up to the house. Don't be afraid...it is only me. It is Hank and you are safe in my arms," he reassured softly.

I wrapped my arms around his neck as he finished carrying me up to the house.

"What happened, Hank?" Mom asked as she saw us approaching. "Is she alright?" her voice was somber. "Did she fall off Lacey?" her voice rose the closer she got to us. "I saw Lacey come galloping up to the barn full tilt with Katie riding her. I thought she was going to run right through the barn." Mom placed her hand on my forehead as she spoke.

My eyes were closed and my head was pounding.

"Just take her up the stairs to her room, Hank, and I will be right up to put her to bed," Mom suggested as he walked past.

Hank nodded. He took two steps and as soon as I felt him alight the stairs, I let out a blood-curdling scream.

"No, please don't! No, please!" I screamed. "I beg of you, please let me go. Please don't hurt me!" Another scream escaped my lips..."NO!"

Hank stopped on the fourth step. I was incoherent and he could not understand a word I said. I begged him not to take me up the stairs: "Please…no…no…no."

Fear and terror consumed my mind. I went limp as I passed out. I did not feel the tears that fell silently from Hank's eyes as he stood on the step holding me close in his arms. I did not feel his heart pounding in his chest as he carefully turned and went back down the stairs. I could not feel his body shaking from anger at what had happened to me so long ago. I could not see or feel anything.

"She has passed out but I can't find it in my heart to take her up the stairs." Hank went on to describe to Mom in detail the preceding events. "Katie talked to me when she came back from her ride. Lacey had taken her to the woods and she knows that is where she was running that night." He added, "Katie knew that the event was connected to the woods but she did not remember what happened." Hank went on somberly, "She implored me to tell her but I did not."

He continued in a weak voice, "When the lightning hit the rock and the thunder boomed in the sky Katie panicked and turned to run from the office. I grabbed her just as she was about to hit the floor," Hank explained. "Where do you want me to put her?" he asked.

"Here, Hank. Put her on the sofa and I will cover her up and let her sleep until she wakes," Mom said with abject concern in her voice.

Dad had come running in the room when he heard me scream and was pacing the floor unsure of what to do. "Do you want me to call the doctor for her?" Dad said unable to think of anything else to do.

"No, she will be okay for now but I might just call Dr. Goodson later. Maybe we can set up an unscheduled meeting at a place for them to run into each other and he can coax her into coming to his office?" Mom sounded extremely worried for my well-being.

Hank laid me down on the sofa and covered me with a blanket. He sat on the edge of the sofa and just watched me as I slept.

"You don't have to wait, Hank," Mom said. "She will be alright now. She will sleep."

Hank replied, "I just want to sit here for a few minutes to make sure she is alright and then I will go, if that is okay with you?"

"Sure you can sit as long as you like. I am going up to bed. Just turn off the light and lock the door behind you," Mom said as she headed up the stairs to go to bed.

Hank looked at Katie remembering how much help she had been to his wife before and after she fell terribly sick. Both he and his wife could count on Katie being there and helping her out. Katie was like the child they had never had. What was to become of her now? What would be the repercussion from her remembering about the woods? The doctor had said that she would remember one day but not to push her to do so. Today she encountered that part of her past that she was beginning to remember only in her nightmares. Could she handle what happened? How long would it take now that she saw the woods for the first time since it happened? She had buried it so far inside herself that Hank thought it would never resurface. Katie had been so different after it had happened...so quiet and so afraid of everything. Over time she had begun to return to the Katie he knew but she held back and would never let herself go. She was easy to startle and shied away from many outings. She stopped dating and wanted to stay at home behind locked doors. As the thoughts were running through his head he drifted off to sleep. His head fell forward and his chin rested on his chest.

"No...no...no. Please no." Katie was beginning to dream again. As she spoke Hank opened his eyes and watched her. Not sure what her reaction was going to be he sat forward in the chair. She began to thrash around on the couch kicking off her blankets but after a little while she was still again. Her breathing gradually calmed down. *Good, she is sleeping again and not dreaming* Hank thought as he sat watching her. All of a sudden Katie sat upright on the sofa. Hank watched her carefully not sure if she was awake or still sleeping.

"You bastard," Katie spat out viciously through pursed lips glaring at Hank who just sat there unsure if he should speak or not. Katie was looking at him but her eyes were dull and glassy. *She is not awake* Hank thought to himself. *She is back in the past.*

"How dare you do this to me?" Katie continued her voice louder this time. "What right do you have?" Katie almost spat out the words.

She stopped talking and just looked straight ahead as if speaking to someone in front of her. Her eyes moved slowly from one side of the room to the other as though she were watching someone walking around. She tried to move but could not. It was almost as if she were paralyzed or somehow restrained. She looked down and then back up to the person she had been addressing.

"Answer me!" she uttered in a very low voice so unlike her own. When she spoke her voice was filled with hate and anger.

"How could you do this to me?" she asked. "Go ahead and kill me because if you don't I will one day get my revenge on you for what you have done to me."

Katie sat very still and Hank was thinking that maybe he should talk to see if he could get her to say the name of the person she was with. The name that nobody else knew. Only Katie could tell them but until now she had never gone this far in her nightmares. Hank cleared his throat thinking maybe she would turn and talk to him and call him by name. Should he push her or should he just let her continue and hope that she would say it?

Katie did not hear or even notice when Hank had cleared his throat. *Better not push her…it is best she do it at her own pace* he thought. She is remembering more and sooner or later she will remember the whole ordeal. Her eyes continued to watch the person moving but she did not speak again. As if someone had come up and pushed her she fell back down on the sofa. Her eyes closed and she did not utter another word.

Hank got up and walked over to the sofa to cover up Katie again. As he gently put the blanket back over her, she began to stir. Her eyes opened and she looked at Hank. "What happened, Hank?" her throat hurt badly and she could hardly speak above a hoarse whisper.

"You were in the office when the storm started. You turned to run up to the house and got dizzy and passed out," Hank replied. "Do you remember anything?" Hank asked trying to sound nonchalant about it. Katie shook her head.

"Can I get you anything, Katie?" he asked hoping to change the subject.

"Could I get a glass of water, please? My throat hurts really badly and it is very dry."

"Sure," Hank replied and got up and went to the kitchen to get her water. He came back and handed a glass of water to her. I had got up from the sofa and was folding the blanket. "Thanks for the water. It feels good on my throat," I said as I slowly sipped it.

"Do you need anything else?" Hank asked.

"Yeah, a shower and a nice warm bed," I said, laughing.

"Let me run you home, Katie." He continued before I had a chance to speak: "I would feel better knowing you got home safe." Hank got up and went for his keys.

"I will be alright now, Hank. Thank you for taking care of me," I said.

I turned and started to walk towards the door but stumbled as I did so. Hank reached out to grab me but I stopped and told him that I was fine.

"I guess I am still a little dizzy," I told Hank as I sat at the kitchen table.

"That settles it. You write your Mom a note to explain why your car is here and I will go get the truck and run you home," Hank told me as he walked to the door.

"You really don't need to bother, Hank. I can make it home by myself," I said with more confidence than I really felt.

Hank went out the door while I grabbed the notepad on the table and told Mom that Hank would run me home and that I would be out the next day to get my car. I also apologized to Mom for the argument earlier and said that I would talk to her tomorrow. As I signed the note I heard Hank pull up in the truck. I turned out the lights and locked the door shutting it behind me.

"This really isn't necessary, Hank. I can get home by myself," I said as I slipped into the seat and fastened the belt.

"You had two choices, Katie," Hank said as he laughed. "You could stay here at the farm or I can run you home. Those were your choices."

We both laughed as he put the truck in gear and drove off.

"You can turn the radio on if you would like to, Katie," Hank told me as we were driving along.

"No, I think I would rather leave it off Hank. I have a splitting headache and I think the music will make it worse," I informed him. "I think I will just close my eyes and relax. Just wake me when we get to the house." As I spoke the words I felt a twinge go through me. I rested back against the seat and closed my eyes. The whine from the tires made me drift off to sleep again…Bright lights. The blinding bright light was back and I forced my eyes shut to keep from looking at it.

"Stop, please stop!" I cried out.

"What's wrong, Katie? Are you okay?" Hank slowly pulled over to the side of the road.

"Are you feeling sick? Do you need to get out for a minute?" Hank was deeply concerned.

"Please, stop. Please…I can't see," I screamed.

"Katie, it's Hank. You are with me and you are safe," he reassured.

"Oh, Hank, please make it stop," I said as fear consumed me.

"What do you want me to stop, Katie?" Hank asked as he tried to figure out what had brought on this sudden panic attack in me.

"The lights…the blinding lights. Please, Hank, please make it stop…turn it off, please. I can't see," I begged.

"Katie, we are alone on this road. There hasn't been another car that has passed us." Hank explained, "We haven't seen a car in either direction since we left the farm. I have turned off the interior lights and just the headlights are on."

Hank continued softly, "Katie, it is me, Hank, and you are safe. I am not going to let anyone hurt you." Hank was gradually calming me down but he was still not sure about the light that I had mentioned.

"Oh, Hank. I think I'm going crazy. I am seeing things that are not there and I am afraid of things that I can't see," I choked through my tears. "Is this ever going to end, Hank? Please help me…help me understand…help me remember," I sobbed.

Hank held me close to him as I cried. After a few minutes I calmed down and sat back in the seat.

"You were just sleeping Katie and maybe in your sleep you thought you were somewhere else but everything is okay and you are safe. Nobody is going to hurt you while I am around." Hank sounded very confident as he spoke and I felt very safe. I did know that while he was with me nobody would hurt me.

"It's okay, Hank. We can go now," I told him at last after I was relatively calmer. "I think I am back to normal now. Well, as normal as I can be," I giggled nervously.

Hank reached over and started up the engine again and we headed back down the road.

He sat wondering as he drove along what blinding light she could be referring to. That was the first time that she had ever mentioned a light. The trees and woods she had, in passing, mentioned before but never really put the two together. That night she ran in the woods for her life and the same woods she once again revisited today. Did she unknowingly run Lacey to that exact spot or did Lacey remember the spot and knowing that Katie was upset took her there? Hank had ridden Lacey that night he went searching for Katie. That was where he had first seen her running bare footed and in deep shock. What impact would today's ride have on her? Would it bring back the memories? Would she be able to handle the ordeal she went through? What about tonight? Who was she talking to? Why would she not mention a name so that one would know who was responsible for it? She came so close…only to stop just before yelling out a name. In time Katie you will know what happened and you will know who did this to you. But how will you handle it? Will you tell one of us first or being the independent person that you are will you directly confront your attacker? Which will it be?

The rest of the ride home was uneventful. I sat quietly against the seat and never said another word. My eyes were open but luckily we never saw another car. Hank pulled up to the house and backed into the driveway. He turned the motor off and waited for me to say something. I sat very still without moving or talking. Should he say something or just wait to see what she had to say? Slowly I turned to face Hank and in a very cheery voice said, "Thank you, Hank, for driving me home but I still think that I could have got here by myself."

"Think nothing of it, Katie. I was happy to do it for you," Hank replied. "Now let's get you into the house," he added.

Hank walked around the truck and opened the door for me. He had the door open before I had had a chance to protest.

"Do you have the keys to your house? I will open the door for you and if you feel like it we can talk for a bit," Hank offered.

He shut the door and walked beside me up the steps. After unlocking the door he returned the keys.

"How about it, Katie? Feel like talking or having some tea?" Hank asked. "I am not really tired and would love some tea if you are up to it," Hank coaxed.

"You know, Hank. Maybe some tea would be good and we can have a talk." My voice sounded tired even though I was not going to admit it.

I walked over to the sink and poured some fresh water in the kettle and placed it on the stove. We sat down at the kitchen table and waited for the water to boil.

"There are so many questions that I have, Hank," I began. "I am a little worried too because I don't remember all of what happened. Today I know I took Lacey out for a run and was upset when I left," I admitted.

"I let her run and gave her full rein to go wherever she wanted to go. It gets a little fuzzy here and I can't remember much after that until I woke up on the sofa and you were sitting in the chair watching me." I watched Hank's face as I continued: "I know there is a lot that happened in between the times but it seems to have disappeared from my mind. I didn't fall off Lacey and bump my head did I?" I asked chuckling.

Hank was a little unsure of how to answer the questions but he knew that if he did not I would withdraw into myself like I had done all those years ago and not talk.

"What do you remember about the ride, Katie?" Hank began.

I did not respond.

Hank went on slowly: "I am not sure exactly where you went but you were gone for about three hours. We had the storm coming in so I was getting ready to saddle up and come looking for you," he continued.

Without realizing it Hank had picked up the card that was lying on the table and was twirling it between his fingers as he spoke. Just as he was about to start talking again the tea kettle started whistling. I jumped up and went to the stove to turn it off. Pouring two large cups of tea I brought them back to the table.

"You still drink it plain don't you, Hank?" I asked as I set the cup in front of him.

"Yes, plain is the way I like it," he replied.

Still holding the card in one hand he picked up the cup and sipped the hot tea. *Should I tell her about her trip to the woods or should I wait and see if she asks me again?* he mused. Hank was trying to decide when he suddenly noticed the card that lay between his fingers. He flipped it around so that he could study it closely. After reading it, he looked at me. I sat there with a grin on my face and said, "Hank, you have been playing with that card in order to avoid telling me what happened today."

A sheepish grin came over his face and he asked, "What is the card for, Katie?"

"That is a card that Carol gave me for a doctor friend of hers," I explained, smiling as I did so. "She wants me to go see him so that the wonderful doctor can cure me." I was still smiling as I continued, "Carol gave Mom a card and she put a couple on my desk at work. Mom has also tried to give me the card so that I could set up an appointment to go see him but I told them both that it wouldn't do a lot of good going in to see him when I could not remember anything about what had happened to me."

After a brief pause I asked, "What do you think, Hank? Do you think it would do any good to see the doctor?" Before he could answer, however, I went on, "I only have the dreams and nightmares—nothing that I can really tell him about my past; so it seems such a waste of time to me. It seems like I would just be going to see him because everybody keeps pushing me to go," I frowned.

"Katie," Hank began slowly as he looked evenly at me. "Katie, it is up to you and I am not going to push you either way because you know how you feel and you also know that the doctor may or may not be able to elicit events related to your past." Hank looked very serious as he continued. "Are you ready to go in and talk to him and are you willing to take the chance if he can't bring it out? You have been pushing your Mom, Dad and me for the past few months to tell you and you are getting very upset when we won't talk about it."

I sat watching Hank as he continued, "You will know when you are ready to talk about it and tell him what you do remember. When that day comes, by all means Katie, call him." Hank advised, "If you don't feel ready, don't go just to please others. Does that make sense to you?"

I nodded.

"I know that you are anxious to have the nightmares go away but simply remembering about the events might not necessarily get rid of them. There is a chance that it could even make them worse," Hank explained. "Go easy with it, Katie. Don't push yourself. Just know that one day you will remember and at that time you will be ready to face the past and will be able to move on with your life without looking back."

I watched him closely as he continued.

"Your mind is a tricky thing and it will let you remember everything when you are ready to know the truth."

I sat there looking fixedly at him and finally understood what he was telling me.

"You know, Hank, you are the first person that I have talked to that hasn't pushed me to go to the doctor and I really appreciate that. I value your opinion very much." I smiled as I went on, "I still think that it is too soon to go to the doctor but with everyone telling me to go I thought maybe I was just being silly in not wanting to go." I blushed and said, "I wanted to thank you for helping me today. I am not sure of all that has happened but just like everything else I am sure one day it will make sense to me."

Hank finished his tea, got up and placed his cup in the sink.

"Well, Katie, I think I better get going now." Hank walked to the door and I followed him. I reached up and gave him a tight hug and kiss.

"Thank you, Hank. Drive carefully and I will see you in the morning when I come to get the car. Thank you again and I love you."

"I love you too, Katie. Talk to you tomorrow," Hank replied.

I watched him as he went to the truck, got in and started it up. He waved to me as he drove off. Locking the door and turning off the light I walked into the bedroom. I turned down the bed covers, slowly slipped out of my clothes and threw them in the clothes hamper. I quickly climbed into bed and switched off the light. I felt exhausted but my mind was not ready to sleep yet. I lay gazing outside the window at the stars. A full moon was glowing in the sky and the stars were bright and twinkling. It was a very quiet night with no breeze. The window was open but no air seemed to be coming in. The more I tried to relax and drift off to sleep the harder it was for me to do so. As I lay in bed, my mind started going back to the ride. *No, don't think about that now.* I tried to push it from my mind and think of nothing but the beautiful fluffy clouds that started the day. I slowly began to drift off to sleep but once again I saw myself on Lacey's back riding through the field. Resolutely pushing everything else from my mind and thinking only of the stars I could feel my body eventually begin to relax and soon exhaustion took over and I fell asleep. For the first time in a long time I slept through the night. No dreams or nightmares creeping into my sleep and haunting me with frightening memories. I fell into a very deep sleep.

I awoke early the next day. The sun was just beginning to rise in the sky and a warm, gentle breeze was blowing in through the window. I could hear the birds chirping close by in the trees. I felt groggy. I had slept soundly and for a long time. I had not been awakened by any nightmares. My head began to pound as I lay there. *Maybe I should go back to sleep and I would feel better when I woke up?* I tossed and turned on the bed and decided to get up. The jumbled thoughts ran through my head. *A nice hot bath would help clear things up for me* I thought.

I went in to run the water and then checked the messages on the machine. As I walked closer to the phone I could see the red light blinking which indicated that I had messages. Three messages were on the machine but I didn't feel like hearing them yet. I put some water on for tea and went back to turn off the bath water. I was getting everything ready when the kettle began to whistle. I walked back into the kitchen to take it off and grabbed a cup as I walked by the cupboard. I filled it and slowly walked by the telephone again. I decided to see who had called in case there was an emergency. I pushed the button as I sipped my tea. The first message was from Carol wanting to know what I had planned for the day. The second message was from Scott reminding me about the special board meeting Monday morning. The last message was from Hank informing me that he would be there around noon to pick me up to go get my car. I smiled when I heard the message from Hank. He was such a wonderful man. He had always been there for my family. I glanced at the clock and it was only 9:30am so I had plenty of time before he got there. I slipped into the tub. The water was hot and relaxing. I leaned back, closed my eyes and started to relax.

As I sat relaxing I decided to try to make sense of the jumbled thoughts going through my head. I tried to think back over the ride. I had ridden Lacey many times over the years but yesterday's ride was so different. *Why did she take me to the woods? Did I subconsciously turn the reins making her go there?* I remember looking into the woods many times but I never really noticed them until yesterday. I knew that was the exact location that appeared in my nightmare. *Why did part of me want to go in and look further into the woods? Did I think that I could have seen who I was running from? Would it help me get past my fear of the woods?* I could walk Lacey through and if I got too upset she could walk me back out. *Should I go in and walk around...maybe that would jog some memories?* I thought about what Hank had told me. I finally had one of my questions answered. I wasn't crazy...*something had happened. The doctor said not to talk about it to you* Hank's words echoed in my mind. *Who had been the doctor? Was I injured and needed medical help? Did the doctor try to talk to me?* I seemed to have more questions now than I did before.

I let out a sigh and continued my thought processes. Trying to sort it all out was not going to be easy. I wanted very much now to remember and to try to figure out the details and find someone who would talk to me. *How many people knew about this ordeal? Had I talked to Carol before about the nightmares or had she first mentioned those to me?* I knew she could usually tell when I had had a bad episode with the nightmares just by looking at me. Mom had the same ability and would always ask me if the nightmares were back but now that I think back about it she never asked me *what they were about.* She always waited to see if I went into detail. If I didn't, she never pushed. *If I am not supposed to talk about what happened why is it that everyone around me wanted me to go see Dr. Goodson?* I did have something now that I remembered. It was not a lot but it was a start. *If I did start to remember I wondered if I should talk to anyone about it?* Hank was the one that told me the truth about something happening and that the doctor had told everyone not to mention anything to me about it. *Maybe I should talk to Hank if I started to remember more details about that night?* He told me that I could talk to him any time and I knew that I could trust Hank's sincerity. We had always confided in each other and I knew that he would help me in any way he could. He also told me that the doctor believed that one day I would remember and know who had hurt me that night. *Would I know if I ever saw or spoke to my 'attacker'? Could it be someone that I actually knew and have been around since that night? If so, would he say or do something to trigger my memory? Would my memory come flooding back all at once or would it return in bits and pieces for me to sort out?*

It was all so confusing. One day at a time. That would be the best way to handle it. The blinding light. *How did the light fit in? Was it the headlights of a car? Could there have been an accident?* Oh, it is all so confusing to me! Try as I might I just could not seem to remember. *Maybe if I tried to concentrate on one thing at a time it would be easier for me to remember?* The running through the woods seemed to be a significant part of my nightmares and I was at that exact location yesterday. *If I go back to the woods and retrace my steps maybe it would take me back to the spot where I began?* It was a possibility. The woods covered a lot of ground. *How would I know if I was going back the same way that*

I had run that night? In my nightmares I was running but I did not seem to be doing so in a straight direction. Rather I seemed to be zigzagging through the woods as though trying to hide and get away from someone. *Was it only my fear or was there really someone chasing me? Did I run into a tree and was that why the doctor was there?* I did not seem to have any scars though. *I will set off to the farm today* I thought. I will ride out to the woods and see if it helped me to remember anything. The cooling water made me shiver and I decided it was time to get out and get ready. I dried myself and walked into the bedroom to throw on some jeans and a tee shirt. I looked at the clock and it was 11:30am. Hank would be coming soon.

I went into the kitchen to quickly wash up the dishes that were left in the sink. I watched the birds as they splashed around in the birdbath. I giggled as they threw water all around them. At one point there were so many birds standing on the edge that I didn't think another bird would fit. One bird was scolding a squirrel that happened to wander a little too close. A couple more kept swooping down close to his head in hopes that it would scare him away. Standing his ground the squirrel sat eating sunflower seeds very slowly as if to irritate the birds even more. I enjoyed watching the antics of these creatures and could have watched them all day long. Just as I finished washing up I heard Hank drive up. He knocked on the door and walked in.

"Hi, Katie," he said as he walked across the kitchen to give me a hug.

"Hi, Hank," I replied. "You are right on time," I laughed. "I could set my watch by you."

Hank tossed his head back and laughed.

"Are you ready to go Katie or do you have something to attend to first?" he asked.

"I would like to talk to you for a minute if you don't mind," I replied watching him closely for his reaction.

"Sure, Katie," he replied. "I've got all day."

"Good, "I giggled. "Here, sit down and we can talk," I said as I motioned him to sit on the chair. "I have been thinking about what happened yesterday and I would like to see if I can get your help on something," I began tentatively.

Hank watched me closely as I continued, "I don't remember everything that happened yesterday but I do remember going to the woods. What I would like to do, if it is okay with you, is go back to the woods today and if I start to remember anything I would like to talk to you about it." I went on before he had a chance to respond, "I am not sure if I will remember anything but I would like to have someone to talk to about any memories and you have always told me that you would be there for me," I reasoned.

He looked down at the table so I wasn't sure what he was thinking.

"Hank, if you would rather not I will understand and I won't hold it against you but I really need someone to talk to. I won't ask you any more questions but will only tell you what I have remembered," I stated.

After a pause I continued, "I don't want to talk to Mom or Carol about it because they will merely push me to go to Dr. Goodson and I am not ready for that yet. I don't know when or if I will ever go to see a doctor but it would help me to know that I have you to turn to if I need someone." I paused and waited for his reply.

Hank was still looking down. He slowly looked up at me and with tears in his eyes he began to speak. "Katie, I am honored that you have so much trust and respect for me." He continued, "I will gladly do anything that I can to help you and I won't pressure you to remember. I don't like the idea of you going to the woods alone. So please let me go with you and I won't say anything. I will wait in the distance and let you do whatever you need to do. I just don't like the idea of you being out there by yourself," he finished.

"Hank, I have been out there many times and I have never had any trouble. I think it would be better if I went out alone. That way I would not be distracted," I said trying to sound convincing.

I could see that he was disappointed by my decision but I thought it would be better to go alone. I would wait to see how I felt once we went out to the farm.

As we drove out to the farm the sky darkened and the rain clouds were moving in fast.

"Looks like your ride may have to wait, Katie," Hank said as he gazed outside the window at the fast darkening skies.

"Guess you're right, Hank. I don't want to go out in a storm," I replied, a little disappointed. "I have an early meeting in the morning so I better get things ready for it. We can always take a ride the next time I come out," I suggested.

I sat back and did not speak for the rest of the ride. Hank was also quiet. I could tell he was thinking about something but I did not feel like asking. It seemed that when I talked it was always about the same thing and I never seemed to get any answers…

Chapter 4

It was late by the time I got home. I had stayed to help Hank clean up the barn and brush out the horses. I took extra time in brushing out Lacey. My mind was a blank as I brushed Lacey. I was tired of trying to sort things out! If the memories were going to come to me they would have to surface on their own. I decided that I wasn't going to push it any more.

I went in and took a long hot shower. I put some water on for some tea to help me relax before going to bed. As I walked into the kitchen I saw the light flashing, indicating that I had messages on the machine. I pushed the button to check it out. The first message was from Carol.

"Hi, Katie. I just wanted to call and remind you that we have a special board meeting in the morning," her voice sounded excited as she spoke. "They are going to make some announcements and I am very excited about it. Don't be late." She continued, "I will wait for you in your office. See you in the morning." Click and she was gone.

The next message on the machine was from Scott.

"Hi, Katie. It's Scott. I don't know if you got my last message because you did not call back. Don't forget about the special board meeting in the morning. See you then. Bye."

He spoke fast as though afraid of using up all the tape on the answering machine.

I deleted the messages and went to the stove and poured myself some tea. I walked out on the deck to sit on the swing. I left the yard light off because I could see quite well with the kitchen light on. As I sat on the swing I slowly rocked it back and forth. It was very relaxing as I was tired from helping Hank all day long. I closed my eyes and listened to the night sounds. The rain had stopped earlier in the evening and it was a clear night. There was a full moon and the sky was full of twinkling stars. I set my cup down, closed my eyes and leaned back as I slowly rocked. All I could hear was the sound of the chirping crickets and a lonely bullfrog croaking off in the distance. I let out a deep sigh as the tea began to work and I could feel my body relaxing. I began to feel very tired so I stood, grabbed my cup and went back into the house. On my way into the bedroom I placed the cup in the sink. I walked into the bedroom, turned down the bedding and slipping out of my robe I climbed into bed. Sleep came quickly.

I woke early and after a shower I quickly got dressed. 'Important board meeting'…'special announcement'…'special board meeting'…Carol's and Scott's words kept going through my mind. I kept wondering what the special announcement was going to be. The proceeds from the auction had put us over the goal in the money we had hoped to raise. They had already had the board meeting regarding that so it was something else that was going to be announced this time.

As I drove up to work I could see the construction workers busy working. They had progressed rapidly on the new wing. They should have it completed within the next month or two. It was amazing how quickly they could build it. Once it was completed it would have the best updated state-of-the-art equipment to facilitate the needs of disabled children from anywhere in the world. They were also going to install computer uplinks; so doctor conference calls could be made to provide the fastest and most efficient diagnosis possible. If needed, even emergency surgeries could be performed via computer screens from anywhere in the world. It was truly amazing to think of the endless possibilities that would one day be performed here.

I was the last one to arrive at work and as I went into my office I saw half the board members waiting. I giggled and asked if the meeting was going to be held there. We all sat around waiting for the meeting to be called to order.

"Why don't we go down and wait in the boardroom?" I suggested as more people began to arrive. "There is more room down there and we can all sit down comfortably. Besides it is almost time for the meeting to start," I said as I got up from my chair and walked towards the door with everyone following.

Carol came up to me and started asking questions: "Katie, do you have any idea why we are having this special meeting? I wonder what the announcement is going to be? When was the last time we had a special meeting? Do you think they are going to be giving out promotions today?" Carol's questions kept coming.

"Carol, I am not sure of anything," I laughed as I interrupted her questions and for the first time all morning she was finally quiet. "I am sure we will all find out soon enough. It is almost time for the meeting to begin and we will all know shortly," I assured her.

Everyone had taken their seats and we were just waiting for Mr. Sweeney to come in and call the meeting to order. A few minutes later he walked in and there were two other people with him. I had never seen either one of them before and I had no idea who they were. Carol was sitting next to me and stopped chatting when they walked in. She looked at me and smiled. I figured she must know who they were and was happy to see them.

"I would like to call this meeting to order," Mr. Sweeney began. "We have a lot to cover so I want to get started."

As I glanced around the room I could tell that some of the board members knew who the guests that had come in with Mr. Sweeney were. I smiled to myself every time I looked at him. He reminded me of Santa Claus with his build; he had white hair plus the characteristic white beard and moustache.

"As all of you are aware," he commenced, "we surpassed our money goal this year." Clearing his throat he continued, "With the money that was left over from our budget for the new wing we have decided to add on two more positions. I have called this Special Board Meeting so that I could introduce you to the new members who will be joining our staff." He took a sip of water and continued: "First, I would like to introduce to you Dr. Sara Jenkins," he informed us. "She will be assisting in most of the surgical procedures that we will be undertaking."

"Next, I would like to introduce Dr. Shawn Goodson who will be working as our counselor and psychologist. Dr. Goodson will be working with all the families that are sent here for treatment. Now let's give them both warm heartfelt thanks for deciding to join our staff." He paused as we all clapped.

Once the applause had ceased Mr. Sweeney resumed, "Now we will need to make some changes around here. But first I want you all to get a chance to learn more about our two new staff members so we will have brunch after the meeting. Please help them with anything they need and answer any questions they might have," he said as his speech drew to a close.

"Let's break now and get something to eat and drink," he said laughing.

We all stood up to go to the cafeteria but he interrupted us and said, "Katie, could you stay for a minute, please? I would like to talk to you alone."

He waited for everyone else to leave and he shut the door behind them. I felt a feeling of dread overcome me.

"This will only take a minute and then we can join the others," he began. "I have given careful consideration to this and I know that you are going to be pleased with what I have to tell you."

He paused momentarily as he studied my expression and continued, "I am going to be moving you out of your office and you are going to be working with Sara and Shawn." He explained, "You have had the most extensive training and with your love for children you are the best qualified person for this position." Without giving me a chance to speak he added, "I have discussed this matter with both of them and they are pleased and excited to have you working with them. They were looking over the employee files to find the best candidate to fill the position and stopped once they saw your file and your credentials." His words had an unmistakable ring of conviction attached to them.

"Katie, this is something you have worked very hard for and you have the opportunity now to fulfill your dream." He quickly added, "They will be bringing their files over and the three of you can get everything set up and we can start taking appointments." He had a big smile on his face when he finished speaking.

"I am not sure if that is something that I want to do Mr. Sweeney," I began. "I like doing the work that I am doing now. Isn't there someone else that would be more suitable for the job?"

"Oh, Katie," he said and laughed. "You are joking, right? This is exactly what you want to do and you have been pushing for donations to help get the new wing built; so don't tell me now that you do not want to do it."

I looked at him blankly while he continued, "It is already settled and you will begin working with them tomorrow when the first set of files start coming in."

"Well then, I guess that is what I am going to be doing," I said trying to keep my voice steady even though I was very upset with the change. "It doesn't sound like you are giving me a choice on the matter."

"Good," he stood up as he spoke. "I will introduce you to them when we reach downstairs and they can tell you what time they want to get started tomorrow for setting up the files and paperwork."

I stood up but did not speak. Neither one of us spoke as we walked down to the cafeteria. As we got closer we could hear everyone laughing and chatting. I just wanted to go back to my office and sulk. I was still trying to decide who was really behind the decision for me to be the one to work with them. I knew he was right when he said it was the job that I had been waiting and working so hard to get. Maybe if it wasn't Dr.

Goodson I would have been happier about it. It seemed everyone around me was pushing me to visit him and have him figure out my nightmares. Now I would have to be working with him on a daily basis and I was not happy with that thought. Did both doctors pick me out like Mr. Sweeney had said or had Mom, Dad, Hank or Carol been the one to sway their decision? I guess that would be another thing that I would have to wait and find out.

As we entered the cafeteria I could see Carol sitting and talking with Dr. Jenkins. When she saw me she smiled and winked at me. She would be the first that I would question about it. The rest I would get around to asking later.

I went up and got some fruit to eat. I was not hungry right now and I did not want to eat. However, I didn't want to explain to anyone why I had lost my appetite either. I took my bowl and turned around. Carol was sitting alone so I walked over and sat down beside her.

"Took you long enough to get here," she laughed. "What did Sweeney want to talk to you about?" She looked curiously at me and continued, "You don't look very happy about it, whatever it was," she observed pausing for me to respond.

"So you don't know what he wanted to talk to me about?" I inquired.

"No, I don't. Remember I was the one that was trying to figure out all weekend why we were having the Special Board Meeting." She giggled and asked again, "So are you going to tell me or not?"

"He wanted to tell me that I was going to be the one working with Dr. Jenkins and Dr. Goodson," I replied.

Carol squealed and said, "Oh, Katie! That is wonderful news. This is exactly what you have trained so hard to do!" She calmed down and resumed, "You are going to love working with them. They are both exceptional doctors."

"You are always pushing me to go see Dr. Goodson. Did you speak to Mr. Sweeney about me working with him so that he could help me with my nightmares?" I asked Carol as I sat watching her eyes to make sure she was being honest with me."

"What would make you think that, Katie? Besides when does Sweeney ever listen to any suggestions I have. Plus remember I was bugging you to find out what the special meeting was for," Carol convincingly replied, acting hurt that I would even suggest such a thing.

"I am not sure I want to do it, Carol." I shrugged my shoulders and went on, "But Mr. Sweeney said they both picked me out from my employee folder based on my credentials. So I guess I am going to have to start from tomorrow."

I sighed and continued, "Maybe if it wasn't Dr. Goodson, I would feel better about it and be more excited."

"Oh, Katie. You will see. He is wonderful to work with and he is truly gifted and skilled while working with people, especially children, just like you are."

Carol looked very serious and continued, "He is a caring and compassionate person and is very genuine with respect to his passion for helping anyone that needs it. Once you start working with him you will see and understand him better."

"Don't sell him short, Katie." She advised, "Just observe the response he gets from those he helps. You will soon see he does not consider his patients as dollar signs. He really does his best to help them."

I sat and pondered about what she had said and before I could comment Mr. Sweeney came up to me and asked me to accompany him so that he could introduce me to the new doctors. I got up and Carol smiled at me and gave me a 'thumbs up' motion.

We first went to Dr. Jenkins. Mr. Sweeney waited until she had finished, before speaking: "Hi, Sara. I wanted to introduce you to, Katie. She is very excited about the prospect of working with you."

"Hi, Doctor Jenkins," I said as I extended my hand to her. Sara was in her early forties and was almost six feet tall. Her hair was red and she had blue eyes. She had a full figure and a bubbly personality and I liked her right away.

"Hi, Katie and please call me 'Sara'," she replied. "We are going to be working together so we might as well keep it informal. I like it much better that way."

After releasing my hand she continued, "We have a lot of work ahead of us. Are you ready to start?" she asked. "They are bringing the filing cabinets in the morning and we can work together to get them sorted out."

She laughed as she saw my anxiety-ridden expression and explained, "I would like to get everything done as soon as possible, so I hope you don't mind if we work a little longer every day."

"No, that sounds fine with me," I replied. "I like to have everything in order so that we can access a file if we need it."

"I will be seeing my regular patients starting next week, so we need to get things set up by this weekend," she said as a warm smile of reassurance lit her face.

"I will start moving things around as soon as I leave and the area will be ready for the filing cabinets by morning," I informed her.

"That sounds wonderful!" Then turning to Mr. Sweeney she said, "I know that we picked the right person for this job."

Turning her attention to me once again Sara said, "I am really glad that you decided to work with me, Katie. I know you will enjoy it as much as I do."

Mr. Sweeney interrupted and informed Sara that we had to go over and see Shawn before he left. He took my elbow and turned me around.

"See you in the morning, Katie and I look forward to working with you," Sara said as we started to move away.

"See you then, Sara," I said as Mr. Sweeney pushed me along.

Dr. Goodson was sitting on a chair along the wall and had just finished talking to Scott as we walked up to him.

"Hello, Shawn. I wanted to introduce you to Katie before I had to go," he said. "Katie, this is Shawn."

"Hello, Dr. Goodson," I said and extended my hand.

He took my hand in his and covered it with his other. He was in his mid-thirties; brown hair and soft dark brown eyes. He was six feet tall and had a medium build. His chest and arm muscles were well developed from working out.

"Please, Katie. Call me 'Shawn'," he said. "I prefer first names because it makes it more casual and people respond better when the atmosphere is more relaxed."

When he talked he had a soft-spoken, soothing, calming voice. I understood what Carol meant when she said he would be easy to talk to. He had an inner compassion that showed through his eyes, smile and voice.

As Shawn talked to Katie he observed that she was a few inches taller than five feet with long auburn hair and hazel eyes. She had a medium build and a sadness you could see in her eyes. Carol had told him about the nightmares and flashbacks that Katie was experiencing and he wondered how long it would be before he would be able to get her to open up to him.

He continued, "I am very glad that you decided to work with us. Sara and I are really looking forward to working with you."

"Thank you, Shawn, but I am not sure after talking to Sara if I am ready for the daunting task ahead of us," I replied laughing. I elaborated, "She needs everything set up by this weekend for her patients next week so we will be working hard all week long."

"Don't worry, Katie. We will all be working together and we will get it done quickly," he said and smiled. He had a very calming voice as he spoke: "My filing cabinets won't be coming until next week. That way we won't get anything mixed up during the transit."

"I will get my office cleared out to make room for both of your patient file cabinets, so it will be easier when they are brought over," I informed him.

"Sounds great," he said convincingly and added, "I will see you in the morning and I wanted to thank you again for your decision to come work with us."

"See you in the morning," I said and turned and walked out of the cafeteria and went to my office to start moving things around.

When I entered my office there was a big box sitting on my desk. There was a note attached that read: *'Katie here are the computer disks from my office.*

If you want to start downloading them onto your computer it would be greatly appreciated. Looking forward to working with you' and it was signed 'Sara'. I looked through the box and a feeling of panic gripped me. I wasn't sure if I was going to be able to get them all installed and get everything moved out. Just as I was trying to decide where to start I heard someone come through the door.

"Hi, Katie," Scott said.

"Hi, Scott" I answered.

"I am here for two reasons," he said. "First, to congratulate you on your new position. You must have sucked up big time to get this one," he laughed and continued, "and secondly to help move everything out for you so you will have room for the make-shift office that is coming in the morning."

"Scott," I explained, "I didn't know anything about them joining the staff. It was just as much of a surprise to me as everyone else. Mr. Sweeney told me they went through all of our employee files and chose me to be the one to assist them," I told him.

"Yeah, whatever you say, Katie," he said. "It just seems everything always goes your way."

I was a little annoyed by his remark so I decided to start downloading the files before we got into an argument. I told him I had things I needed to get started on and he could begin whenever he wanted to.

Scott began moving the file cabinets out of my office and took them down to Carol's office. She was going to be taking over my position once the new wing was finished and my new office was ready. I took out the numbered disks and started downloading them onto my computer and putting all the patient records onto our system. Scott finished up and tried talking to me again but I did not feel like talking or arguing with him so I just ignored him. He left when he discovered I wasn't going to stop my work. Carol stopped in to see what I thought about the new doctors.

"Well, what do you think now that you have had the chance to talk with the doctors?" she asked.

"Sara seems quite bubbly but I am not sure if that is just the excitement of everything going on or if that is what she is really like," I told Carol.

"And..." she paused momentarily. "Well, come on...what did you think of Shawn?"

"He seemed nice," I replied.

"Nice! Is that all you have to say?" She frowned and continued, "I thought you might have more to say than that."

"What do you expect, Carol?" I asked her. "We only said 'hi' and that it would be nice working together." I laughed and continued, "I am sure I will know more about him after tomorrow. So ask me tomorrow night."

"You will enjoy working with him, Katie. He is a really nice person". With that she got up and walked to the door.

She paused and said, "I know you don't want to hear this but he will be able to help you too, Katie, if you just let him."

I looked up and she could tell I was upset by what she had just said.

"Carol, I will not discuss that issue ever again," I snapped, "so you might just as well drop it."

"You'll see." She quickly added, "One day he will help you." She didn't look back but just walked down the hall.

I worked the rest of the afternoon and into the evening trying to download as many disks as possible. It was late and I was getting very tired so I decided to stop for the night and start afresh in the morning. Maybe I could get Carol to help me get the rest done? I would ask her in the morning. She had left early and didn't say anything when she had walked by my office.

I drove home. After entering the house I put some water on the stove for tea. I wanted to get to bed so that I would be well rested for work in the morning. It would be another long day and we would be working into the evening. The kettle began to scream, so I took it off the burner. After making myself a cup of tea I went into the bathroom to take a hot shower.

After I was done I dried off and didn't bother to put on my robe. I picked up my cup, walked into the bedroom, turned down the bedding and then slipped into bed. I was tired and the tea tasted good. I turned on the light and thought I would read a little until I was sleepy. I read a couple of chapters in the book that I had on the night stand before I dozed off.

I hadn't been asleep long before the dreams started coming. Bright lights…Blinding lights and I could not see anything. Splash! I was back in the water struggling to get free…to get to the surface so that I could breathe. Back in the house again…Over and over the flashbacks kept coming. My screams woke me. I sat up in bed while I calmed myself down. *Someday*, I thought to myself, *these nightmares will be gone and I will be able to sleep all night through.*

I turned off the light and lay back down trying to force myself to sleep. *Why bother?* I thought. I will go to sleep only to wake again in a panic. *Damn*, I thought, *maybe Carol was right? Maybe I should try to discuss with Shawn these flashbacks and nightmares? If nothing else maybe he could suggest how I should handle them so that I could get some sleep? I will wait and see if I feel comfortable talking with him before I mention anything to him.*

I kept watching the clock but I could not go back to sleep. I got up and walked into the kitchen. *Maybe I just needed to move around and I would get tired and would be able to sleep*? I went out on the deck and sat on the swing and rocked back and forth trying to relax and not think about the flashbacks. It was no use. The pieces would flash through my mind no matter how hard I tried to block them out. I sat there for over an hour. I was feeling very tired and sleepy. I got up and went back in and crawled into bed. I lay down and turned on the radio. It would be a change and maybe the music would help me sleep.

I lay there half listening to music until I drifted off to sleep. I was back in the woods again. I would run until I could run no more. I stopped and caught my breath and ran again. This time the dream wasn't as vivid and I finally fell asleep…

Chapter 5

The morning started out dark and gloomy. I woke up late and was still tired from the sleepless night the night before. It was going to be a busy day and I wasn't ready for it. My mood was very restless. I put the kettle on for some tea while I quickly got dressed. I threw on some jeans and a tee shirt because we were going to be moving files around. I would be more comfortable dressed casually and would be able to get more done. It was to be a new beginning for me at work but I didn't feel the excitement that I had hoped for. Maybe I would feel differently once I got to work and got started?

The kettle began to whistle and it brought me back to reality. I took the kettle off the stove and poured myself some tea. I sat at the table to drink it and put on my shoes. A quick glance at the clock informed me that I better get moving. I took another sip of tea and rushed out the door.

When I arrived at work Sara and Shawn were already there. The file cabinets had already arrived but were still in the hall and had not been moved into the office yet.

"Hi, Katie," said Sara with a big smile on her face. "Are you ready for the day?" she giggled as she asked me.

"Hi, Sara," I replied. "Sorry, I am late coming in. I got a late start."

"That's okay. You are here now and we can get to work," she said.

"Hi, Katie." Shawn got up and walked over to me.

"Hi, Shawn," I said and continued, "How are you doing? Are you finding everything you need?" I inquired.

"I am trying to decide where to put everything," he said looking around the room.

"We can move the desk against the far wall if you would like to help me?" I suggested.

"That should give us plenty of room for the cabinets and we will still have room left over for yours when they arrive," I added.

"Hi everybody," Carol called out. "Need some help?" she asked. We all laughed together.

"I still have some patient diskettes, if you would like to help me download them onto the computer," I requested.

"Sure I can help. Let's move the desk and I will be out of everybody's way while you get the rest of the things situated and set up," she said.

"Sounds great," Shawn said and continued, "You girls grab one end of the desk and I will take this side and we can move it so that Carol can get started."

We got the desk moved and the computer set up and I gave Carol the box of diskettes that needed to be downloaded. She feigned a cry and took the box over to the desk to work.

While she was working, the rest of us started moving in the file cabinets and put them against the wall closest to the door so that they would be easier to access. After we got them in place we started bringing in all the boxes that were filled with the patient folders. Just when it seemed like they would never end Sara brought in the last one.

The morning flew past as we worked at getting the office set up. Sara had to leave because she had a patient she needed to talk with. They were going to be leaving the area and they needed to pick up their son's medical files for the new doctor they were going to be seeing. Later in the afternoon she had to assist in surgery so she would not be there to help us.

"I am sorry that I have brought all this work over and now I have to leave and can't help," she apologized. "I know Katie that you will be able to sort everything out. I have confidence in you," she added as she picked up her purse and walked out the door giving us a wave as she left.

All morning while we were trying to work we had people stopping in to say 'Hi' to Shawn. He was very courteous and would stop and talk a few minutes with each one. I had grabbed another box and was setting up the file cabinet trying to get another box done before we stopped for lunch.

"Break time!" Carol yelled from the corner. "I am starving and I am not going to be able to do another thing until I eat something," she cried as she placed the back of her hand to her forehead and sighed.

We all laughed and decided to stop and take a break to get something to eat.

"Let's go out to get something," Carol suggested as she looked at us to get our reaction.

"Sounds good to me," Shawn replied.

"You two go ahead. I am just going to go down to the cafeteria and grab something and bring it back up here," I informed them.

"Let's go to the restaurant at the corner, Shawn. They have good food," Carol suggested.

"Okay, I am up for that," he replied. "Are you sure you don't want to go, Katie?" he asked.

"No, I am not very hungry and I want to get back to the files," I said. "Go and enjoy yourselves," I added.

I went down to the cafeteria and grabbed a salad and tea and went back up to the office. I figured I would just eat as I worked. I sat on one of the boxes and looked out the window as people walked around. It was still very cloudy and had begun to drizzle. I set my salad down and started massaging my neck. My eyes were tired from sorting the files and it felt good just sitting with my eyes closed for a minute.

"Katie, Katie, Katie," a voice squealed with excitement and I could hear it coming all the way down the hall.

I looked up and smiled as Paul wheeled into my office. He had come in for his physical therapy treatment.

"Hi, Katie!" he cried excitedly.

"Hi, Paulie. I am so glad to see you," I replied.

He came over and gave me a hug. We sat talking and he told me how his therapy session had gone. His eyes were very wide and he spoke very fast like he was afraid he would forget to tell me something. I giggled as he chatted so quickly and that made him giggle. I loved to hear him laugh. Everyone around him always joined in when they heard him laugh. He always came in to see me after his session was over. It was his reward for working hard. He had brought me a card that he had made for me. It was a picture of a barn with Lacey standing in the door. I got up and got a piece of tape so I could hang it on my wall. I hung it right next to the picture he had drawn for me the week before.

When I came back and sat down in front of Paul he started to tell me a funny story about something he had seen and was waving his hands in the air for emphasis and rocking back and forth. He looked quite a sight and we both got giggling and laughing when suddenly a laugh broke out behind us. I quickly turned around looking to see who was standing at the door. Shawn was standing there smiling and laughing at what he had just witnessed.

"Oh, I am sorry. I didn't see you come in," I said.

"I just got here and I didn't want to interrupt. It looked like you two were really enjoying yourselves," he said smiling. "Sorry, I didn't mean to laugh and interrupt you both," he added.

"Paul, this is Dr. Goodson and he is going to be working here at the hospital," I told him.

"Hi, Dr. Goodson. It is good to meet you," Paul said with a big wide smile on his face.

"Paul came in for his therapy treatment and he always stops in to see me when he has finished his session for the day," I informed Shawn.

"Katie is my best friend," Paul explained to Shawn.

"You are very lucky to have a friend like Katie," Shawn replied.

There was a knock at my door. I looked up and it was Shirley.

"Hi, Katie," she said. "I knew he would be here," she added.

"Oh, Mom! Do we have to go already?" Paul protested.

"Yes, Paul. We have some more stops to make. Tell Katie 'goodbye, we need to go'," she replied.

"Shirley, I would like to introduce you to Dr. Goodson. He has joined our staff and will be working here," I explained.

"Dr. Goodson this is Shirley Knight," I said as I introduced them.

"I am sure we will be seeing a lot of each other," Shirley said to Shawn.

"I look forward to that," he replied.

As Shawn and Shirley stood chatting to one another Paul and I continued talking.

"Do you like your picture?" Paul asked me.

"I love it Paul. You did a beautiful job on it," I replied. "It looks just like Lacey," I told him.

"Do you think I could still go for a ride on her, Katie?" Paul asked anticipating the answer. "I had so much fun riding the pony and I would like to ride Lacey like you said we could," he leaned forward in his chair and looked at me expectantly. "Please, please, please, Katie," he begged.

"Of course we can," I told him.

"Yes!" he exclaimed excitedly.

He was waving his hands in the air saying 'yes' and moving from side to side in his wheelchair as if he were dancing around after my reply. We both started giggling.

Shirley and Shawn walked over to us to see what all the excitement was about.

"Mom, Mom, Katie is going to take me for a ride on Lacey!" he squealed. "Do you want to go Dr. Goodson?" Paul asked in his excitement.

"Paul, Dr. Goodson is a very busy man and he doesn't have time to go riding," I said before Shawn had a chance to speak.

"Actually Katie, I would love to go riding if you don't mind. It has been a while but I enjoy riding," he said smiling as he looked at me.

"Sure, if you would like to. We have plenty of horses and I will make sure you get a good one," I told him hoping he couldn't see my hesitation.

"Great. Just let me know when you are going and I will be ready," he said.

"I am going to be pretty busy all week so how about Saturday? Is that day okay with you Shirley?" I inquired.

"That will be fine. Are you sure it's okay, Katie?" Shirley asked me.

"It will be wonderful," I replied.

"How is Saturday for you, Dr. Goodson?" I asked Shawn, hoping he would have other plans.

"Saturday is great for me," he replied.

"I will make a picnic lunch and I will drop by and pick up Paul on my way out to the farm," I told Shirley.

"Tell you what, Katie. I will pick you up and we can stop by and pick up Paul on our way," offered Shawn.

"Oh, I don't want to impose on you, Dr. Goodson," I said trying to evade his offer.

"Are you kidding?" Shawn laughed. "I am the one that seems to be imposing on your plans."

I kept silent and he continued.

"There it is settled, Katie" said Shawn. "What time shall we go?" he asked.

"Let's figure on noon," I replied and continued, "If that is okay with you, Shirley?"

"That is fine with me. I will have him ready for you to pick up," Shirley said. "Thank you, Katie. He enjoys spending time with you and talks about you everyday," she added.

"He is such a joy to be around. He makes me laugh and forget about everything when we are together. So I am not sure who enjoys it more: him or me," I told her.

"We need to go now, Paul. We have interrupted them long enough," Shirley said.

Paul unfastened his seat belt and held his arms up to me. I reached down and picked him up and gave him a warm hug. I turned him around a couple of times before placing him back in his wheelchair.

"Bye, Paul. I will see you Saturday," I said and waved to him as they went out the door.

Turning to Shawn I said, "Sorry about the interruption, Shawn, but Paul has always stopped to see me after each of his therapy treatments. It seems to help him knowing he can come visit me and he tries really hard," I said.

"Don't worry about it, Katie. He seems to love you very much," Shawn replied.

"He has brought a lot of joy to me too. I love spending time with him," I said. "Now I think I have wasted enough time so I better get back to work," I said laughing.

"Hello everyone," Carol said as she waltzed in the door.

"Hi," we replied in unison.

"Don't mind me. I will just be slaving away in the corner," she laughed.

"Thanks for helping," I told her.

"Anything to help and I get to watch Shawn do some physical labor for once," she laughed and winked at me when she spoke.

I did not mention anything to Carol about going riding or the picnic that we had planned. Carol did not like horses and wouldn't want to go. I was hoping that something would come up and Shawn too would not be able to go. He seemed nice enough but I wasn't ready for an afternoon with him. I would not know what to say. We had the rest of the week and maybe something would come up.

Shawn had gone back to putting the file cabinets together and I went back to the stack of papers that I had set down when I had taken a break. The tapping of the keys on the keyboard was the only sound in the room as Carol typed the labels that we needed and downloaded more of the patient diskettes on the computer. Time seemed to fly past as we worked. We seemed to get a lot done but there was always much more to finish.

"Are you two going to work all night long?" Carol asked breaking the silence.

We had been working so hard that I did not pay attention to the time. I looked up at the clock and it was 6:30. I stood up and stretched myself. I looked at Carol and smiled.

"Sorry, I didn't realize the time," I told her.

"That's because all you do is work, Katie," she replied.

"I have finished the labels you need and there are a few more diskettes to download but I will finish them tomorrow. I am beat and I am going home," Carol said.

"I think I am going to stay and finish up what I am doing. Then I will go," I told her.

"Are you going to stay and slave away too, Shawn?" she asked him.

"I think I will stay just a little longer to finish up this last cabinet," Shawn replied.

"Okay, I will see you both in the morning," she said as she went out the door.

I went over and picked up the labels that Carol had typed for me. Shawn had finished the last cabinet and pushed it against the wall.

"There, that is the last of the cabinets," he said delightedly. "My work is done," he laughed as he spoke. Then he asked, "Is there anything I can do to help you finish up, Katie?"

"I am just going to put these labels on and I am going to stop," I told him.

"Here let me take some and we can get it done faster," he said as he took some of the labels.

"That is okay, Shawn. I can finish it up. You probably want to get going," I said.

"No, I will stay and help so that you can get it done quicker," he said.

We finished working in silence. It had been a very long day setting up the new office. I appreciated Shawn staying to help me finish up. We worked for another two hours before finally deciding to stop for the night.

"There that is all the labels. Is there anything else that needs to be done, Katie?" Shawn asked.

"No, I think we have done enough for today," I replied and added, "I will get a fresh start in the morning."

"Would you like to stop and get something to eat?" Shawn asked.

"No, I am tired. I think I will just go home and collapse," I laughed.

We continued talking while we walked down to the car garage. My muscles were aching from the long day that I had worked. Shawn walked me to my car and waited for me to get in and start the motor before turning and walking to his own car. He waved as I drove off.

By the time I arrived home I was so tired I just took a shower and went to bed and hoped that sleep would come quickly. It had been a long day and I was exhausted. I lay thinking about Shawn. He seemed like a nice, sincere person. I felt a little nervous around him, not knowing how much Carol had told him about me. Did he know about the flashbacks and the nightmares? I would feel embarrassed if he did. I did not know him and I did not want him knowing too much about me either. I would have to talk to Carol in the morning to see what she had told him. Shawn had a very soothing, calming, soft-spoken voice when he spoke. Paul liked him and wanted to spend more time with him but he liked everyone. Shawn seemed genuine when he talked and in terms of his concern for other people. I guess in time I would get to know him better now that we were working so closely. I will know if I felt comfortable enough to talk to him.

The rest of the week continued on the same lines. We worked late every night trying to get everything done so that the patient's files could be accessed quickly. The new patients would start arriving from Monday. So we wanted everything ready for them to make the move easier for everyone. As the week progressed some days Sara would stay and help and Shawn would have appointments to handle. Other days Shawn would stay and help and Sara would have to leave early. Carol stayed and helped me throughout the week. We all got to know each other a little better as we worked together. We all talked and laughed and complained about our aches and pains from pushing ourselves to get done.

Finally, Friday arrived and we had set a goal to have everything done. Every file relabeled and put in the file cabinet. Sara had a meeting to attend, so she was leaving for the weekend. She stopped at the office on her way to the airport to see how things were going. I told her that we would be finished by the time we left and she was very pleased with our progress. She was running late and had to rush off.

It was late afternoon and as I put the last folder in place I pushed the drawer shut. Carol and Shawn both applauded as the drawer clicked shut. We all laughed together.

"Let's go celebrate," Carol suggested.

"We are not there yet," Shawn joked.

"I am going home for a hot bath and bed," I told them.

"Oh, come on, Katie. Come with us," Carol pleaded. "It is still early. We can eat, have a drink and we can all go home," said Carol.

"Yes, Katie, come with us." Shawn continued, "You deserve to enjoy the victory dinner too. You worked very hard to get it done staying late to make sure we would meet the deadline."

"I don't know. I am very tired," I told them as they watched me.

"You are going, Katie, and we are not going to take 'no' for an answer," Carol said pouting.

Then turning to Shawn, Carol said, "Come on, Shawn, before she changes her mind," giggling as she did so.

We all walked together down to the parking garage.

"I'll drive," Shawn said. "Carol you grab Katie so she doesn't get away," he continued.

I laughed and replied, "I can drive. That way you won't have to bring us back, Shawn."

"No, get in girls." He chuckled and said, "If you drive, Katie, you won't go. See I am getting to know you and your tricks."

I blushed because I knew he was correct. I would have just driven home and not gone to the restaurant. We talked and giggled all the way there. We were all so very tired that everything that was said was funny to us. Shawn gave a toast to the hard work and great job that we had all accomplished. Carol gave a toast to new friends and I gave a toast to new beginnings. After we had eaten Shawn suggested we go. He had promised me that we wouldn't stay out late and true to his word we left as soon as we had finished dinner. He drove us back to the office to pick up our cars. Carol's car was first and we dropped her off and waited for her to start her car and backup. We waved to her as she left. Shawn then took me to my car.

"I need to get your address, Katie, so that I can pick you up tomorrow," Shawn said.

"Shawn, it is okay. I can pick up Paul and meet you out there," I told him.

"No, Katie. I would feel better picking you up and together we can stop to get Paul," he said.

I gave him my address and phone number too. He could call to let me know in case something came up and he couldn't make it.

"I am excited about going, Katie. I think it will be a lot of fun," he said. He inquired, "Is there anything that I can bring?"

"No," I laughed and continued, "I called Mom and she is preparing the lunch in the morning. All we have to do is pick up Paul and everything else is ready. You will understand once you meet my Mom," I laughed.

I got out of Shawn's car, unlocked my own and got in. Shawn waited until the engine started and I backed out of the parking space. We waved to each other as I drove by.

I walked in the door and kicked off my shoes. I filled the tea kettle and went in the bathroom to run a hot bath. I lit the candles around the tub and went in to get the tea. I walked in the bedroom and grabbed my robe. I turned the water off and the steam rose from the tub. I slowly climbed in and sat down. I lay back and for the first time all week I finally relaxed. I watched the fire on the candles as they swayed and danced. I closed my eyes and let my mind go blank. I did not want to move or think for the next hour. The water had started to cool and I stepped out of the tub. I dried myself off and slipped into my robe. I grabbed my cup and took it to the kitchen and put it in the sink. I stood looking out the window for a few minutes. I was feeling very tired and relaxed after my bath and decided to go to bed. I turned down the covers, took off my robe and climbed into bed.

I felt my body relaxing and I fell into a deep sleep. I began tossing and turning as I felt my body begin to run. *Run, don't stop.* Bright lights blinding me…*Help me, please! I can't see! Running, I am running as fast as I can…I am panting and my lungs feel like they are about to explode.* The light flashes again and I cannot see. *Run, don't stop! Run, they are going to catch you*! Fear and panic envelop me. The light disappears and I blink trying to adjust my eyes so that I can see where I am going. *Run, run, run*! That is the only thought going through my mind. *Faster, run faster they are catching up and they are going to grab you*! The light is back in my eyes and I cannot see. Splash! Everything is black and it feels like someone is holding me. I can't move and I am fighting against something. Nothing happens as I try to move my hands to protect myself. I feel myself sinking deeper and deeper in the water. I kick my feet trying to fight my way to the surface. I am struggling to breathe and I can feel my lungs ready to explode. *Air…I need air.* I can feel my body sinking further down into the water. I struggle hard trying to move my hands and arms and as if my restraints had suddenly disappeared I could finally move. I frantically kick my feet and using my hands and arms I fight my way back up. I am fighting hard. I don't know how long my lungs are going to last. *Faster, harder, I push myself.* I get to the surface and gasp for air. I am on my hands and knees in the middle of the bed. I am gasping for air trying to fill my lungs again with air. My chest is heaving and my heart is pounding in my chest. The room begins to spin and everything goes black…

Chapter 6

I slowly opened my eyes to see the morning light permeating through the bedroom window. I lay still for a few minutes, not wanting to move. I was trying to come to grips with the horrible nightmare from the night before. I slowly crawled back under the covers and the tears began to flow. Total frustration enveloped me and I began to sob uncontrollably. Why? What could have happened to me? How long must I endure these nightmares? The tears streamed unabated as I tried to get up. Every muscle in my body ached and screamed out in pain as I tried to move.

I looked at the clock. It was 10:15. Shawn would be there at 11:30 to pick me up for the picnic with Paul. I was not feeling up to the ride or the picnic but I did not want to disappoint Paul. He was looking forward to the expedition eagerly. I forced myself to stand up, grabbed my robe and went to the kitchen. I put some water on for tea and walked around the kitchen hoping to loosen up my tight muscles. Nothing I did seemed to help. The kettle began to whistle, so I took it off the burner and filled my cup. I walked into the bathroom and turned on the shower. I stood under the shower head and let the hot water pour on my skin. I turned around letting the water fall on my back. I tilted my head back under the water and just stood there. It felt good as the hot water eased my aching muscles.

After showering, I wrapped myself in a towel, stepped out of the shower and examined myself in the mirror. I looked horrible. My eyes were swollen from crying and my cheeks were puffy. I grabbed a wash cloth and ran it under cold water allowing it to soak up the water. I dabbed my eyes with the wet cloth; then held it there for a few minutes before repeating the procedure with my cheeks. My eyes hurt and the cold wash cloth soothed them. I looked back in the mirror and the swelling had subsided greatly.

I went in the bedroom and got dressed. After I was dressed, I sat on the bed and put on my shoes. My mind went back to the water. *Did I fall into the water or was someone trying to drown me?* It always happened so fast that I did not know how I got in the water in the first instance. Confused, I pushed those thoughts out of my mind for the moment. I quickly glanced at the clock again. It was 11.20. I had time for another cup of tea before Shawn would arrive. The water was still hot so I poured myself another cup and stood looking out the kitchen window at the birds. Shawn had driven up and was at the door but I had not seen him. He stood watching me for a few minutes. He was trying to decide if he should interrupt my thoughts. He knocked loudly on the door while I was deep in thought, startling me. I jumped dropping the cup which shattered in the sink. I turned and looked towards the door which Shawn had opened quickly as he entered.

"Are you okay, Katie?" he asked. "I didn't mean to scare you. I thought you heard me drive up," he explained.

"I was thinking about something and did not hear you," I said as I picked up the pieces of the cup and threw them into the trash.

"Are you ready for the ride?" I asked trying to avert his concern.

"Yes, I am. In fact, I am really looking forward to it. That is, if you are ready?" he watched me as he spoke, uncertain about what had just happened.

"Okay, let me grab my purse and we can go pick Paul up. I am sure he didn't sleep much last night knowing we were going riding today," I laughed as I spoke hoping Shawn would not notice my hands shaking.

I grabbed my purse and we walked to the door together. I turned on the porch light and locked the door as we got ready to leave. I could feel Shawn watching me as I talked and we walked to the car. I knew he was trying to analyze me by the way he was looking at me. *Maybe this wasn't such a good idea?* I should have called and told him I didn't feel well and postponed the trip for another day. I could not do that to Paul. He was so excited about going. We got in the car and put on our seatbelts. I explained to Shawn the route to Paul's house. We talked a little while driving but I was very guarded on how I responded to his questions. When we pulled up in the driveway, Paul was sitting in his wheelchair on the deck. We could hear him squealing with excitement.

"Hi, Katie! Hi, Dr. Goodson!" he yelled delightedly.

"Hi, Paulie," I said laughing.

"Hi, Paul. Are you ready to go or did you change your mind?" Shawn teasingly asked.

"I am ready!" Paul said and he wheeled his chair as fast as he could to the car.

"Hi, Katie!" Shirley yelled from the house. "He has been ready since five this morning," she added laughing.

"Hi, Shirley. I knew he would be up early and ready to go," I told her.

Paul had come up to the car and Shawn helped him in and folded up his wheelchair and put it in the trunk.

"I am not sure what time we will be back, Shirley," I said.

"If Paul had his way he would move in out there," Shirley replied. "We aren't going anywhere, so whenever you get done we will be here waiting. So there is no rush." She continued, "Have a safe ride and we will see you later."

Shawn had got in the car and I walked up and climbed in and we were ready to go. Paul started talking and never stopped until we got to the farm. I giggled at his excitement about the ride. Shawn sat there smiling at us as Paul and I teased and joked back and forth. We drove up the driveway and Mom and Dad were sitting on the porch swing rocking back and forth. They stood up when we parked the car. Shawn got out and opening the trunk of his car removed Paul's wheelchair and helped him in it. He did this effortlessly as though he had done it many times before. Shawn pushed Paul and I walked along beside them.

"Hi everyone!" Mom called out as she waved to us.

"Hi Grandma!" Paul shouted and waved back.

"I am so glad to see you, Paul. I have missed you," Mom said as she clasped her hands in front of her.

We walked up on the porch so I could make the introductions. "Mom, Dad…I would like you to meet Dr. Goodson," I said knowing the reaction I was going to get from Mom.

"Shawn, I would like you to meet my parents…Marge and Bob Stevens," I introduced to him.

"Good to meet you Dr. Goodson," Dad said as he extended his hand.

"Hello Bob…and please call me Shawn," he said shaking my Dad's hand.

"Hi Marge," Shawn said as he shook Mom's hand.

"Hello, Shawn. It's very nice meeting you," Mom replied as she gave me a quick glance.

"Hi, Paulie," Dad said as he ruffled up Paul's hair.

"Hi, Grandpa," Paul replied giggling.

"So you are going to ride the big horse today, huh?" Dad teased him.

"I am going to ride Lacey today and I can't wait," Paul said with big excited eyes.

"Katie you look tired. Are you feeling okay?" Mom looked inquiringly at me.

I could tell she knew that I must have had another nightmare so I tried to stop her before she said too much in front of Shawn. I was afraid she would take any opportunity to mention the nightmares in front of Shawn in hopes that he would get me to talk about them.

"Mom, please don't start. Not now," I told her.

"Everything is packed and Hank has put the sandwiches and other surprises in the saddlebags for you," Dad said quickly during the uneasy pause that followed Mom's query.

"We can have some fresh pie when you get back and Paul you can tell us all about your ride," Mom told us.

"We are going to the pond. So if anything comes up and you need to get in touch, you know where we are," I informed Mom as we descended the steps.

"Okay. Be careful and have fun. We will see you later," Mom told us as we started walking down towards the barn.

Just as we got to the grass I looked at Paul and asked him if he wanted to race to the barn. I stood shifting my weight from one foot to the other like I was anticipating running a marathon.

He giggled and replied, "Count it down for us Dr. Goodson."

"On the count of three. Ready, one, two…three!" he shouted.

I started running slow and Paul was pushing his wheelchair when all of a sudden Shawn came up behind him and grabbed on to the handgrips and started running with Paul. Paul squealed and we ran all the way down to the barn door. Laughing and gasping for air we stopped just inside the door.

"It's a tie," we heard Shawn's voice coming from behind us.

Hank came walking out laughing and told us he thought he was going to have to open the back barn door because he didn't think we would be able to stop. We all stood laughing while we went over the strategy of how we could have perfected our run.

"Hank," I finally said once I regained my breath. "I would like to introduce you to Dr. Shawn Goodson."

"Dr. Goodson, I would like you to meet Hank," I completed the introductions.

Hank held out his hand and shook Shawn's.

"Please Hank…call me Shawn," he replied.

"Well, this is a pleasant surprise," Hank stated and continued, "I have heard a lot about you, Shawn."

"You can't always believe what you hear," laughed Shawn.

"Katie, you look a little tired today. Are you feeling alright?" Hank asked with concern in his voice.

"Not you too! I have already heard it from Mom. I am fine thanks," I said as I looked away from him.

"Can we go now, Katie?" Paul was rocking in his chair. He was so excited.

"We can go if you are ready," I responded.

"Okay, let's go" he said.

"The horses are ready. Let me grab the saddlebags and put them on the horses," Hank said.

"Can you carry them, Hank? I know Mom always fixes too much," I giggled.

"I may need the tractor but I will try to carry them out for you," he joked.

We walked over to the horses and Hank handed Shawn the reins of the horse he was going to be riding. He put his foot in the stirrup and skillfully lifted himself up on to the horse's back. Hank came over to me and cupped his hands and I put my foot in his hands as he lifted me up on to Lacey's back. He then went over and picked Paul up and handed him to me. I placed him in front of me and he leaned back against me for support. Hank then handed the saddlebags to Shawn who placed them on the horse's back. We were all set to go but Hank stopped us.

"Just a minute. I want you to take some binder twine with you," he said and ran back into the barn to grab it.

He walked over to me and had the spool in his hand along with a knife in case we needed to cut it. In the meantime, Shawn had brought his horse up so that he was standing next to Lacey.

"Here you go," Hank said. As he leaned towards me the twine brushed against my wrist. A bright light and flashback hit me. I screamed and my hand recoiled as though burnt. Hank grabbed my wrist. I felt a surge of panic envelop me. Hank could see the terror in my eyes.

"Katie, Katie…it's me. It's Hank," he spoke softly to me, his eyes filled with concern as he looked at me. "Katie, are you alright?" Hank asked.

I sat there for a moment. The flashback had caught me by surprise. *What did it mean?* The twine had not scratched me. *Why had I reacted this way when it touched my wrist?* I sat looking a little dazed and confused. Paul had tensed up. I could feel his body stiffen as he leaned against me. Shawn had leaned forward in the saddle and had extended his hand to grab me in case I slid off.

"I am alright, Hank." I looked at him feeling myself blush from the embarrassment that I was feeling.

"Sorry, I didn't mean to scratch you," he said lying for me so that Shawn would not become suspicious at my reaction.

"It's okay, Hank. I know you didn't do it on purpose," I replied giving him a quick thank you wink.

"You scared me, Katie!" Paul exclaimed.

"I am sorry. I was caught off guard. I should not have reached for it at the same time Hank was handing it to me," I told him.

"Are you up for the ride, Katie?" This time it was Shawn who expressed concern.

"I will be fine, Shawn. Let's go," I replied but avoided looking his way.

Paul let out an excited squeal and I turned Lacey around and Shawn's horse followed. We walked the horses slowly while I composed myself, still tying to figure out what had happened. Shawn rode his horse up next to mine and I hoped he did not want to discuss what had just happened. *Oh, why did this have to happen today of all days?* I didn't want Shawn to see any of my flashback reactions or talk about my dreams. Not today. I just wanted to push them from my mind. Today I wanted to enjoy myself and not think about blinding lights or flashbacks or sinking in the water. Please just let me get through the rest of the day.

"It's a lovely day for a ride, don't you think?" Shawn asked trying to break the silence.

"Yes it is. I try to go riding as much as I can. It makes me feel so free," I replied.

"Can we run, Katie?" Paul finally spoke.

"You want to run really fast, Paul?" I giggled as I asked him.

"Yes!" he exclaimed.

I turned and looked over at Shawn and he seemed to be enjoying the ride. We had been walking the horses and they were ready to run. I was ready to run too.

"Okay. We can run now," I told Paul.

I looked at Shawn and asked, "Are you ready to run?"

"Sure," he said laughing. "I will try to keep up."

"All you have to do, Paul, is tell Lacey 'to the pond' and she will run to the pond," I told him.

"To the pond, Lacey" Paul yelled.

Lacey took a few more steps and started to trot. Then she galloped and soon went into a full run. Paul laughed as we started running. I looked back to see if Shawn was coming and he was still right alongside us. I could tell by the way he was handling his horse that he was quite an experienced rider. He looked very skillful as he held the reins and leaned forward in the saddle. We galloped the rest of the way to the pond. Lacey slowed down the closer she got. Paul had the reins and control of her but Lacey knew she would stop at the pond. I was concerned a little that Lacey might once again run past the pond and go to the woods. I was not ready for the woods today. This was the first time I had been back out since that day and I had forgotten about it until we got closer to the pond.

"Pull back a little on the reins, Paul, and she will stop so that we can get off," I told him. "This looks like just the right spot for a picnic, don't you think?" I asked.

Shawn had stopped his horse, dismounted and came over to us. He reached up and took Paul down for me. He reached back up and offered to help me down too. He waited because he could see my hesitation but he was not going to move until he helped me down. He slid me down the side of Lacey and held me in his arms until I touched the ground. I hoped he didn't see me blush as I felt embarrassed by his help. Once I was on the ground he looked into my eyes and was about to speak but decided against it. He let his hands fall to his side. He picked Paul up again as I pulled the blanket from the duffle bag that Hank had given me.

I looked around and picked a grassy spot under the tree and spread the blanket out. Shawn walked over and sat Paul down and he went back to the horses to grab the saddlebags. Hank had put the small radio in so we could have some music to listen to. I opened the saddlebag. Hank had put some carrots in for the horses. I told Paul he could give each of the horses a carrot. Shawn picked him up and carried him over to the horses as he gave one to each of them and watched as they ate them. When they were done, Shawn carried Paul back and they both sat down on the blanket. I took out the paper plates, silverware, and napkins and set them on the blanket. Shawn picked up the radio and turned it on. Shawn and Paul were chatting to each other as I got everything out. Mom had sent sandwiches and cut up vegetable with dip, along with fruit, cookies and brownies. I opened the other saddle bag that I thought had the juice in it but when I opened it the knife and twine were there instead. I stared into the bag, motionless. For a moment I thought about reaching in and touching it to see if I could or if the same terror would consume me. When I looked up Shawn was looking at me so I quickly shut it and set it aside.

"Wrong bag," I announced. "I will grab the other bag and I will be right back," I told them as I got up and walked over to retrieve the correct bag. I returned and sat back down on the blanket. I opened it and the juice was in there. I took out the bottles and set them on the blanket.

"Okay, let's eat," I suggested.

We sat listening to music and eating our lunch. We laughed and chatted and listened as Paul told us some jokes. After we were done eating I grabbed the trash bag Mom had sent and cleaned up the blanket. I looked up at the sky and it was full of fluffy white clouds. I told Paul to lie down on his back and look up into the sky. We all lay down looking up at the clouds trying to pick out different things that we saw. Paul was the first to spot something.

"There is a car," he said pointing it out to us.

"I see an airplane," Shawn said as he pointed up at the sky.

We spent most of the afternoon looking at the sky and we picked out as many different things as we could. Each time we looked around we saw a new form appear before us and pointed them out to each other. Some of them you had to really use your imagination in order to see it. Time passed quickly and I didn't realize how late it was getting.

"I see a bug," I laughed and pointed at the sky.

"A bug? What kind of bug? Where…I don't see it?" Paul looked all around the sky.

"Right there," I pointed straight above us and added "do you see it?"

"What kind of bug, Katie?" Paul asked still trying hard to see the form in the sky.

"A tickle bug!" I exclaimed as I leaned over Paul and tickled him. He let out a squeal and started to laugh.

"I have never heard of that kind of bug," Shawn laughed.

"Show Dr. Goodson the tickle bug, Katie," Paul giggled.

"Too late. It is gone now. He was only here long enough for me to tickle you," I replied.

I sat up and told them that it was time to clean up and return.

"Oh, do we have to, Katie?" Paul asked and continued, "I am having so much fun. I don't want to leave yet."

"Grandma and Grandpa Stevens want to see you for a little while before you have to go back home," I explained to him.

"Okay, I guess I am ready then," he replied.

Shawn got up and took Paul and they went over to the field. I put the rest of the things back into the saddlebags and put it on Shawn's horse. I picked up the blanket and folded it and put it back into the duffle bag and strapped it on to Lacey. I was not paying attention to the guys or what they were doing. When I turned around Shawn was standing there with Paul who was holding out his hands to me with a bouquet of wild flowers.

"These are for you, Katie," Paul smiled as he handed me the bunch of flowers.

"Thank you, Paul. They are beautiful," I responded. I inhaled their fresh fragrance and said, "They smell wonderful, Paul. Thank you so much," I cried out as I hugged and kissed him on the cheek.

"I am going to take Lacey over to the stump so that I can mount her. I will walk her over so that you can hand Paul up to me, Shawn," I told them my plan.

"No, here…I can help you up," Shawn volunteered and he sat Paul down and cupped his fingers together and looked at me waiting. I just looked at him for a moment and then put my foot in his hand and he lifted me up on Lacey's back. He turned around, picked up Paul and handed him to me. Feeling more confident Paul sat up and took the reins. We waited for Shawn to get on his horse and Paul pulled the reins and Lacey turned around and we started walking back towards the house.

"Can we run again, Katie?" Paul asked me.

"Sure, just tell Lacey 'to the barn' and she will run for you," I told him.

"Are you ready to run Dr. Goodson?" Paul asked.

"Just give the command," Shawn laughed.

"To the barn, Lacey," Paul yelled. Lacey began to trot, then went into a gallop and soon changed to a full run. Paul leaned back against me for support as Lacey ran. We ran through the meadow. It was beautiful with all the flowers in full bloom and the mixture of fragrances filling our nostrils. Lacey ran until she got to the field leading up to the barn where she slowed back down to a walk.

Hank was working on something in the coral and stopped what he was doing so he could take the horses from us. When we got closer to the barn we could see that Shirley was there. I hoped everything was okay because she had told us that she wasn't planning on going anywhere. When we got to the barn Hank walked over to us and Paul handed him the reins.

"How was your picnic, Paul?" Hank asked.

"It was so much fun I didn't want to return this soon," Paul said and continued, "Guess what kind of cloud Katie saw in the sky?"

"I am not sure, Paul. What did she see?" Hank inquired.

"A bug…it was a tickle bug too and she tickled me," Paul said laughing.

"You don't get to see one of those everyday," Hank giggled. "I can get the horses. You kids go on up to the house," he continued.

"If you would like I can help you bring them in," Shawn offered.

"No, go on up to the house. I have been getting the aroma of freshly baked pie all afternoon and I think it is waiting for you guys," Hank told him.

Suddenly Hank said, "You must have lost one of the saddlebags, Katie. I only see one of them here."

"I can ride back and get it, Hank," I said. Turning around to Shawn I said, "Why don't you take Paul up to the house and I will ride back and get it?"

"No, that is okay, Katie. Go on up to the house. We can get it later," Hank told me.

The three of us walked up to the house discussing our picnic and ride. Paul suggested we go again the next day. We walked up the steps and Shirley met us at the door. She had stopped to pick up Paul. They were over at a neighbor's house helping them pack up because they were leaving town to go to another city.

"Aw, Mom…do we have to go?" Paul pouted as he asked.

"Yes, we are going to help them get packed up so we need to get going now," she told him.

"Here, let me help you, Shirley," Shawn suggested.

"Thanks, Shawn," Shirley replied.

Shawn pushed the wheelchair down to her car and put Paul in the back seat and put the wheelchair in the trunk for her. He waved goodbye to Paul as he went around the car.

"Thank you Shawn and Katie for taking Paul for the ride and the picnic. I am sure I will hear all about it for the next few days," she laughed.

"You're welcome, Shirley. I think we all had fun today," I replied.

Shirley got in the car and drove off. Paul was waving in the back seat as they pulled away.

"Are you two coming in for some fresh pie?" Mom asked us.

I looked at Shawn and told him to go on up for pie while I took Lacey and rode back to get the saddlebag.

"If you don't mind, Katie, I would like to ride with you. I enjoyed my earlier ride and I wouldn't mind going back out if you don't mind," he suggested.

I looked back up at Mom and told her we had forgotten one of the saddlebags and we were going to ride back to get it. I told her that we would be back soon for the pie. She waved, turned and went back into the house.

"I can do it, Shawn, unless you really want to ride again," I stated.

"I don't mind at all. It has been some time since I rode and I didn't realize how much I missed it until I got back on," he replied.

We walked back down to the barn just as Hank was bringing the horses around. I told him we were going to ride back and get the saddlebag and I could take care of the horses when I got back if he had something else planned. He handed Shawn one set of reins and me the other. He helped me up on Lacey and walked back towards the office.

We turned the horses and started back across the field. I didn't feel much like talking so I asked Shawn if he wanted to race to the pond.

"If you are unsure we don't have to race. You don't have to worry. Both horses have their own trail leading to the pond and once we get started that is where they are going to go," I told him.

"I am ready if you are, Katie," he laughed.

"To the pond, Lacey," I yelled.

Lacey responded and started running. Shawn's horse was right beside mine. It felt good to run again…feeling the wind blowing my hair back and the warm sun shining down on me. It was an invigorating experience. I tightened my knees and screamed at Lacey to run faster as Shawn began to take the edge on me. Faster she ran and I could feel her strong muscles working below me. We were getting closer to the marker we had picked as the finish line. I was ahead by only inches as we crossed. We stopped the horses, laughing breathlessly. I slid off Lacey's back and Shawn dismounted. He congratulated me on my big win and gave me a bow to admit his defeat.

We began looking around for the saddlebag and finally found it under the tree. Shawn walked over, picked it up and carried it back while I stood absent-mindedly gazing at the woods.

"Do you want to go to the woods, Katie?" he asked.

"No, why would you think that?" I asked bewildered.

"You have been looking at the woods off and on all day as though you were expecting something or someone to come walking out," he responded.

"I didn't realize I had been looking at the woods," I replied and forced myself to look away from it.

He turned and walked over to his horse and threw the saddlebag over the horse's shoulders. Without realizing it my eyes had gone back to the woods. I stared deep into them. I didn't know what I was expecting to happen. Shawn silently walked up behind me but didn't say a word. He just watched me, wondering what I was searching for.

Waiting and wondering if he should speak, he stood and looked for himself at the woods to see if he could find anything there. I started to turn when all of a sudden a flashback stung my eyes. My head was pounding with severe pain. I opened my mouth to speak but nothing came out. My eyes dilated in fear as I saw a movement. My body wanted to run but I could not…I was petrified. Terror consumed my mind and body and I felt myself falling. I felt numb all over and everything went black. Shawn grabbed me as I passed out and fell backwards.

He carried me over to the tree and slowly sat down with his back up against it. Shawn put his arm around me and held me gently as he waited for me to regain consciousness. He sat watching me and wondering what could have brought it on. Carol had told him that I had been experiencing bad dreams, flashbacks and nightmares but didn't go into it. She had told him that she had tried to convince me to go to him. *What has happened to you, Katie?* Shawn thought to himself. *Why won't you open up and talk about it? How much do you remember? Just talk to me Katie and I will help you get through it.* He sighed and leaned back against the tree to relax as he held me close to him.

I slowly opened my eyes and tried to sit up but the pain was still there. I moved my eyes looking around to try to figure out where I was. It slowly came back to me and I could remember. I sat there for a few moments before I realized that someone was holding me. I lifted my head expecting to see Hank and with shock I realized it was Shawn that was holding me. I blushed with embarrassment and sat upright.

"Are you okay, Katie?" Shawn asked.

"I think so. I am sorry, I am not sure what happened," I replied.

"You were looking into the woods. Your eyes dilated in terror and you fainted. I caught you before you hit the ground and brought you here under the tree where you could relax," he explained.

I sat upright, slid my feet up, placed my elbows on my knees and began to massage my temples. My head was still pounding and I wasn't thinking clearly yet.

"Do you want to talk about it, Katie?" Shawn asked in a soothing tone.

"I can't, Shawn," I replied.

"You can't Katie or you just don't feel like it?" he queried.

I could feel the tears stinging my eyes as I held them back. If only I could talk about it. If only I could remember and could open up and spill everything to him. I would feel better and I am sure the nightmares would stop. I wanted to speak but my throat felt constricted, so I remained silent.

"It will help you if you talk about it, Katie," he said and continued "you will be surprised at how much better you will feel."

"Don't you understand…it isn't that I don't want to talk about it…I can't talk about it because I don't remember anything about it!" I said feeling my anger rise within me.

"You will remember if you try talking about the things that you do remember," he offered.

"Oh, so now you are going to put me under the microscope and analyze me?" I continued defiantly, "I didn't ask you to help me and I don't want you to help me. Sooner or later I will remember and I will be able to figure it out on my own," I told him as I met his glance on an even keel.

"Okay, it is entirely up to you, Katie. I was just trying to tell you that I am here and willing to listen but it is obvious you don't want my help," he replied calmly.

I tried to stand up but felt weak. So I leaned back against the tree. *Why did he have to come out here with me?* I didn't want any of this to happen in front of him. He must think that I was crazy.

"Are you ready to go now?" I asked him.

"Yes, we probably should head back," he replied.

He stood up, turned around and held his hand out to help me up. At first I thought I would rather do it on my own but decided I should have him help me since the last time I tried to move I was too weak. I took his hand and pulled myself up. He told me to stand there and he would get the horses. He brought Lacey up and stood with his hands clasped together and I slowly walked over to him and put my foot in his hands and he lifted me up on to Lacey's back. I sat there a minute not sure if I was ready for the ride back. In the meantime Shawn had mounted his own horse and had come over to me.

"Are you feeling well enough to ride, Katie?" he asked.

"I think so but could we go slow until I am ready, please? I still feel a little shaky," I replied.

"Did you want to ride together so that you can lean on me until we get closer to the house and then I will get back on my horse?" he asked looking at me.

I just looked at him uncertain about what I wanted. I didn't want to rely on him but I wasn't sure if I was going to be able to ride alone. He could sense my hesitation and before I could speak again he got down from his horse and grabbed Lacey's mane and pulled himself up behind me. He slid up close to me and gently pulled me back so that I was leaning against him. He took the reins and turned Lacey and she started back towards the barn.

"Just close your eyes and lean back against me," he suggested. "I will steady you and won't let you fall off. You are safe in my arms, Katie," he said reassuringly.

I did as instructed. I could feel his heart beating against my back as I lay back relaxing as we rode on. Neither of us spoke again until we got up closer to the house. He stopped Lacey and spoke.

"Katie, do you want me to get back on my horse or do you want me to take you the rest of the way?" he said speaking very softly.

I opened my eyes and sat up trying to decide if I could finish the ride by myself. Shawn was very patient and just sat and held me while I thought about it. It would be easier to just let him finish taking me up to the barn. If I did that Hank and Mom would both be filled with questions for me. As I was trying to make up my mind Hank came out of the barn and looked towards us. He took a couple of steps towards us like he was trying to figure out what was going on. He wasn't sure if I was hurt or if we had decided to ride back together. Hank put both hands up in the air in a questioning gesture as he waited and watched for a response. Without thinking I raised one arm up in the air which was the signal to him that everything was okay.

"What do you want me to do, Katie?" Shawn asked again.

"Please just take me up to the barn. He has already seen us so it won't matter now," I replied.

"Come on, Lacey" he said.

Lacey started slowly walking again, heading for the barn. Hank stood and watched as we approached him. He waited until we were closer. He started walking towards us and Lacey stopped as she waited for him to take the last few steps. His eyes were on me the whole time.

"Katie!" Hank only spoke my name but his voice was full of concern for me.

"I am fine, Hank," I tried to reassure him.

"Katie!" Hank repeated my name not wanting to say much in front of Shawn. I sat up as Shawn dismounted before reaching up and lifting me down. He held me and watched my eyes as if waiting for a sign from me. I slowly smiled and he knew that I was okay and could stand. Shawn let go of me and turned and took the reins of his horse.

"Katie?" Hank said in a questioning tone.

"I had another flashback and fainted," I told him being very brief.

"Why don't you go on up to the house Katie and Shawn and I can take care of the horses," Hank suggested to me.

I turned to Shawn and told him how sorry I was about the episode. I invited him to come up to the house when he was done for some pie.

"I will be up when we are done," Shawn replied.

"Hank, you come up too. We can all enjoy some pie," I smiled and said to him, then turned and started walking up to the house. Hank and Shawn each took a horse and walked into the barn. Hank was the first to speak.

"Thank you for taking care of her, Shawn," he said gratefully.

"Hank, I know I shouldn't ask you but I am sure you wanted me to stay behind so that you could ask me more about what happened. I know you didn't need help with the horses," Shawn remarked.

"I don't know if I should talk to you about it, Shawn," Hank replied. "Katie is the one that will have to talk to you and discuss what has been happening. It is just that I am so worried and concerned about her," he explained.

"I can tell you what happened if that will help you, Hank," Shawn suggested.

"I think I can probably tell you Shawn. It had to do with the woods, didn't it?" he inquired.

"Yes, it did. All day her eyes kept going back to the woods. Most of the time I don't think she even realized she was looking. A flashback hit her and she grew weak and fainted. Luckily I was close and caught her before she hit the ground," Shawn explained. "When she came to, she was very weak and she had a migraine so I rode with her to keep her on her horse," Shawn stated.

"It is funny we have all been pushing and pressurizing her to go see you about the flashbacks, dreams and nightmares but she would not have any part of it." Hank continued, "Now today you are with her when it happens and she still won't talk to you."

"Hank, I am more than willing to help her and would love the opportunity to bring her back to her normal self but she has to be the one willing to talk and try to slowly remember. Without her willingness there is no use of me trying to bring it up and talk about it," Shawn replied.

"You saw her at the woods today, Shawn. It is only getting worse. I hope and pray that she remembers slowly and the memories don't come flooding back to her all at once," said Hank.

"If the flashbacks and nightmares are coming closer together and with more severity then it won't be long before she starts talking to someone about them," Shawn said. "If I am there I can help her but I am not sure who she will turn to," he stated.

"She will come to me, Shawn. She had asked me some time back if she needed someone to talk to if she could come to me. So I know that she will and after today she will probably be back out tomorrow or the next day to talk," Hank confided.

"I would like for you to do something then, Hank." Shawn went on, "If she comes and talks to you please write it down after she leaves so that you will be able to refer to it later if necessary."

"Sure, I can do that. I just hope that she can cope with my help alone," Hank said.

"I will continue to subtly try to get her to talk and open up to me," Shawn explained and then added, "She is a great girl and I can help her if she trusts me."

"I will do anything I can to help, Shawn. Just let me know if there is anything else I can do," Hank said as he shook Shawn's hand.

"The one thing that everybody needs to do is not push her to come see me as a patient. She will fight coming and then won't talk to me," Shawn advised.

"I will let Carol and her folks know that they need to stop pressurizing her and we will see how it goes," Hank replied.

They had put the horses in their stalls and Hank fed them while Shawn poured fresh water. Once the doors were shut and locked they decided to head up to the house. Hank promised that he would keep Shawn informed on any changes that he saw in Katie. He also promised that he would keep notes on anything they talked about. Shawn told Hank that he was going to give Katie some time and not talk or pressure her about what had happened out at the pond. They walked together up the steps to the house. When they got inside everyone was sitting at the table waiting for them. Katie looked upset and one could feel the tension in the room. I was the first to break the silence and speak.

"It is about time you guys got here," I said pouting.

"Are you ready for some fresh pie?" Marge asked.

"Would either of you like some coffee or tea? I just made a fresh pot," Bob offered.

"I will have some coffee with my pie," said Hank.

"I will have tea please with mine," replied Shawn.

Marge got up and cut them both a big piece of pie and brought it to them while Bob got up and got the coffee and tea. We made small talk while eating but nobody mentioned what had happened earlier in the day. We discussed the picnic and the ride but nothing was said about the flashback. When we were done I got up and cleared the plates. I placed them in the sink and asked if anyone wanted more coffee or tea. Both declined. Hank said he had some business to take care of and excused himself and went back to the office. Hank got up and walked to the door as I followed him. Once we were outside I took the opportunity to speak with Hank.

"I am sorry, Hank. I couldn't talk to you with Shawn there but I will try to come out tomorrow or early next week and if you don't mind I would like to talk to you," I told him.

"I would like that, Katie. You know where to find me if you need me. I am either here or at the house. Either way please feel free to come and talk to me," Hank told her.

"Thank you, Hank. I love you," I gave him a hug and turned and went back into the house.

Feeling the tension and my uneasiness Shawn told me that he was ready whenever I wanted to go. I seized the opportunity and said I was ready right then. I bade goodbye to my parents and Shawn thanked them for letting him come out and go riding. He hoped that he could do it again sometime. He thanked Marge for the picnic goodies and the wonderful pie. They both walked to the door and went to the car.

Once in the car I sighed. We both put our seatbelts on and Shawn started up the car. We spoke very little on the way back to my house. I was embarrassed by what had happened and did not want to talk for fear that he might bring it up.

It was getting dark by the time we pulled in the driveway. I had left the light on just in case it was dark by the time we got back. As Shawn stopped the car he turned off the motor and turned to look at me.

"Would you like some company or are you tired?" he asked.

"I am feeling really tired, Shawn. Maybe another night, okay?" I suggested.

"That will be fine but I would like to say something before you go, if it is okay with you," Shawn told her.

"Sure, go ahead," I said but felt concerned about what I was afraid that he might say.

"I just want you to know that I am here if you ever need anyone to talk to. I am not trying to pressure you. I just want you to know that I am a good listener and if you need me I will always be just a phone call away," he told me reassuringly.

"Thank you, Shawn. I will remember that and I also have your card with your number," I explained. I continued hesitantly, "I would like to thank you too for not mentioning anything to Mom and Dad about what happened. I am sure Hank talked with you but I also know that he didn't tell you everything."

"Katie, Hank loves you a lot and is willing to do anything to help you and keep you out of harm's way," Shawn remarked.

"I know but I am just not ready to talk and it seems like everyone around me is getting very anxious for me to spill my guts out over this and the very sad thing is I don't remember anything," I confessed.

"Don't rush it, Katie. You will know when you are ready. I just want you to know that I am here if you need me," he explained.

"Thank you, Shawn," I said as I opened the door and got out of the car.

Shawn watched as Katie went up and unlocked the door. She paused in the doorway and waved goodbye to him. He started up the motor and backed out of the driveway and drove down the road.

I could not wait to be alone. I had had a horrible day and just wanted to forget about everything. I went inside, filled the bath and stepped in. I lay back and enjoyed the warmth of the water. I cleared my mind of all thoughts and relaxed.

After an hour I got out and dried myself off. I then put on my robe and walked into the kitchen. I placed Shawn's card by the phone in case I decided I wanted to call him so I would know where it was. Just as I turned to go to the bedroom the phone rang.

"Hello," I answered.

"Hi, Katie...this is Shawn. I just wanted to see if you were okay or if you needed anything. I also wanted to thank you again for letting me come along with you and Paul today. I had a wonderful time and hopefully we can do it again," Shawn suggested.

"I am glad you enjoyed yourself, Shawn. We can go riding again sometime. It was fun," I replied.

"Have a wonderful sleep and if you need anything I am just a phone call away," he told her.

"Thank you again, Shawn and I hope you sleep well too," I replied.

"Goodbye and goodnight," he said.

"Goodbye and goodnight to you too," I replied.

I hung up the phone and smiled. *Well, Dr. Goodson you got a taste of what I have been going through. Do you still think you can help me?*

I turned off the kitchen light and went into the bedroom. I took off my robe and climbed into bed. Not wanting to think about what had happened I cleared my mind and lay back hoping to sleep. I chuckled to myself when the thought of bringing a life jacket to bed crossed my mind. I thought about what Shawn had told me but wasn't sure if I felt comfortable talking with him. He seemed very nice and he appeared to be genuine but still I felt hesitant not knowing where to begin when all I had was bits and pieces of dreams, flashbacks and nightmares. As I lay there in my bed thinking I felt myself drifting off to sleep...

Chapter 7

I awoke very early next morning feeling a little apprehensive. Today is the day, I told myself, that I am going to go to the woods and face it down. I will stop and talk with Hank but if I am ever going to be able to get past these memories I am going to have to start somewhere.

I got out of bed and went to the kitchen and made some tea. After it was done I grabbed the cup and went into the bathroom to take my shower. After my shower I looked in the bathroom mirror and watched myself as I was braiding my hair. *Yes, today was going to be the day.* Determination… *Yes, I could do it and I would feel better after I went to the woods. I would sit there all day if need be because nothing was going to stop me now. Nothing!*

I went in the bedroom and quickly got dressed; eager to finally confront my past, ready to face whatever demon that lay in store. *I could do this after all. I had been fighting the demon for eight years now where he had had the upper hand, but not this time. I would confront him and put an end to all the dreams and nightmares. The demon had been in control of my life long enough. Face to face he and I. Only this time I would choose the battleground and not he. He was the one that felt the need to sneak into my world and take the coward's way to attack me. Not today…I was ready! I will take control of the situation and finally put an end to it once and for all.*

As I walked through the kitchen I grabbed my purse and keys feeling an inner strength that I had not felt before. *Yes, I am ready.* I got in the car and pulled out of the driveway. It was a cloudy overcast day and I just hoped that it would not storm. I didn't want anything to stand in my way. I was ready today…tomorrow I might not be.

I pulled into the driveway and drove down to the barn. Mom and Dad had left for the day so they would not be home. That was one thing I was glad about because I did not want to argue with them again. They had both lectured me the night before when Shawn and I had got back from our ride out to retrieve the saddlebags. I pulled up and got out of the car and went into the office to see if Hank was in there. He was busy working on some papers but looked up when I walked in.

"Good morning, Katie," he said with a big smile. "You are up early!"

"Good morning, Hank," I replied with a smile. "Hank, can we talk?" I asked him.

"Sure, Katie. Pull up a chair and sit down. What would you like to talk about?" he asked.

"About the woods and what happened yesterday," I replied.

"What would you like to know, Katie?" he asked.

"Hank, I know that what happened to me has something to do with the woods. The day Lacey took me there I had flashbacks but could not make any sense out of them," I said frowning.

"You know that it is going to take time, Katie. Just give it time and you will remember," he reassured me.

"Yes, that is what everyone keeps telling me but I am tired of waiting. I cannot deal with the flashbacks any longer," I told him as I looked out the window.

"Are the flashbacks and nightmares coming more frequently now?" he asked looking puzzled. "I thought you only had them once in a while," he added.

"No, Hank. They are coming regularly and I do not know how much more I can take it," I replied.

"Did you want to talk to me Katie or did you want to talk to Dr. Goodson…Shawn?" he inquired.

"I would rather talk to you Hank, if you don't mind. He seems nice and all that but I would rather not talk to him. I think I can handle it on my own," I said.

"Well, I am here for you Katie and I will help you in any way I can. Just let me know what you need," he spoke softly.

"I am going to go out to the woods...alone, to see if anything happens or if I can remember something," I announced.

"I will be happy to go along with you, Katie," he volunteered.

"No, Hank. This is something that I have to face alone and I think it will be easier if I am alone," I replied.

"I don't like the idea of you going out there alone, Katie," he said frowning.

"I will be okay and I feel that today I am ready to face the woods and hopefully something will come of it," I responded.

"I can wait back by the pond and will not bother you, Katie. That way I will be there if you need me," he suggested.

"No, I am going alone and I do not want you to follow me because this is my chance to face it head on and I need to do it alone," I said adamantly.

"Okay, but if you are not back in a couple of hours, I am going to come out to make sure you are alright," he replied.

"I will be back. Do not worry about me," I told him with more confidence than I really felt.

I got up and walked out of the office and went down to Lacey's stall. She neighed when she saw me coming. I unlocked the door and led her out of the stall to a bucket. Stepping on the bucket I pulled myself up on her back. I held the reins and led Lacey out of the barn.

"Bye, Hank. I will see you later!" I yelled as we went out the door.

"Bye, Katie. Please be careful!" he yelled back.

As soon as I had left, Hank reached in the drawer and took out his notepad and started writing. He put the date and time with 'Katie's Talk' in big letters across the top. He wrote down all that we had talked about and how I was feeling. He didn't know exactly what to write. Shawn had only told him to keep track of what we had talked about. He felt like he was betraying Katie by keeping a notebook on their talks but he had to do something to help her. Shawn said that it could be used later and he was the doctor so he should know what he was talking about.

Hank continued writing and after he was done he carefully tucked it away in old ledgers so that nobody could find it if they opened the drawer. He would take it back to the house with him each night and bring it back each morning. That way he would know that nobody else saw it and read the things he had discussed with Katie. He sat looking out the window thinking about how sweet and precious she had always been to him. He shook his head sadly and wished there was more that he could do for her. His mind went back to the night that he had found her in the woods screaming and running until she finally collapsed just outside of the woods. *What had happened that night he wondered to himself? What would he do if he ever found out who was behind the events that had happened that night?* She was like a daughter to him and he would stop at nothing to get back at anyone that had dared to harm her.

Lacey galloped across the field kicking up dust as her hoofs hit the ground. Katie was thinking to herself, unsure of what she should do or how it would turn out. *Would she finally be able to face the woods and whatever that lay within? What was she hoping would happen? Did she expect someone to come walking out and be able to confront this person face to face?* Her mind was racing as fast as Lacey's galloping hooves and she still could not reason with herself on how to handle the particular situation.

Lacey ran to the pond and stopped. This was the usual routine and she always followed it. I turned the reins and urged her to keep going. Lacey hesitated at first but started walking slowly towards the woods. When we got to the edge of the woods I pulled the reins and Lacey once again stopped. I slid from Lacey's back to the ground. Taking the reins I walked Lacey over to the grass so that she could graze while I waited for the arrival of my demon.

I walked to the edge of the woods. I put my hands on my hips and looked first to the left side of the woods as far into the woods as I could see before shifting my gaze to the center of the woods. Still seeing nothing, I looked to the right in the woods.

"I am here and am finally ready to face you," I announced.

My eyes scanned through the woods as though I expected someone to materialize and come walking towards me.

"Come on you coward. Come face me on my terms now when I am ready for you!" I yelled.

Nothing happened. I took my hands away from my hips and moved closer into the woods. I would walk a few yards and then stop and look around again, careful to keep within a safe running distance of Lacey in case I had to ride to safety. I stopped and leaned against one of the trees and stared ahead of me intently. Except for some birds and a couple of squirrels nothing else moved. The woods were very quiet as though tempting me to come in deeper to be grabbed and held hostage.

The minutes turned into hours but still nothing eventful happened. Tired of walking and searching aimlessly through the woods I slowly walked back out. I sat on the grass at the periphery of the woods watching and waiting…still nothing happened. My anger mounting, I stood up abruptly and yelled defiantly at the woods, "What are you waiting for? I am here right now. What is the matter? You shy away from facing me now but only appear when I am sleeping and defenseless?…I will stand and fight because I am not afraid of you!" I screamed defiantly.

Agitated I yelled in desperation, "I have had enough of you and if you are not willing to expose yourself then better stay out of my way!" I demanded. "Confront me here and now or stay out of my life forever!"

Everything remained calm. I threw my hands up disgustedly as a final surrender. I walked over to Lacey and grabbed on to her mane as I mounted her. I took one last look at the woods as I screamed, "Coward!"

With that I turned around and just as I was about to grab on to the reins an owl screeched from directly above me which startled Lacey. She reared up and I lost my balance and fell to the ground hitting my head when I landed. Everything went blank around me. Lacey took off galloping across the field as she headed for the barn.

Hank gazed outside the window at the fields. Shawn had called and Hank was discussing with him what Katie had spoken about. Hank could see Lacey running towards the barn and smiled thinking that they were safe and finally returning home. As Lacey got closer, however, he noticed that Katie was not on her.

"Shawn, I am going to have to call you back. Lacey is galloping across the field but Katie is not riding her," he cried in alarm. Hank continued, "I am going out after her and I will call you when I find out what is going on."

"I am on my way. I will be there in twenty minutes," Shawn said as he hung up the phone.

Hank ran out the door and gently walked up to Lacey.

"Good girl. Whoa, Lacey," he spoke softly as he grabbed the reins. He jumped up landing sideways across Lacey's back and swung his foot around. He grabbed the reins, turned Lacey around and kicked his heels into her sides as Lacey took off galloping across the field.

Shawn got up from his desk and headed out the door. He jumped in his car and started down the road to the farm. With increasing concern he pushed harder on the gas as his car sped off.

Hank was using the ends of the reins to slap Lacey and get her to run faster. He was fearful of what could have happened to Katie. He was getting closer to the pond but still could not see Katie anywhere.

"Katie!" he yelled but got no response.

"Katie, where are you?" he cried in panic.

He stopped Lacey and looked around but could not see her anywhere. Suddenly he remembered her saying that she was going to the woods. He kicked Lacey's sides and she took off again headed towards the woods. When he got closer to the woods he spotted Katie sprawled out on the ground. Hank pulled the reins to stop Lacey and he jumped off her back and ran up to Katie.

He knelt down beside Katie and looked at her. She looked like a rag doll that had been tossed aside. Not knowing how badly she was hurt he was not sure if he should move her.

"Katie…it is Hank. Can you hear me?" he asked but she did not respond.

He put his fingers on her throat to check her pulse. She was alive. He put his hand on her cheek and spoke.

"Katie, I am going back to get the truck. Hold on and I will be back soon," he told her not knowing if she could hear him or not.

Hank ran to Lacey, mounted her and yelled, "Back to the barn, Lacey." Lacey took off racing towards the barn. As Hank got closer to the barn he could see Shawn driving up and jumping out of his car. He ran to the barn but soon came back out. He began pacing back and forth as he looked impatiently towards Hank approaching. When Hank was finally within hearing distance Shawn asked, "Did you find her?…Is she alright?"

"She is lying sprawled on the ground…I'm not sure what happened…I rushed back to get the truck" he informed Shawn as he put Lacey in the coral. Hank dashed into the barn, grabbed his keys and headed for the truck. Shawn was right beside him.

"Do you have a blanket? We will need it if she is in shock," Shawn told Hank.

"Sure. I will grab one out of the office," Hank replied.

Hank ran into the office and grabbed a blanket that was lying in the corner. He ran back to the truck again as Shawn joined him quickly. Hank started the truck, jammed it in gear, hit the gas throwing gravel everywhere as he sped across the field. He drove as fast as he could. Neither he nor Shawn spoke much. Both were very anxious to get to Katie as soon as possible. Hank was feeling guilty about allowing Katie to ride out to the woods alone and finally told Shawn of his feelings. Shawn did his best to console him. They drove past the pond and could see Katie still lying there. She lay very still. Hank drove up to her, switched off the motor and hastily jumped out of the truck. Shawn quickly got out too and ran alongside Hank over to Katie. They both knelt down beside her and Hank was the first to speak to her.

"Katie, can you hear me?" Hank asked speaking softly.

There was no response. Shawn took her hand and felt for her pulse on her wrist. He opened her eyelids and checked her eyes but there was still no response.

"Hank, we need to get her back to the barn. If you carry her I will get in and you can put her on the seat between us," Shawn told him. He continued, "Be as careful as you can although I have checked and she does not seem to have any broken bones."

Hank carefully picked Katie up and carried her over to the truck while Shawn followed. After seating Katie comfortably between Shawn and himself Hank started the truck and slowly drove back to the barn. The bumpy field caused Katie to bounce around so Shawn put his arm around her and pulled her close to help steady her. They were almost through the field when Katie started to squirm in the seat.

"No, please!" her voice just above a whisper.

"Katie, it is Shawn. Can you hear me?" he asked.

"Katie, we are here. Do not worry! You are safe," Hank reassured her.

"Stop now! No, please, please!" Katie screamed out her words this time.

She spoke through closed eyes. She appeared to be somewhere between reality and nightmare. She then began to thrash about as if she were fighting off an attacker. Shawn held her tight to keep her from injuring herself. Katie inhaled deeply as though ready to scream again but instead fell back against Shawn's arm. She remained subdued during the rest of the ride back to the barn.

"She is either having a flashback or a nightmare," Hank stated.

"How often does she have them?" Shawn inquired.

"She has been having them quite frequently and we have tried to get her to talk to someone about them but she refuses," he replied.

"I tried to get her to talk to me but she avoided me so I did not push it," Shawn explained.

"She talks to me when they get really bad," Hank confided to Shawn.

"That is good. She needs to talk to someone and she will talk to the one she feels the most comfortable with," Shawn replied.

"At first, when she had the nightmares she didn't speak, only tossed and turned but now she speaks and from what she says it must be the one that had terrified her that night," Hank said offering more information than he had planned.

"Is there anything that triggers her fears?" Shawn prompted, "A word, a sound, a smell…anything at all that you can think of would help me."

"There are a few things that I have noticed. One was the other day when I handed her the twine and she screamed as her hand recoiled. I could see the terror in her eyes and it upset me," Hank confided.

"Good…is there anything else you can think of? Her terrified reaction suggests that perhaps twine could have been used to harm her in some way and she is giving subtle hints and suggestions through her subconscious self without even realizing it. That is what she needs to do in order to get it out of her system. With increased occurrences she is going to soon start remembering events in greater detail," Shawn explained.

"The thing that sparks off her fears the most is thunderstorms. During a storm she tends to pace the floor, is very flighty, and will run if spooked," Hank said trying to offer helpful detail.

"Thunderstorms?" Shawn said aloud as he furrowed his brows thoughtfully.

"Yes, we were having a horrible thunderstorm the night it happened and when it turns dark and the thunder is rumbling in the background you can see her tense up and she will start pacing the floor," he added.

"I will watch her the next time we have a storm so that I can analyze her reactions," Shawn suggested.

"I think I will just take her over to my cottage where she can lie down and relax. She is not going to want her folks to know about it," reasoned Hank.

They drove past the barn and took the drive leading up to the cottage. Hank pulled up and got out of the truck and came around the truck to get Katie. Shawn opened the door and helped slide her across the seat. Hank picked her up and carried her in his arms up to the house.

"No, please, please please," Katie begged softly as the tears rolled down her cheeks.

"You are safe, Katie. It is Hank and I am not going to let anything happen to you," Hank said reassuringly.

Shawn opened the door and closed it behind Hank. He took Katie inside the room, lay her on the bed gently and covered her with the quilt. Shawn sat on the bed next to her and checked her pulse and pupils again. Her heart rate was back to normal and her eyes were responsive. She began to move and Shawn put his hand on her cheek and talked to her.

"Katie, listen to me as I am speaking to you," Shawn began slowly.

"Please stop. No, please...I beg of you," Katie was barely audible as Shawn leaned closer to hear her.

"Katie, listen to my voice...only my voice. Katie you are safe. Nobody is going to hurt you. Relax Katie and listen to my voice. It is Shawn and you are safe at Hank's. Relax, Katie...relax...sleep Katie...you are safe," Shawn soothed her gently.

Shawn watched her and once again repeated what he had just said. As he spoke he could see her body relaxing and her breathing slowing down as she drifted into a deep sleep. Hank was standing in the doorway watching Shawn as he sat talking to Katie. Shawn had spoken very softly so Hank had not heard what he was saying but he noticed that Katie responded to his voice. Shawn looked at Hank and smiled at him and continued speaking to Katie. Hank walked over to the bed and talked to Shawn.

"Is she okay?" he asked.

"She will have a terrible headache when she awakens but she will be fine," Shawn reassured him.

"Can I get you anything?" Hank asked.

"I could use a cup of tea if you have some," he replied.

"Sure, coming right up," he announced and turned to go get some.

Shawn sat for a minute watching Katie and once again repeated his words to her. She lay there sleeping and did not move. Shawn rose silently from the bed and walked into the kitchen where Hank was filling the cups.

"Go ahead and have a seat," Hank invited.

Shawn sat where he could observe Katie as she slept in case she stirred. Hank sat down and Shawn could see fear and concern written all over his face.

"She will be okay, Hank. Once she wakes up she can tell us what happened," Shawn said trying to alleviate his concern.

"I feel so helpless. I just don't know what to do. I want to really help her but I don't know how," Hank said dejectedly.

"Just being there for her Hank is the best thing you can do for her," Shawn comforted him.

After tea, Shawn got up and walked into the bedroom to check on me. He gently sat back down on the bed and began speaking softly to me again. He would say a few words and stop and watch her. He picked up my hand and put it in his and he took his other hand and placed it on top of mine. He began talking to me again very softly, gently rubbing my hand as he spoke. I slowly opened my eyes and groaned as I tried to move.

"Katie, it is Shawn. You are at Hank's and you are safe," Shawn reassured.

I slowly opened my eyes again and looked around. I tried to move but my head throbbed painfully.

"Ohhhh!" I groaned. My eyes slowly took in my surroundings.

Hearing my groans Hank came up to the door. He smiled at Shawn as he continued speaking softly to me.

"You are at Hank's, Katie, and you are safe," Shawn said as he continued rubbing my hand gently.

"Hank, can you get her something to drink, please? Water or tea...either will be fine," Shawn told him.

Hank went to the kitchen and presently returned with a glass of water that he handed to Shawn.

"Here, Katie. I want you to drink just a little bit for me," he requested. Shawn held the glass and put it to my lips as I took a sip. "You need to drink just a little more, Katie," Shawn urged.

I took a few more sips, closed my eyes again and laid my head back down.

"Katie, can you talk to me?" Shawn asked. "Open your eyes and look at me," Shawn requested in a soft-spoken voice.

I opened my eyes and looked at Shawn. I tried to sit up but grimaced in pain so I lay back and looked at Shawn.

"I am okay. Thank you," I said weakly.

"How do you feel?" Shawn asked.

"I hurt all over. Thank you very much!" I giggled.

"Good! I am really glad to hear that," Shawn chuckled.

"My head is pounding and it feels like it is about to explode," I told him.

"Do you remember what happened?" Shawn asked.

"Yes. I went to the woods and when I was about to ride back an owl screeched and frightened Lacey. She reared and I fell off her and that is all I remember," I told him.

"Good. I have checked you over Katie and you don't have any broken bones but I am sure that your head hurts. Do you want something for it?" he asked me.

"I think as long as I lay here with my eyes closed I will be okay," I replied.

"If you need anything just let me know. I will be in the other room," Shawn told me.

As he started to get up I held on to his hand and said, "Thank you, Shawn."

"You're welcome. Now try to get some sleep and if you need anything let me know," he Shawn suggested.

He got up and went back to the kitchen where Hank was sitting at the table. He looked up at Shawn as he walked in.

"She will be okay, Hank. She is talking now. I have checked her and she doesn't have any broken bones but she is going to be very sore for a few days.

"It is late, Shawn. If you would like you can sleep on the couch in case she wakes up and needs you," he offered.

"All I need is a blanket and I will be set," Shawn replied.

"I want to thank you for coming out and helping Katie. I had no idea how to handle it," Hank confided.

"Don't worry, Hank. She will be fine," Shawn reassured him. "She can remember what happened and that was what I was concerned about," he explained.

"I will leave the light on in case you need to get up," Hank said. "See you in the morning, Shawn," Hank called out as he bade Shawn goodnight.

"Goodnight!" Shawn replied.

I slept through the night. I awoke late the next day. When I opened my eyes I could feel the pain in my body. I tried to get up and groaned loudly. I tried to stand up but my legs were wobbly. I took a few unsteady steps and sat back down on the bed. I put my hand up to my temples hoping I could massage away the throbbing pain.

"How are you feeling?" Shawn asked.

"A little tired…a little sore…and a lot embarrassed!" I chuckled putting on a resolute face as I continued rubbing my temples.

"Would you like something for your headache?" he asked.

"I think so. It doesn't seem to be going away on its own," I replied.

"Here, lean on me and I will take you out to the kitchen and get you some tea," Shawn offered.

"That would be wonderful," I smiled briefly through my pain.

Shawn helped me to the kitchen table and sat me down on the chair. He put on some water for the tea. He sat down as Hank entered.

"Good morning all!" Hank greeted cheerily.

"Good morning," Shawn and Katie echoed in unison.

"How are you feeling, Katie?" Hank inquired.

"I am fine but just a little sore. My head is still pounding," I replied. "Thank you, Hank, for coming to my rescue again!"

"I will always be there for you, Katie. You know that," he smiled and kissed me on top of my head.

Shawn got out the cups, poured tea for all and handed it round the table. He sat down and looked at Hank and smiled back at him. Katie and Hank sat and talked about what had happened and how she was feeling. Shawn sat and listened to what she had to say, not offering much to the conversation. Hank and Katie soon forgot Shawn was there as they continued talking. Katie confided in Hank about going to the woods…her sense of discouragement at realizing that perhaps she might never remember what had happened…how tired she was of fighting the flashbacks and nightmares…

"I think I am just going to go home now and take a hot bath," I told them.

"I will follow you home to make sure you get there okay," Shawn offered.

"I can do it; you don't need to trouble yourself," I replied.

"No, I will follow you. So whenever you are ready just let me know," Shawn stated.

"I am ready now," I replied.

I stood up and groaned as the pain stabbed through my body. Hank stood and helped me walk to the door.

"I will go up and get your car. You wait here," Hank suggested.

"I will go with you and grab my car too," Shawn stated.

Hank and Shawn walked up to the barn so they could talk about Katie briefly. Shawn reassured Hank that Katie would remember the painful events of her past and that she would be able to make it through.

When they got to the barn Hank got in Katie's car and Shawn got into his own and they both drove back to the house. Katie was waiting outside for them. Hank got out and then helped walk Katie over to her car. He gave her a hug and kiss and helped her in. She kicked the engine to life and drove off with Shawn behind her.

I pulled into the driveway as Shawn pulled up his car behind mine. He got out of his car, went up to mine and opened the door for me.

"Why don't you give me the key, Katie, and I will open the door for you?" he suggested.

I was tired and in pain and just handed him the keys. Shawn helped me out of the car and walked with me up to the door. After unlocking the door he helped me into the house and I sat down at the kitchen table.

"Is there anything else you need? I can stay for a while if you would like," he offered.

"No, I am fine. Thank you Shawn for everything that you have done," I said gratefully and added, "I am just going to take a hot bath and go back to bed."

"Okay, you have my number. If you need anything don't hesitate to call," Shawn offered.

"Thanks, I will," I replied.

"I want you to take a few days off from work, Katie. You hit your head pretty hard. You have a concussion and it would be best if you rested," Shawn advised.

"I will wait to see how I feel in the morning," I replied.

"I'm the doctor and you work for me so I am ordering you to take a few days off." Shawn smiled and added, "I would have any of my patient's that had a head injury like you do the same. The main thing you need is to take it easy for a few days at least."

Shawn looked back and smiled at me as he walked out the door, locking it shut. I heard him start the car and drive off. I started rubbing my temples to soothe the pain. I got up and walked to the bedroom. I was sore all over and decided to just lie down for a while and try to sleep. I undressed, crawled into bed and quickly drifted off to sleep...

Chapter 8

The water felt good as I eased into the tub. I let the warmth of the water soothe and relax my aching body. My muscles ached from the fall that I had had the day before; the bruises visible in dark multi-colored patches all over my body. I lay back and sipped my tea as I let my mind mull over the events of the past. What did I hope to find? Who was supposed to come walking out of the woods? I inhaled deeply holding the air in my sore lungs and then exhaled slowly. Nothing lost, nothing gained I thought to myself. Maybe I was trying too hard to remember? The flashbacks and nightmares always seemed to surface when least expected. Forcing the memories only caused them to bury themselves deeper into the recesses of my mind. If only I could summon them whenever I wanted to deal with them…take them step by step and work with only one flashback at a time. I was hoping that by going to the woods I would be able to face one portion of the nightmare, analyze it, put it behind me and then move on to the next one…coming to terms with them one step at a time. Why did my mind want to jumble them all up and offer me only fragments that made no sense to me? Just when I thought I could handle the fragments of the flashbacks my mind decided to throw in new ones.

Were the flashbacks real or was I merely dreaming and mistaking fiction for reality? I had tried to go and face the woods which was a major portion of the flashbacks and nightmares but that had got me nowhere. If only I could just remember a full episode of any event I am sure it would bring back all the memories to me. Frustration and hopelessness crept in and my eyes filled with tears.

The water was beginning to cool. I let half of the water out and turned on the hot water. I slid my feet up closer to me as I wrapped my arms around my shins and let the hot water swirl around me. I rested my chin on one knee as I gazed at the water from the spout falling onto the waiting water below which was causing a rippling effect. I was mesmerized watching the turbulence in the water as it continued to gush onto the water below. The hot water began to scathe my skin and jolted my mind to the present. I quickly turned off the hot water and using my hand I began to swirl the water around mixing it with the cooler water behind me. Soon the water temperature was even and I once again lay back and relaxed. The crashing water reminded me of my nightmare and how I was being sucked down deeper into a vortex of water…the sensation of my lungs gasping for air. *Where could I have been* I wondered? The pond did not seem to bother me so it must have happened elsewhere. The water in the tub did not affect me so it could not have happened there. *Was I taken somewhere outside of town to another town perhaps? It had been a year since I had been down to the park and the lake there. Is that where I was? Is that the water from my nightmare? Should I try another attempt to face my demon? Would I remember anything if I did go there or would it just be a repeat of the incident at the woods?* A confrontation of no consequence and feeling foolish and frustrated afterwards. *Maybe I should talk to Hank and ask him if he remembered or knew anything about the water from my nightmare? Maybe he could provide me with information that could help me?*

The phone rang, startling me. I jumped getting water all over the floor. With a disgusted sigh I sat up, released the lever and allowed the water to go down the drain. I stepped out of the tub and grabbed a towel to dry myself. Wrapping the towel around myself I picked up my cup and went into the kitchen. As I walked past the phone I clicked the button to retrieve the message.

"Hi, Katie…it is Hank. How are you feeling? A little sore I bet. If you need anything just give me a call. I will be home and not at the farm," he informed me and ended with, "I love you…talk to you soon. Bye."

The message ended. The machine deleted the message and the tape rewound itself. I set my cup down and turned to go and get dressed. I was not moving fast as my body still ached. I grabbed a tee shirt and a pair of shorts and slipped these on. I walked back to the bathroom to clean up the floor. I threw the towels in the basket and went to the mirror to look at my face and brush out my hair. I had a big bruise on my left cheek. *Makeup would cover that* I thought to myself. I put my fingers up to touch it and grimaced in pain. I decided to wait and put the makeup on shortly before I had to go to work. The phone rang again.

"Hello!" I answered thinking it was Hank calling back.

"Hi, Katie. It is Shawn," the voice replied.

"Oh," I said stammering and continued, "I thought it was Hank calling back."

"I just called to see if you needed anything," he said.

"No, I am fine. I was just getting ready to head out the door," I informed him.

"Any place in particular?" he asked.

"Just for a ride to sort out my thoughts and I also want to stop and talk to Hank," I replied.

"Well, if you need anything just give me a call," Shawn suggested.

"Thank you. I will remember that," I responded gratefully.

"Have a nice ride and I will see you later," Shawn said as he hung up.

"Bye," I replied.

I hung up the phone and grabbed my cup. Filling it with more tea I sat down at the table to gather my thoughts. I knew what I had planned to do but was beginning to wonder if I should go alone or call Hank to meet me there. *Don't be foolish* I thought to myself. *Just stop there for a minute and then go out and talk to Hank. Stop and see if you remember anything first.* I slowly sipped my tea trying to muster up the courage that I would need. I slipped on my shoes, grabbed my keys and headed for the door.

As I was driving I tried to decide upon a plan of action...*should I go to the lake or go out and talk to Hank instead? My last attempt to confront my past went horribly wrong so I had no reason to assume that this time would be any smoother. What if I did remember something?* At this time of the day the park would be filled with people picnicking and sunbathing on the beach. *Should I execute my plan then or perhaps was it more sensible to wait until later when there would be less people around? To the lake first* I finally decided. *It would only take me a few minutes and after that I could go and talk to Hank.*

The park was crowded with people. I parked way off to the side of the parking lot closest to the boat launch. There were not as many people there and I could always work my way down the beach if I wanted to. I pulled up and parked the car and got out. I stood by the front of the car for a few minutes getting up my nerve to continue. *So far I felt nothing...but what was I expecting? What should I be feeling? This is stupid* I thought as I contemplated getting back into the car and leaving. *No,* I pushed myself on. *Just go to the water and stand there.*

I stood up and walked towards the water. The seagulls were screeching overhead. I walked up and stood looking out over the water as though searching and waiting for a loved one to come back to me. I kicked my shoes off and waded into the water as the sand squished between my toes and the minnows quickly swam away. My feet buried into the soft wet sand. I looked up into the sky as the sun moved behind a cloud and I felt the warm gentle breeze as it blew my hair back from my face. I felt very serene and at ease. I watched as a couple started loading their boat onto their trailer. One of their oars had fallen out of the boat which they had not noticed. I ran and retrieved the oar, then walked back towards the dock. I called out to the couple to let them know that I had their oar. The man came over and I handed his oar to him with a smile.

"Thank you," he said gratefully. "I didn't see it fall out but I would have missed it when I got home," he remarked.

"You're welcome. I am glad I saw it before you pulled out," I replied.

He turned and walked back towards his truck. I stood watching the next person waiting to put his boat into the water. I took a few more steps towards the dock when I began to feel very uncomfortable. I turned slowly and faced the water again as I looked out over it. I walked further out into the water which had come up to my knees now. I decided to walk past the dock to the other side to see if that would trigger any memories. I slowly started walking towards the dock. I was in no particular hurry. I had almost reached the dock when I suddenly froze. An overwhelmingly uneasy feeling enveloped me. Fear gripped me like a vice. *Run…get out now!…Run before they get you* were the sole thoughts that obsessed me. My body shivered violently as my mind raced. I swung round to face the shore and headed desperately for it, splashing water all around me. I ran across the beach until I finally got to my car, panting hard. Groping around for the key in my pockets I unlocked the door with unsteady hands, climbed inside and slumped on the seat exhausted as I closed the door behind me. *Deep breaths* I told myself. *Calm down…you are safe.* I lay back and inhaled deeply as I gradually calmed myself down.

After a few minutes I started the car and backed up. Putting the car in gear I slowly drove off. Feeling calmer and more in control of myself I was able to think more clearly as I drove. I was going over to talk to Hank to discuss what had happened to see if he could help in any way. I was not sure how much he knew about that night or if he would talk to me after the doctor had told everyone not to mention anything to me until I had started to remember for myself. Well, I was beginning to remember portions of my flashbacks. *Maybe that was an indication of more flashbacks to follow?* I could remember the woods and realized that it might feature significantly in my nightmares and flashbacks as did the water which had terrified me only moments before. *Should I tell Hank about the water or should I just keep trying to figure out the pieces of the puzzle on my own? My last attempt almost got me killed* I thought as my fingers went instinctively to rub the bruise on my cheek. Even the nightmare where I was sinking in the water was getting more realistic. During the last nightmare I could feel my lungs collapsing from lack of air as I passed out on my bed. *Should I really be pushing this or should I just let the memories slowly come back on their own?* I longed to remember but part of me wanted to just lock it deep inside me and not have to dwell about it any more. I simply did not want to have the flashbacks and nightmares tormenting me any more. *Maybe Hank could help me answer some of these questions and help me decide how to handle it before I went insane? Was it the not knowing but the desire to get to the bottom of it that kept pushing me to find the truth?*

I drove up the driveway to Hank's cabin. His truck was there so I knew he would be at home. As I pulled in and turned off the car he opened the door and came out on the porch.

"Hi, Katie. I am glad to see you," he called out.

"Hi, Hank," I replied.

"How are you feeling?" he inquired.

"I'm a little sore but I will survive," I chuckled.

I walked up the steps and across the porch. Hank reached out and gave me a hug. He looked at my cheek and shook his head.

"It looks worse than it feels," I lied.

"Is your cheekbone broken?" he asked with concern.

"No, just bruised," I answered. Before he could say anything further I asked, "Can we talk, Hank? I did something today that has triggered another memory and I am hoping you might be able to fill in some blanks for me."

"What did you do, Katie?" his voice was both surprised and concerned.

"Nothing as stupid as yesterday," I laughed.

"Here, come in and we can have some tea while we talk," he suggested. "The water is already hot. I was about to have a cup myself," he explained.

"Sounds good to me," I replied.

We went inside. I sat down at the table while Hank went over and grabbed two cups and poured us some tea. He came over with the tea and sat my cup down in front of me. I took a refreshing sip.

Hank sat down across from me. Looking at me he advised somberly, "I want you to be careful, Katie. If I had only accompanied you yesterday you would not have been hurt," he reminisced.

"Oh Hank! You know very well that I would have gone out another time alone, so please do not blame yourself for what happened," I said with a hint of a twinkle in my eye.

"What did you do today, Katie?" he asked.

"I went to the lake to see if I could find the water that haunts me in my nightmares," I replied.

"Why didn't you call me, Katie? I would have gone with you," he chided.

"I just wanted to check it out first," I explained.

"And just what did you find out?" he asked in a worried tone.

"First, Hank…do you know anything about the water in my nightmares?" I asked.

"No, Katie. I only knew about the woods," he confessed.

I went on to describe the incident at the lake and how I had experienced the uneasy qualms by the dock. That was where I thought something might have happened. I vividly described the fear that had gripped me and my frantic running from the water to my car. He scolded me for going alone but later told me that he understood why I had to go by myself.

"Hank, I am going to go back there again tonight," I informed him hesitantly knowing his reaction.

"No, Katie! I forbid you to go there!" he spoke agitatedly.

"I have to, Hank. I know something happened there and I know it happened at night. So maybe if I go at night it will help me remember what happened or who was involved," I explained.

"You are not going alone. I will go with you," he announced.

"I will be fine, Hank," I remarked and added, "I will park closer and will not go out into the water."

"No, Katie. I do not think it is a good idea for you to go," he advised.

"I am going Hank with or without your permission. I am a big girl and can take of myself," I replied defiantly.

"What time are you going?" he asked.

"I am not sure," I said and continued, "besides, if I tell you when, you will be there waiting. So I am not going to tell you."

"Are you going early evening or are you waiting and going after dark?" he asked anxiously.

"I do not know for sure and besides, I may chicken out and not go at all," I said chuckling.

"I know you better than that Katie Lynne. You are going. You just don't want to tell me what time you are going," he said with growing anger in his voice.

"I should not have told you I was going at all," I snapped.

"I am glad you did. Maybe I can talk some sense into your head and keep you from going?" he replied.

"You were the one that told me that I would remember one day. If there is something that I can do to jog my memory then I think I should do it," I retorted.

"Katie, I did not say you should not try to remember. All I am suggesting is that you should have someone with you instead of going alone," he explained.

"Why should someone be there?" I asked.

"The lake is not a safe place to be. You never know who is going to be there," he replied.

"I will be careful and I will not take any unnecessary risks. I know what I am doing," I announced with more confidence than I really felt.

"Why don't we just go back down to the lake now?" he asked me.

"Because when there is someone else around nothing seems to happen," I explained.

"I think it is too risky to go alone," he repeated.

"I am not going to argue with you about it," I replied.

"I still think you would be better off talking to Shawn about it and not going to the lake alone. He is willing to help you and he told me himself that he could," Hank suggested.

"I do not want to talk to Shawn about it. Besides, I cannot seem to remember anything, so what am I supposed to talk to him about?" I asked.

"Tell him what you do remember," he said and added, "tell him about the flashbacks and nightmares. He can help you sort through it. He is a good doctor and he wants to help you."

"Now you sound just like everybody else…'Go to the doctor…good ole Dr. Goodson can help you. He is amazing and with a snap of his fingers can rid you of your past,'" I lashed out at Hank. "Seems like everybody wants me to go see him and talk to him but yet he has been around on two separate occasions when I was having the damn flashbacks but not once did he offer any helpful hints or suggestions to me!"

"Katie, you have to sit down and talk it over with him. He wants to help but you have to be willing to help yourself and listen and do what he asks you to do," said Hank as he tried to convince me.

"This is something that I need to do and I need to do it alone if anything is to come of it," I replied.

"Oh, Katie! Why won't you listen to reason?" he asked shaking his head.

"It depends on whose reasoning you want me to listen to! We both feel we are correct and know the right thing to do. It just happens that there are different reasons," I replied.

Hank groaned knowing that there was nothing he would be able to say or do to change my mind.

I was going whether or not he agreed with me. I had to find out for myself if I could force the memories back. Why couldn't I make anyone understand that I needed to find out what happened? The flashbacks and nightmares were coming closer together and getting more intense each time I experienced them. I could not go on like that much longer. I had come to the point where I was afraid to go to sleep for fear of those horrible nightmares slithering into my mind while I slumbered. Was it real or just dreams from my imagination? I had felt something at the lake today. Something had happened there and maybe if I went out there tonight after dark it might jog my memory. Besides, there was no harm in doing so. I would be very careful and I would not go out into the water. I would stay by the water's edge and have my car parked close by. At that time of night there should not be anyone around. I could do it and it had to be done alone.

"Would you like some help with the chores?" I asked Hank hoping to change both the subject and his mood.

"I can get them but thanks for the offer," he replied.

"I am going up to brush Lacey, so I can help if you wish. It might loosen up these tight sore muscles," I laughed.

"Suit yourself," he replied curtly.

"Would you prefer it Hank if I did not go to the lake?" I asked.

"Yes, I would feel better if you did not go or even if you let me go with you. I would feel better about it," he replied.

"I am going to be too tired to go after helping with chores so I will wait and let you know when I am ready to go," I said lying to him.

"That would be great. Now make sure that you follow through with it," he looked at me shrewdly as he spoke.

"How about next week when I am not so sore?" I chuckled.

"Any time you are ready. Just let me know," he laughed.

Hank drove us up to the barn. We chatted and giggled while we did the chores just like old times when I would come home from school and run down to help. The earlier tension faded and both our moods had improved. After we were done, he went into the office and I went in to brush Lacey. Once Hank was in the office he took out the notebook he had hidden and started to write down what Katie had talked to him about. Carefully remembering to put the date and everything he could remember regarding their talk, how she felt and how she was acting. He was also advised by Shawn to write down her mood or if she was upset. Shawn had also instructed him to try to get her to talk and see if she mentioned anything that she might have remembered. Today's talk gave him more information than any of the other talks that they had had before.

Hank sat wondering if Katie had really meant it when she told him that she would wait to go to the lake and take him along. She had been so intent on going there tonight and going alone too. *Did she really change her mind or was she just trying to convince him otherwise?* He would give Shawn a call after she left and discuss it with him. *Maybe Shawn could talk some sense into her?* Hank had already planned on calling her later to make sure that she was home and not out searching for answers.

Hank closed the book and placed it safely back between the ledgers. He took care of the farm receipts that he had been working on. *Enough work for tonight* he thought to himself. He walked out of the office and stood and watched Katie as she brushed Lacey. If only her life could be so carefree and uncomplicated. He wondered what would happen to her once she found out about that night. *Was it better for her not knowing what had happened and experiencing the fear and pain of the flashback and nightmares or would it be easier for her knowing what had happened and facing it once and for all?* She was beginning to remember more and more and it would not be long before she would piece together the events that had happened that night. He would do anything he could to help her but she always wanted to do it on her own. 'Face my fears head on,' is what she always told him.

If only she would not be so stubborn and just try talking to Shawn. He seemed sincere in wanting to help her. He was basically helping her already. If only she would just offer him a little help and tell him the different things that he needed to know to help her she would feel better. It might even be possible for him to help alleviate some of the flashbacks and nightmares. Trying to suggest this to her was a waste of time. She did not want to listen to reason. She was adamant that she could do it on her own. She had always been strong and independent. *Maybe a little too much for her own good?* If only she would understand that by confiding in Shawn the things that she was starting to remember he could possibly help jog her memories and would be there to help her cope with whatever it was. *Maybe soon she would see that and talk to him?* Hank sighed and walked towards Katie.

"You are going to brush her hair out if you keep brushing," Hank said laughing.

"It helps me think when I brush her out," I replied giggling.

"Are you feeling hungry?" he asked.

"Yes, a little I guess," I admitted.

"Well, get finished up there and we can either go to town or I can grill us up some burgers. You get to decide," he offered.

"Are you kidding?" I asked jokingly and continued, "Grilled burgers."

"You put Lacey back in her stall and I will lock up the doors and then we can go and eat," he suggested.

"Sounds great!" I said eagerly.

Hank went to the back of the barn and slid the door shut and latched and locked it. He glanced around at the animals as he walked back through. Katie put Lacey back into the stall and locked the door. She picked up the brushes and took them back to the tack room.

"Ready to go?" Hank asked.

"Yes!" I affirmed.

Hank switched off the lights in the office and closed the door. He pulled the barn door shut and latched it. Katie walked over and got in the truck. Hank got in, started it up and drove towards home. He pulled in the driveway and turned off the engine. They got out of the truck and went in the house.

"I will get the burgers ready, Katie, if you could make the salad," he requested.

"Right on," I agreed.

Hank started up the grill as I got out the salad and started cutting up the fresh vegetables that were going into it. I was mulling over my decision about going back to the lake. *Maybe I should wait and go another night* I thought. *Hank would feel better if I waited and had him come with me. Oh why does my life have to be so complicated!*

I set the table and went out the door to see how Hank was fairing with the food.

"You know Hank, I have been thinking over what you said and maybe I am pushing myself too hard to remember," I confessed.

"I will gladly go with you Katie if you want me to. You know I am willing to do whatever I can to help you," he reassured me.

"I think there has to be something with the dock from the way I felt earlier but I am not sure if I want to fight it tonight," I told him.

"I will go with you whenever you are ready. I will wait at the car unless you want me to walk with you," he explained.

"I don't know what I want. Sometimes I think it would be better to know and have my memory back but at other times I do not really want to know," I replied. "I don't know if that makes any sense to you or not," I said confusedly.

"I understand, Katie. I am sure that it is very hard not knowing and having that void in your memory. Honey, you will remember someday and maybe it is better to be patient and not force yourself too hard," he said soothingly.

"I guess you are right. Everyone else keeps pushing me to see the doctor. I did not want to go see a stranger and open up my past to him but everyone kept pushing. So I thought I would try it on my own and we both have seen what that got me into," I said.

"It will come in time. You just have to be patient…something you have always had trouble with," he said with a chuckle.

"I know. But I have been patient with this. It has been eight years now," I said sadly.

"It seems like forever to you I know; but just because you try to force the issue doesn't mean that it will make things come back any quicker," he explained.

"You are right. But what do I do in the meantime, Hank? Wait doing nothing? That seems senseless to me," I rued. "These flashbacks happen at all times…remember the twine? I had no idea it was going to happen, much less what it meant," I confessed.

"It is something that is coming back to you, Katie. It is something that happened and your mind is not ready to deal with it. That is why your mind only shows you bits and pieces and lets you think about it and analyze it and each one gives you a little more of the memory," Hank explained.

"I would much rather have it happen in my time. I want to be in control of it. I don't like when the flashbacks come at will," I confessed.

"Your mind is giving you bits and pieces whenever something triggers the flashback and there is no way to control it," Hank replied.

"That is why I want to force it, Hank. I want to confront my fears when I am ready; not when I am with a group of people. I want to face it on my own terms," my voice quivered as I spoke.

"I wish it were that easy, Katie but things never happen that way," he said. "The mind is a very complex thing and it will work out…in time," Hank said reassuringly.

"Oh!" I sighed.

"The burgers are ready. Are you hungry?" Hank asked.

"Starving," I giggled.

We went in and sat down to eat and continued our conversation. After we were done eating, I got up and made tea. Later I cleared the table and washed the dishes. When it was all done I sat back down at the table with Hank.

"It's getting late. I think I'm going to go," I announced.

"Thanks for coming out, Katie," he said.

"I needed someone to talk to and you are the only one I feel comfortable talking with," I said.

"You are going home, aren't you?" Hank asked.

"Yes, I am tired and still a little sore. I am going home for a hot bath and bed," I replied.

"Good. Drive carefully. I love you. Talk to you soon," Hank said as he gave me a hug before I got in the car.

"Thanks, I will…and thank you again for listening to me! I love you too…bye," I bade Hank farewell.

"Bye, Katie. Take care," he said waving as I drove off.

Hank turned and went back into the house. He refilled his cup with tea and went and sat down on the chair. He sat debating about calling Shawn to seek his advice. Hank did have more information to share Shawn. Maybe he could help Hank decide the best way to help Katie. Shawn did seem anxious to help her. The phone rang interrupting his thoughts. Hank got up to answer it.

"Hello," he responded.

"Hi, Hank. It is Shawn," replied the voice at the other end.

"I was just going to give you a call," Hank chuckled.

"Is everything okay?" Shawn inquired.

"Oh it is about Katie. I am not sure what I should do so I was going to call you to ask your advice," Hank replied.

"What's wrong?" Shawn asked.

"She is okay but she did something today and it brought back a memory from her nightmare. She was going to go back tonight and check it out," Hank explained.

"She should not go alone, Hank," Shawn replied with concern.

"I tried all day to persuade her to let me go with her but she was adamant to go alone," Hank replied.

"Do you know where she is going?" Shawn queried.

"Yes, she told me she was going to the lake just outside of town but she told me that she was going to wait and let me know when she was going. She said she was going home to take a bath and go to bed," Hank stated.

"Do you believe her?" Shawn asked.

"You know 'Katie'," Hank chuckled. "She has a stubborn defiant streak in her," he said slightly amused.

"Do you think she will go?" Shawn wondered.

"I am going to call her in an hour's time. By that time she will have bathed and if she does not answer then I would know that she has gone," Hank reasoned.

"The lake is not a safe place for her to be by herself, especially at night," Shawn emphasised.

"I know but she doesn't always listen to reason and wants to do whatever she can to remember what had happened to her back then," Hank replied.

"I will go down to the lake if you think she will go there," Shawn offered.

"I am going to call her after about an hour. If she is not at home I think it would be a good idea to go over to the lake, even if I have to just sit back and watch her. At least that way I will be there if she gets into trouble," Hank explained.

"Let me know and I will meet you there if you don't mind," Shawn said.

"No, not at all. Besides, you can help her more than I can," Hank confessed.

"Sure. Just give me a call and let me know what is going on and it will not take me long to get to the lake," Shawn suggested.

"I will let you know either way when I call her," Hank promised.

"Thanks, Hank," Shawn replied in gratitude.

"No, thank *YOU* for all your help. I will talk to you later," Hank said.

"I will be waiting to hear from you," Shawn replied.

They both hung up the phone. Hank felt much better knowing that Shawn would meet him at the lake if Katie did decide to go.

Shawn sat wondering if Katie would go to the lake or not. He pondered about what the best way would be to get through to her to make her realize that he could help her. *If she would only trust me I could help her* he thought. *I have been trying the slow gentle approach. Maybe I should push a little harder? If she is starting to remember the places where it happened and the feelings in the nightmares then she is getting closer to remembering and it will not be long before she begins to fit the pieces together. If I can only somehow get her to trust me it would be so much easier for her. I will figure some way to get through to her* he decided.

I pulled into the driveway and got out of the car. I unlocked the door, went inside my house and slumped on the chair. I leaned over to remove my shoes and moaned, as my muscles were still very sore. I rose and put the kettle on for some tea. As I waited for the water to boil I pushed the button and listened to the messages on the answering machine. I decided to take a hot shower after hearing and deleting these. I filled my cup and walked into the bathroom. The hot water felt good on my bruised and aching body. I stood under the shower head and let the warm water fall gently on me. The warm water helped soothe my sore muscles. After showering, I wrapped a towel around me, walked into the bedroom and slowly sat on the bed. I sat thinking about what my next move should be…

Chapter 9

I looked at the clock. It was 10:30. I felt rejuvenated after my shower. I was torn between going to the lake to see if anything came back to me or just going to bed. I did promise Hank that I would not go that night. He would be angry with me if I did without informing him. Yet if I asked him to go along and nothing happened it would be an exercise in futility. If I did remember something I could always go and discuss it with him the next day. I could even go that same night if it was not too late. The force inside me that kept pushing me to go on eclipsed the worries about Hank's feelings. I quickly got dressed, walked through the kitchen, grabbed my keys and was out the door. I got in the car and paused for a moment wondering if I was doing the right thing. Then I started up the car and backed out of the drive and slowly drove heading for the lake.

Hank picked up the phone, dialed and waited while it rang. *Pick it up, Katie* he kept thinking. Three rings but the phone had not been picked up. One more ring and the machine would automatically record the message. *Come on, Katie...be there* he was frantically thinking. *Click* and the machine started giving Katie's message. Hank's shoulders sank as he realized she was not there. He would give it one more try to see if maybe she was not answering. The beep sounded and Hank pleaded into the phone.

"Hi, Katie. It is Hank. If you are there please pick up." He waited and pleaded, "If you do not pick up I will think that you are at the lake and will come to get you. Please pick up."

Hank waited a few more seconds but there was no response. He slammed the receiver down and did not know who he was angrier with…Katie, for disobeying him and going to the lake alone or himself for believing her.

Hank picked up the phone again, dialed and waited.

"Hello," Shawn answered at the other end.

"Hi, Shawn. It is Hank. I called Katie but she is not there," he informed him.

"Want me to meet you at the lake?" Shawn asked. "Or if you don't mind, could you pick me up? I am on the corner of Broadway and Perry and it is on your way," Shawn explained.

"I know right where it is and I can be there in fifteen minutes," Hank replied.

"I am ready and will be waiting for you," Shawn responded.

"I'm leaving right away," Hank blurted.

"See you soon," Shawn replied.

Click, click they both hung up and Hank turned and headed straight for his truck. He jumped in and started it up. The wheels of the truck threw gravel as he backed up and put it in gear.

Shawn put on his shoes and grabbed his medical bag and went out to wait on the porch for Hank to get there.

Hank pulled up and Shawn ran to the truck and jumped in.

"I am going to spank her like a child who refuses to listen," Hank informed him.

Shawn laughed and said, "Hank, you need to calm down. She is only trying to get through to her past. It is very normal and the last few attempts have failed. She feels the need to do it alone. There are reasons why, in your eyes, you feel that she is defying you but to her she is only doing what she thinks is best," Shawn elaborated.

"Going out in the middle of the night to face who knows what, is best for her?" Hank shouted. "Are you sure you know what you are doing? Are you really a doctor or are you just winging it here?" Hank asked angrily.

"Yes, I am a doctor and I have the diplomas to prove it," Shawn replied poker-faced.

"I'm sorry…I am just so worried that she keeps doing these things. The other day she could have died and I begged her to let me go with her but she would not hear of it," Hank explained.

"She will fight you every step of the way, Hank. I know what I am talking about." Shawn added, "Why do you think is she fighting me so hard and will not talk to me?" Shawn asked.

"Because she is so stubborn and will not listen to reason," Hank replied.

Shawn chuckled and said, "Hank you need to calm down before we get there or you are just going to upset her even more and make her angry."

"I am not going to go and pretend that I am all happy and excited that she went out there alone. She needs to know that I'm serious about the danger she put herself in," Hank burst out.

"To her and through her eyes she does not see it as 'dangerous'. She sees it only as a way to fill that void…the void she cannot remember. Each time she comes across something that jogs a memory she is going to go after it," Shawn explained.

"Even if it means she could get badly hurt or worse yet killed in doing so?" Hank asked in disbelief.

"Her mind does not see it as risky or dangerous. Her mind sees it as finding answers to questions that she has been looking for," Shawn explained.

"I will shake it out of her," Hank threatened.

"Hank, please calm down before we get there. You will only make matters worse and she will resent you for sticking your nose in," Shawn explained.

"We are almost there. She said she would be at the dock so that is where I will head for," Hank replied.

"Let's try something first," Shawn suggested. "Do not go right up to her car. Park somewhere back so we can watch her. She will be safe because we will be within a safe distance to get to her if she needs us," Shawn explained.

"Okay. I can see her car and she is still sitting in it," Hank informed Shawn.

"We will wait and observe her. If nothing happens she can go home thinking it is just another failed attempt but if something does happen we are here to help her," Shawn explained.

"I will wait for a few minutes before going to her," Hank replied.

"Hank, for the last time, please calm down," Shawn pleaded. Speaking calmly he continued, "I know you want to help her but if you go down there and get her all upset you will be setting her back and I know you do not want that."

"Okay, I'll try to be calm now," Hank replied. After a few minutes he chuckled and asked, "What is she still waiting for in the car?"

"She is getting up her nerve to go out and face whatever it is she hopes to find," Shawn explained.

"Is she going to sit there all night long?" Hank asked surprised.

"She is trying to find the courage to face this entity and she may not get out of the car if she feels she is not ready," Shawn elaborated.

"You mean she could just sit in the car all night and never get out?" Hank asked.

"She has to feel prepared or she will not be able to do it," Shawn replied.

"I just wish she would listen to me and not take such risks," Hank said somberly.

"She will get through this," Shawn spoke optimistically. He added, "She is doing things the hard way but eventually she will trust me enough and will talk to me or once the memories start coming back she will talk to you."

"I just hope she is ready to face it," Hank mused.

"She is strong…she will get through and we will be there for her too," Shawn reassured him.

There was a big bonfire burning on the beach and a group of lads were playing music while they danced, laughed and talked loudly. Hank and Shawn watched them almost as much as they were watching Katie. Every once in a while one would let out a loud whoop and everyone would laugh. Hank and Shawn were not sure if Katie's hesitation was due to the group of lads being there. They waited and watched.

The door opened and Katie got out of the car. She stood by the car and waited as she stared at the water. She walked slowly across the beach and headed for the water. She stopped when she got to the water's edge and gazed at the group of people. She would take a few steps towards the dock…then stop, turn and face the water.

"What is she doing?" Hank asked just above a whisper.

"She is trying to revive the feeling again, the one she felt earlier; but she is being distracted by the rowdiness of the young men," Shawn replied.

"I do not like the looks of this. I am going to pull up closer," Hank informed him.

"No, do not move the truck. She would be able to see it and she will be angry and lose her thought processes," Shawn explained.

"I hope you know what you are doing, doc," Hank retorted.

"I know exactly what I am doing. Just wait…she is within a safe distance from us," Shawn pacified Hank.

Katie moved closer to the dock and could be seen under the dock's parking lights now. She stood and waited, looking out over the water. A couple of youth from the party noticed her and yelled out to her. She did not turn or look their way. Thinking that she was ignoring them two of the guys jumped up and started running down the beach towards her.

"That is it. I am going for her," Hank said as he rose swiftly.

"No, Hank!" Shawn physically restrained him. "Wait just a few more minutes, please. I know this is hard for you but you need to trust me on this," Shawn said calmly.

"Just how long do we have to wait, Shawn?" Hank asked.

"Not much longer. I want to see her reaction to the confrontation and then we can get out and start walking towards her," Shawn replied.

"Okay, but I cannot wait much longer," Hank quipped.

The two guys yelled out to Katie as they walked towards her. She turned and watched as they got closer. Shawn and Hank could not hear what she said as she was not within ear shot.

The youth were trying to convince Katie to come join them at their party. Katie refused. When they realized she was not going to, they started to move closer towards her. After a while one of them walked up and stood right before her. Katie stepped back but did not seem intimidated by him. The other one had stayed back at first but started inching towards Katie stealthily from behind.

"I am not waiting any longer, Shawn. I do not like the way one of them is coming up behind her," Hank said agitatedly.

"We will get out of the truck, quietly close the doors and slowly start walking towards her," Shawn replied quickly.

"I will walk slowly unless one of them grabs her. Then nothing is going to stop me," Hank shot back.

They got out of the truck. Shutting the doors quietly, they started working their way towards Katie. They could see that the youth approaching Katie from behind was very close to her but were not sure if Katie was aware of his presence. The rest of the party-goers were yelling out to their friends to return but they took no heed.

One of the lads closed in on Katie from behind as the other grabbed her wrist. Katie let out a loud blood-curdling scream. The group of merry-makers had turned up their music so they did not hear her scream. The lad who was standing in front of Katie grabbed one of her wrists while his companion grabbed the other.

"You are a sweet little thing. Let's go have some fun," the first lad taunted.

"We will treat you real good," his friend said leeringly.

"That is it. I am not waiting any longer!" Hank yelled over his shoulder as he ran to help Katie.

Hank and Shawn sprinted towards Katie. The guys were trying to pull Katie along but she was fighting them off.

"What's the matter baby?...Don't want to go to the party?" the first guy asked sarcastically. He added with a malicious wink, "That's okay. It is more private here. Are you ready?"

"Hey, get away from her right now!" Hank bellowed.

"Let's get out of here," one of the lads advised hastily.

The youth took off sprinting for the parking lot. They jumped in a car and quickly drove off laughing as the tires of their car skidded past.

Hank was the first to reach Katie. He tried to hold her but as soon as he reached out to her she screamed. Shawn quickly caught up.

"Hank, do not touch her. Just talk calmly to her," Shawn cautioned.

"Katie, honey, it is Hank. You are safe now," Hank spoke calmly.

"I am going to come up behind her and slowly walk around to the front of her. While I am doing this I need to have you move around so that I can stand in front her. Please, it is very important that you do this," Shawn instructed.

"Katie, I am here and I am not going to let anyone hurt you," Hank said reassuringly.

"Slowly start stepping to the side, Hank. Then I need for you to go get your truck and bring it up by her car. She is going to scream and fight me but I need to do this. She will be fine. Do not worry. I am helping her. I am going to become her attacker. I need to get her fully agitated to trigger her memory. Then I can calm her down. She is in shock and having a flashback. So whatever she does or says do not come near her," Shawn emphasized.

"Katie, you are safe. It is Hank, honey," he said and slowly edged out of the way so that Shawn could stand in front of her.

Hank looked at Shawn and Shawn nodded his head in approval. Hank turned to go and get his truck. He ran across the beach and slowly pulled the truck up to her car, the bright headlights reflecting on them as he drove up. He got out of the truck but kept his distance from Katie as Shawn had advised. Hank watched, fighting back his reaction to run and grab Katie and hold her safely in his arms.

Shawn looked into Katie's eyes and could see that they were glassy and that she was in shock. She stood looking in his direction but her eyes were not focused. With another step he was directly in front of her. Without hesitation Shawn purposely grabbed both her wrists with his hands. Katie screamed and fought back against his grip.

"What is the matter, Katie?" Shawn taunted.

"Let me go, now!" I yelled at him.

"You want it, Katie and I am going to give it to you," Shawn said as he pulled me closer to his body.

Hank wanted to run up to Katie but forced himself to remain where he was as Shawn had instructed. He could not bear to hear Katie scream and beg to be let free. Hank would pace a few feet, then turn and come back, waiting and watching as Shawn teased and mocked her. Shawn appeared to be egging Katie on by lifting her wrists in front of her and tightening his grip on them.

"Come on, Katie. What are you waiting for? I will tell you when I am through with you but until I do, you are mine," Shawn taunted.

Shawn took a few steps into the water holding Katie very firmly as he did so. He pulled her into the water, stopping when she was in ankle deep water. He continued taunting her. Katie was quiet for a few minutes and Shawn was wondering what she was thinking when all of a sudden she took her right leg and with all her might kicked. Her foot caught Shawn along his left hip with such force that he lost his balance. He was caught off guard and as he fell he held on to her wrists and she fell on top of him, water splashing all around them. Shawn held her out of the water as he tried to stand back up. Katie started twisting and squirming as she tried to free herself from his grasp.

"I am not through with you yet, Katie. You are mine," Shawn continued to taunt her.

"Hank, help me please!" I screamed.

Instinctively Hank ran to Katie's aid. For the first time she had screamed out his name and he was going to be there for her this time. *Oh Katie…I am here. You are safe* he thought to himself.

"Hank, do not come any closer!" Shawn warned as he fought with Katie in the water.

"She called me. I need to help her," Hank replied.

"She does not know you are here. She is only calling your name," Shawn responded. "If you do not want to hear her then go to the truck and wait. She is fine...I have her," Shawn reassured.

How much longer? Hank thought as he went back to the truck to wait, not knowing if he would be able to control himself if she cried out his name again.

Shawn focused again on Katie as she fought against his hold on her. She was fighting and struggling as hard as she could. She freed her hand again and as she struggled her head went in the water and it gave Shawn the chance he needed to get up. He pulled her up on her feet and out of the water. As soon as her face touched the water she began fighting, kicking and screaming. Shawn pulled her back on shore still holding her wrists firmly in front of her.

"Please, please let me go. Please, please, please," I begged.

"Let's go back in the water, Katie. Feel like a swim?" Shawn laughed as he taunted her.

"No, let go of me!" I demanded.

Shawn held her wrists and took a few steps back into the water. As soon as she felt the water getting deeper Katie screamed and fainted. Shawn grabbed her before she could fall. He carried her in his arms and started walking across the beach to her car. Hank saw Katie's limp body and ran towards them.

"I will put her in the car and drive. You follow us," Shawn suggested.

"Is she okay, Shawn?" Hank asked, his voice shaking.

"She's fine. She passed out but I tell you she put up a good fight," Shawn replied.

"The keys are in her pocket. Let me get them for you," Hank offered.

"I am going to take her to my house, Hank. It is closer and I want to be able to work with her as she comes round," Shawn explained.

"Just help her that is all I want," Hank requested.

"This is a very critical time for her and I need to be able to work with her while she is in this state," Shawn replied. "Here, take my keys. When you get to my house please open the door and I will carry her in," Shawn instructed.

"I will meet you there in a few minutes," Hank replied as he jumped in the truck and drove off.

Shawn placed Katie on the seat. After fastening her seat belt he closed the door behind her and then ran to the other side of the car. Shawn got inside and started the car. He backed up slowly, put the car in gear and drove off. He kept glancing at Katie as he drove. They had almost reached his home when Katie sat up and looked around.

"Stop, oh please stop," I begged. "I cannot see…the light is blinding me. Please, please make it stop. Please turn it off."

"Katie?" Shawn started to speak but checked himself and watched her.

As soon as Katie heard the unfamiliar voice she screamed and frantically felt around with her hands as though she were blind. She groped around for something but Shawn was not sure what she was trying to find. It did not take long for his thought to be answered. She grabbed the door handle and pulled. The door was locked so she could not open it. Panic engulfed her. She used both her hands forcefully to unlock the door.

"Katie, do not fight me," Shawn said quietly and waited for her reaction.

"No, no, no," I begged and my body went limp.

Shawn drove into the driveway and pulled up to the house. Hank had left the door open and was standing in the doorway waiting for them. Shawn unlocked the doors and got out of the car. He ran around to the other side and opened Katie's door. Hank came out onto the porch and waited. Shawn picked Katie up from the car seat and held her in his arms close to his body.

"I thought you would never get here," Hank said worriedly.

"She woke up and started fighting me again. She was begging me to turn off the bright light," Shawn explained.

"She did that with me too one night when I was taking her home from the farm," Hank admitted.

"She will be fine. I just need to talk with her. I am going to lie her down on my bed where she can get some rest and not hurt herself," Shawn informed Hank as he walked past him.

"Is there anything that I can do?" Hank inquired.

"Yes. Please bring my bag from the truck," Shawn responded.

Hank ran out to the truck quickly and returned with Shawn's bag.

"She has wet clothes on. I have some jeans and a shirt. I'd be grateful if you could put them on her for me. I am sure she would rather you did it instead of me," Shawn suggested.

With that Shawn left the room and closed the door behind him. Hank leaned over Katie, unzipped her pants and slid them off her. He then slid the dry ones on her and zipped them. Next he lifted her wet shirt off her head and gently replaced it with Shawn's dry one. He went to the door when he was finished, opened it and handed Shawn the wet clothes. Shawn took them aside and put them in a bag. He then went into the bathroom to change his own wet clothes. When he was done he came back out and walked over to Hank.

"There is coffee or tea if you would like to make some. I am going to go in and talk to Katie and I will have some with you when I am done," he told Hank.

"Shawn, is she going to be okay?" Hank asked worriedly.

"Hank, she will be fine. I will know for sure when she awakens. I can give her something to help make her sleep if she is very upset," Shawn replied. "So I am going to go back in now to talk to her. If she screams out, she is fine. I know that telling you not to worry is not going to do any good but just remember that I do know what I am doing," Shawn explained as he smiled at Hank gently.

"As long as I know she is okay I will be fine. That is all I am worried about," Hank confessed.

"I know you are concerned but this could be the break that we have been waiting for," Shawn responded. "Why don't you make us something to drink and I will come out and tell you more when I am done," Shawn promised.

"Is tea, okay with you?" Hank asked.

"Tea will be just fine," Shawn replied as he turned and walked towards his bedroom door.

Shawn walked into the bedroom and dimmed the light so that it did not shine brightly on Katie. He walked over to the bed and sat down next to Katie gently. He sat for a minute looking at her. He slid up so that he was closer and began to run his finger across her forehead. Soft, gentle strokes. He moved his hand lower and rubbed his two fingers on her cheek. Very soft, gentle strokes. After doing this for a few minutes he took her hand in his and covered her hand with his other hand as he softly began to talk to her.

"Katie, it is Shawn. You are safe now." Shawn's soft-spoken, comforting voice had a calming effect on her.

"Nobody is going to hurt you, Katie. You are safe and I am with you," he told her.

Shawn continued gently rubbing her hand. As he spoke to her he moved his hand back up to her forehead and gently rubbed his fingers across her forehead. He continued speaking softly to Katie. Shawn would stop and watch her for a few minutes and then resume. He could see her body responding as she began to breathe at a slower pace and her muscles began to relax. He stopped talking and watched her again. She began to stir but stopped after a moment.

"No, no, no…please stop," my voice was just above a whisper.

"Katie, you are safe. I am with you," Shawn repeated softly.

"No, no, no, no," I continued pleading.

"Katie, listen to my voice," Shawn began.

"No," I murmured. "No, no, no…" my voice trailed off.

"You are safe, Katie. Listen to my voice. I am with you and nobody is going to hurt you," Shawn reassured.

Katie stopped talking and her body relaxed again. Shawn went back to rubbing her forehead, temples and cheeks. He would stop every few minutes and watch her. She was breathing slowly. Shawn got up, covered her with a blanket and went to the kitchen. Hank was pacing the floor in the other room.

"She is relaxing Hank and I did not have to give her anything," Shawn informed him.

"That is good news," Hank responded eagerly.

"Now let's have some tea and I will explain some things to you," Shawn suggested.

Shawn poured them each a cup of tea and walked over to the table and set the cups down. Hank was anxious to find out more; to learn what had happened and to make sure that Katie was going to be okay.

"Katie had her first experience tonight of reliving a part of her past," Shawn explained.

"Are you sure she is going to be okay?" Hank asked.

"Yes, she will be. I am not sure how much she will remember but she was reliving the past tonight," Shawn stated.

"I am glad that we went and saved her from an attack by those lads," Hank confessed.

"It was the confrontation with them that put her in the state that we found her in," Shawn replied. "Up until the time that he grabbed her wrist I am sure she was fine. Once he grabbed her she went back to the past and began to fight. That is why I told you not to touch her and I finished the confrontation with her. As I spoke to her I taunted her forcing her to remember. I did not count on her fighting back so hard. The most important thing for me to do once I had her back in the past and in a fighting state was to calm her down," Shawn elaborated.

"Do you think she will remember who did this to her?" asked Hank.

"I am not sure. I kept trying to get her to call me by a name but she would not; so I am sure she does not know who it was…as yet," Shawn replied.

"That was very hard for me not to go to her when she screamed for help," Hank remarked.

"I know it was and that is why I told you not to come closer," Shawn reminded him.

"It is not easy working your way through these kinds of things," Hank replied.

"She will find her way through this and she will know exactly what happened and also who did it to her," Shawn responded.

"I just hope she does not do any more stunts like this again," Hank said shaking his head ruefully.

"Hank, there is a chance that she will not remember what happened tonight," Shawn explained. "We will have to wait until she wakes up and see what she has to say," he suggested.

"Oh, great! Another suppressed memory. That is just what she needs!" Hank said dejectedly.

"Let's wait and see how she handles things when she wakes up," Shawn advised.

"What happens if she does remember?" Hank asked. "How much do you think she will know?"

"I do not know. We will have to wait it out," Shawn replied.

"I wish it would just be over for her. She went all those years without remembering anything. Now she is remembering bits and pieces and never knows when the flashbacks are going to resurface," Hank said sadly.

"Did you say that she was with you one time when she was blinded by a bright light?" Shawn asked.

"Yes. I was taking her home after she had had a flashback. While I was driving she begged me to turn the light off. She screamed for me to stop, which I did. I told her there were no other cars or lights around but I had a hard time convincing her of that," Hank replied.

"We will work on it Hank and slowly she will remember," Shawn reassured.

"I just want the old Katie back," Hank responded.

"I think I'll go and check on her again," Shawn replied.

Shawn quietly walked into the bedroom and sat on the bed. He watched Katie for a few minutes and softly began to talk to her again. Once again he repeated the same words that he had been telling her earlier. He took Katie's hand and rubbed it gently as he spoke to her. Katie's body was now relaxed and her breathing had stabilized. Shawn stood up and walked back to the kitchen.

"She is sleeping soundly now," Shawn updated Hank.

"Good. I only hope that after everything she has been through that she does not have a nightmare," Hank said.

"She may sleep all night," Shawn explained.

"She needs her sleep so it would be good if she did," Hank replied.

Hank and Shawn sat talking about their lives as they got to know more about each other. Every hour they took turns going in to check on Katie. Every time Shawn would go in he would repeat the same process with her. He would touch her cheek and rub her hand, each time reassuring her that she was not alone and that she was safe. He would wait and watch her as he did so.

Katie had been sleeping for five hours now without waking. The sun was beginning to rise and both Hank and Shawn were tired but did not want to sleep until Katie had awoken. They sat back down and started talking again. Suddenly they heard movement in the bedroom and both men got to their feet.

"Hello, anybody there?" I asked quietly.

"I am here, Katie," Hank called out.

"Hank, help me, please help me!" I cried.

Hank looked at Shawn who nodded. Hank went to the bedroom. He looked in and found me sitting up in bed, confused about my whereabouts. Hank went over to the bed and sat down. I had tears rolling down my cheeks and hugged Hank as soon as he sat down. Hank put his arms around me and pulled me close to him.

"You are safe, Katie," he said comfortingly.

"Where am I?" I asked looking around.

"You are at Shawn's house but you are safe," Hank told her as he rocked her in his arms like a baby.

Shawn came to the door to look in on me and I looked up as he walked in.

"Do you remember what happened, Katie?" Shawn asked.

I sat and thought about it before finally speaking.

"Yes. I went to the lake and was walking along the water," I replied.

"Do you remember anything else?" Shawn asked.

"Only that someone grabbed me and I did not want to go," I replied.

"You are safe in my arms, Katie. I am not going to let anyone hurt you," Hank reassured me as he rocked me gently in his arms.

"Oh, Hank! I am so sorry for going out alone. I did not think anything would happen," I cried as I spoke.

"I should give you a sound scolding Katie for not listening to me," Hank replied sternly.

"I'm sorry. I won't do it again," I promised.

"You were lucky, Katie. When we got there you were having a confrontation with two young men. Do you remember the incident?" Shawn asked.

"One of them grabbed my wrist and told me that I had to go along with him. Then someone came up from behind me." I shuddered as I spoke.

"Yes, that is when we got there. They ran off when we yelled at them to stop," Shawn explained.

"I remember going into the water. I kicked someone and I remember fighting," I responded.

"Yes, that was me that you kicked," Shawn replied and lifted his shirt to reveal a large bruise on his hip.

"I'm so sorry! I did not realize it was you," I replied taken aback.

"I know you did not know. It's alright," Shawn reassured. "It may take a few days for you to remember everything but you were safe the whole time Hank and I were with you."

"I feel so stupid," I remarked.

"You are trying to recall your past Katie but you are fighting yourself," Shawn explained.

"Katie, Shawn is willing to help you. All you have to do is talk to him," Hank suggested.

Katie looked at Shawn and said, "I do not need help and I do not want help. I can do this on my own. Are you so anxious to help a crazy lady, a real nut case lost in the past?" I asked sarcastically.

"Katie, you watch your tongue young lady. I called Shawn and asked for his help and you dare to speak and treat him this way?" Hank yelled at me, shocked at my response.

"I'm sorry, Shawn but I can handle this on my own. But I'd like to thank you for all the help you've given me," I looked down as I spoke.

"Just keep in mind, Katie that I am here if you ever need anyone to talk to," Shawn replied.

"I just want to go home. Do you know where my car is?" I asked.

"It's right outside. Will you be able to drive yourself home?" Hank asked.

"I said I am fine. I just want to go home," I repeated.

I swung my legs off the side of the bed and stood up. I looked down at myself and did not recognize the clothes. Instinctively my hand touched the jeans and shirt. Shawn explained that Hank had put some of his clothes on me because I had been soaked from falling in the water at the lake. I told Shawn that I would presently return his clothes to him and once again apologized for snapping at him. I bade both Hank and Shawn goodbye and walked out to my car. I got in, started it up and drove off.

"I'm sorry, Shawn. I do not know where her attitude came from. She should have been grateful for your help," Hank told him

"It's a normal reaction, Hank. Don't worry about it," Shawn replied.

"Normal for speaking so rudely to you?" Hank asked sounding confused.

"You have to remember…I am the attacker that her mind is first to remember because it is fresh in her mind," Shawn explained.

"Yes, but you did not have anything to do with the original attack on her," Hank replied.

"No, I did not but I can stand in and fool her mind into remembering and that is what I did. Her reactions to me were similar to the same she used that night," Shawn explained. "She remembered that something had happened there from when she went there earlier in the day. When she went last night she was confronted by those lads and it took her back to that night. She experienced the same fear and terror that she had felt that night and she had surely reacted in a similar manner. That is why I told you not to touch her because you would not have grabbed her. Instead you would have tried to comfort her. She was reacting to the things that had happened long ago and holding and comforting her at that time would have confused her and she would have stopped. I needed to take her farther into the flashback to get her to remember more about it. She needed to go through the whole thing. That is why I taunted her and took her out farther into the water. Something had happened in the water. By triggering events while she was having a flashback she is likely to remember and help it resurface. It has been in her subconscious, only releasing bits and pieces of memories that made no sense to her. Tonight I brought it back out into her conscious mind and she will begin to remember more and more of it until she remembers the whole thing. I am not sure when that will be but the more she thinks about what happened last night the clearer it will become to her. That is why it was so important that after I taunted her I had to talk to her in her subconscious state so that she would not confuse my voice with the person that attacked her. I had to let her know that I wanted to help her and that I was not the bad guy. That is part of the reason she snapped at me and was rude not because she was angry but the sound of my voice confused her a little and it is a normal reaction. She probably will not remember it so that is why I did not say very much," Shawn concluded.

"Wow, doc! I'm sorry I gave you such a hard time. I know that you want to help her and I was almost as bad as Katie in giving you a hard time," Hank said sheepishly.

"Does that make it clearer for you and give you a better understanding?" Shawn asked.

"Yes and I appreciate you taking the time to explain it to me," Hank replied.

"I will try to explain anything I do to help her so that you will know what she is going through and have a greater appreciation for why she keeps on insisting that she can do it alone and does not want any help," Shawn offered.

"I think I better get going. I have to get the crew started on a project and the Stevens' will wonder where I have been if I do not return to the barn soon," Hank told Shawn.

"I think I will try getting some sleep. Please give me a call later if you talk to Katie to let me know how she is doing," Shawn requested.

"I will give her some time to cool down first. I will call her later and update you," Hank replied.

"She will calm down and think about what happened. Hopefully she will remember more and you are the first person that she is going to approach," Shawn told him.

"She still had no right to speak to you that way," Hank replied.

"It is difficult for her Hank because everyone has pushed her to go and talk to me. She does not think I can help her because she cannot remember on her own," Shawn explained. "She will remember more and I am sure that eventually she will come and talk to me," he reasoned.

"I hope so. I do not know how to handle any of this and I do not want to cause her any more problems than she already has," Hank said somberly.

"She will come round and when she does I will be there to help her," Shawn promised.

Hank reached out his hand to shake Shawn's and said, "I want to thank you for everything you have done. I really appreciate it."

"I am glad that I have been of help. Give me a call anytime," Shawn replied.

Hank turned and went out the door. He got in his truck and drove off waving to Shawn as he did so. Shawn waved and went back inside. He was tired as a result of the preceding events. He went in and lay on the bed trying to get some rest. As he lay on the bed he accidentally touched his hip and flinched in pain. Shawn lifted his shirt to look at the bruise inflicted by Katie's kick. He smiled wryly, lay back down and soon drifted off to sleep…

Chapter 10

I pulled into the driveway and stopped the car. I continued sitting in the car…thinking. The tears were sliding down my face. I leaned forward and rested my head on my hands that were on the steering wheel. At the moment I did not care about anything or anybody. The words from last night were still echoing through my head. The 'whys' were all I could think of. Why won't it stop? Why can't I remember? Why the flashbacks? Why the nightmares? Why the dreams? Why do I care? Why do I have to remember it now? Why, why, why? I do not care anymore. I do not care if I ever remember what happened that night. I am tired of it and I am not going to think about it any more. I am through trying to figure it out. I am tired of everyone trying to help me. I am tired of everyone trying to analyze it for me. I am tired of everyone telling me to talk to Shawn. I AM SIMPLY TIRED OF IT!!!!

I opened the car door and stepped out slamming the door so hard that it shook the entire car. After a short while of restless pacing outside, I unlocked the door and went in. The tears were still rolling down my cheeks. I threw the keys up on the counter and kicked off my shoes. I walked over to the sink and poured some water for tea. I slowly paced the floor unknowingly as the tears continued to fall. *I will not do this anymore* I thought to myself. *It is not worth it. Besides, if I am going to remember it is going to have to come back on its own. If I have anymore flashbacks I will just ignore them. I have kept this deep inside of me for eight years. I can force it back and not think about it for another eight years. I am done with it! Done…*

The kettle whistled. I turned off the burner and poured my tea. I walked out onto the deck and sat on the porch swing. I watched the birds as they flew up to the birdfeeder. Whenever a thought occurred to me I made a conscious effort to stop and force it back. *I will not think about anything that is related to my past. I will not think about it or mention it again to anyone…not even Hank.*

The phone rang. Not really wanting to talk to anyone at that moment I paused before answering it. *Maybe I will just let the machine get it? No,* I decided. *I better answer it myself* I eventually reasoned.

"Hello," I snapped into the receiver.

"Hello, Katie," Hank replied trying to ignore my anger.

"Did you call to see if I was home, Hank?" I asked sarcastically. "I am here, so you do not have to go chasing all over town for me. You do not have to worry. I do not plan on going anywhere, so you can take it easy," I said dryly.

"Katie, I just called to find out how you were. I was not planning on chasing you anywhere," Hank replied.

"I have decided that I am not going to worry anymore about my past. I will deal with it somehow when it resurfaces. Until then I will not be bothered by what happened," I told him.

"Maybe that is the best thing to do," Hank said slowly to improve my mood.

"So, is there anything else you wanted?" I asked rudely.

"No, Katie. That was all I wanted. I am glad you are safe. I just wanted to tell you that I love you and I am here for you," Hank said paternally.

"You have a funny way of showing your love," I replied wryly.

"Katie, it is because I love you that I want you safe. That is why I want to make sure you are okay. However, I am sorry if you see it any other way," Hank answered feeling hurt from my biting words.

"Well, I am here and I am safe. Now you can call Shawn and let him know that he does not have to go out chasing after me either," I snapped. "In fact, neither one of you has to worry about me ever again."

"Katie, I know you are upset and angry but I do want you to know that I love you and I would do anything to help you," Hank reiterated.

"Are you going to analyze me now and tell me how I am feeling?" I queried sarcastically.

"No, I am not. I just wanted to call to tell you that I love you and I am here for you but you seem intent on hurting me and saying vicious things so I will just let you go," Hank responded.

"Goodbye, Hank," I quipped. "I love you too but I am a big girl and can take care of myself so you do not have to worry any more," I retorted.

"Goodbye, Katie," he said and hung up the phone.

I slammed the receiver down. I was not sure why I was so upset but I was hurting and I did not care who I hurt. I looked down and saw that I was still wearing Shawn's clothes. I went into the bedroom and took off his clothes and threw them on the floor. I then slipped my robe on and sat on the bed. For a minute I thought of going out to ride Lacey but decided against it because I did not want to talk to Hank any more that day.

Why take it out on Hank I thought to myself. *He was only trying to help and if he had not come along where would I be now? I know he loves me and wants to protect me but I needed to do it on my own. What must Shawn think of me? Every time he is around I seem to act like a crazy person. I wish I could control the flashbacks and be able to stay calm when they struck. I will not let them control my life anymore. If they recur I will act as if nothing is happening, so nobody will suspect I am having one. If I can just learn to quickly push them aside and not think about them…I will concentrate on something else and not allow myself to be consumed with trying to figure out what it means or where I was when it was happening. I will be strong and hope for the best. I can do this. I have to do this. I do not have a choice.*

I thought about calling Hank and talking to him but I was still angry and I knew that we would only end up arguing. Besides, he would want to talk about what had happened and I wasn't prepared to discuss it with anyone at the moment. *I will stay away from the woods* I decided *and I will not pass by the lake. Hopefully that will curb the flashbacks. If I downplay the memories maybe they will gradually fade away and I will be able to get on with my life. I had not thought about the past for eight years. I could easily bury them again deep inside me if I focused on other things.*

I lay back on the bed looking up at the ceiling. That always seemed to help me think better. *Now how do I handle the flashbacks?* I wondered. *There had to be a way to control my reactions if I did happen to think about the past; a focal point to concentrate on when memories were triggered. When the flashbacks occurred what should I do? They always caught me off guard. I had always tried to keep the flashback fresh in my mind so that I could remember every little detail. How could I undo all the things that I had programmed my mind to do? There had to be a way to do it* I thought. I felt confident I could come up with an easy answer. *When the flashbacks occurred they were always at a different setting each time. Besides, I could never predict when they would occur which constrained using a thought association to divert my thinking. Perhaps I could use Paul…his sweet innocent face to be the focal point of my thoughts when a flashback struck? He always made me smile and feel better. That would work as long as I was not with him when I had a flashback—so using him was a good idea but one fraught with risk as well. Now for a place…where do I feel safe and enjoy being?* I mused. *The pond* I thought smiling. *I loved it there; the cool water relaxing my mind and body. There I could purge dismal thoughts from my mind and focus on nothing else other than the birds singing or the wildflowers with their exquisite beauty and their aromatic fragrance filling my nostrils. Maybe I should use the pond and think of the warm sun shining down on me and the breeze gently blowing my hair back? Oh, but what if I had a flashback about the woods again? The pond was too close to the woods and I might not be able to direct my thoughts to only the pond. Thinking of the pond might be too risky too.* I sighed and casually looked around the room hoping to think of something that I could use. *Well, scratch 'person' and 'place' off my focal point list* I chuckled to myself. *So that left 'thing' or 'object'. This was not going to be as easy as I first thought it would be. Come on, I could come up with something* I thought, still looking around and thinking.

Okay, break it down and think of things in isolation. What brought me joy and could make me smile when I looked at it or thought about it. Lacey had always brought me great joy; my rose bush that, when in full bloom, was not only spectacular to look at but filled my nostrils with the most wondrous fragrance. Other things that calmed me were big white fluffy clouds with the shapes that seemed to appear within them; a rainbow with the vibrant colors that seemingly reached out to me to brighten my day; a waterfall, a smiling baby, sunrise or sunset. I could go on but I still needed to pick one thing that I would be able to concentrate on if a flashback hit me. But of all the things that I loved how do I pick out a single thing? I let out a disgusted sigh, breathed deeply and held my breath for a while, then exhaled slowly.

Relax, I told myself. *You can do this.* I closed my eyes and cleared my mind of all thoughts. The room was quiet and I felt very peaceful. My plan was to think of nothing for a few minutes and then when I opened my eyes, the first thing that came to mind would be chosen as a focal point. Process of elimination would be the determining factor. *Maybe I should just toss a coin and decide that way?* I giggled at the thought. I would leave it up to my mind to make the final decision. After all, it would be my mind that needed that one thing to think about, that one object to concentrate on. I would let my mind pick out its own thought association.

I sat up, opened my eyes and in my mind's eye I pictured a rose. A beautiful yellow rose bud just starting to bloom. A perfect picture appeared in my mind. I got up and went to the deck and sat on the swing, looking at the roses. I selected the one that resembled the rose I had envisioned in my mind's eye and concentrated on that single rose. I moved closer and sat trying to fixate and etch it into the recesses of my mind, trying to remember every detail about the flower, every leaf and every contour of its petals. I would close my eyes and think only of the flower before me. Feeling sure I had it just how I wanted to remember it I stood up and went into the kitchen, grabbed the scissors and went back out to the roses. I carefully cut the stem at an angle and leaving a long portion of the stem I took it back in the house. I tied a piece of string to the end of the stem and taking it to the closet hung it upside down to dry. After it dried I would put it in a vase with some baby's breath and set it on the kitchen table so that I would be able to refresh my memory; a constant reminder that would help me remember that I could do this. I was strong and I could conquer this demon and get past it. It had happened a long time ago and there was no need to drag it all up again. Push it back deep into my mind where I would not think about it any more. *If I did not dwell on the flashbacks and nightmares they would soon cease recurring. I could do that* I kept telling myself *and it would work. I will forget about that night and everything that happened; it was strictly mind over matter.*

I closed my eyes as I concentrated on the rose once again, remembering every detail carefully. I would open my eyes and repeat the process until I remembered every single detail. I was ready and I felt very confident that the rose would be my constant companion no matter where I went. As the days, weeks and months went by I would continue from time to time to bring up this image to refresh my memory if needed. Plus I had the rose drying that I could look at in case the image of the rose faded. I was ready and would be waiting for the next flashback.

"No!" I said aloud, "*I will not let this take over my life anymore.*" I was ready and I would fight it no matter where I was, no matter who was with me, whether I was ready or not. I would busy my mind with other things.

I will go back to reading more, take more trips to the museums and do volunteer work. I will not give my memory a chance to come back to haunt me. I will outsmart it and finally be able to have some peace.

I got up to put the kettle on to make some more tea. I had a renewed confidence in myself, a self assurance that I had not felt for a long time. I stood looking out of the window while the water got hot. The phone rang and I went to answer it.

"Hello," I answered.

"Hello, Katie. I just wanted to call to let you that we are home," Mom said cheerfully.

"How was your trip?" I asked.

"It was wonderful and we had such a good time," she responded. "We are both a little tired but I wanted to let you know we were back and safe," she said.

"I am glad you had a good time. It seems like all you do is work around the farm and never spend any time having fun," I told her.

"Did anything happen while we were gone?" she asked.

"No, not really," I lied not wanting to tell her about my fall and what had happened at the lake.

"So we did not miss anything, huh?" she chuckled.

"No, real boring couple of days," I laughed.

"I am going to let you go so that I can get everything unpacked. I will talk to you soon," she said.

"Okay, Mom. Bye for now," I replied.

"Bye, Katie. We love you," she added.

"I love you both too," I said.

Click. We both hung up and I went to get the kettle that was now screaming very loudly. I was going to have to avoid my parents for a couple of days until my bruise healed. It had faded but was still noticeable. I should have told her in case she talked to Hank and he mentioned it to them. No, he will not say anything. He would wait to see if I said anything to them. I knew I could always count on him and I also knew that I needed to talk to him and apologize to him for talking so rudely to him before. Sigh...it seemed I had a hard time trying to keep my tongue once I started to get upset or angry and it seemed like I always took it out on Hank.

I poured my tea and went out on the deck to enjoy the sunset. It was a beautiful sunset with purple, pink and red colored clouds surrounding it as it disappeared from the sky. As I watched the sun setting I thought of my renewed attitude and I felt as though this sunset was the end of the old me and the next day's sunrise would be a new beginning for me. A new start for me with new challenges and a renewed feeling that I could conquer the world if I wanted to. A feeling that was growing stronger within me, rejuvenating my confidence to face the world with a smile without the inner fear that they might know something about my past and what had happened that night eight years ago. I no longer cared about that part of my life and I was ready to shrug it off and forget all about it. If in time the full memory resurfaced I would face it with the same renewed confidence that I had recently acquired and it would not bother me as much. That was the old Katie and I was now the new and improved version. I chuckled to myself as the thoughts ran through my mind. When I went to bed tonight I would be leaving the old me and when I woke in the morning I would be a totally changed person and ready to embark on a new beginning…

Chapter 11

The alarm went off. I opened my eyes and stretched my body under the covers. Tilting back my head I took a deep breath. Then I sat up and moved my legs over to the side of the bed. I looked out the window. For some reason everything looked different to me. Maybe it was my new outlook on life? I felt more alive and more in control as I felt no longer a slave to my past. I had mustered courage to bury it deep inside me. I was not going to let my past rule my life anymore. This was the 'new me' and I was really beginning to like the self-confidence infused within myself. I was sure, like everything else, that I would have a setback or two but I was determined not to let the past consume me anymore. This was a new day, a new beginning, a new me…

I went to the kitchen to make some tea. While I waited for the water to boil I busied myself tidying up the kitchen. Presently, the kettle began to whistle. I poured myself a cup of tea. After I was done I went in to take my shower. The water felt good as it relaxed my body. After showering and cleaning up the bathroom I began to get dressed for work. I went to the kitchen and grabbed my keys that I had thrown there yesterday when I had been so angry. *Not now* I thought. All my anger had gone and I was in control. I would not let the anger of my past take over. I went out the door, got in the car and drove to work.

The construction crew had finished their work and was just loading up the last of the materials into their trucks. The work had gone very smoothly and they had completed the project before schedule. I stood looking at the new wing, admiring the work that they had done. I walked through the door and was looking around when I ran into Bob and John. They had also gone in to take a peek at the new wing along with other colleagues. They came up to me while I was reading the dedication plaque.

"Hi, Katie!" Bob was the first to speak.

"Hi, Bob. Hi, John," I greeted them.

"Hi," replied John.

"Beautiful isn't it?" I asked them as we looked around at all the new equipment that had been moved in.

"Amazing work and done in such a short time. And they certainly did an exceptional job too," Bob said appreciatively.

Carol and Sara had come in and were walking around glancing at everything. They presently joined us. Sara stood and read the plaque before she spoke: "Now that the new wing is done, do you realize how many people it is going to help? Just think of the number of families that walk through that door who are uncertain of their future once they hear the devastating news of their loved ones having a fatal disease. The new equipment will not only help them live longer but also alleviate some of their pain and give them a better quality of life."

"It's amazing, Sara, and for so many years it was only a dream. We never thought we would ever get the funding to accomplish it. Now with the funding the new wing has been built and we are about to start a whole new era in the field of rehabilitation. It will be so exciting and gratifying to help those that do not have the money for services like this," I told her.

"The new wing will not only help the local families but it will bring in families from all over the world for surgeries and physical therapy that they cannot get elsewhere," Sara noted. "Even the operating rooms will now be different. With the closed-circuit, satellite hookups we can help with emergency surgeries with other hospital computers. It is truly amazing how far technology has come."

"With advancements in science it makes you wonder what the future will be like. Hopefully most of the diseases that we work on now will be a thing of the past. Each day researchers are coming up with new and exciting ways to find out about the different diseases and most times can detect it even before new parents start their families," I replied confidently.

"Maybe one day our skills will only be needed for accident emergencies, to set broken bones and heal them up quickly," Sara said.

"Oh, wouldn't that be wonderful!" I responded enthusiastically.

"But until that day comes we have a lot of work to do. Are you ready to start again, Katie?" she asked.

"Have they started bringing in Shawn's file cabinets yet?" I inquired.

Sara chuckled as she replied, "They have brought them in and they are in the old office waiting for you guys to get started on them."

"I don't know if I am ready for another marathon change over," I laughed.

"I am free to help you this morning, if you want my help," Carol offered. "Just let me put my stuff in my office and I will be down to help," she said and turned to go to her office.

"Sorry, I will not be much help for you. I have two meetings today and a late surgery," Sara said apologetically.

"I think you do that on purpose," I told her chuckling.

"No, it only seems that way," replied Sara, winking as she walked with me towards the office.

"We will be able to set the filing cabinets in the receptionist's office, so that we won't have to move them again. That will be a bonus," I remarked.

"Shawn came in early and has been working on them so you will have a head start on it," Sara stated.

"Oh, I don't mind working on the files. It helps me familiarize myself with the new people that will be coming in," I explained.

"I like your attitude," Sara said, chuckling.

"Shawn has a lot of interesting cases and I am looking forward to working with all of them," I confessed. "It will not be long before we have everything set up. It will make it so much easier," I remarked.

"I just hope we have everything done before the dedication of the new wing. That is only a few days off," Sara replied.

"I will stay overtime if I have to and it will be done in no time," I said rolling my eyes in a comic gesture.

"I love your sense of humor Katie and I know we will enjoy working together," Sara said in appreciation.

We walked into the office and Shawn looked up from his work. He had been working for two hours and was making great progress in the files. Sara apologized for not being able to help and turned to walk out the door so she would not be late.

"Good morning, Katie," Shawn greeted me.

"Good morning," I replied and asked, "Where do you want me to start?"

"I have the file cabinets set up in the other office. So we can take the folders in that room. It will be easier for you to get them set up," he explained as he looked around at the boxes all over the room.

"I am getting really good at this. I could do this for a living," I said laughing.

"I think we should have started on mine first and got warmed up before we did Sara's," Shawn said laughing.

"I think it was a good thing we did hers first otherwise I might not have the strength I need to get yours done," I answered jokingly.

"Do not worry, people. I am here to save the day…again," Carol said cheerily as she bustled into the room giving us both a wink as she walked up to us.

"I have a good start going and a couple of the guys are coming up to help take these boxes into the other office. So we will not have to keep going between offices," Shawn informed us.

"Do they have the computers set up in the other office?" Carol asked.

"Yes, they got them hooked up yesterday. So they are all set. Are you ready then?" Shawn asked.

"Just hand me the box you need me to get started on," Carol replied.

Shawn grabbed a box for Carol and they walked into the other office. I grabbed the box of folder labels and went over to the stack of boxes. I had opened the first box when I heard someone come in the room.

"Hi, Katie!" Scott barked.

"Hi, Scott. Did you get elected to be the mover today?" I asked.

"They said they needed a man with muscles, so everybody looked at me," he replied as he puffed out his chest in a mocking gesture.

"All the boxes in this section need to be moved over to the other office. So you can get started anytime you are ready," I told him.

"So, how does it feel to be working with the top dogs, Katie?" Scott asked.

"I did not realize I was," I replied, irritated by his question.

"Seems you and the doc are getting a little chummy?" he insinuated.

"Seems that you have your information wrong," I replied coolly.

"Oh, I don't know. First, you take him riding up at the farm and the other night your car was parked at his house overnight," he sneered. He walked over to me and took a piece of my hair and twisted it in his fingers as he glared at me.

"Following me?" I asked him annoyed at his insinuations.

"If you needed someone to talk to Katie you always know where I am," he replied. Then he added as an afterthought, "But maybe the doctor can offer you more than I can?"

"Actually, it is none of your business what I do Scott," I replied as I felt my anger rising.

"I bet that telling Shawn all your deep, dark secrets makes for great pillow talk?" he smiled mockingly.

"I am not telling him anything, not that it is of any concern to you," I answered evenly.

"Is that how you got your new position? Did you sleep your way to the top? I never thought you were like that," he said with disgust in his voice as he pulled harder on my hair.

"I imagine that is how your shallow little mind thinks," I spat the words out at him and continued, "If you remember, Mr. Sweeney gave me this position. I did not apply for it. So if you have a problem with it, go see him."

"I do not have a problem with that. I do not care who you are sleeping with," he said as he slid his hand around my hair. He placed his arms on my shoulders to prevent me from moving and added, "But I get lonely too. You can come to my bed anytime."

"You are supposed to be moving the file cabinets and not harassing me. So if you will just take your hands off me and get back to the job you were sent here to do I would appreciate it," I replied more than a little flustered.

"Oh, but Katie it feels so good to have my hands on you," he sneered.

"Well your touch repulses me so I suggest you let go of me or you will regret the big mistake you are making," I warned.

"Just keep in mind that you can come to my bed anytime you feel like slumming," he laughed in my face.

We stood glaring into each other's eyes neither one of us backing down as Shawn returned. He stopped in the doorway and watched us closely. I stood holding my hands in tight fists from the anger within; my nails cutting into my palms. Shawn coughed to let us know that he had entered the room. Scott did not move. He left his arms on my shoulders while holding my hair back in a ponytail with his hand. I tried to move but his grip was very firm. Slowly Scott removed his hands, turned around and went to the boxes. He had brought a two-wheel hand cart to help in moving the boxes. He slid the jack under one of the stacks and pulling the cart back towards him he turned and walked out the door.

"Is everything alright, Katie?" Shawn asked me.

"Everything is fine, Shawn. Nothing I cannot handle," I replied.

"You just seem very agitated. He obviously said or did something to upset you. Would you like me to get someone else to help?" Shawn asked.

"Do not worry about it. He said what he had to say and now he will leave it alone," I assured Shawn.

We went over and marked the boxes for Scott to move. Some needed to be cross-referenced; so those were put in a different stack. Scott came back in with a smile on his face and he looked at me out of the corner of his eyes. I turned my back so that he could not see how much his words had hurt me. Scooping up another stack he turned and wheeled them out of the room. Shawn watched our exchange and wondered to himself what Scott had said to me. He could tell that whatever it was that was said had upset me and that I was not willing to talk about it.

I took the lid off the top box of each stack and put a box of folders and labels inside so that it would be easier to work with. Scott came back in to get another stack and paused while I put the lid back on the box. He made a mocking 'kissing' gesture towards me while I glared back at him for his childish act. He slid the cart under the stack and he was back out the door. Feeling very flustered I excused myself to Shawn and walked to the door where I stopped, trying to decide which way to go. *Do I just go to the bathroom and splash some cold water on my face or do I go down and confront him? If I talk to him will it just make it worse or will he listen and stop? The old 'me' would just drop it and let it go. That was yesterday. Today it was the new 'me' and the new 'me' had more confidence and was willing to take on the challenge.* I turned and went to the other office. *Besides, if I let him get away with it this time he would figure he could pull his childish stunts whenever he felt like embarrassing and degrading me. I would show him first hand the new 'me' and I was no longer going to be the timid and shy girl I was before.*

I walked in the door to the other office where Scott was joking and laughing with Carol. I walked up to him and stood in front of him staring him in the eyes. He stopped talking to Carol and looked at me unsure about the confrontation he was about to have.

"What the hell do you think you are doing?" I asked him.

"Did I strike a nerve?" he chuckled when he spoke.

"I am not sure if you are really that ignorant and think you are being funny or that you are just plain stupid and do not realize what comes out of your mouth?" I asked him.

"Where did that come from?" he asked.

"I was not impressed and I will not have you talking that way to me to degrade me even if it is only the two of us in the room. I certainly hope you understand that! If not, I will gladly say it again…only slower and with pictures if you need it to get through your head. If you cannot say something that resembles an intelligent conversation you do not need to talk to me at all. Am I making myself clear to you?" I asked him.

"You are a little spitfire today. I like that," he responded.

"You are not going to like what I have to say if you do not stop. I am not joking and I will go to higher authorities if you continue to speak to me that way or ever lay hands on me again," I informed him.

"Are you threatening me, Katie?" he asked in an undertone.

"I am not threatening you, Scott. I am making you a promise…do it again and we will go together to have a little discussion with someone that can really solve the problem," I replied.

"So is that what your good ole doc has taught you, Katie?" he asked falteringly and I knew that my words had got through to him.

"I do not need to be taught on how I should be treated but maybe you did not listen well enough when it was being taught to you," I said as I continued looking into his eyes.

"You certainly have changed over the last few days. I am not certain I like the change that has come over you," he replied.

"Why, because I will not let you get away with your treatment of me? If so, that is something that has gone on for too long and I have enough respect for myself to put an end to it whether you like it or not!" I spat back.

"Guess you are too good to be hanging around your old friends now that you have a new position. Gotta watch who you are seen with," he responded hoping to get me agitated again to have the upper hand.

"Where I go, what I do, who I am with and what we do is of no concern to you. In fact it is none of your business. I will do whatever I want, with whomever I want, whenever I want and I certainly will not answer to the likes of you…ever," I replied in an even, unruffled tone. I was determined to be in control of this conversation.

"My, my, my…you certainly have changed. You are not the quiet, timid, shy, little thing any more, huh?" he noted.

"Just tired of listening to you run your mouth and saying nothing of interest," I responded.

"I will remember what you said Katie and from now on, do I need to ask your permission to speak to you?" he asked sarcastically.

"Maybe that would be a good idea if you cannot speak intelligently," I replied matter-of-factly. I walked to the door but turned back to tell him one last thing.

"Oh, just to clear something up for you. You said you saw my car at Shawn's house the other night all night long. I just wanted to let you know that if you would have been a little more observant you would have also noticed that Hank's truck was there all night too. We were working on a project and it was not at all what you were thinking," I retorted. "Sorry to have disappointed your little fantasy but nothing happened and I left before Hank did. So Shawn and I were never alone in the house. So next time before you try to start any vicious rumors you better substantiate all the facts before doing so. Are we clear on that?" I asked viciously.

"Perfectly," he replied sheepishly and went back to his work.

I walked out of the office and went down the hall to the bathroom. I wanted to splash some water on my face. This was the first time that I had stood up for myself and for the first time I was not the least bit shaken by the confrontation. I walked past the office. Shawn was still working on the files so I went past the door and walked into the bathroom. I walked up to the sink, looked into the mirror and smiled at myself, proud of the stand that I had taken. My heart was beating hard and my knees were a little shaky but I was very pleased that I had had the fortitude to challenge Scott. *This was the new 'me'* I said to myself, puffing out my chest and straightening my shoulders. I giggled at my reflection in the mirror. *One point for me* I thought to myself. *Score one to one. You want to turn this into a match, Scott? Well, the game is in play with the score tied. We are even and the ball is in your court. I learned a long time ago not to match wits with an unarmed opponent but in your case I will make an exception and gladly take you on. Game, point, match, win!* This round I beat him and would be better prepared for his next attack. I looked in the mirror and liked the confident, self assured person I saw looking back at me. *Now back to work* I chuckled as I winked and walked out the door.

I walked back into the office. Shawn looked up at me not knowing what the confrontation was about and he appeared hesitant to ask; so he kept working. Scott came in to get the last stack of boxes but never looked at me. Instead he turned his attention to Shawn and spoke briefly with him.

"This is the last of the boxes. So unless you have something else you need me to do I will go back to work," he told Shawn being careful not to look in my direction.

"No, that is all I needed to have done. Thanks for your help," Shawn replied.

"Glad I could be of help," he chuckled and turned to go.

"Thanks, Scott," I said and he turned around to look at me.

"Sure, Katie. Any time I can be of service to you just give me a call," he replied.

"I will keep that in mind," I responded with a smile.

Scott turned and walked out the door just as Carol came walking in. He stepped back and let her enter and he walked out without saying anything else. Carol looked at Shawn and smiled and came up to me with a puzzled look on her face.

"Okay, you want to let me in on it. I have been trying to figure it out since you left the office," she said.

"I thought it was pretty self-explanatory Carol," I said chuckling.

"I asked Scott about it after you left and he said he was just as dumbfounded as I was but something tells me he knew exactly what you meant," Carol replied.

"He knows exactly what I was talking about. Do not let him fool you," I explained.

"I am just not sure where it came from," Carol said laughing. "The look on his face was priceless…oh to have had a camera!" she lamented.

"I am tired of his treatment and I am not going to put up with it any more. I think he got the message that I was through with it," I said.

"You made a believer out of me girl but Scott, on the other hand, might be a different story," she replied.

"My next step is positive reinforcement and he really does not want me to go any farther if you get my meaning," I told her.

"I am not sure what has come over you Katie but I like it. You seem more confident in yourself and for the first time in a long while you are more like your old self," she remarked.

I winked at her and replied, "You haven't seen anything yet. I am just getting warmed up."

"Just make sure you let me know in advance so that I can be there for the next round," she said with a grin.

"You will be the first one I call," I chuckled.

"I came down to see if you two were going to break for lunch any time soon?" she asked.

"Sounds good to me. How about you, Katie?" Shawn asked.

"I am starving. Let's go," I replied.

"Quick, Shawn, before she changes her mind. You grab one arm while I grab the other," Carol teased.

"Oh, I don't know about that. She seems to be in a feisty mood today. I don't want to take any chances," he chuckled.

"Hell knows no fury like Katie scorned," Carol announced and we all laughed.

We walked down to the parking garage. Shawn drove us all to the corner café. We sat outside in the warm sunshine and ordered our food. We passed the time discussing the new wing and the great possibilities that were about to begin with the opening of the new facility. Shawn told us about the new equipment that had arrived and how it would be used. He answered all of our questions. I was truly amazed at the advanced technology that I was going to be a part of and the unbelievable things that were possible because of it. The time raced by so quickly that none of us realized it. After checking the time we knew we had to get back to work if we were going to get the files done.

We returned to the office presently. As we walked down the hallway of the office building Carol turned off to go into the first office while Shawn and I kept going down the hall to the other office. We walked in and started to sort out the folders that were left over. Carol had made great progress in downloading Shawn's patients' files into our computer system. In between downloading the disks she had been typing up the new labels for the folders and putting them on. Shawn and I finished up the last of the folders and he picked up the box and carried it into the office where Carol was working. I followed, carrying the extra folders and labels.

"Are you done yet, Carol?" I giggled.

"I have been done for hours. What has kept you two? I have been waiting for more work to do," she answered.

"Never fear, Carol. We are here with more work for you to do," Shawn replied.

"Bless your heart. I was afraid that I would just be sitting here the rest of the day with nothing else to do," Carol said as she crossed her eyes.

"I can always find you tons of work to do," Shawn teased.

"That is what I am afraid of," Carol laughed.

"Alright. It looks like you two have it all under control so I guess I will just go home," I said chuckling.

"Lock the doors, Carol. Quick, before she escapes," Shawn urged.

"I will make you a deal, Carol. You go for the door while I distract Shawn and we can both make a break for it," I said laughing.

"I have a better idea," Shawn said. "Let's all make a break for it while the coast is clear," he suggested.

We all laughed and decided if we wanted to get anything done we better get back to work. We spent the rest of the afternoon working and Carol only stopped once to go get us all something cold to drink. I was working on the first file cabinet and had everything labeled. Three of the four drawers were filled and all set up. I sat down and looked around. Carol was still typing away. She only had twenty more patient disks to download. Shawn was putting the patient name labels on the folders. I looked at the clock. It was eight-thirty and I was tired.

"Do you want me to start on the next drawer?" I asked Shawn.

He looked at the clock and was surprised at the time: "I did not realize it was that late. I think we should call it a night and start afresh in the morning."

"I can do that if you will, just for tomorrow, consider noon a fresh start," Carol proposed.

"I'm sorry. I did not realize how late it was getting," Shawn apologized.

"We did get a lot done today," I noted.

"Must be we are getting better at this," Carol remarked. "Just think if we had one more office to set up how fast we could do it."

"Oh, no!" I replied.

"Okay, girls. Let's lock up and go home," Shawn suggested.

"I'm right behind you," Carol replied.

"I think I will just sleep here. I don't think I can move," I said grudgingly.

I stood up and the three of us walked out the door and down the hallway leading to the parking garage. We had all parked close together. Each of us went to our cars and opened the doors.

"See you two in the morning," Carol called out.

"Get some sleep and drive carefully," I replied.

"Thanks for a great job, girls! See you both in the morning. Please drive carefully," Shawn advised.

I got in the car and started it up. We all took turns backing out of our parking spaces and we drove off in different directions for home.

As I drove home I felt more alive with a confidence that I had not felt for a long time. I was thinking about our confrontation earlier. Scott was just the first of my adversaries that I had to face and in time I would be forced to face the demons from my past. But today was not going to be that day. I will wait to fight the demon another day but I knew that I would be ready to face whatever it was that happened and I would be victorious. I felt stronger, knowing that I could and would do it when the time came.

I pulled into the driveway and stopped the car. I got out and walked up the steps to the house. I was totally exhausted. I walked in the door, put my keys on the counter and turned the light over the kitchen sink on; then walked into the bedroom. My mind and body were both drained from all the work I had done. I slowly took off my clothes and climbed into bed. Pulling the covers up around me I closed my eyes and presently fell asleep…

Chapter 12

I pulled into my parking space at work and turned off the car. Carol's car was not there so she had not yet arrived. Shawn's car was parked a few spaces down from mine. I looked at the car seat next to me and at the paper bag lying on it. The contents of the bag were a final reminder of that night at the lake. It contained Shawn's clothes that Hank had put on me that I had gone home in. I should have taken them back the next day after I had washed them but I did not want to face Shawn and the questions he would have had for me. Maybe I will just check his car and put them in the backseat? I thought That way I would not have to take them in and nobody would know about it. If I took them in and someone was in the office with Shawn it would be a little hard to explain. How could I explain why I had Shawn's clothes? It was early and there were not many people at work yet. I had to make up my mind and get going I thought to myself.

I grabbed the bag and got out of the car. I walked over to Shawn's car and tried to open the door. It was locked. So I had no alternative but to take them inside the office and return them to him. Besides, I needed to thank him for helping me that night. Since that night neither one of us had mentioned it. I was very grateful for that. I did not need to be told how stupid it was of me to go to the lake on my own. Hank had reminded me several times already. I realized now what a risk I had taken. I did not need any further reminders. Besides, I had put it all behind me and I would not be doing any more flashback experimentations. I did not care anymore what happened.

I walked into the building and down the hall to the office. Shawn was not there. I set the bag down on the file cabinet and would give it to him when he returned. I grabbed the folders that Carol had finished. Sitting on the floor I sorted them out and then placed them in the drawer. I was almost finished with the stack that I had when Shawn entered. I kept working as I had not heard him come in. After putting the last of the folders in the drawer I stood up to grab some more. Turning around I noticed that Shawn was standing there. He startled me because I had not heard him enter.

"Good morning," I greeted him.

"Good morning. It looks like you wanted to get an early start this morning. I have not seen Carol but it is not noon yet," he said chuckling.

"Before anyone else comes in I wanted to give you this," I told him and grabbing the package I handed it to him.

"Oh, I love surprises," he said with a smile.

"I was going to put them in your car so that nobody would see them and start any rumors but your car was locked so I brought them in. I hope you don't mind," I said hesitantly.

"Thanks for bringing them back. You could have waited to return them to avoid any unpleasant questions. However, there isn't anyone here now so I will keep them safely behind my desk," he suggested.

"Thank you," I replied. "I have not had the opportunity to thank you for helping me that night. I just want to say that I appreciated it very much," I stated.

"I'm glad I could help, Katie. I realized you did not wish to discuss it so I have not mentioned it to you," he explained.

"Thanks. It seems it gets discussed a little more than I prefer but it seems everyone wants to help me out," I said with a sigh.

"You know you can talk to me about it if you feel comfortable in doing that," he offered.

"I know and I appreciate your offer but it seems everyone wants to help me talk about it but there is one major problem with that," I admitted.

"What is the major problem?" he probed gently.

"I cannot remember much about it. So when everyone keeps telling me to talk about it I cannot because all I have is bits and pieces that mean nothing to me. I cannot piece them together to make any kind of sense of those fragmented bits of memories," I explained.

"You will eventually remember, Katie. You just have to be patient and not push yourself too hard. It will come to you," he said reassuringly.

"I don't want to remember any more," I admitted.

"Why is that??" he asked surprised at my candor.

"All I have to go on is fragments that come to me in flashbacks and nightmares. But whenever I try to sit and analyze them they seem to fade as quickly as they came to me," I confessed.

"So what do you plan on doing about it?" he asked.

"Forget the memories. Push them back into my mind and not think about them anymore," I said.

"Do you think that is really going to work for you?" he asked.

"It will work for me," I said chuckling.

"You know the flashbacks and nightmares are not going to stop," he replied. "You may be able to suppress them for the time being but they will return," Shawn explained.

"Thanks. I really needed to hear that," I said sarcastically.

"You told me they were coming more frequently. Have they stopped completely now?" he asked watching my reaction.

"I have not had any nightmares since the night I went to the lake and I have not had a flashback in a few weeks now," I responded.

"That is good, but I just want to warn you that they will return," he cautioned.

"I will not be concerned or think about them. Instead, I will busy myself doing other things and they will fade from my thoughts. I have done it before when it happened and it will work for me again," I said confidently.

"I thought you wanted to remember and that is why you went out searching for the answers you were so desperate to find?" he queried.

"Yes. I was searching and trying desperately to get the answers I wanted but nothing that I did seemed to help me remember anything. So I just do not care now if the memories ever come back to me," I confessed.

"So after all your efforts are you going to just let it drop and not try anymore?" he asked.

"You got to enjoy my previous two failed attempts. I almost got killed at the woods and I still do not want to think what could have happened at the lake if you and Hank would not have been there for me," I answered sheepishly.

"You should not be so hard on yourself Katie because even though you feel that you have failed you have learned something from those attempts to get nearer the truth," he replied.

"Yes, I found out that I am not a very good detective and I should not take up that line of work as my profession," I chuckled.

"Your mind is showing you things even though they might seem stupid and confusing to you. Your mind is giving you bits and pieces that you will be able to handle and think about and come to terms with before it starts giving you the more difficult things to handle," Shawn explained.

"I am just tired of trying to analyze the thought processes that my mind gives me. I want more and if my mind would only sort through the unnecessary things and give me the memories that would help me I would want to continue and pursue it. So until that happens I will just drop it and go on with my life. I have spent enough hours wading through the flashbacks and memories and have wasted enough time because I come up against a brick wall every time I think that I am getting somewhere," I explained.

"It will come to you eventually and you will be able to come to terms with it. Your mind will be able to walk you through all of it piece by piece," he said.

"Well, until that day comes I will just let it be and not focus so much time and effort on what seems to be an impossible task," I answered. "I just wanted to thank you for coming to my aid that night since I have not really had a chance to do so," I said.

"You're welcome and always remember that I am here if you want to talk. I will not pressure you to discuss anything that you do not feel comfortable with," he suggested.

"Until I remember more it really will not do me any good to talk about it," I replied.

"Do you remember any more of what happened since that night you went to the lake?" he asked.

"No, not really. In fact, I have not thought much about it. I was very angry the next day and that was the day I decided I was through trying to figure out what happened. I have not allowed the memories to permeate my thoughts," I replied.

"I thought maybe it might have brought back some memories because you were having a flashback when Hank and I reached you," he explained hoping to get me to start thinking about that night again.

"All I remember about that night is that I went to the lake. I had walked up to the beach and stood looking out over the water. I did not have the same fearful feelings that I had had earlier in the day. So I walked farther down the beach when a guy came up to me and…" I stopped as my mind slowly went back to that night as I started talking about it.

"Yes, you were by the water and the guys came up to you. Do you remember anything else?" Shawn asked.

"They wanted me to go somewhere with them. I did not want to go. I told them I was waiting for someone." I opened up without realizing that Shawn was making me think back and remember the events that had happened.

"You kept talking with them and there was a party going on a few yards down the beach from where you were. Do you remember the fire and the other people that were there?" Shawn pressed on.

I stood and thought for a few minutes before I spoke: "I do not remember much of the party. I mainly remember them coming over and interrupting me while I was trying to recall the flashback that I had had earlier in the day," I replied.

"Do you remember the one guy grabbing you and trying to pull you?" Shawn queried.

"I remember him telling me that I was to go with them. I recall someone grabbing me from behind," I admitted as I remembered more of the events that had happened.

"Yes, there were two. One walked up to you as he talked while the other came up from behind. That is when Hank yelled and we came running to help you," Shawn said.

I stood and looked out the window as I thought more about that night. I could remember more about it and how the first guy kept telling me that I was going to party with them. I remembered how angry I was because he had interrupted me when I wanted to be alone. I had felt something earlier when I was there and I knew by going back at night I would have remembered more but that guy would not leave me alone.

Shawn smiled confidently to himself knowing that he had got me thinking back and forcing me to remember what had happened. He watched me as I began sifting through old and new memories. He longed to ask me what I was thinking and remembering but was aware that if he interrupted me he would also stop my thought processes. He realized that I needed to be gently pushed forward or else he risked the chance of me burying it back deep into my memory.

"Water…I cannot breathe. Coughing…fighting to get to the surface again, so I can get air. My lungs need air," I said aloud without even realizing it.

"Fight harder," Shawn responded, speaking very softly and gently so as not to interfere with my thinking. He waited and watched for my response. As he did so he gently picked up my hand and began to softly rub it relaxing me without my realizing it.

The memories came flooding back but they were different from the ones that I had been used to. I was in the water but someone was holding my wrists, holding them so tight that I could not move. They were holding me so tight that it hurt and my fingers were going numb. *Who was holding me?* Usually in my nightmare I was alone fighting my way to the surface but now someone was in the water with me. *But who and why were they forcing me into the water?*

"Help me! Somebody please help me!" I spoke louder this time without even realizing it.

"Look, Katie," Shawn spoke just above a whisper. "Look at the hand...look higher, Katie. Look at the arm...you can see, Katie. Look up to the shoulder," he pressed firmly.

"I can see his hand, his arm, his chest and his shoulder," I said excitedly.

"Now look at the face, Katie. Who is holding you?" he asked quietly as he watched me staring outside the window in a trance.

Shawn continued urging me on: "Katie, slowly look at the face...you know his face. Slowly look and remember. You are safe. You are with me. I will not let him hurt you," he said repeating the words he had said to me over and over again during my last two episodes. He had gently taken my hand in his again and was softly rubbing it as he talked to me.

"I'm afraid to look. He is holding my wrists so tight that I am hurting. I am very afraid. Please, help me...please make him stop," I implored as I stared outside the window but visualized my faceless attacker in my mind's eye who was holding and hurting me. Every muscle in my body was tense as I was remembering. I could visualize my attacker in front of me...his chest, his hands, his arms and his shoulder.

"Katie, listen to my voice. It is Shawn. I am here with you. Nobody is going to hurt you. I am here with you, Katie. You are safe. I am holding you in my arms. He cannot hurt you. Slowly lift your eyes up and just look at his face. I am here with you, Katie. I will not let him hurt you." Shawn spoke slowly, his soft-spoken voice calming me. "You only have to look up and see his face, Katie. I am here with you and I will be here with you while you face him. Look up, Katie," Shawn urged me gently as he gently pressed forward to figure out the attacker's identify. Shawn watched my eyes as they slowly started to look up.

My eyes slowly worked their way upwards searching hard for the face I so desperately wanted to see to get past my ordeal.

"Good morning all," Carol said cheerily as she walked into the office.

I was startled by Carol's entrance and jumped, breaking my concentration. I stood blinking as I gazed outside the window. Shawn slowly let go of my hand and turned to look at Carol. I reached up and wiped the tears that had begun to slowly fall…thinking back on the man's form that had, just seconds before, stood there so clearly but now was gone. I turned and after greeting Carol I immediately excused myself and walked out of the room.

"Well, wasn't that touching!" Carol announced.

"Good morning, Carol. It must be noon," Shawn said chuckling.

"I decided to come in a little earlier but it looks like I came at a bad time and I must have interrupted something," she replied.

"No you did not interrupt anything. We were just talking," Shawn responded.

"It looked a little more than 'just talking' to me," Carol snapped.

"I just got here a few minutes ago, so you really did not interrupt anything, Carol. You are letting your imagination get a little carried away," he said laughing.

"Maybe I should go talk to Katie and ask her what was going on?" she suggested.

"I have something that I was hoping you could help me with. But if you think you need to go ask her, I guess it will have to wait," Shawn said hoping to change her mind.

"Sure, Shawn. I guess Katie can wait. What do you need help with?" Carol asked.

"These papers need to go out today and I am not sure where I am supposed to take them. Can you take them and get them sent out for me, please? You would really be doing me a huge favor," Shawn said smiling at her.

"I know just where they need to go. Don't worry. I will run them down and they will be sent out within the hour," she stated confidently, willing to do whatever she could to help him.

"You are a real life-saver, Carol. Thank you so much. I am still trying to learn where everything is around here. I am used to my old little office so this is going to take me some time to get used to," he said chuckling.

"Consider it done," Carol said as she took the papers, turned and walked out the door.

Shawn went over to the boxes. He lifted the cover and took out another stack of folders. As he continued working I reentered the office. I walked over to the desk and picked up the folders, then went over to the file cabinet.

"Are you okay?" Shawn asked smiling.

"Yes, I am just a little shaken, but I will be just fine," I replied.

"Did you want to finish our conversation?" he asked.

"No, I do not think I want another interruption. But thank you for taking me as far as you did," I replied.

"We do not have to do it here, Katie. You can stop by my house or I could come over to your place. On the other hand, if you prefer we can wait until everyone leaves and we can do it here in the office. It is up to you," he suggested.

"I do not think so but thanks for the offer," I replied.

"Katie, you were so close. Why stop now? You would have known if Carol would not have come into the office when she did," Shawn noted.

"I know. That is how it always seems to work. I always get within inches of knowing and something happens and it is gone. I am tired of trying to chase the elusive attacker. It gets very frustrating, so I will just let him go and stop tormenting myself with it," I answered.

"I will respect your wishes if that is what you really want, but always remember I am here if you want to talk. You saw how easy it was to jog your memory. It will be just as easy if we continue with it now but if you let it go it will take longer to for the memory to resurface," Shawn explained.

"Well, I guess it will be gone. I am done with it. . . finished," I admitted.

"Okay, if that is how you feel. Now let's get this office ready for the dedication," Shawn suggested.

"I will start with this box and maybe you can get started on that stack. I will be able to get the files in place in no time at all," I said confidently.

I grabbed the top box and went back over to the file cabinet. I sat down on the floor, opened the drawer and started placing the folders in. Shawn started on his stack. He pulled the files out and put the new labels with the new patient numbers on the folders and placed them face down on the desk. Carol came back and without saying a word went to the computer to finish downloading the last of the patient files.

We worked long into the afternoon before stopping for a well-deserved break. We had gone through three of the seven stacks that were still there. Carol stopped and got our orders and called for take-out meals, so that we would not have to stop work and could get done faster. We worked until our meals got there and finally stopped to eat. We set up the desk as our table and sat down and ate.

After lunch I cleaned up our mess and went back to the file cabinet. I had finished up the drawer and was ready to start on the next one. I grabbed all the folders that were done, opened the next drawer and started lining them up. Carol was done downloading the patient's disk on the computer so she offered to help us with the boxes. She opened the lid on the top one and started pulling out folders. She then put the new name labels on them and placed them face down on the desk. Shawn started on another stack and as I finished the ones I was working on I would grab more and continue placing them into the file cabinet. We had a fast efficient system of working and were moving along smoothly. As we finished off the boxes they were thrown over in the corner. Shawn went over, sliced open the bottom and flattened out the boxes. He set them by the door for maintenance to pick up and dispose of. We had finished off three more boxes and only had one more to go. Shawn looked at the clock and it was six-thirty. We had finished all but one stack of boxes.

"It is getting late, so if you girls would like to go that will be fine. I think

I will stay and finish up this last box before I go," he informed us.

"I can stay and help you get finished if you would like me to. That way it will be done and if we work together it will get done faster," Carol chimed in.

"I do not have any plans; so if we continue like we have been doing it will not take much time at all and it will be completed," I added.

"That way tomorrow all we will have to do is finish cleaning up and we will be all set for business," Shawn chuckled.

"Let's get started and get this done," I laughed.

Shawn and Carol opened the box while Carol grabbed a stack and started working on it. Shawn grabbed another stack and worked on it. Meanwhile, I opened the file cabinet and started putting in the files. We kept working non-stop and had it all done in just a couple of hours. Our system was working so well that we finished the final boxes off faster than all the rest of them. We cleaned up the remaining paper mess and were finally done.

"Yes, we are finally done. Who is up for some celebrating?" Carol asked.

"Not me. I am going home for a long hot bath," I replied.

"I am out too. Sorry, Carol. Maybe another night?" Shawn suggested.

"You guys are no fun," she complained.

"I am fun. I am just tired," I told her laughing.

"We did not come in at noon today, Carol. We started early and now we are ready to collapse and you are ready to party," Shawn said teasing her.

"I will take you both up on the rain check for going out another time," she told us.

We grabbed our purses and Shawn grabbed the paper bag that I had brought him. We walked out the door and turned off the light. We walked down to the parking garage and each went to our cars and got in. Carol pulled out first, honking and waving. I backed out next and waved as I drove away. Shawn had got in his car and he pulled out just after I went by.

I drove home thinking about how Shawn had brought me so close to finding out who my attacker was. *Should I go ahead and let him work with me on it to get it over with once and for all?* I would have known if Carol had not come in when she did. The hand and shoulder looked so familiar to me. *Maybe if I think about it I can remember?* There was no watch or ring to identify with but I knew it was someone that I knew…someone that was close to me. *I will sleep on it and maybe I will feel differently about it in the morning when I awaken* I thought. Shawn was very patient and I felt very safe with him there with me. *I was sure he could help me but did I really want to know after all this time? What would be gained by it now?* It was so confusing to me at times. I did want to know so badly that I could hardly stand it but now it did not really matter to me any more. *Sleep on it* I thought to myself…*wait and decide in the morning.* I was too tired to think right now.

I pulled into the driveway and walked up to the house. *Yes, sleep on it and in the morning I will be able to think when I was fresh after a good-night's sleep.* Besides, everything was clearer in the morning light and I would know what to do…

Chapter 13

We had a special board meeting scheduled this morning so I had to get up early and go to work. After all the planning and fund-raising events it was finally coming together and the new wing was now built and ready to start taking patients. As I drove up, I looked at the new wing and was amazed at how quickly everything had come together and how the construction crews had worked non-stop to get it finished. The dedication was scheduled and the board members wanted to talk with us before it commenced. Most of the members had already arrived. The camera crew was busy setting up and getting their anchor people organized and ready to start filming. All the news agencies from around the country had sent representatives to provide full coverage of the dedication event. It was a beautiful sunny day and one could feel the excitement in the air.

I went up to the board room as everyone slowly worked their way to their seats. I walked in and took my seat as I waited for Mr. Sweeney to arrive.

We all sat talking among ourselves, laughing and joking about the day we were about to face with the media's presence everywhere. Mr.

Sweeney finally entered and called the meeting to order.

"Today will be an eventful day, not only for us but for everyone. As you can see we are receiving extensive coverage from the television and news media. I am not sure if those yet to arrive will be able to find their way in. Please feel free to mingle around and answer all the questions of the media. Remember that we have all waited a long time for this new wing and we want everyone to know that we wish to help those in need," he announced. "A buffet table with a luncheon has been set up so I would appreciate if you would all stay here for your lunches and encourage everyone to eat," he chuckled.

"For those of you that will be working in the new wing, please try to stay in that area so that you can show the people how the different machines work and how it will benefit those that will be using them. Remember these people helped fund this new wing and we want to show our appreciation for reposing their trust in us. We need to convince them that their money was well spent. So, unless you have any questions, this meeting is adjourned. Oh, and don't forget to hand out the brochures to everyone so that they can take these home and read about the new technology that we have to offer. Have a wonderful day and now let's all go for the inauguration ceremony," he invited.

Thunderous applause rang out after he was done speaking. We stood and filed out through the door, each of us heading to our designated areas while Mr. Sweeney and the rest of the board members went outside for the ribbon-cutting ceremony. The mayor and prominent city leaders had all arrived for the ceremony to pledge their support for the new wing. As they walked out the door the flash of the cameras started and faces lit up in smiles. Our chaplain from the hospital was on hand to give the blessing for the opening of the new wing and the benediction. The local school band was there to play the national anthem. People were starting to gather around the section that had been roped off at the main entrance doors where the big, red ribbon with the words "Grand Opening" was written on it. Spread out across a table lay brochures about the new wing, a large cake that had been donated by one of the local bakeries and a pair of oversized scissors that would be used to cut the ribbon. The band was all set to play, television cameras moved in and started taping while the news media stood with their tape recorders in their hands just waiting for the announcer to begin. Mr. Sweeney walked up to the podium to commence the ceremony.

"Could I have your attention, please?" Mr. Sweeney requested into the microphone as the gathering stopped talking and all eyes turned towards him.

"I would like to begin the ceremony. May I request Chaplain Smith to come up and give the blessing first? I will speak once he has finished," Mr. Sweeney told the crowd.

The Chaplain came up to the microphone and gave the blessing. Mr. Sweeney then walked up to the microphone. He began his speech by thanking everyone in the community for coming together to make the new wing possible. He went on to tell everyone how the new wing was 'state of the art' technology and would be able to assist in helping not only the local community but, with its satellite hook up, it would make communication internationally available for assisting surgeries wherever it was needed. He also told them that behind the new wing there was a heliport for helicopters to bring in patients that needed special care. The people would clap each time he announced the new advantages that were being made possible thanks to the new equipment that was now available. Mr. Sweeney went on to tell them how all the technicians and assistants had taken extra courses to learn how to use the new equipment and how it would speed up the physical therapy sessions that were presently underway. He concluded by urging the gathering to go through the new wing and check everything out. He informed everyone that there were hospital personnel throughout the wing that could answer any of their questions. Everyone clapped after he had finished speaking.

When the clapping had finally subsided Mr. Sweeney announced that they would cut the ribbon while the band played. The Chaplain would then give the benediction and everyone would be allowed into the new wing. The crowd clapped once again. Television anchors and newspaper crew all came up close to get a close-up as Mr. Sweeney and the mayor both took a side of the scissors and cut the ribbon. The crowd applauded emphatically and whistled animatedly. The band began to play the national anthem. When they had finished, the Chaplain stood up and gave the benediction. Mr. Sweeney returned to the podium and thanked everyone for participating. He also suggested that everyone should walk around the new wing and check things out. The mayor and he then walked up to the doors and held them open as the crowd began to filter in through the open doorway. They talked and joked with the people as they passed by. As people started entering, the television anchors moved in and taped portions of the new wing; then left so that they could edit it for the daily news report. The newspaper crew stayed longer and stopped and talked with the technicians and assistants so that they could get the full story for the next day's front page report.

The morning raced by quickly. We took turns going down to the luncheon to eat and invited the people viewing the new wing to stop and eat as well. I went to the office to grab some more brochures and went around filling the tables to make sure that there would be enough for everyone to take a copy. I grabbed some more brochures and returned to my station in the new wing. Shawn and Carol came up. While we stood discussing the ceremony Shawn's beeper went off. He checked the number but it was not familiar to him. He went to the phone to return the call while Carol and I continued chatting to the visitors. Sara came up looking concerned and motioned for me to come over to her. I excused myself and walked up to her.

"Hi, Katie. Have you seen, Shawn?" Sara asked.

"He got a message on his beeper and went to call the person back. He is down in the office if you need him," I replied.

"I got the same call. I will go down and talk to him about it," she informed me.

"Okay, I will talk to you later," I replied. She turned and went down the corridor to the office and I went back to keep Carol company.

It was late afternoon and most of the people had started to leave but there were a few still looking around. Shawn started walking down the corridor in my direction and when I looked up he motioned for me to come over to him. I excused myself and walked towards him.

He smiled and said, "Hi Katie. I know it is getting close to the time where we will be wrapping up but Sara and I just got a call and we will be getting a new patient in. We would like to know if you could possibly stay a little longer and help us with him?" he asked.

"Sure. It won't be a problem. When will the patient be arriving?" I inquired.

"He will be flown in and should be here in about four hours. You can go home for a while if you wish and come back around seven if that is fine with you. You have a lot of experience in this and we think it would be a big help if you could assist us in getting him settled in and evaluated," Shawn explained.

"I will be fine. I will go down and eat, then return to the office and get some work done while I wait," I replied.

"Thanks, Katie. You will be a big help. Sara was hoping you didn't have any plans and could stay," he stated.

"What happened to the patient?" I asked.

"He was in an automobile accident and is not responding. His vital signs are stable but he has not spoken since they brought him in. His parents live here which will help in his recovery. The doctor felt our facility would be best for him," Shawn explained.

"Just page or call when you need me. I will be in the office and will come down to help," I replied.

"Thanks again, Katie. I will let Sara know that you will be staying to help," he said.

I walked back to Carol and told her that I was going to go down and have something to eat. She decided to go along with me. There were only a few people left and they were making their way to the door. We went down, filled our plates and went over to the table to sit.

"I don't know about you but I don't think it was such a good idea to wear a new pair of shoes today. There was way too much standing and walking," Carol giggled.

"I wore my most comfortable shoes for today. I learned a long time ago 'comfort over style' any day. You knew you were going to be on your feet all day," I chuckled in response.

"So what did Shawn want?" she asked.

"We have a new patient coming in tonight and Sara asked him to see if I could stay and help them," I replied.

"Oh, our first patient in the new wing! Isn't that exciting?" she squealed.

"I was really hoping that the new patients wouldn't come so quickly," I responded.

"What and let all this technology get dusty?" she asked. "I think it is exciting…just think we can cure people quicker and send them on their way," she added.

As we sat eating we had people come up and join us to talk with us some more. The day had been great with a wonderful turn-out. It made all the work we had invested to get to this stage worthwhile. We talked about the fund-raising events that we had had over the last two years and how everyone in the community had come together to help make the new facility a reality. Carol finally decided she was too tired to sit any more. So she bade all of us farewell and walked out the door leading to the parking garage. I got up and went down the corridor that led to the office. I went in, sat at my computer and started typing up some of the paperwork that had been left on the desk. I looked at the clock…it was five-thirty. It would be a while before our new patient arrived. Our first patient…it seemed so unreal to have the new wing finally built and ready for patients. I continued working on the list of patients of the previous day. We had not scheduled many patients this week, knowing that we would be investing time in the dedication ceremony. I continued working and finished up all the files that had been brought to me. I labeled them and put them away in the cabinet. I started cleaning up the office. We had stayed late the other night and did not have a chance to do a thorough job; so as long as I had a few minutes I started cleaning up. The phone rang and I went over to answer it.

"Hello," I answered.

"Hi, Katie. It's Sara. The helicopter has just arrived. Can you come down please when you are ready?" she requested.

"Sure, Sara. I will be right down," I replied.

"Thank you. Bye," Sara responded, keeping the conversation short.

"Bye," I replied.

I hung up the phone and went out the door, closing it behind me. I walked down the corridor and waited as the helicopter's blade slowed to a stop. Shawn and Sara were waiting and walked up to the helicopter once the blade had almost stopped spinning. They slowly pulled the gurney from the helicopter and snapped the legs down in place. I opened the doors as they approached and glanced at the person on the gurney. He had tubes in his nose and mouth; plus IVs in his arms. The oxygen mask that they had put on him covered most of his face. Shawn and Sara wheeled him into the first examination room while I followed them in and grabbed the patient chart that was attached to the gurney. I flipped it open and caught my breath when I read the name on the chart. *Matthew James Sinclair*. I slowly looked over the chart and read what was written down. I could feel the tears welling up in my eyes but I forced them back.

"Katie!" Sara yelled. "Katie, what is the matter? I need the information!"

"I'm sorry," I replied apologetically.

I read them off the doctor's notes and filled them in with all the information that they needed. I relayed the medications that they had given him and read off the vitals that they had taken just before the helicopter landed. I provided them with the background of the accident and the medications they had given him. Sara took the oxygen mask off. His vital signs had stabilized so they removed the tubes but left the IVs in.

We had been in the examination room for almost two hours. Also present were Dr. Samuel Brown—the neurologist; Dr. Calvin Baker—specialist in internal medicine and Dr. Hannah Peaks—orthopedics specialist, all of whom had been called in on the case. They had prepared the patient's room in the ICU. Shawn and I were going to take him up while Sara, Sam, Cal and Hannah would look over his tests thoroughly and try to decide what steps needed to be taken first. They had taken more ex-rays, MRI and a cat scan to look over the injuries that he had sustained in the accident.

We wheeled the patient into the elevator and I pushed the button to take us to the floor that we needed. I kept looking at him and trying to remember the last time that I had seen him. It was hard seeing him this way thinking back on how he was and remembering what I had read in the doctor's report. This was a severe spinal injury and it was very doubtful that he would ever walk again. Possible paralysis from the neck downwards.

I watched him as the elevator moved from floor to floor. *How long had it been since we had seen each other?* I wanted to reach out and hold his hand but I did not want Shawn to know right now that we knew one another and what we had once meant to each other. *Time goes by so quickly…it seemed like yesterday that we were running in the woods and having picnics at the pond* I reminisced. The elevator stopped and the door opened. We exited the elevator and pushed him to his room. I hooked up the machines and pushed the timer so that the nurses would know when it was time to come in and turn him. He was put on a rotating bed and was strapped in so that the bed could be turned without causing him any more injury. The bed was new and this would be the first time it had been used. Every two hours the timer would go off at the nurse's station and they would come in and rotate the bed. It kept the possibility of further injury down because he could be moved while remaining stabilized at the same time. Shawn was adjusting the straps and Matthews' eyelids began to flutter.

"Matthew, can you hear me?" Shawn asked but there was no response. He continued: "Matthew, I am Doctor Goodson and you have been in an automobile accident. Can you hear me?" there was no response.

"Matthew, if you can hear and understand me please open your eyes," Shawn requested.

"Ka ka ka," Matthew whispered incoherently.

Shawn repeated, "Matthew I am Doctor Goodson and you have been in an automobile accident. You are in the hospital and we are going to take care of you."

Matthew did not speak or move. Shawn looked at me and said that he would try again later to get a response from him. He told me that we were done and we could go. I told him that I wanted to stay for a few more minutes. Shawn looked at me quizzically, then turned and left the room. I went up to the side of the bed and looked down at the patient. The tears that I had been holding back now fell, sliding down my cheeks as I watched the machines that were hooked to him.

"Matt…it's Katie. Can you hear me?" I asked but there was no response. I sighed and pulled the chair over next to his bed. I grabbed his chart and began reading the words that were written on it, as if by reading it again I could change the words that stared back at me.

"Ka ka ka," Matthew repeated.

"Yes, Matt. It's Katie. I am here with you. Can you hear me?" I asked but he did not respond to my voice.

I sat down on the bed and held his hand very gently as the tears streamed down my cheeks. I wondered where he had been and what he had been doing over the past few years. I sat with him patiently for two hours. I was beginning to get very tired and decided that I should go home to bed. Two of the nurses came in to turn the bed. They asked if he had awoken or if he had said anything. I informed them that he had whispered something incoherently. I gave him one more look and then told the nurses that I was going home. I stopped at the door and turning around watched how the nurses rotated the bed. Matt's lifeless body never moved and he did not wake up or say anything as they did so. I returned to my office. I grabbed my purse and keys and then went down to the parking garage. Part of me wanted to stay with him and hold him close. But another part of me reminded me that I could not erase the past and that we had both moved on. There had been a time that we were very close…but that was years ago. *Would he remember now after the accident?* The report said that there was the possibility of brain damage in addition to his spinal injury. *How would he handle the thought of never being able to walk again?*

As I walked to the car I ran into Matt's parents. They were just coming in after receiving the call about the accident.

"Hi, Katie" they greeted me.

"Hi, Joe. Hi, Mary," I replied.

"Matt has been in an accident Katie and they are bringing him here," Mary told me.

"I know, Mary. I was just up in the room with him. I assisted the doctors when he was brought in," I informed them.

"Oh, Katie. Is he alright? They were so vague when they called us and they wouldn't tell us anything except that he was being flown in for treatment here," Joe remarked.

"He is in the new wing and he is getting the best treatment possible. He has two of the best doctors that we have on staff working on him," I explained.

"Did you talk to him, Katie?" Mary asked.

"No, Mary. They have given him medicine that is making him sleep. They have run tests on him and Dr. Jenkins is going over the results as we speak," I replied. "He is in ICU...Room 305. He was flown here so that he can be looked after properly," I added.

"Katie, we don't want to impose but could you please go in with us and tell us what the test results mean?" Joe inquired. "We are not very good at understanding these things and we know that you are trained in this," he observed.

"Sure, Joe. I would be happy to accompany you. I can look over the chart and see if they have put in the new information," I replied reassuringly.

We walked in the door and I showed them the way to get to his room. I did not want to go back to the room. I did not want to tell them the bad news that their son may never be able to walk again. There was also the possibility that he would never talk or even remember them. I guess it would be 'best' coming from me instead of Sara but it did not make it any easier knowing what their reaction would be.

As we got closer to the door I explained to them that he was on a rotating bed and that they could hold his hand but because of the IVs and the straps that were holding him in the bed they would not be able to hug him. I also reminded them that he had been given medication to make him sleep so he probably would not respond to them. I just wanted to prepare them for what was to come. They both told me they understood. I slowly opened the door and they went inside.

"Oh, Joe!" Mary cried out in shock as she saw her son.

"Be strong, Mary. We need to be strong for Matthew," Joe told her as Mary began to cry hysterically.

Sara was checking his vitals and looked up when we walked into the room. The ex-ray films were hung up on the screen. The light was still on and I could clearly see the broken bones.

"Hi, Dr. Jenkins. I would like to introduce Matthew's parents to you. This is Joe and Mary Sinclair," I said.

"Joe...Mary...this is Dr. Jenkins and she will be one of Matt's doctors," I explained as I completed the introductions.

"Will he be alright?" Mary asked Sara.

"We are going to do everything we can to help him, Mary," Sara replied.

"Can I talk to him? Will he be able to understand and answer me?" Mary shot the questions at Sara.

"We are not sure right now how much he can hear and understand. We will have to wait until he wakes up. He does have some broken bones that we will need to set but right now we want him to remain on the bed until all the tests are run and we know exactly what we are working with," Sara explained before excusing herself to get the results of the other tests.

"Katie, please explain to us exactly what all of this means. You can read the chart and the ex-rays. You know exactly what it means," Mary pleaded.

I took the chart and read what had been written on the pages. I explained everything to them and let it sink in before going on. I told them how the accident had occurred and what the doctors from the other hospital had given for his prognosis. I explained in detail how there was a great possibility that he would have brain damage and there was a chance that he would be paralyzed from the neck down. I showed them, on the ex-rays, the number of broken bones that he had. I explained what the tests showed as Matt's parents stood holding and comforting each other while the tears fell from their eyes. As I talked they both stood looking at Matt. After I had offered them all the information that I was aware of I asked if they had any questions. They told me that they would have to wait until he woke up and all the test results were back. Until that happened they would still hope and pray for a miracle for their son.

"Ka ka ka," Matthew spoke again.

"What do you need honey? It's Mom...your Dad is also here." Mary went over to the bed to talk to Matt hoping that he would speak again.

"Matthew, it's Dad. We are here and we are going to stay with you son," Joe said reassuringly.

As we stood waiting Matt didn't speak again. He just lay there with his eyes closed. Mary kept talking to him hoping that he would open his eyes and say something. After an hour I knew I had to go but just like them I was hoping that he would awaken and say something. Mary sat on the edge of the bed and would speak to him and wait. When he didn't respond she would wait and try again a few minutes later. I was getting very tired and knew I had to leave.

"It is getting late and I need to go," I explained.

"Thank you very much Katie for explaining everything to us. We really appreciate your help," Joe said as he hugged me.

"It was good seeing you again, Katie. It has been a long time. I just wish it were under different circumstances," Mary sobbed as she gave me a hug.

"I will check on him in the morning and give you a call to let you know how he is doing," I promised.

"We will be staying until we hear what is going on. So we will see you in the morning," Mary informed me.

"See you in the morning," I replied.

I turned and walked out the door. I was exhausted and just wanted to go home to bed. I walked out to the parking garage and was feeling very depressed. I knew that he was going to get the best possible care but I wished there was more that could be done. I wish there was a better prognosis for him. There was the possibility that the first tests could be wrong but it would take time to know for sure.

I got in the car and drove home. I pulled into the driveway and parked the car. I slowly walked up the porch and went into the house. I didn't bother to turn on the lights. I locked the door and went into the bedroom. I turned the covers down, slipped out of my clothes and climbed into bed. I lay on the bed gazing outside the window as my mind went back to the happier times that Matt and I had spent together. I wondered what would happen now. I finally closed my eyes and drifted off to sleep…

Chapter 14

The dark clouds were gathering in the sky as I drove to work. The weather report called for thundershowers lasting into the evening. I had awoken early so that I could go and check on Matthew before I went to work. I still found it hard to believe about the accident and his predicament. I hoped that the first test results were not accurate. That sometimes happens when one was in a bad accident. The swelling could sometimes give false readings. The ex-rays did show a lot of broken bones, so there was no reason to believe that the test results that the other hospital had sent were incorrect. Sara and Shawn had both ordered more testing to be done and the results should be in soon. With the new wing we had a full staff twenty-four hours a day and test results were ready within a few hours instead of having to wait for the day crew to come in to read them. I would know soon enough what the new results were and I could discuss them with Joe and Mary. I thought back about last night and how I had mixed feelings about seeing them again. I had not seen them for over two years and it had been almost eight years since I had last talked to Matthew.

They looked the same, only older. Mary was tall and thin. Her black hair was beginning to turn gray but her eyes were still as blue as ever. Joe was a few inches shorter than Mary. He was a burly man with brown eyes and was balding. Mary was very straight-laced and proper while Joe was more laid-back with a wonderful sense of humor. I often wondered how they had ever remained together.

I pulled up into my parking space and got out of the car. There were only a few people there for the day crew and it was too early yet for the change of shift. I could see that Shawn's car was already there but I did not see Sara's car. I entered the hospital and walked down the corridor to Matt's room. As I got closer to his room I could see the "oxygen in use" sign implying that they had had to hook him up to oxygen during the night. Although this was common practice for serious accident cases to help patients breathe easier, I could not help but wonder if there was more wrong with him than we had anticipated. I stopped at the door and looked in before entering. Joe was sitting on the chair next to the bed with his arms crossed and his head bent forward while his chin rested on his chest. Mary was sitting on a chair next to the bed. Shawn was checking Matt. The machines were hooked up and one could see Matt's heart rate and blood pressure on the monitor. I stopped, unsure whether I should go in or not when Mary looked up and saw me. She stood up and headed for the door, so I opened it and walked in.

"Oh, Katie! I am so glad that you are here," Mary cried out.

"Good morning, Mary. Good morning, Dr. Goodson," I said. Joe had not moved so I knew he was still sleeping. Shawn looked at me but did not speak.

Mary hugged me tightly as I held her shaking body close to mine.

"Have you had anything to eat, Mary?" I asked.

"Not since yesterday afternoon. But I'm not hungry," she replied.

"When Joe awakens you really should go down and get something even if it is only juice. You need to keep your strength up," I advised.

"Maybe when Joe wakes up...if he is hungry, we will go. I really don't want to leave Matthew," she said.

"I am going to read his chart and help Dr. Goodson. I will let you know what the new report says," I informed her.

"Thank you so much Katie for being here!" she replied in gratitude.

"I am glad I can help," I responded.

I walked over to the bed and looked down at Matt as he lay there with his eyes closed. I looked over at the monitor and his vital signs were normal. I looked at Shawn as he worked on Matt and I wished I knew what he was thinking.

"Good morning, Dr. Goodson," I greeted.

"Good morning, Katie," he replied without looking at me.

"How does he seem to be doing?" I inquired.

"He is resting comfortably. We gave him something to keep him sleeping to let his mind and body rest but it should be wearing off soon. I would like to see if I can get him to respond to me but I am not sure if he will or won't," he explained speaking very professionally. I wondered if that was because of the presence of Joe and Mary in the room.

"I see that he is hooked up to oxygen. Is it necessary or just to help with his breathing?" I asked.

"He was having trouble breathing during the night, so I had them put the oxygen mask on. But I am going to take it off presently. If he has trouble again I will have them put the oxygen tube back on," Shawn replied in a terse, professional manner but I could tell that something was bothering him.

I assisted Shawn as he removed the mask off Matt. I unhooked it from the wall and placed it on the monitor in case we needed it later. I looked at Shawn but he avoided my glance. I was not sure what seemed to be bothering him. I thought maybe Matt's condition was worse than he first thought and perhaps he did not want to mention anything in front of his parents. I had not had a chance to look at the chart, so I was not sure if all of the results had come back yet or not.

"Has he awoken or tried to speak since his arrival?" I asked.

"He only seems to mutter and has not spoken any words. So, as far as I am aware, he has not regained consciousness. He might not be able to open his eyes. I'm not sure," Shawn replied. There was something inexplicably different about Shawn today.

Shawn checked Matt's reflexes. He went to the foot of the bed and checked his response to foot massage but there was still no reaction. Matt moaned as Shawn moved his left foot. Shawn began rotating the foot to see if he could get Matt to respond again. Matt's eyes began to flutter slightly and Shawn tried speaking to him.

"Hi Matthew. I am Dr. Goodson. You were in an automobile accident and you are in the hospital." Shawn paused before continuing, "Can you hear me Matthew? Open your eyes if you cannot speak."

Mary came and stood by the bed waiting and hoping that Matt would say something. There was no response from Matt. Shawn repeated his words in a very calm and soothing manner. He had a very soft-spoken voice that put you at ease whenever he talked to you. I had noticed that before when he was talking to me during my previous two flashback episodes.

There was no movement from Matt and the monitor showed no change. Mary looked imploringly at Shawn hoping he could do something...anything to get Matt to respond so that she would know that he was okay. Shawn picked up the chart and began to write down the information regarding Matt's response to the foot massage and his reflexes. It was time for the bed to be rotated and the buzzer went off. I came over to the bed to help Shawn turn the bed. Joe woke up when the buzzer sounded and Mary backed away from the bed so that she would not be in the way. They were used to the routine already and did not particularly like the present moment because part of the time Matthew would be obscured from their view while the bed rotated slowly. Shawn suggested to Joe and Mary that they go down and get some coffee or something to eat. Joe agreed and they left for the cafeteria.

I started to key in the new information on the keyboard for the bed rotation. Shawn went over and pushed the intercom button and asked the nurse to come down to help him. I was a little surprised because I was already there and could have helped. Shawn was very quiet and had only said a few words to me.

"I can help you with the preparations," I suggested.

"That won't be necessary, Katie," he replied curtly.

"But I am already here and it won't be any trouble. I have already typed in the new sequence that you wrote down," I explained.

"The nurse is on her way and she is going to help me," Shawn answered but still evaded my glance.

"Are you okay, Shawn?" I asked, hoping that I could get him to talk to me or at least look at me while I tried to figure out his sudden quietness.

"I am fine, Katie; just a little busy right now. So if you don't mind..." he replied.

"Fine. It is early for me to work yet but I will get out of your way. You don't seem to want my help now," I quipped back sharply.

"I have the nurse coming and I may need to change the configuration. Moreover, they are going to set some of the broken bones and we will not be able to use the rotating bed once his broken bones are set," he replied in a very professional tone.

"You're the doctor," I said as I turned and walked out the door. I was upset by the way he was treating me and I had no idea where the change in his attitude had come from. At any other time when we were working with a patient he was always very casual but today he was totally different. I went down to the office and began working. I had been working for an hour when Shawn came in to get Matt's papers that had been faxed over to him. I did not look up. I just kept on working.

"Are these all the papers that were faxed over?" he asked.

"That's all of them," I replied as I kept on working without looking up.

"They are going to send him down to have another MRI and more x-rays. So when we get the results back they are going to set the broken bones," he informed me.

"You may want to have the nurse inform his parents so that they won't worry when they come back to the room and don't find him there," I told him as I continued working.

"I just thought you might want to do that," he suggested.

"My help wasn't needed before so I am sure you can find someone else to inform them," I retorted. "I have to get the patient's therapy sessions ready. The first one will be coming in shortly," I stated.

"I just thought you might like to tell them," he suggested again.

"Maybe that is what's wrong," I quipped. I stood up and walked to the door without looking at him and headed down the corridor to the therapy room.

Shawn watched as Katie stood up and walked out the door. He had thought about calling her back but he wasn't sure exactly what he wanted to say to her. He had talked with Matthew's parents and they had told him how Matthew and Katie had once dated and had planned to marry but with both of them going off to college and not spending time together they had parted on friendly terms. That was eight years ago. *What difference did it make now? What would happen now that he was back in town?* It still wasn't certain if Matt would come out of his present critical and non-responsive predicament. When he was brought in, it took Katie by surprise and Shawn had noticed the pained look in her eyes as she watched Matt. *I guess time will tell what happens* he thought *but for now Matthew needed all the help he could get and if Katie can help get him to respond maybe he should not have chased her out of the room and upset her by getting someone else to help him…*

What is wrong with Shawn I wondered? I have never seen him act this way before. If he doesn't want my help with Matt why did he call me in on the case? Is it because Matt is in such critical condition and he does not want to put me through it? Did Mary tell him that we had once dated and he feels it is a conflict of interest having me on the case? I still found it hard to believe about Matt's accident but the feelings I had for him back then were now gone and he was just like any other patient. *Maybe I should talk to Mr. Sweeney and see if I can be transferred to just Sara's cases?* But that would not work because if Shawn had any patients that needed physical therapy I would need to help and get their files from Shawn. I could always tell Mr. Sweeney that it wasn't working out and I would rather go back to just working in the emergency room more and not in physical therapy. I knew he wouldn't believe me. I had worked very hard to get where I was, taking every class that was available. Mr. Sweeney knew how much I had wanted this position and would want to know what had happened to change my mind. Sigh...*I guess I will just have to face Shawn and ask him what the problem was* I realized. He was the only one that was going to be able to tell me. The one thing I did know was that I was not going to go through this every time we got a new patient. *Why did he request that I work for them if he was going to push me aside and not let me do my job? Maybe I should talk to Sara and ask if I could be put specifically in her department?* Just as I reached the therapy room door my pager went off. I checked and it was Shawn paging me. *Now what!* I thought to myself as I turned and went to the phone to call him back. I dialed his extension and waited as the phone rang.

"Hello," Shawn said as he answered the phone.

"This is Katie," I told him and continued, "What did you need?"

"Could you come back up to the office, please?" he requested.

"I was just going in to set up the machines for the incoming patients," I answered.

"I have Matthew's results back and I wanted to go over them with you," he informed me.

"Are you going to talk to me about it or do you want me to send the nurse in my place?" I asked sarcastically.

"No, I am not planning on calling the nurse. So if you could come up to the office, I would appreciate it," he replied, ignoring my sarcastic remark.

"I will be right up," I answered and hung up without giving him a chance to say anything else.

I turned around and went back down the corridor and headed straight to the office. I passed Joe and Mary as they were going back down to Matt's room. They smiled as they walked past me. I was glad that they did not ask me if I had heard anything yet. I knew Mary was in a hurry to get back to the room to check on Matthew. So we just kept walking our separate ways. I walked into Shawn's office. He had Matt's folder sitting on his desk and was still looking over the results as I walked up to his desk. I sat down in the chair that was pulled up to his desk.

"You wanted to see me?" I asked using the same professional manner that he had used with me earlier.

"I wanted to go over Matthew's results with you and let you know what we were going to do next," he replied.

"You could have just left a note on my desk. You really didn't need to call me in. I do have patients coming in and I need to get things set up for them," I responded.

"I am sorry. I guess I started this and I should have let you help me this morning instead of calling the nurse in. I'm sorry and it will not happen again, Katie. I value your input and I know that you are well qualified and it was wrong of me to treat you the way I did," he stated.

"Well, that is what I am trained for and you did request that I get this position because of my extensive training," I replied.

"I know. Believe me it won't happen again," he said reassuringly.

"What do the test results show?" I asked.

"As you already know we gave him medication to put him in a drug-induced coma when he was brought in to slow everything down," he responded.

"Yes, and he did improve to where he did not need the oxygen any more," I interjected.

"He has been off the medication now for over twenty-four hours and he should be responding now or at least trying to move and open his eyes," Shawn replied with a worried look on his face.

"Do the test results show anything more?" I asked.

"No, not really. I was hoping that something would show up but there is nothing out of the ordinary that has been picked up," he answered.

"So what are your plans for him now?" I asked.

"Well, for right now I am going to send him down to have his bones set. I will have the nurses and therapy go in and work with him to see if we can get him to respond. But I am not sure yet how best to go about treating him," Shawn answered.

"What does the brain scan show?" I inquired.

"There is nothing abnormal but still a lot of swelling around the brain," he replied. "The scan also shows that there is still activity going on and he can breathe without assistance. I am not sure why he is not responding," Shawn said aloud, baffled.

"So we don't know as yet if the paralysis is going to be permanent or if it is only being caused by the swelling around the brain?" I mused.

"He doesn't seem to be responding to anyone and he has not yet opened his eyes. However, he did react when I was testing his reflexes but it was only his foot. He didn't respond to anything else," Shawn admitted.

"Have you talked with his parent's yet?" I asked.

"I am going down to talk to them after we get done," he informed me.

"So for now it is just a waiting game and there really isn't anything we can do for him," I said more as a statement than a question.

"We will just keep working with him and hopefully it won't take long with all the stimuli that I will have going on for him," Shawn replied.

"I am sure that his parents will also help. I can get Mary to read to him in between the time that we work with him," I suggested.

"Well, hopefully it will work. But the main thing we have to work on is to get him to wake up so that we can find out exactly how much he remembers," he explained.

"The swelling around the brain can be causing it. The brain scan shows that there is brain activity still…so that is a hopeful sign," I said trying to sound encouraging.

"Well, I better go down and talk to his parents to let them know what is going on and what we plan to do," Shawn replied.

Shawn got up and picked up the folder that held the test results. He also took along the latest x-ray films that had been taken earlier that morning so that he could go over them with Joe and Mary. Shawn needed to let them know that they were going to go ahead with treatment even though Matt was still in a coma-like state. It still wasn't definite from the results whether or not Matt's paralysis was going to be permanent or not. The longer it took for him to awaken from his present state would mean the longer it would take to work with him and help him. It had already been a week and we could find no reason for him to remain in a coma.

Time was of the essence and it was time that Matthew was running out of…

Chapter 15

It had been two months and there was not much change in Matthew's condition. He was still in his coma-like state. The swelling was gone. The test results showed that he had spinal injuries and that he would be paralyzed from the waist down. He had been taken off the machines. The casts had been removed because his broken bones had healed.

Mary spent most of her days reading and telling Matthew about the things that were going on around him. She read the newspaper to him everyday, even though it was doubtful if he could hear her, let alone comprehend what she was saying to him. We spoke when I would go in to give him his physical therapy sessions. She filled me in on the things that he had been doing over the years since our breakup. He had been dating but his girlfriend had decided that she wasn't willing to spend the rest of her life with a crippled man and had walked away from him.

I was giving Matthew therapy sessions everyday even though he would not be using his legs again. I spent the time working his leg muscles but I concentrated more on his arms because he would be using them the most with the wheelchair and the daily chores that he would need to do. Mary informed me that he would be going home to live with them once he left the hospital. She was still in denial phase and believed that as soon as he woke up he would once again be able to move and be the normal person that he was before the accident. It was hard to imagine him in this predicament, knowing how active he had once been and how he had enjoyed playing sports. I wondered how he would react to the devastating news about the accident and about being told that his girlfriend didn't think he was worth staying with any more.

As the days went by, even his friends that had been coming in to see him and check on his recovery had stopped doing so. Carol had been the only one that came to see him every morning before work and she would stop by again each night before she went home. There were six of us that used to hang around together from grade school through graduation day. After graduating, we all went to different colleges so we didn't get to see each other very often. Even now we would try to get together at least once a year to catch up on what we had been doing. Matthew had started college but decided he didn't want to study any more and had pursued different interests. He never got together with the rest of us.

I was deep in thought as I sat looking out the window at the rain. Carol would be coming soon. We had to go over the upcoming state fair project. We had to organize the booth that we would have there. This was the beginning of the fund-raising events that we organized every year. It was a week-long event and people came from all over to attend. We would have the new wing to promote. We had help from the fire department who brought over the fire engine for the kids to get in and get a closer look at. They turned on the flashing lights and the siren and let the kids watch the water as it pumped out from the hose. The kids would cover their ears from the noise and laugh at the flashing lights. The local businesses had given us free items to pass around to the people that stopped at the booth. We also had a raffle each year and this year we had two large items to raffle off. A local car agency had donated a car while another business had donated an all-expenses-paid week's stay at a local resort. This would be the first year that the proceeds would not be going towards the new wing. With the new wing completed all the proceeds this year would go for the renovations of the hospitality house. Although it was called a house, it was really a motel. The hospital had purchased it from the owner so that families that did not have the money to stay somewhere else could stay for free while their loved ones were at the hospital. Over the years, many of the families had made donations for the hospitality house because it had meant so much to them being able to be close to their loved ones at a time of crisis. They had set up a registry that people signed after indicating the name of the patient they were attending to and a brief description of the patient's predicament. Each year the book was replaced and the information was entered into the database. The books were placed in the library for safe-keeping. Along with saving the data each year the computer would print out holiday cards to send to the families. It was a personal touch. Some of the families would reply and that information was also placed in the patients' folders.

Carol was running late as usual and it was getting close to the time for me to go up and do Matthew's therapy. I was just getting ready to leave her a note when she finally came in.

"I am finally here!" Carol said chuckling.

"It's about time you got here. I don't have much time. I have to do Matt's therapy soon," I informed her.

"I was busy calling the businesses to get their support. So I wasn't just wasting time," she answered.

"I have the poster and raffle information ready. I also have the sign-up sheet down in the break room for those that want to sign up," I replied.

"I know that Sara isn't going to be able to be of much help. She has a seminar to attend but I am sure that Shawn will help out along with some of the technicians. I saw the assistants discussing it and they plan to sign up to help," she informed me.

"We always seem to have a good turn out for this," I stated.

"The raffles should bring a lot of profits this year. I am surprised we got such great items," she squealed.

"Great tax write-offs for them and great items for us. It is a win-win situation for everyone," I replied.

"It will give us a good start on the fund-raising," noted Carol.

"Yes, it will be the first time that the fund-raising hasn't been for a new wing and I hope we remember to promote the correct place," I chuckled.

"Now, wouldn't that be embarrassing…promoting the new wing with it being completed? But we have been working on that project for several years," she said mockingly waving her hand in front of her face as though it were a fan.

"Guess we better start practicing our speech before we start on the public," I laughed.

"I had the donation jars put around the businesses. The television and radio stations are going to promote it for us too," she said.

"That's great! They seem to do more every year for us," I remarked.

"Well, hopefully it won't take us years to get enough funding," she replied.

"I hate to cut this short but I need to give Matt his therapy session," I informed her.

"How long do you think it is going to take before he finally wakes up?" she asked.

"I don't know. I thought he would have come around by now," I replied.

"Mind if I go up with you while you work?" she inquired.

"I don't mind if he doesn't; but I guess he won't know will he?" I said.

"I can always talk to Mary while you work," Carol suggested.

"Yes, she is having a very hard time with this," I replied.

We got up and walked out the door going towards the corridor that would take us to Matt's room. We discussed the fair as we walked along. Most of the work had been done. We mainly needed to get the volunteers to sign up and show up in their time slots.

When we reached Matt's room Carol opened the door and held it for me to enter. Mary was sitting in the chair by the bed reading to Matt. She looked up and smiled when we walked in.

"Hello girls," she greeted us. "Now that brings back memories of years ago when you both used to come in the house to see Matthew," she reminisced.

"Hi, Mary! How are you?" Carol asked.

"I am fine. I just wish that Matthew would wake up so that I could take him home," she said as she looked over at the bed where Matt lay.

"I'm working on it, Mary. It is up to him now," I replied.

"I know Katie and I appreciate everything you have done for him," she said gratefully.

"I guess I better get to work and stop chatting," I said jokingly, hoping to lighten the moment.

Carol and I walked up to the bed each approaching from either side. Carol took his hand and stood looking at him. I started getting the tray ready to give her a few minutes to talk with him before I began.

"Hi, Matt. It's Carol," she said and paused as though waiting for him to answer. "Your Mom and Katie are here too and we are all very anxious to talk to you, Matt," she explained.

"I have tried repeatedly talking to him and hoped that he would answer but I have heard nothing except some mumbled words," Mary said sadly.

"Matthew, can you hear me?" Carol asked. "Katie is going to start your therapy so I will talk to you again when she is done," Carol said.

"Hi, Matt. It's Katie. I am going to begin your therapy sessions," I said aloud.

Carol let go of his hand and stood looking at him when Matt's eyelids began to flutter. She looked at me and back at Matt. He moved his fingers slowly, very slowly, making a loose fist.

"Katie, did you see that!" Carol screamed.

"Ka-ka-ka-ka," Matt responded, speaking very slowly.

"Katie, he is moving his fingers and trying to speak," Carol exclaimed joyfully.

Mary jumped up and ran to the end of the bed. Carol fumbled for her pager, finally pushing the button.

"Katie, get him to talk. He will respond to you. Please, please try, Katie," Mary begged.

"Matt, it is Katie. I am here with you but I need you to talk to me.

Please say something to me," I said hoping for Mary's sake that he would open his eyes.

"Hello," Shawn answered the page.

"Shawn, come as quickly as you can. Matthew is moving and speaking. Hurry!" Carol exclaimed speaking very quickly and with great urgency.

"Ka-kaaa-ka," Matthew responded slowly.

"Matthew, honey, it is Mom. Please open your eyes," Mary spoke and watched, hoping for a response.

"Ka-k-k-kaaa," Matt muttered slowly.

"Hi sweetheart, it's me and I want so much to talk to you," I spoke softly as I did so many years ago hoping to get a response that way.

Matthew didn't speak but he moved his fingers that were on my side of the bed. I picked up his hand to see if he would hold on to my hand. He slowly moved his thumb and stopped. The door flew open as Shawn ran in and came up to the other side of the bed. Carol and Mary stood back to give him room.

"Hi, Matthew. I am Dr. Goodson. You were in an accident and you are now in the hospital. Can you understand me?" Shawn asked as he had so many times over the past few weeks.

Matthew did not respond. Shawn looked over at me and looked down my arm to my hand that was holding his. Shawn repeated his words again and paused to see if Matt would respond. Matthew did not move or speak. Shawn asked me what had transpired and I told him. He repeated his words to him again but once again there was no response.

"Try speaking to him again, Katie, to see what happens," Shawn suggested.

"Hi, Matt. It is Katie. Can you hear me?" I asked. I paused and waited before releasing his hand slowly.

"Try again, Katie. He seems to respond to you and your voice," Shawn remarked.

"Hi, sweetheart. I need to talk to you. Please, honey, open your eyes and talk to me," I said using the same approach that had worked the last time.

"Kaaa-ka," Matt muttered very softly.

"Again," Shawn said looking at me.

"Hi, sweetheart. I need to talk to you, honey. Please, talk to me," I softly begged for his response.

Shawn watched me closely and watched more for my response than Matthew's.

There was no response. Shawn told me to continue talking to him and also start the therapy. He thought that maybe the therapy would trigger some response. I began talking to Matt as if we were back in time and were still together.

I could see a different look in Shawn's eyes as he stood watching Matthew and I felt uncomfortable talking to him like that. He seemed to respond more to me when I talked very softly and using words that I had spoken to him years ago when we were together. Matthew's eyelids fluttered again but his eyes did not open. I started his physical therapy session and concentrated on his arms first, thinking that with the stimulation he might respond more quickly. He had moved his hand and fingers earlier. Maybe if I started working his muscles he would begin to move his fingers or even open his eyes. It had been over two months and he should have awakened. I continued talking to him but he did not respond as I had hoped he would.

Shawn stood talking to Mary but kept looking over to see if there was any change in Matthew. He then walked over to the bed, picked up his chart and jotted down what had happened and how Matthew had moved his fingers. Mary and Carol had been talking softly and when Shawn walked over to the bed Mary came over and stood looking down at Matthew.

"I had hoped that he would open his eyes and talk," Mary said shaking her head sadly as she looked at Matthew.

"It's OK, Mary. He did move and there is always hope that he will awaken soon. Until that happens we need to continue as we are doing," Shawn explained.

"I don't know how long I can do this," Mary answered with tears welling up in her eyes.

"I know it is hard but you can only do so much. The rest is up to him and I think with his response today it may not be long before he comes to," Shawn reassured her.

"Why does he start to speak—and today he even moved his fingers—but he only starts and that is all. Why doesn't he continue speaking so that we can understand him?" Mary asked.

"With a head injury it sometimes takes a long time. On top of that he has a spinal injury too. I don't know how long it is going to take," Shawn replied.

"He will one day awaken won't he?" Mary asked pleadingly.

"I am going to send him down for another brain scan to see if there are any changes. Hopefully we will get some new information and will know more," Shawn told her comfortingly.

"I just wish I knew if he could hear me. I would think that if he could hear me he would open his eyes or squeeze my hand to let me know that he knew that I was here," Mary spoke sadly.

"Mary, would you like to go down to the cafeteria and get some coffee?" Carol asked.

"Yes, I think that might be a good idea," Mary replied.

"I need something to perk me up," Carol said.

"I know. It sounds good to me. Let's go. I don't want to be gone too long in case Joe comes," Mary said.

Carol and Mary walked up to the bed as I was taking away the tray. I had finished the therapy session and just wanted to go out for some fresh air. Shawn had finished writing down his notes and had called to have the assistant come up to take Matt down for the brain scan. Shawn was keen for the results as soon as they were available.

"I need to go now, Matthew. I will stop in to see you in the morning," Carol said as she gave Matthew a kiss on his forehead.

"I am going down for a quick cup of coffee, Matthew. I won't be gone for long," Mary called out to him as she smiled at me before walking towards the door.

Carol and Mary left the room and headed for the cafeteria. Shawn hung up the phone and came back over to the bed. He wrote down the tests that he had ordered on the chart and slipped it back into the folder. I had taken care of everything and was ready to leave.

Shawn had been very quiet and I didn't feel much like talking either. I pushed the tray back against the wall and turned around. I walked over to where Shawn was standing and told him that I was done and was going back up to the office. Shawn was finished too so we walked back to the office together.

"The tests are all set up. I will let you know when the results are in if you wish," Shawn told me.

"I don't think there is going to be much of a change so I will just ask you in the morning," I said.

"Oh, I thought you might want to know right away," he remarked.

"Please don't get the wrong impression, Shawn. Matthew responds if I speak to him like I did back when we were together," I replied. "That was a long time ago. We are not together now but if it helps I will talk to him that way until he awakens and realizes the truth," I explained.

"I didn't mean to imply or suggest anything about your feelings towards Matthew. I just thought you would like to know," he replied a little surprised at my frankness.

"As I watch him and work with him now I can't help but remember the things we did, the things we said to each other and the love that we had once shared, the hopes and dreams we once had; but like I said, that was a long time ago and we have both changed. Now he is just another patient to me," I reminded him.

"You never know, Katie. Once he awakens you will be spending even more time with him in therapy. Your feelings might change and you both may get a chance to reconsider your relationship," Shawn remarked as he watched my eyes for a response.

"There were a lot of hurtful things said and done back then. I am not sure about a lot of things but right now the one thing I do know is that although I feel bad about his accident I don't feel anything else for him," I admitted.

"Katie, does working with Matt bother you?" he asked.

"I see him as just another patient and nothing more," I repeated.

"You say that Katie but I can't help but feel that as I watch you working with him there is something deep inside you that you are trying to come to grips with," Shawn observed.

"Very observant, Dr. Goodson," I replied chuckling. "Are you analyzing me now as I work or is this just an observation you came up with?"

"If you wish I can get someone else to do his therapy and that way you won't have to come in and face this inner struggle every day," Shawn suggested.

"Now what kind of person would I be if I could not set my feelings aside and work with a patient be it someone I know or a total stranger?" I asked as I looked into his eyes.

"Katie, this is different. There is a lot of history between the two of you and nobody would hold it against you if you would rather not continue working with him," Shawn replied.

"Let me see how the next few sessions go and I will let you know how I feel about working with him," I responded.

"Katie, you know I am here for you if you need someone to talk to. We can talk here or at either one of our houses. If you would feel better we could go to a restaurant or to the park and talk," he suggested.

"I know Shawn and I really appreciate it but for right now I think I can handle it. If I change my mind I know where to find you," I replied.

"Just give me a call if you want to talk. I am a really good listener," he said chuckling.

"I know, but don't you get tired of coming to the rescue of this crazy lady?" I asked.

"Katie, you are not crazy. You are trying to come to grips with a past you don't remember and now you have another jolt in your memory with Matthew coming back into the picture," Shawn replied.

"I am going to go home and take a long hot bath. It will clear my mind and I will start afresh tomorrow," I answered.

"Okay. See you in the morning," Shawn smiled at me as he spoke.

"See you in the morning and have a good evening," I replied as I turned and went out the door.

I reached in my pocket for my keys but they were not there. I checked my purse and they were not in there either. I rechecked my pockets and tried to think where I might have left them. I emptied my purse but I still could not find my keys. I had had them just before I had gone in to do Matthew's therapy. *I must have dropped them in Matthew's room* I thought to myself. I walked down the corridor heading back to his room. I had not reached into my pockets while I was in there so I could not imagine what had happened to them. I would have to retrace my steps in order to find them. My mood was not very good already and this did not help. I walked into Matthew's room and saw that Mary had not yet returned. I walked over to the tray and checked but the keys were not there. The keys were not on the floor either. As I was looking around something caught my eye on Matthew's bed. I walked over to the bed where I spotted the keys lying under Matthew's fingers. I could not imagine how they were there. I had to move Matthew's hand because the keys were underneath it.

"Stealing my keys now?" I asked Matthew jokingly as I went to retrieve them.

"Yes," Matthew replied.

"Matthew!" I exclaimed as I pulled my hand back because his voice had startled me. I looked at him and he slowly struggled to open his eyes.

"Ka—k," Matthew began as he tried to speak.

"Matthew, can you hear me?" I asked him excitedly.

"Yes," he replied.

"Let me get the doctor and your mother," I told him excitedly.

"No!" he ordered.

"Matthew, can you understand me?" I asked.

"Yes," he answered as he opened his eyes and looked at me.

"Do you know where you are and what happened?" I asked.

"Kat-t-t-ie," he began slowly as he tried to speak.

"Yes, Matthew. I am here. You were in an accident and you are in the hospital now," I informed him.

"I know," he answered.

"Your mother is going to be so pleased when she gets back!" I exclaimed delightedly.

"NO!" Matthew spoke loudly this time.

"You don't want me to tell her?" I asked in disbelief.

"No," he repeated.

"Matthew, she has been so worried about you and has stayed day and night with you," I explained.

"Only…you…" he spoke slowly.

"You have to tell your mom," I begged.

"No," he repeated.

"She will be back soon and she will see your eyes open and your lips moving. She will know," I reasoned with him.

"Please," he begged.

"Okay, for now I will not tell her but you cannot let her go much longer without letting her know," I replied.

"Thanks," he responded speaking a little more clearly this time.

"How much do you remember, Matt?" I asked.

"Most," he replied.

"Your mom will be back soon, Matt. I need to go before she gets here or she will see you speaking to me and will not stop until you talk to her," I informed him. I needed to get some fresh air. I was not ready for this…not then. I needed to sort my feelings out first before speaking to him.

"Please…stay…Katie," he begged.

"Matt, I can't stay long but I will stay until your mom comes back," I promised.

"Ho-o-l-l-l-d me," Matthew stammered his request. I moved closer and held him in my arms. I could feel the tears welling up in my eyes.

"Kisssss…Kat…," he requested as the tears fell from his eyes. I looked for a moment into his eyes, the same eyes that I had looked into all those years ago. I closed my eyes and softly kissed his lips. I heard the door open and Mary walked in.

"I need to go, Matt. Your mom is back. I will have them bring you down to physical therapy and we can talk more. Please rest for now," I whispered so that Mary would not hear me.

"Thanks," he replied as he closed his eyes. "Love you…" he softly whispered into my ear.

"Hi, Mary," I said as I turned to go out the door.

"Hi, Katie. Did he talk your ear off while I was gone?" she asked jokingly.

"Yes, he did. I didn't think he was ever going to quit talking," I replied with a wink as I walked towards the door.

"See you tomorrow, Katie. Thank you for everything," Mary responded gratefully.

"See you in the morning," I answered and quickly walked out the door.

I walked to the office to see if Shawn was there but the lights were off so I walked down to the parking garage. As I was walking up I could see that Shawn was talking to someone. The man walked off before I reached them. Shawn reached for the door handle to open his door.

"Shawn!" I yelled.

Shawn turned to see who had called him and smiled at me as I walked up to him.

"Hi, Katie. I thought you had already left," he said.

"Shawn, I need to talk to you," I told him still shaking from the effect that Matthew's kiss and words had had on me.

"Sure, Katie. Would you like to go back up to the office or for coffee?" he asked. "Are you okay? You look a little shaken," he asked with concern.

"We can talk here. It won't take long if you have the time that is?" I asked.

"Okay, let's go over to the bench where we can talk," he replied.

We sat down on the bench. I struggled unsure if I should tell him or just wait as Matthew had requested me to do. We sat down and I just looked at Shawn for a moment. I could see the concern in his eyes as he waited for me to speak. He was very patient and didn't push me to speak or hurry with what I wanted to tell him. The tears began to well up in my eyes again but Shawn just waited and did not speak. I could tell he was very concerned and had no idea what I was about to tell him.

"Shawn, I need to have you do something for me," I began falteringly.

"Sure, Katie. What do you need?" he asked me still looking into my eyes.

"Shawn, I was asked not to tell you this so please don't react until I finish," I explained.

"Katie, are you alright? Did something happen?" he asked with concern.

"I am fine, Shawn...a little shaken but I am alright," I said trying to sound convincing.

"What do you need me to do, Katie?" he inquired.

"Shawn, Matthew opened his eyes and spoke to me. I need you to cancel his tests for tomorrow," I spoke slowly still letting it sink in.

"He spoke? Katie that is wonderful...that is what you wanted isn't it?" he asked.

"I am not sure what I want right now. He begged me not to tell anyone and he doesn't want his mother to know yet either," I continued.

"Just a minute," he requested. Shawn took his cell phone out of his pocket and dialed a number. He called and canceled Matt's tests telling them that he wanted to wait a few more days.

"There, Katie, that is done," he smiled as he looked at me.

"He won't talk to anyone else, Shawn. He told me he would only speak to me," I informed him.

"Does he remember what happened and where he is?" Shawn asked.

"Yes, he said he knows but he speaks very slowly and only answers in one or two words," I replied.

"How do you feel about it, Katie?" Shawn asked as he watched closely for my response.

"I am not sure how I feel or what I feel. I am a little confused right now," I replied.

"That is normal, Katie. You will have time to sort out your feelings but don't rush. You need to look at all aspects before you come to your decisions," he advised neutrally.

"There is something else I need for you to do, Shawn," I requested.

"Sure, Katie. What else can I do for you?" he asked.

"I told Matt that I would have them bring him to me for therapy tomorrow so that he could speak to me and let me know what he has to say," I informed him.

"I will write the instructions in the morning and have them bring him down," Shawn replied reassuringly.

"I am not sure if I want to talk to him, Shawn. I am not ready yet," I confessed and the tears began to fall slowly down my cheeks.

"Katie, what else did he say to you?" Shawn asked as he reached out and started to put his arm around me then changed his mind and put his hand back down on his lap.

"He asked me for a hug and then he wanted a kiss; so I gave him both after which his mom entered. At that time Matt whispered in my ear that he loved me," I blurted out and the tears began to stream down my face.

"What are your feelings, Katie?" Shawn asked as he watched me closely. "Do you still love him?"

"No, Shawn. I don't love him anymore and I want to help him but I cannot handle this right now. I can't handle my emotions right now. I thought I was through having to think about my past. Now this happens and it forces me back. I have the past thrown into my face as memories come flooding back," I admitted.

"I can still have someone take over for you, Katie. He will eventually talk to someone else," Shawn suggested.

"No. I will continue on for right now but I will let you know if I do decide that I would like someone else to take over," I replied. "I need to go. I just wanted to let you know that he has awakened and can speak," I explained.

"Are you sure you are going to be okay?" Shawn asked.

"I will be fine. Thank you, Shawn, for listening and being there for me," I told him.

"I will always be here for you, Katie, whenever you need me," he replied reassuringly.

"Thank you, Shawn. I will see you in the morning," I bade him farewell.

"See you in the morning. I will be home if you need someone to talk to, Katie," he offered.

"Thank you, Shawn," I replied.

I stood up, walked towards my car and drove home. I waved to Shawn as I drove past. He was still sitting on the bench and smiled as he waved. I had planned on going out to the farm but with what had happened I decided to go home instead. I pulled into the driveway and walked into the house. I put the kettle on as I walked past the kitchen. I went in to run my bath water. I stood looking into the mirror and wondered what I was going to do next. Just when I thought I knew what I was going to do everything changes. I didn't think I still had any feelings for Matt but when I hugged and kissed him the emotions came flooding back to me. The tea kettle whistled so I turned the bath water off and went to get the tea. I took it back into the bathroom and slipped my clothes off and slowly sank into the hot water.

I tried to clear my thoughts so that I could just relax but the more I tried the harder they fought to remain. I tried sorting out my feelings by putting things back into perspective but no matter how much I tried I could not get past the feelings I had experienced when holding Matt. He had told me that he loved me. *How many times before had he spoken those same words to me? Did he love me or was he just afraid of what was happening to him? How much did he know* I wondered. *He must know by now that he could not move his legs but did he know that it would be so for the rest of his life? Did he realize that his girlfriend was not there and had told Mary that she wanted nothing to do with him anymore? Did I feel sadness for him or was it pity? Was I still in love with him?* I had loved him all those years ago and had planned on spending the rest of my life with him. After we broke up I did not start to date again. Instead I poured myself into my studies and after I had finished one course I would jump to the next. It kept my mind occupied and I was happy with the work that I was doing. *Why was it that when I tried to think back on when we had broken up I still had a hard time remembering everything?* It seemed foggy. *Was that why I was struggling with my feelings and emotions?* No, I thought. He had left me once and didn't want to stay together. *What made me think that he meant it this time? Was he just trying to hang on to me because he feared the future and the possibility of being alone the rest of his life?* I would just take a day at a time and try to keep in mind that he needed to sort his feelings out and had a long way to go. I was not going to rush anything.

I stepped out of the tub and dried myself. I grabbed my tea and went into the bedroom. Sitting on the bed I gazed absently out the window. I did not want to think any more nor consider the future. Not now…I did not need to put myself through that.

I slipped into bed and slid under the covers. I was through thinking about it tonight. I just wanted to sleep. I gazed out the window and could feel myself drifting off to sleep…

Chapter 16

I awoke early. I had tossed and turned for most of the night. I could not help but think about Matthew. I was confused by my own feelings and the emotions that had stirred within me. I had thought about the times that we had been together and the fun times that we had had over the years. But along with the good times, I also remembered the bad times and the arguments. I was not sure what I was feeling but I knew that I had to come to terms with my feelings soon. At first I had no doubt in my mind on what I wanted and how I was feeling, but after being held in his arms the emotions that had stirred within me had taken me by surprise. We had gone our separate ways and had moved on with our lives. I was not ready for the turmoil that I knew could follow. He had a girlfriend or at least he did before she found out he would never walk again. How would he handle that news once he found out that she had walked away from him? Did he remember her at all or was he instead waking and still living in the past? It would be hard to know until I talked with him today. We did have all those promises that we had once made to each other and the love we pledged that would last forever. But that was many years ago and my heart had hardened and I never thought that I would be able to love again. Life had so many twists and turns and one never knew what to expect. Did he speak with only shallow words muttered at the spur of the moment or was he actually speaking from his heart? Did he realize that he was paralyzed? Did the fear of being alone for the rest of his life scare him into speaking of love to me again? I will not let my heart go through that pain again. I wondered just how much he did remember and how long he had been pretending to be asleep. The questions just kept coming and I knew that it was going to be impossible to go back to sleep. What difference did it make now? I thought to myself. Yes, we did make promises to each other and we had talked of undying love but that was a long time ago and I would not fall into his trap again. I would not let him use me to get what he wanted. I could not do that again. I guess I knew deep in my heart what I wanted but my life was different now and there was no turning back…or was there?

I threw the covers back more confident of my feelings and got up to start my day. It was still early but I couldn't sleep as the thoughts kept running through my mind. I would go into work early. Working would take my mind off everything else. I would know soon enough exactly what I was going to do.

I pulled up and parked the car. Shawn's car was already there. I was surprised to see him there that early. He must be catching up on work too. I went through the door and headed for the office. I decided to stop at the cafeteria to grab some tea before going up. I stopped and chatted with Mary who had run down to get some coffee. She was still in hopes that Matthew would soon awaken and that she would be able to take him home. It was hard for me to look at her worried eyes knowing that the day before I had talked with Matthew but had promised him that I would not tell anyone. I hoped with all my heart that he would not make her wait much longer. It would mean so much to her knowing that he could speak again.

We turned and started walking down the corridor together. I told her that I didn't think it would be much longer before Matthew would respond and awaken. I was going to try again today to get him to tell her. *Why did he want to keep it from everyone else?* He must have known with her pleading for him to open his eyes and talk just how much she needed to hear his voice. I guess he had his reasons even though they didn't make any sense to me. We got to the corridor that I needed to turn down. I told Mary that I would see her later and informed her that Matthew was going to be brought down for his therapy session. Mary bade me farewell and kept walking towards Matthew's room while I turned to go to the office. As I neared the office I could see the light in Shawn's office. *He must be in the office working already* I thought. I opened the door and walked in, setting my tea down on my desk. Shawn was pulling folders from the file cabinet.

"Good morning, Katie," he greeted.

"Good morning, Shawn. You are here early," I noted.

"I had trouble sleeping, so I thought I would come in and catch up on some files," he replied.

"That sounds familiar," I said chuckling.

"You couldn't sleep either?" he asked.

"No. I tossed and turned all night long and when I couldn't sleep I decided to come in and work to get my mind off things," I replied.

"Anything you want to talk about?" he inquired.

"Not much to say," I answered.

"Just couldn't sleep or did you have more nightmares?" he asked, looking at me.

"No nightmares. I was just thinking about Matthew and his sudden change in feelings. I guess I was just unprepared for his sudden show of affection," I confessed.

"You know, Katie, he might think that he is back in time and doesn't realize the years that have passed," Shawn suggested.

"I know…that is what I keep telling myself," I replied.

"Are you hoping for more, Katie?" he asked.

"I am not sure what I am feeling right now," I said. "There is a part of me that remembers the bad part of the past that we shared but there is also a part of me that remembers the loving, wonderful times we shared together," I explained.

"I don't think you should rush into anything, Katie. Take your time and really think about what you want," he advised but there was a strange look in his eyes.

"Are you saying that I would be making a mistake by going back with him?" I asked.

"That is up to you, Katie, but I think you should really think it through carefully before acting," he advised.

"That is all that I have been thinking of which is why I am here at work at this early hour," I replied.

"Katie, he may only be using you too, knowing how you once felt about him," Shawn suggested.

"It sounds to me like you are really trying to discourage me from going back to him," I remarked.

"You have to remember, Katie, that he left you once even after he had pledged his undying love to you and had had no concern about your feelings at that time," Shawn reminded me.

"We were much younger at the time and we have both had a chance to mature," I replied as though I were making up excuses for Matt's past actions.

"So does that make it alright for the treatment he gave you?" Shawn queried. "So now that you are older will it be okay with you if he decides in a week, a month or even a year from now to just leave you again?" he asked.

"So are you saying that the only reason he wants me back is because he is hurt and will again one day leave me?" I mused.

"I don't know what his plans or schemes are and neither do you. I just want to warn you that he might not be revealing his true feelings to you. He may still only be remembering the past and may tell you that he loves you and wants you, but once he remembers everything that might not necessarily be his true feelings," Shawn warned.

"You seem to be more concerned with this than I do. What difference does it make to you?" I asked him a little irked at his pushing.

"I just don't want to see you get hurt. That is my only concern," he replied looking deeply into my eyes as he spoke.

"I guess if I fall for his lies again it is my own fault and I have nobody else to blame," I responded.

"Katie, I just want you to think with your head and not your heart. That is all. Just make a decision based on your thoughts. Remember that he left you once and is capable of hurting you again, if you fall for his false attempts to win you back," Shawn reminded.

"I don't even know what Matthew is thinking and you could be giving me all these warnings for nothing. He may not have any plans of getting back together," I confessed.

"I think that would be wonderful news if he had no plans of getting back together for both you and Matthew," he stated.

"I will wait and see what he has to say to me today," I replied.

"That is another thing I don't like about this whole thing, Katie. Why is it that he does not want anybody else to know that he has awakened?" Shawn wondered. "He knows how much his mother is hurting, yet he would rather let her think that he has not come out of his coma-like state. Now what kind of man is that? Is that really the kind of man you want to spend the rest of your life with? Is that what you consider loving and compassionate?" Shawn asked.

"I am not sure why he doesn't want her to know yet, but I am sure that he has his reasons for it," I replied.

"Selfish reasons if you ask me," Shawn quipped.

"Well, I don't ever remember asking you for your opinion on this but you certainly have offered it," I answered.

"I just want to warn you and remind you how important this could be for you," he replied.

"I am sure that when the time comes and I make my final decision I will have thought it through very thoroughly. If you wish I can then tell you my decision for your final approval," I replied sarcastically.

"I think it will be interesting to find out just what that final decision will be," Shawn replied ignoring my sarcasm.

"Well, I guess I will soon find out what he wants. I need to get down to the therapy room. They will be bringing him down shortly," I informed him.

"Please remember what I have told you, Katie," Shawn reminded me.

"How can I forget? You have told me so many times already," I replied.

I turned and walked out the door not waiting for his reply. At that moment I did not want to hear what he had to say. I now had second thoughts about telling him that Matthew had finally awakened. I was excited at first to tell him but his constant warnings and nagging were wearing rather thin on my nerves. I walked into the therapy room to find that Scott had already brought Matthew in and had placed him in the last room. I was a little anxious to find out exactly what Matthew had on his mind and why he wished to continue the charade. I knew that Shawn was right in his warnings but I didn't want to hear it. I did not know why he kept pushing the issue. It really had nothing to do with him. My thoughts were interrupted because Scott was just coming out of the room when I walked up.

"So, Katie, just like old times, huh?" Scott mocked. "He pushes you aside and you come crawling back to him." Scott laughed as he walked around me.

"I am giving him therapy treatments, Scott. I am not running anywhere," I shot back through clenched teeth.

"He speaks and you jump," he replied chuckling.

"Are you trying to make a point? If so, make it and leave," I said firmly.

"You wouldn't listen to me even if I were trying to make a point," he retorted as he walked away.

I walked into the room. Matthew was lying on the bed with his eyes closed. I wondered if I had just dreamt that he had spoken to me the day before. I was angry and thought about leaving and getting someone else to treat him—but I wouldn't know what he wanted to tell me if I did that. I pulled the tray over so that it was within easy reach as I walked up and stood next to the bed.

"Good morning, Matthew. You wanted to talk to me?" I asked. He didn't respond. I repeated my words but there was still no answer from him; nor did he open his eyes. I decided to go ahead with the treatment and send him back up to his room. Maybe he would awaken once I started. I reached over him to release the safety strap that had been fastened while they brought him down. I slowly unbuckled it and as I brought my hand back he grabbed my wrist. I screamed and pulled my hand back, startled.

"Good morning, Katie," he said smiling.

The door flew open and Shawn and Scott charged in. Shawn came running up to me and Scott ran to the foot of the bed.

"Are you okay? I heard you scream?" Shawn asked, his voice filled with concern.

"I am fine. I was just startled. Sorry, I didn't mean to scream," I apologized but Shawn could see that my hands were still shaking.

"Can't handle him, Katie?" Scott asked sarcastically.

"Everything seems to be fine here, Scott. You can go. We don't need your help," Shawn told him but kept his eyes on me.

"Sure, Doc. If you don't need me I will go, but in case you change your mind just have Katie scream," Scott replied and chuckled as he left.

"Are you okay, Katie?" Shawn inquired again.

"Yes, I am fine. Just a little jumpy, I guess," I replied.

"I will be working in the other room. If you need anything, just give a call," Shawn offered.

"Okay, but I should be alright now," I answered.

Shawn walked to the door, looked back over his shoulder and smiled. I stood there still shaking a little. I had to fight the urge not to slap Matthew for what he had done. I wasn't sure now if I wanted to hear what he had to say. So I decided to go slow and talk softly so that the others would not hear if and when he responded to me.

"Not very funny, Matthew," I scolded him. He slowly opened his eyes and looked at me.

"I am sorry. I didn't think you would react in that manner," he said apologetically.

"Last night you said you wanted to talk to me. We are alone, so you can speak freely now," I said reassuringly.

"Katie, it is so good to see you again. Thank you for coming to see me," he said gratefully.

"Matthew, do you know where you are and why you are here?" I asked.

"An accident and I am in the hospital," he answered softly.

"How much do you remember?" I began.

"Some but not all of it," he replied.

"Do you know why you are in therapy, Matthew?" I asked.

"No…not for sure. The only thing I know Katie is that I want to hold you in my arms," he informed me, avoiding my questions.

"Why do you want to hold me, Matthew?" I inquired. I was hoping to find out from his response if he could differentiate between the past and the present.

"I want to hold you in my arms Katie because I love you and I want you near me," he replied.

"Do you know what year it is?" I asked him, trying to get a definite answer from him.

"Yes, I know the year. I also know that I have been a real jerk about how I treated you in the past but I am hoping you can forgive me and we can get back together," he replied softly.

"Yes, you were a jerk to me. You also know that we are no longer dating and that we have both moved on with our lives," I reminded him now that I knew that he was in the present and realized that we were not together.

"I want to change that, Katie. I want you back in my life and I want to spend the rest of my life with you, Katie. I am so sorry for the way I was back then but I promise I will never treat you that way again," he pleaded.

"You have made a lot of promises to me, Matthew and they didn't seem to matter much to you back then, so why should I think that you would be any different now?" I asked him still unsure about my own feelings.

"Katie, I was coming back here to make up with you when I had the accident," he explained.

"Matthew, you were dating someone else. How could you be coming here for me?" I queried.

"I told her of my feelings for you; how I still loved you and wanted to be with you," he replied quickly.

"I find it hard to believe that you could be so much in love with me despite leaving and never wanting to see me for eight long years. Then, all of a sudden, you are in an accident and feel the need to rekindle our lost love," I responded.

"Katie, please give me a chance to show you just how much I really do still love you," he begged as he took my hand in his.

"I can't give you an answer right now, Matthew. I have to think it over," I replied as I felt my heart begin to give in to his words.

"I am not going anywhere, Katie. Please tell me that you will think about it," he requested.

"Matthew, I would be lying if I told you that I didn't still have some feelings for you but so much time has passed and we are both different people now," I reasoned.

"I am not asking you to give me an answer today or tomorrow, Katie. I just want you to know how I feel," he replied.

"I will think about it Matthew but I can't make any more promises to you or to anyone else for that matter," I told him.

"I understand and I am happy knowing that you will think about it, Katie. I have missed you so much my darling. May I please hold you in my arms?" he asked.

"Matthew, you don't want anyone to know right now that you have awakened. If I hug you and someone comes in they will know. Are you willing to take that risk?" I was not sure if I wanted to be held by him. I was still struggling with my emotions.

"I don't care if they know, Katie. I just want to hold you close in my arms," he told me as he held his arms out and pulled me close to him.

"Matthew, do you know what you are doing?" I asked.

"I love you, Katie. I love you so much my darling," he whispered in my ear. He held me close to his body as he whispered in my ear.

"I need to go, Matthew. I have other patients that I need to see." I needed to get away to do some thinking.

"Okay, Katie. Please think about what I have said to you. I mean every word that I have said," he promised as he unlocked his arms from me so that I could move.

"I will come to your room tomorrow for your treatment. So I will see you then," I replied.

I turned and walked out the door. I could feel the tears welling up in my eyes. I was not prepared for what he had said. As I walked out of the room I caught a glimpse of Shawn filling out some paperwork in the corridor. He looked up as I walked out the door. I could see the concerned look on his face. I did not stop to talk to him because I did not want to listen to any more of his warnings that day. I started walking back down the corridor to my office. I was trying hard to fight back the tears that were stinging my eyes. I walked into the office and was glad that nobody was in there. I went over to the window and gazed outside. I didn't hear the door open or the sound of approaching footsteps from across the room. I was thinking only of the words that Matthew had said and was trying to sort out my feelings and the emotions that were consuming me.

"Katie?" Shawn asked.

"Please, Shawn. I am not in the mood right now to listen to any more of your warnings. So if that is what you have to say please just leave me alone right now," I begged softly.

"That is not why I am here, Katie. Please look at me," he spoke softly as he took my arm and slowly turned me around to face him.

"I need to be alone right now," I replied as I looked at the floor trying to avoid his eyes.

"Katie, I am here if you want to talk. I won't give you any warnings or lectures. I am here for you to open up to and I will listen and be here for you," Shawn replied. He took his hand and cupped my chin and lifted my face so that he could look into my eyes.

"Shawn I need…" I began but the tears filled my eyes and ran down my cheeks.

"Katie, I am here for you today, tomorrow or whenever you need me," he told me as he took me in his arms and held me as I cried.

Neither one of us spoke. Shawn held me tenderly in his arms close to his body. I felt safe and secure in his arms and I knew that I did not have to think about anything now that he was there for me. It felt good being held in his arms and I could feel his heart softly beating as I lay my head on his chest and closed my eyes. I felt my body relaxing in his arms.

"Katie...follow your heart and you will get the answers you so desperately seek," Shawn said when he finally spoke to me.

I looked up into his eyes as I replied, "Will I ever get the answers I need to know, Shawn? Everything seems so confusing to me right now. I thought I knew what I wanted and that I was happy with my life except for the void from the past that I could not seem to remember."

"In time you will know everything, Katie. And at that time you will know exactly what you want and who you want to be with." His voice was so calming that at that moment I truly believed every word he had told me.

"Thank you, Shawn, for always being there for me. You seem to know when I need you the most. You are there with the right words to say to me and have the ability to make me see things so clearly," I replied.

"Remember that I will always be there for you, Katie, whenever you need me," he replied as he lowered his head and kissed me softly on my lips.

Shawn held me in his arms for a while as my tears dried. I opened my eyes and looked up at him again. He smiled as he looked at me. In my heart I did not want this moment to end. For some reason I felt comfortable and safe when he held me close in his arms. I knew that nothing else mattered to me right then. I didn't think about my past and I had no thoughts of Matthew and the loving endearing words he had spoken to me just a few minutes ago. My thoughts were only of Shawn and how I was feeling then.

"I need to go, Shawn. I have other patients that I need to get ready for," I finally told him.

"Katie, please remember that if you need me I am only a call away," he reminded me.

"Thank you, Shawn. It is very reassuring to me knowing that you are there for me," I admitted.

He slowly released me from his arms and stepped back. I told him I had to go and turned and walked out the door. Shawn stood looking out the window, unsure of what had come over him. *I had no right to hold her in my arms or take the liberty of kissing her* he thought to himself. *I don't know what came over me…it just seemed to be the right thing to do at the time* he thought trying to convince himself. *There is one thing I need to do and I think now is the time to do it.* He walked out the door and headed down the corridor. He was determined and would stop at nothing until he had the chance to speak his mind. Shawn put his hand on the door knob and slowly opened the door.

"Hi, Dr. Goodson," Mary greeted him cheerfully.

"Hello, Mary. How are you doing today?" he replied just as cheerfully.

"I am doing good," she answered. "I am surprised to see you. I didn't know you were going to check on Matthew today," she sounded surprised.

"I need to check him out so I will need for you to leave the room for some time," Shawn told her.

"Sure, Dr. Goodson. I will go down to the cafeteria and get something to eat while you are working on Matthew," she replied as she stood and walked to the door.

"It will be about fifteen minutes, Mary," Shawn informed her.

"Okay. I know he is in good hands so I won't worry while I am gone," Mary told him as she went out the door.

Shawn stood for a minute just looking at Matthew, unsure if he should go through with it or not. Katie had told him that it was none of his business and she was right. It was between her and Matthew. But Shawn felt that he could not just stand by and let him take advantage of Katie. She was too trusting and naïve. There was something about this whole thing that didn't add up…something a little shifty and underhanded on Matthew's part. If Shawn got to know Matthew's true intentions he would have felt better. If Matthew truly did love her and had indeed planned to come back and renew their love Shawn would have been the last one to stand in their way. There was only one way to find out.

"Hello, Matthew. I am Dr. Goodson," Shawn said and waited for a response. There was none.

"Matthew…it's Dr. Goodson and we need to talk. I am not leaving until you speak to me," Shawn spoke sternly. He did not feel like playing games at that point in time.

Matthew just lay there, breathing slowly, acting as though he had not heard Shawn.

"Okay, Matthew…you want to continue this little game then please let me do all the talking. I don't really care what you have to say," Shawn said, trying a different approach this time. Matthew lay still.

"Stay away from, Katie. She doesn't need the likes of you around her. She is a very caring, trusting and compassionate woman and could easily fall for your lies but you do not fool me for a minute. I will not stand by and let you hurt her again. You have no real intentions when it comes to her. You are thinking of your own selfish wants and will only use her to get what you want for your own personal gain. When she is of no more use to you, off you will go again. You forget you hurt her deeply in the past and she will have trouble getting by that. As time goes by she will see right through you just like I do. You don't love her and I am not exactly sure what you hope to get out of this but I am not going to stand nonchalantly by and let you play your mind games. I am wise to your guile and will fight you every step of the way. My advice to you is to wake up to the world and go on your merry way. Don't look back because I am going to be the one standing there that you will be facing. So keep that in mind while you are trying to connive and manipulate your little web of deceit. Another thing you should think about is that as long as you continue this farce I remain your doctor, whether you like it or not. That won't change until you decide to "awaken" to the rest of the world and tell them that you would like another doctor. So until you do that you are stuck with me and I will use every opportunity I get to make your stay miserable. You should also keep in mind that with the stroke of a pen I can have Katie taken off your case and you won't be able to use your sneaky little games on her. I know you for the conniving person that you are and there is nothing that is going to stop me from protecting Katie. You may think that you have the upper hand here but please keep in mind that I have the ability to help Katie think things through and that I will make sure she knows the kind of man you are. You have proved it to me time and again. You think nothing of anyone else's feelings. You are out for only yourself and won't stop until you get what you want, even if you hurt others in your quest for happiness. I am not sure that you even know how to love in the real sense of the word. You had your chance with Katie eight years ago but decided that she was not what you wanted. When you tired of her you decided to move on, to bigger and better things. You hurt her badly when you left. Once you were gone you never looked back. But now, out of the blue, you tell her you were on your way here to profess your undying love to her and to win her back over. Do you really expect her to believe that after everything you have done to her? In time I will be able to show her just what you have done to her. Yes, I know you had something to do with her attack. I am not sure yet what it was but as her memory returns I am sure that it will emerge that you were a central perpetrator. Mark my words Matthew; you will not win on this attempt. I will be watching you constantly and eventually I will show Katie the real you."

Shawn finally finished speaking but Matthew never once opened his eyes or spoke to him man to man. He felt contempt for Matthew and wanted nothing else to do with him. Shawn realized the sad fact that he too was stuck with Matthew as his doctor. He waited for some kind of response from Matthew but when he didn't get one he thought it best to just leave.

"Have it your way, Matthew. But the longer you pretend to be asleep the longer I have to show Katie what you are really like. I did prove one thing to myself with this talk and that is you are exactly what I thought you were. Someone afraid to stand up for himself and who uses others to do his dirty work even if it is a woman that you say you love. We will have a chance to talk again because I am not through with you yet. So you can look forward to more of these little chats until you become a man and face me," Shawn stated.

Inspite of all that Shawn had said he could not get Matthew to respond. Shawn did not want to be in the same room with him any more, so he turned and walked out the door. Sooner or later Matthew would have to face him because he would not be able to avoid the talk Shawn would have with him regularly…

Nobody noticed as the figure opened the door quietly and walked into Matt's room. He walked over to the bed where Matthew was expecting him. Matthew knew that this man would be the best person to carry out what he had planned on doing.

"It is about time you got here. You need to get rid of Katie once and for all. She is getting too chummy with the good doctor. Once he manages to jog Katie's memory of her past it will only be a matter of time before she remembers and they will be coming after us. I can't move or I would have done it myself. It is all because of you so now you can take care of it before it is too late," Matthew said threateningly.

"You were supposed to be the one taking care of this. It is your loose end, not mine," the figure replied in the same menacing tone.

"I was on my way back here to take care of her once and for all but I didn't plan on the accident now did I? One of us has to do it. I remember what you had told me when you had called to warn me that she was beginning to remember too much and I am not willing to take the chance. So better think of something quickly to get rid of her," Matthew said ominously.

The man walked to the door and started to open it when Matthew added.

"I don't care what you do or how you do it; just get it done and come and inform me when you have finished so that we don't have to worry any more…got it?" Matt asked as he glared at him.

"I will be back as soon as it is done," the man replied and slipped unnoticed out of the door…

Chapter 17

The fair was only a couple of days away. Carol and I had been working hard to get everything ready. All the time slots on the sign-up sheet had been filled. We had good coverage from both the television stations and all the local newspapers. We would be raising money for the hospitality house. The donation jars were filling up quickly. I had stopped at the printers and picked up the photos that they had enlarged for the demonstration. There were photographs of the new wing that showed the improvements that had been made. There were also photographs of the hospitality house and the blueprints showing the changes that were going to be made to it. We would be going down the next day to set everything up in the merchant's building where we had been placed. Everyone was really excited about it and could hardly wait. This was one of the better projects that we had had the most fun doing.

I had continued doing Matthew's treatments in his room. Mary would usually take the opportunity to run down to get something to eat when I came in. Matthew still hadn't let anyone else know that he was awake. He had me bring him food and milk so that he could eat it after Mary had gone home. She had stayed with him day and night when he was first brought in. However, Shawn had recently talked Mary into going home at nights to sleep. She would return first thing in the morning to see Matthew. Shawn had had his feeding tube taken out because he figured that sooner or later Matthew would get hungry enough to ask for food. Shawn was getting very tired of Matthew's role-playing and was trying everything he could think of to get him to stop so that the real treatments could start. I felt uneasy when I would go in to do Matthew's therapy because he would profess his love for me and tell me of a future that we would have together. I was still thinking over his new promises and still hadn't given him an answer. He seemed to be satisfied with the thought that I would eventually make up my mind and come to him. I had brought him some food and he was eating it when suddenly the door flew open and Shawn came walking in.

"So glad you decided to join the real world again, Matthew," Shawn announced as he walked up to the bed.

"Good evening, Shawn," I said not sure where he had come from.

"Good evening, Katie. I see our comatose patient can stay awake long enough to eat but he has closed his eyes again hoping that I didn't see him. The charade is over, Matthew. I stood at the window watching you eat. Now why don't you open your eyes so that we can find out how you are," Shawn snapped.

Matthew slowly opened his eyes and glared at Shawn. "At last we meet Dr. Goodson and my first request is a different doctor. I don't like your bedside manner," Matthew spoke with clenched teeth.

"I will get right on that for you," Shawn promised.

"Right now I don't want you to do anything for me. So please feel free to leave because as you can see I am just fine," Matthew quipped.

"Sorry, it is not that easy. You have to be proved capable of making that decision and I am not sure how long a psychological profile is going to take on you but rest assured as soon as it can be arranged I will gladly sign you over to someone else. But you must also remember that Katie will be taken off the case when I go," Shawn informed him.

"Katie?" Mathew looked at me as he started to speak.

"Yes, Matthew. If Shawn turns you over to another doctor I will no longer be the one to give you physical therapy. You will be assigned someone else," I replied.

"You will still come and see me won't you, Katie?" Matthew asked.

"I am really busy right now with the fair project and I am not sure just how much time I will have during the next couple of weeks," I replied.

"I guess you get your way for now doc but you can set up the profile and I will think about it for the next two weeks," Matthew spoke to Shawn but refused to look at him.

"If you are done Katie I need some help with a new patient," Shawn requested.

"Yes, I was just finishing up. You want me to come up to the office?" I asked.

"You may get your way right now doc but don't get used to it. Soon enough Katie and I will be together and you will not be able to stand in our way," Matthew warned Shawn as he once again turned to look at him.

"I think Katie can decide for herself and doesn't need you to speak for her," Shawn replied.

As the two of them were arguing back and forth Mary came into the room and saw for the first time that Matthew had his eyes open and was talking. She stood still just looking at him for a few minutes before running up to the side of the bed.

"Oh, Matthew! You are awake and can speak darling! Thank God my prayers have been answered!" Mary exclaimed as the tears rolled down her cheeks.

"Yes, Mom. I can speak but I am not exactly sure what else I can do," Matthew replied.

"Let's go Katie so that they can talk things over," Shawn beckoned me.

"I will talk to you later, Matthew. You and your Mom have a lot to talk about," I said.

"Thank you Dr. Goodson and thank you Katie for everything that you have done to bring my son back to me," Mary said tearfully.

"You're welcome, Mary. I'm glad that I could help. Now we can get some real therapy going and it won't be long before you can take him home where he belongs. Isn't that right, Matthew?" Shawn asked as he glanced over at Matthew.

"Yes, it will be really great to get out of here," Matthew glared at Shawn as he spoke.

"I will talk to you later on, Mary. Goodbye, Matthew," I said and pushed the therapy tray up against the wall out of the way as I turned to go.

"I will be back later to check on you," Shawn cried out over his shoulder to Matthew as we walked out the door.

"A little rough on him weren't you?" I asked Shawn as we walked down the corridor.

"Not really. He seems to be the one that wants to play games and I am not going to go along with it," Shawn replied.

"You don't like him do you?" I asked.

"No, I don't. The hospital is for sick patients that need help; not for people that want to play games," he answered.

"Who is the new patient?" I asked in order to change the subject as we approached the office.

"The file is on the desk. I will show you once we get to the office," Shawn replied.

"It is getting late. Do you want me to type up the profile tonight or can I wait and do it first thing in the morning?" I asked.

"You can wait and do it in the morning. I didn't realize it was this late," Shawn replied.

"Good. In that case I will go home to a nice, long, hot, relaxing bath," I said chuckling.

"This will be the first time that I will have been in on one of the fund-raising projects and I am really looking forward to it," Shawn remarked.

"It is a lot of fun. During the breaks we walk through watching the rides and grab something to eat. It makes you feel just like a kid again," I replied.

"Sounds like fun," he said chuckling.

"Well, I am off to the tub and some relaxation," I responded.

"I am going to stay and work a little longer. I want to stop and check on Matthew before I go home. I need to find out what he wants to do now regarding his treatment," Shawn informed me.

"He probably isn't going to give you an answer," I mused.

"Enjoy your bath and I will see you in the morning," Shawn answered.

"Thanks. I will see you in the morning," I replied as I walked out the door.

Although I had considered going back to see if Matthew had thought more about his treatments before Shawn went in to see him, I decided to go home instead. The two of them could not stand the sight of the other. *I will let them fight it out between themselves* I thought. *I don't feel like listening to any more of their sarcastic jabs to each other.* I got in the car and drove home. I planned to stop in the morning to pick up the rest of the papers that were being printed off. We had some brochures of the new wing but these were not enough so they had printed more. I pulled up in the driveway and was really glad to be home. It had been a trying day and I just wanted to relax.

I put the tea kettle on as I walked past the stove and went in to run my bath water. I lit the candles and turned off the water. I went to the kitchen to grab the tea and to sit a minute before going in to relax in the tub. I glanced through the mail and set it back down on the table…*I'll open it later* I decided. All I wanted right now was to get into the hot tub. I slipped out of my clothes, stepped into the water and slowly sat down as the hot water consumed my body. I slid down into the water and lay back as I rested my head on the back of the tub. I closed my eyes and let the heat of the water begin to relax my muscles as I sighed in contentment. I opened my eyes and watched as the candle light danced on the walls and ceiling making different shapes with their glow.

I lay thinking about Matthew's promise and about the answer that I would give him. I didn't like the way that he was being so deceitful and I was wondering if he had changed at all. It was hard sorting through all the times that we had spent together. For every good time we had had, there was a bad time too. Besides, he was the one that wanted to leave me and had decided that I was not the one for him. *Did I really still love him deep in my heart?* I wondered. He left me once and Shawn had reminded me often that if he did it once he would eventually do it again. At one time there was no doubt in my mind but now when thinking about going back there was nothing but doubt. *Could we erase everything and start over or would the painful reminders soon come between us?* I asked myself. We had made promises to each other in the past. I had believed him when he had told me how much he loved me and how we would spend the rest of our lives together. The feelings and emotions that filled me when he held me in his arms and kissed me were different. *What about Shawn's warnings? Why was he trying so hard to discourage me from getting back with Matthew?* I wondered. It was all so confusing to me. I guess in time my heart will make the right decision. *Isn't that what Shawn told me to do…to follow my heart?* Let my heart decide what my real feelings were and how I really felt. In time I would know…that is what Matthew and Shawn had both told me. I reasoned that I would know when the time came just what I wanted to do. Until that time came, trying to weigh the pros and cons just didn't seem to be the answer. *I would always have a special place in my heart for Matthew but was it love or just feelings from the past?* I queried. I did not want to think about it any more. If Matthew really loved me and wanted me he would not pressure me for an answer.

I switched my thoughts over to the upcoming fair, going over the list in my mind to make sure that we had everything ready. Between Carol and myself all the things that we had on our list had been crossed off except the extra brochures that I would be picking up in the morning. We would go down the next day to set up our booth and display the posters and photographs of the new wing. It gave us a chance to get out, have some fun and help raise money for the hospital at the same time.

I was suddenly woken to the realization that the bath water had turned cold…with so many thoughts running through my head I had failed to notice. *In time…*that was what everyone seemed to tell me. I guess they were right and there was no sense in trying to make things happen before time. I got out of the tub and dried myself off, blowing out the candles when I was done. I went in the bedroom and pulled down the covers.

Sliding my robe off, I climbed into bed and snuggled down into the covers, closing my eyes.

I had not been asleep long before the dreams surfaced again. I was not in the car and I was nowhere near the water. I was unsure of where I was. There was no blinding light but I was filled with terror. *Run* my mind told me but I was unable to move. *Run now…run as fast as you can!* I was being restrained by something as I struggled to get free.

Someone grabbed my wrist and pulled me close. I could see his hand. I recognized the hand but I could not place the person. He was laughing…a vicious menacing laugh that sent chills and fear through my whole being. I was lying down, trying to kick my legs and move my arms but I could not move. The more I fought, the more he laughed and mocked me. Soon I saw the blinding light and could feel myself moving. *No, no…*I was back in a car and being taken somewhere. *Run, run…escape.* I tossed and turned on the bed as the covers fell to the floor. Fear and panic enveloped me as my mind sought desperately of a way to get free. I was back in the water…each of my wrists was being held forcefully and I was being pulled in different directions. It felt as though my arms would be pulled from my body. I was in pain and the water terrified me as I struggled to free myself from my captor. The flashbacks began and brief events flashed before my eyes very quickly…so quickly that I did not have time to take it in to make sense of it. Suddenly the flashbacks stopped and I felt myself being thrown down on something hard. *No, no please…Matthew help me! Please, please* I begged him. I sprang upright and screamed out Matthew's name. *Matthew!* I continued screaming out his name before gradually realizing that I was in my own room, sitting up on my own bed. It was only another frightful nightmare! I sat shivering trying to sort things out as the tears started streaming down my face. I grabbed the blanket from the floor and quickly wrapped it around my body to warm myself. The new images had come back into my mind and I was not sure why Matthew was in this nightmare. *Was the fact that I could not move in this nightmare because of Matthew's injuries? His being paralyzed…is that why I couldn't move? No,* I thought to myself *I was being held by something or someone.*

Why did I scream out Matthew's name? In all the nightmares and flashbacks he had never once appeared to me; so why now after all this time would I call for his help? It must be the accident and the fact that he wanted me to reconsider and go back to him. I did not know…it was all so confusing. All I wanted was for the dreams and nightmares to end! I didn't even care any more if I found out what happened. I just wanted to sleep without being terrified by any nightmares.

Frustrated, I let myself fall back on the bed and curled up in the blanket to keep warm. I pushed everything from my mind as I looked out the window into the darkness. *Would I ever be able to overcome this and sleep a night without bad dreams, flashbacks and nightmares? Time*…that was what everyone told me. *In time they would stop and you will remember everything.* The tears continued to stream down my checks as my eyes slowly closed and I fell back to sleep…

Chapter 18

I woke up later than I had planned. My head was still groggy from the dreams of the night before. I dressed quickly without stopping to make my morning tea. I dashed off to the printers first to pick up the brochures before going to work. I pulled up into my parking spot and got out of the car. We needed to get everything down to the fairgrounds so I knew that Carol would be going along with me. I went up to the office. Carol still hadn't come in so I started to get everything organized and put things in boxes to make it easier to carry them. Shawn was in his office going over patients' files but looked up when he saw me pass by. I finished placing the papers into the last box and had moved it beside the door when Carol arrived.

"It is about time you got here," I scolded her.

"I'm sorry. I had to get some things done before I could come in and…" she paused.

I began laughing and said, "Don't worry I've only been here fifteen minutes."

"You! The one that is always thirty minutes before time," she joked.

"Yes. I overslept this morning," I admitted.

"Good morning girls," Shawn called out to us from the doorway.

"Good morning," we answered in unison and chuckled.

"I will type up the new patient's folder and we will be off to set up the booth," I told Shawn.

"I already did it Katie when you weren't here. I had a few extra minutes on hand so I got it done," he replied.

"Sorry, I didn't hear the alarm this morning," I confessed as I felt myself blush.

"Imagine that, Shawn! Our Katie that is always so early…oversleeping!" Carol said chuckling.

"Alright you two. Enough!" I admonished teasingly.

"Are you girls ready to go?" Shawn asked.

"I think I have everything in the boxes but let me check one more time," I said as I took one last walk around the room checking the places where I had set different things.

"You are always so organized, Katie. I don't think you have ever forgotten anything," Carol winked at Shawn as she spoke while he smiled back.

"Okay, we have everything. Let's go," I suggested.

"I'll drive, if that is okay with you girls," Shawn offered.

"It's fine with me, Shawn. I love to be chauffeured around," Carol replied.

"I can…" I began but Shawn cut me off.

"You can ride with us, Katie. You are also good at stopping off somewhere or not going at all," Shawn reminded me.

"Hmmm…you seem to be getting to know me pretty well," I laughed.

"The others are meeting us down there. So if we have everything…let's go," Carol's voice was filled with excitement.

"A little anxious?" I asked her.

"I have always loved the fair, Katie. You know that," Carol responded.

"To be honest, I am really looking forward to it too. I think it is going to be a lot of fun. Plus we will get to promote something very worthwhile," Shawn admitted.

"I don't think I know of even one person who doesn't get excited when the fair comes to town. It helps bring out the kid inside of you," I noted.

We reached Shawn's car. Carol sat on the front seat beside Shawn while I got in at the back. Shawn backed out of the parking space and drove off. I sat looking out the window while Shawn and Carol chatted to each other. I was still trying to make sense of the nightmare from the night before. *What difference does it make? Why bother trying to sort everything out?* I thought to myself. It never made sense to me no matter how hard I tried to analyze it. I was sure that Matthew's accident played a part in my latest nightmare. In all the other nightmares I did not ever remember my sense of immobility. Although there were times when I could feel someone holding on to me and preventing me from moving, this was different. The thoughts of the nightmare and my feeling of immobility brought me back to Matthew's request and promise. I thought I knew where I stood on that issue. I realized that if it was something that I really wanted I would not have trouble making up my mind. The years that had passed and my not having any contact with him seemed to bother me the most. *Why would he think that I would want to get back together after all this time, especially since he had never made any effort to contact me throughout? Did he really mean what he said about being on his way back here to see me to get back with me? Was that just an excuse he was using to get me to reconsider? How long had he been awake while we were oblivious to that? Did he overhear his parents talking about how his girlfriend had left when she had found out about his condition?* I did not understand why I was so hesitant and had not made up my mind till then. There was something nagging at me but I still could not quite put my finger on it. *If I had doubts why didn't they jump out at me so that I could better understand them? Could Matthew be that callous and figure it would be better to be with me instead of living with his parents?* He seemed so sincere while he was holding me in his arms but there was something that was not just right…something that I could feel from deep within me that warned me to stay away…to keep my distance. *Was it our breakup? No* I thought. We had remained friends and even went places together after that. So it must be something else. *But what could it be?* I wondered. I still had feelings for him—not the deep love that I once had in my heart for him—but I did still care about him. *Maybe after his girlfriend thought more about it she would change her mind and return? If given that choice which of us would he pick?* I could call and ask her to come back just once to see Matthew. *Maybe I could get her to confide in me whether or not Matthew had really told her of his plans to come back to me?* I could be very subtle by telling her that Matthew was awake and that if she wanted to see or talk to him that that would be a good time to do so. However, if Matthew had told her of his plans I was sure that I would be the last person that she would want to talk to. Mary had not mentioned her to me so I could not really ask her about it. *Maybe I could ask Mary to call her and tell her of Matthew's change and she would be able to give me the information I wanted without her even realizing it?* I needed to know if that part of Matthew's explanation was true. If so, I could believe the rest of the things that he had been telling me. *Was that what I really wanted or was I just trying to make excuses for not going back with him?* I really hadn't thought much about him the last few years and to have him back in my life I wasn't sure if that was what I really wanted or not.

"Katie!" Carol's shout jolted me to reality.

"What!" I jumped, startled by her shout.

"Welcome back to the real world," she said in annoyance.

"I'm sorry. I was engrossed in my own thoughts while you two were busy conversing," I responded.

"I guess you were in your own little world but now it is time to get back to reality because we are at the fair," she stated.

"Well, let's get going and get everything set up. Then we can go and look around at everything," I suggested.

Shawn had got out of the car and had opened the trunk. We got out and went to the back of the car. Carol grabbed a box and hurried into the building. Shawn took out another box and started to hand it to me but stopped suddenly and looked at me. I felt my face flush as he looked at me. I tried to avert my face so that he could not see my embarrassment.

"Are you okay today, Katie?" he asked.

"I'm fine...I just have a lot on my mind that I need to sort out," I replied.

"No, it's more than that, Katie," he noted as he looked into my eyes.

"I'm fine, really. I was just deep in thought and wasn't listening to what you and Carol had been talking about," I tried to explain to him.

"You had another nightmare last night, didn't you?" he asked.

"What do I have, a sign across my forehead that reads *Crazy lady has yet another nightmare*?" I asked feeling my frustration beginning to mount.

"No," he said chuckling and continued, "I can tell by the far away look in your tired eyes that you did not sleep well and if you didn't sleep well it would have been caused by a dream or a nightmare," he explained.

"Well, that was last night and this is today. I am not going to think about it or let it ruin my day," I answered with a confidence that I had hoped would convince him.

"I know you better than that, Katie. Carol called your name a few times before shouting at you to get you to respond," he informed me.

"You two had been talking and I had blocked out what you were talking about. So when she finally did say something I didn't realize she was talking to me," I explained.

"It was about Matthew, wasn't it?" he asked.

"I don't feel like getting into it right now," I answered.

"You will never want to get into it, Katie," he replied. You always hide from it and push it out of your mind only to have it come back later to haunt you. It won't get any better until you open up and talk to someone. If not to me, at least consider talking to Hank about it," he suggested.

"I told you before that I am not going to talk to Hank about any of this any more," I reminded him.

"Maybe you can talk to Carol about it. You don't seem to want to talk to me and I am the one that can help you get past this; but you either don't trust me or you think I will judge you on what you tell me," he said as he tried to get me to talk.

I looked deep into his eyes for the first time and I could see compassion in them as he looked back at me with an honest concern. He had very dark brown eyes that were filled with care and understanding. My heart told me that I could trust him and tell him anything I wanted but

I didn't feel like re-opening the old wounds that I bore...at least not while I was still trying to sort out my feelings about Matthew. I always felt safe and secure when I was with Shawn and I knew that he was concerned for me and was only trying to help but it was not the right time. We always had a good time when we were together. Shawn could make me laugh and forget about anything that was bothering me. He had a genuine consideration that I had never seen before in anyone else.

"Are you going to help some time today or just stand and gaze at each other?" Carol asked as she walked up to the car.

"We are coming," Shawn answered as he continued looking at me.

"It looks like you are just holding the boxes," Carol said jokingly.

"Actually we just wanted you to do all the foot work and save us the trouble," I chuckled as I answered Carol.

"Okay, hand me another box and each of you grab a box and we will all go in together because I am not going to unload the car by myself," she retorted.

We all grabbed a box and set off towards the merchant's building. Carol grumbled all the way about all the hard work she had to do while we wasted our time talking. As we walked into the building one could see everyone working on their projects and getting their booths set up. Scott and his colleague Larry had borrowed the tall ladder and were putting up the banner. Larry was strong and stood well over six feet. He had blue eyes, a full beard and long black hair that went down to his shoulders.

We had the corner booth and it had the most room. Everyone kept going around to the other booths and socializing. It was a good chance to take a break and meet everyone.

"Hey, Katie! Want to come up the ladder and help?" Scott mocked.

"I could get it done faster than you are doing," I yelled back at him.

"Oh, I forgot you don't like heights," Scott said trying to annoy me.

"I will get the banner done and have everything set up before you are going to get it done," I replied trying to get back at him.

"If you think you can get it done faster climb on up this ladder," Scott said trying to egg me on.

"I have more important things to do. Apparently you can handle the simple job of placing the banner on the hook," I said and laughed back at him.

Scott mumbled something but I could not understand him. I knew that I had dented his ego and would not have to listen to him for a while as he figured out a suitable reply.

Shawn had set up the table and chairs. Carol grabbed the table runner while I measured and cut it. Shawn secured it snuggly under the table with tape and we stood back looking at it to make sure it looked fine. Larry and Scott had the banner hung and were carrying the ladder back. Scott just gave me a dirty look as he passed by but didn't say a word. I smiled as he walked past because I knew that would irritate him more than anything that I could have said to him. We set the brochures on the table, stood up the tripods for the pictures and placed the donation jars at both ends of the table. We had everything set up and decided to take a walk through the fairway.

It was late afternoon and the people had been streaming in most of the day. Carol was hungry so we decided to stop off at one of the food vendors and try out some of the fantastic aromatic food. We ordered, went over and sat at the picnic table. We sampled each other's food so that we could get a taste of everything. After we finished we sat watching the kids run from ride to ride. Everyone was laughing and talking as they ambled about checking the games and feeling the excitement in the air.

Shawn was the one to remind us that we needed to get back to the booth. Carol grabbed our empty plates, walked over and threw them into the trash can. We slowly walked back stopping briefly to watch some of the rides as we passed them. We heard people screaming on their rides and laughed as we reminisced our childhood days. We giggled as we remembered how terrified we were as we went through the haunted house. Shawn told us a funny story of one of his trips to the fair when he was a child and how frightened he was of the clown head that bounced over one of the tents. We walked back into the building as Larry and Scott returned. The five of us had signed up for the same time and I didn't look at the list until it was too late to change my time. Scott had always been an arrogant, irritating person to me and I tried to avoid going anywhere near him. Matthew and Scott had been the best of friends at school. While Matthew and I were seeing each other Scott would come around often and try to get Matthew to go out with him. Scott loved excitement and would do anything on a dare. Most times he did not care if someone got hurt in the process as long as he had his fun; that was the only thing that was important to him.

"Looks like we finally get to spend an evening together, Katie?" Scott noted sarcastically as he winked at me.

"Only because we are being forced together. I would never do it any other way," I answered.

"I am going to set you two in a corner together until you can get along," Carol suggested as she laughed.

"We would end up killing each other," Scott chuckled.

"I would never get close enough to touch you let alone kill you, so you are safe," I retorted.

"You know you love me, Katie," Scott said chuckling and added, "but with Matt back in the picture I guess we will never know who you really want."

Scott's words stung me. I walked over to him and spoke very low so that only he would hear me: "You will never be half the man that Matt is and may you rot in hell for the unconscionable person that you are."

"Okay, you two. That is enough. We are trying to promote a good cause here and we don't need you two arguing and keeping the people away," Carol told us.

I walked over to the other end of the table and sat down. I could feel Scott looking over at me but I would not reduce myself to his level nor did I feel like exchanging any more words with him. As the people stopped to talk to us I soon forgot about him even being there. Thankfully Carol and Shawn sat between us and Carol kept him busy. The time passed by quickly and soon the next group came in to relieve us. We stood up to let them take our seats and briefly talked to them before we left.

"Come on, Katie, let's have some fun," Scott said as he grabbed my wrist and pulled me towards him.

He had caught me completely off guard and I fell against him. He laughed, turned and started walking as he pulled me along with each step he took. Watching this Shawn took a step to come over to us but Carol stopped him. Using all my might I pulled back on my arm breaking free from Scott's hold on me.

"I will say this and I will only say it once so you better listen and listen well," I spoke through clenched teeth. "If you ever touch me again I will lay you out on the floor. I don't want to and will never go anywhere with you and if you touch me again you will find out just how serious I am," I responded fiercely.

"Don't you remember the good times we had, Katie?" he smirked. "Oh, I forgot you don't remember that part of your life," he mocked.

"Just remember what I just told you or you will regret the day you met me," I warned.

"Katie has it under control, Shawn, and it would have only made matters worse if you would have stepped in," Carol explained.

"Why does he constantly taunt her?" Shawn asked.

"I am not sure. It has been going on for years and Scott does it mainly because he knows how much it irritates her," Carol confided.

"Guess that just shows the kind of man he is. He causes distress and purposely hurts Katie knowing the pain from her past and what she is going through after Matthew's accident," Shawn remarked. He stopped speaking and watched Katie come up to them.

"I am going to go with Jim who will be giving me a ride home. You two are on your own so you both better behave," Carol said with a wink as she turned and walked away with Jim.

"Are you ready to go?" Shawn asked.

"Let's walk through the fair. I would like to get something before we go. I don't feel like cooking," I replied.

"Sounds good to me. Nothing like a fair at night with all the lights shining," Shawn observed as his eyes sparkled like a child's with excitement.

We walked out of the building. The lights from the fair were brightly lit: red, yellow, green, blue with white blinking lights. As we walked along we could hear the music change from ride to ride. Kids were running to get to the next ride laughing and talking about the last ride they had just been on. Shawn and I laughed as we watched them. As we walked closer to the exit Shawn stopped and I stopped and turned around to look at him. He was looking up into the sky and my eyes followed the direction in which he was looking. The Ferris wheel was the object of his gaze.

"Katie, I love the Ferris wheel. Would you like to go on it with me?" Shawn asked and waited for my reply.

"I would love to," I answered.

"Great! I will get the tickets and be right back," he replied.

Shawn queued in line for buying the tickets. He looked back at me and smiled. It was not my favorite ride but I was ready for some excitement of a different kind. Shawn came back with the tickets and we stood in line waiting for the Ferris wheel to stop so that we could get on. It slowly came to a halt and we climbed up into the seat. Shawn pulled the bar down over us. We slowly began to move, stopping each time they put someone else on the ride. We were at the top and it stopped again. We looked out over the fair laughing at how small everything seemed from the height that we were at. Something caught my eyes and I couldn't help staring at it. It was the huge search lights that were rotating back and forth. Shawn looked at me and followed the direction of my gaze.

"Katie?" Shawn called out to me.

I kept staring at the lights but could not speak. The brightness was blinding my eyes but I could not look away. I was mesmerized as the tears welled up in my eyes and slowly rolled down my cheeks. I grabbed the safety bar and tried to raise it but Shawn quickly lunched forward and held it down firmly.

"No, please," I whispered.

"Katie, please look at me. Do not look at the light," Shawn spoke in a calming tone.

The ride finally began to move. I continued staring at the light until it was obscured from view. We began our ascent going higher and higher. My eyes searched for the light and watched it again until it was out of sight. The tears continued to fall down my cheeks and I hadn't noticed that Shawn had taken my hand and was gently rubbing it. He begged me to look at him and away from the light that he realized took me back to the nightmares from my past. The ride began to slow down as the people were being let off. Once again we stopped at the top.

"Please don't," I whispered as I gazed into the brightness.

"Katie, I am with you and you are safe. I will not let anyone hurt you," Shawn said soothingly.

"Why? Please just tell me why," I begged as I continued staring at the lights.

The ride began to move again and it stopped to let us off. Shawn got out first and reached over and lifted me out of the seat. He kept his arm around me and I walked along with him numb to everything going on around me. We got to the car. He opened the door and helped me in.

"Shawn, I need to get my car. I know what happened and I need to talk to someone," I told him.

"Katie, what do you remember?" he asked.

"The lights…I know what the lights from my nightmares mean now. While I gazed into the light it came back to me…slower flashbacks showing me exactly what happened that my mind recognized and remembered as it took me through it," I explained.

"Talk to me, Katie. I will take you wherever you need to go," he suggested.

"I need to talk to him alone. I have to find out why," I answered, anger taking control of me.

"Katie, you are not thinking clearly right now. Let's go for a cup of coffee and we can talk," he suggested.

"I need to talk to him alone. He is the only one that can give me the answers that I need to know," I replied angrily as my body trembled.

"Katie, we will stop for some coffee first. I will take you wherever you want to go but you need to think and talk about it while it is fresh in your mind," Shawn advised.

I paused and took a deep breath before going on, "Last night it was the nightmare and tonight while looking at the blinding lights I remembered what happened and why the light kept blinding me that night," I explained.

Shawn started up the car as he took my hand and gently pulled me close to him. I slid closer to him while he put his arm around me and held me close to him. My mind and body were exhausted. I closed my eyes and rested my head on his chest as he drove. I didn't care where he took me. I felt safe and I knew nothing could hurt me while I was with Shawn. He had always been there for me and I knew that the words he spoke to me were right and that I needed to think before going out and facing the person. I needed to think clearly about what I was going to say before just going up to him and blurting out words that made no sense. Shawn continued driving but I kept my eyes closed and I had no idea where we were. I didn't want to open my eyes and see the blinding light again. I knew now what that light meant and what had happened. The car came to a stop but I didn't open my eyes. I didn't want to know where I was. I only wanted to block out what was going through my mind. I didn't want to face what happened. The only thing I wanted was to know *why*.

Shawn turned off the engine and opened the door of the car. He got out, reached in and lifted me gently from the seat and carried me in his arms. I wrapped my arms around his neck as I opened my eyes and looked at him. He was such a caring man and had always been there for me. If he only knew what I was about to tell him I was sure he would not be holding me in his arms and have the same level of concern that he was feeling then.

Shawn opened the door to his house, carried me to the kitchen table and sat me down on a chair. He cupped my chin and lifted my face up to look at me. I tried to avert my face so that he would not see the humiliation I felt. He held my chin and smiled as he reassured me not to worry and that he would help me through that. *How could he help me?* I thought. *How could anyone help me? Why would any man want me now?* His feelings would surely change once I revealed to him what had happened.

Shawn went to the sink and filled the tea kettle and set it on the stove. He took two cups out of the cupboard and set them on the counter. Taking a lighter from a drawer he walked over to the table and lit the candle that stood on it. Shawn looked at me and smiled. He came over and sat on the chair next to the one I was sitting in.

"Katie, everything will be alright. I know you don't think so right now but there is nothing you can tell me that I would ever hold against you and it will not change the way that I feel about you." Shawn's soft-spoken voice was very calming and soothing as he spoke.

"Maybe you better wait until I tell you what happened before you make that decision," I replied keeping my eyes averted.

"Katie, whatever happened was not your fault. You must understand that first," he consoled me.

"How can you say that? You don't even know what happened and why should you even care?" I asked as I felt my anger growing once again inside me.

"If it had been your fault Katie or if it was something that you had wanted your mind would not have blocked it out for all these years. You would have been able to remember everything from the moment that it had happened," he explained.

"But maybe it was something that I had unknowingly wanted and my mind wasn't sure," I replied.

"It doesn't work that way, Katie. If it did then anyone who did something wrong could easily block out what they didn't want to remember. Your mind didn't want you to remember because it was something bad that you did not want," Shawn said reassuringly.

The tea kettle began to scream which startled me. I started to stand up but Shawn stopped me. He got up and went over to the stove and made a cup of tea for each of us. I watched as the candlelight danced on the ceiling. The aroma that it exuded was very relaxing. I was not sure that I wanted to explain to Shawn what had actually happened. Maybe it was not a good idea after all. *Shawn had been such a good friend and had always helped me but maybe sharing the past would change his mind about me? Maybe I should just tell him that the memory was only fleeting and had faded? No, he knew better* I realized. He knew that I had remembered and I did not have a car to leave…so I was stuck. Shawn came back to the table with our cups of tea and placed mine in front of me.

"Thank you, Shawn, for taking the time to comfort the crazy lady once again," I said gratefully.

"You are not a crazy lady and I do not want you to ever say that again, okay?" he answered.

"But that is how I feel. You are always coming to my rescue and that is not fair to you," I replied.

"If I didn't want to help you Katie I would not be here now and I would not have been there for you before," Shawn responded.

"I just want to go confront him and ask him 'why'. That is the only thing I want to know and he is the only one that can tell me," I answered.

"Okay, Katie. Take a sip of tea, hold it in your mouth for a minute and slowly swallow and tell me what you remember," Shawn suggested and I did as he asked me to do.

"I don't know where to begin or how much you want to know," I began.

"Start at the beginning from where you remember and continue through and tell me everything you can remember, no matter how unimportant you think it is," he answered.

I took a deep breath as I looked at the dancing candlelight and fixated my gaze on that because I could not meet Shawn's gaze. I slowly began to talk and tell him what had happened all those years ago…

"We were sitting at the beach and talking. We would soon be leaving for school and would be going to different colleges. He was telling me that he wanted to stay together and didn't think that we should date anyone else. He told me that I was his and that he didn't want another man coming around me. I had explained to him that I had no intention of doing that and I loved him and would always wait for him. He in turn promised me that I was the only woman for him and he would love me forever. After exchanging our promises to each other he stood up and took my hand and we walked in the shallow part of the water. He wanted to go out a little further and we soon were in thigh-level water. He began to teasingly push me trying to get me wet and I was doing the same to him. Then he grabbed my wrist as he pushed me under water. I came up screaming. I don't know if I can do this, Shawn," I paused.

"You are doing great, Katie. Don't stop now. You can do this. Please continue," Shawn gently pushed me to talk.

"He started to hurt me. I tried to get away and run back up to the shore but he grabbed me and once again pushed me back under water. This time after resurfacing I kicked him and he lost his grip and fell. I headed for the shore but he was right behind me." I stopped speaking as I could feel my body trembling.

"You are doing very well, Katie. Drink some more tea, relax a minute and go on," Shawn coaxed gently. "I know how hard this is for you but you can do it and remember I am right here and nobody is going to harm you now. You are safe as I am with you," Shawn reminded me.

I did as he told me to do and slowly continued, still fixating my gaze on the light from the candle. "He chased me up to the shore and tackled me half way across the beach. He straddled me holding my wrists over my head. I asked him to stop because he was hurting me but it was as though he did not hear me. *I don't know if I can trust you, Katie, while I am gone* I remember him saying to me. I told him that I would be faithful to him for as long as we needed to be apart. Another promise that I had made to him…one that came from my heart."

I was very upset and suddenly stood and began pacing the floor as the tears rolled down my face. Shawn just sat and watched me not sure what I was going to do next. He sat on the edge of his chair in case he needed to catch me.

"You are doing well, Katie. You are upset and angry and have every right to be. He was the man you loved and he was hurting you. You did nothing wrong, Katie. You pledged your promises to him but he was still insecure. It was nothing that you did," Shawn reassured me in a calming tone.

I paced back and forth in the kitchen, not wanting to speak. After remembering for the first time what had happened I was so angry that I only wanted to face my attacker. I did not want to wait any longer. I wanted to know *why* immediately...not after I had had the chance to calm down. He hadn't given me an option that night and I should not give him any option either. I wanted the face off right away!

I did not notice that Shawn had risen from his chair and had come up in front of me. I was busy pacing and plotting my revenge. I paced forward and ran straight into Shawn. I looked up at him and he put his arms around me gently pulling me closer to him. He held me firmly and did not speak. I could feel my tense body begin to relax but my anger was still very strong.

"You have done nothing wrong, Katie. It was not your fault so don't blame yourself. I know you are very angry and you have every right to feel that way but don't let your anger take control. Let out the anger, Katie. Finish telling me what happened. Don't let him win by letting what happened because of him make you feel any different about yourself," Shawn advised as he held me close to his body and comforted me.

"But I am a different person now because of him," I said in a voice just above a whisper.

"No, Katie. You are not different. You are a stronger person now knowing what happened and you will be able to get past it. Just remember it was not your fault and you did not want it to happen," Shawn repeated his assurances. "Finish telling me what happened, Katie. Get it all out. Don't leave it now...don't let your anger win. You can do it, Katie," Shawn urged.

I gave a big sigh and resumed: "I remember telling him how much he was hurting me but he would not stop. He only laughed. He ripped my shirt off me and threw it to the side. Next he yanked my jeans down. His next words were very cutting. I kicked and fought as hard as I could to get away from him."

"Katie, you are safe. I am with you and nobody will ever harm you again," Shawn reassured me again as I faltered.

I took a deep breath and continued, "As I begged him to stop he laughed in my face and ripped off my underwear leaving me naked underneath him. *No, please don't. Please stop. Please, please* I begged him but he didn't stop. Instead he held me down, laughed and mocked me and said what he had to say to me. *You know you want this, Katie, so stay still. You are mine and I am going to make sure that no man will ever want you. When I am done with you there will be no man that will ever look at you the same way. Then you will really be mine and mine alone. You are soiled now and you are mine.* I was filled with fear and fought as hard as I could but I could not stop him. I screamed for him to stop but he raped me. I am not sure what happened after that because I blacked out."

My body shook uncontrollably and the tears from my burning eyes streamed down my face. Shawn held me close and firmly but didn't speak. I cried until I thought I had no more tears left. My body had stopped shaking and I felt exhausted. Shawn held me tight in his arms and never let go just as he had promised.

"I told you that I was not the same person and I won't blame you if you never want to see me again. No man will ever want me now," I remarked but could not lift my face to look at his.

Shawn cupped my chin with his fingers and lifted my face up to look at me as he finally spoke, "Katie, you are a beautiful person and what happened to you was not your fault. You did not want it to happen. His words were meant to hurt you and make you feel embarrassed and disgusted about yourself but they were spoken in fear of losing you and by a man that had no real appreciation of the person that you are. Any man would be proud to have you, Katie, and what had happened to you will not matter," Shawn reassured me.

I looked into Shawn's eyes and could see the sincere compassion that he had as he spoke to me. He lowered his face closer to mine pausing momentarily before kissing me. I put my arms around his neck relieved that what I had just told him didn't change the way he felt about me and that we would still remain friends.

"I need to go now to face him and let him know that I have finally remembered what he did to me," I informed Shawn.

"Let your anger settle down first, Katie. You can confront him in the morning. Right now you need to let everything sink in. You need to be able to handle yourself when you confront him or you will not be able to go through with it," he suggested.

"But I am angry and he needs to feel my anger and frustration. Why should I not be as aggressive as he was to me? What choice did I have?" I said and I could feel my anger rising again.

"If you go in now you will only start with what you want to say before your anger kicks in and you will not be able to finish. By waiting you will have time to go over it in your mind and will be able to tell him exactly what you want to say to him," Shawn advised.

"Oh, no!" I exclaimed and stopped abruptly.

"What's the matter?" Shawn asked.

"That is not all that happened, Shawn," I answered.

"What do you mean?" he asked.

"Shawn, there is more. Remember I had told you that Hank said he was riding Lacey at the time I came out of the woods? Hank said that he had later brought me home," I recounted.

"You are not ready to face that part of the attack yet. Are you sure it happened that night?" Shawn asked.

"Yes, because I remember the bright light. It was headlights of a car and there were people that got out of the car and came up to us. The rest I can't remember," I replied.

"You will remember, Katie, just like you remembered tonight. Don't worry about it right now," Shawn advised.

"But don't you see? Someone else knew about it but never said anything or came to me to tell me? They let it stay buried and I don't know who they were and I don't know why they held their silence," I answered as I started shaking again.

"Don't worry about it now. Just let all of it sink in and think about what you want to say to your attacker. That is all you need to focus on right now," Shawn suggested.

"But Shawn…" I started to speak but he stopped my words with another kiss.

"I am here. You have nothing to fear. You are safe in my arms and I will stay with you for however long it takes," Shawn promised.

"Please, no promises. I have found that promises are only made to be broken," I replied.

"Let's sit down and have some more tea. You can be sure that you will have your confrontation soon and he will not be ready for it because he does not know that you have remembered," Shawn remarked.

"How long will it take for me to remember the rest?" I asked.

"It will come when you are ready to handle it all," Shawn replied.

"So it could be years before I am going to remember the rest?" I asked.

"I don't think it will take that long for you to remember," he remarked.

"Is there a way that I can force it to my mind?" I wondered.

"You won't need to force it, Katie. It will come when you are ready," he explained.

"I don't want to wait as long as it has taken for me to remember this," I answered.

"It will come sooner than you think. Now that you have remembered the first part it is only a matter of time and it will all come back to you," Shawn assured me.

"Maybe I can get some answers tomorrow when I finally get to talk to him about it," I said. "That would be the only good thing he could do for me right now."

We continued talking until eventually Shawn had me sleep in his room while he slept on the couch. He promised me that he would take me first thing in the morning for my confrontation with my attacker with whom I would finally be able to have my say…

Chapter 19

I slipped off all my clothes but left my underwear on. Pulling the covers down on Shawn's bed I crawled in and snuggled comfortably under the warm sheets. I could hear Shawn moving around in the kitchen as he turned off the lights. After a while I heard him lie down on the couch. The house was quiet and I felt safe. I could still smell the aroma of the candles and it made me feel more relaxed.

I thought back on the memories that I had had. The same question kept nagging me. . .*why?* I guess I would find out tomorrow. I would finally know why Matthew chose to do what he did. Maybe he would do the decent thing and reveal the rest of what had happened so that I would not have to wait for my mind to reawaken memories of the incident. Shawn was right when he advised me to let my anger settle down before confronting Matthew. I wanted to give Matthew the element of surprise but I now realized that had I gone tonight I would have ended up arguing and Matthew would not have answered my questions. I was determined to have my say in order to find out the *why* that had been troubling me for so long. I tossed and turned remembering the rape and the terror that had filled me that night. My anger began to intensify and I wanted very much at that moment to make Matthew feel the same way that I had felt that night…the fear, the anger and terror. *How could he even consider that I would want to go back with him?* He had to have known that I would one day remember and feel the hatred that I now felt in my heart. Instead he was so flippant about the whole attack and even now he acted as though nothing had really happened. Apparently Matthew thought that I would simply go back to him and love him like I had done before the incident. *Did he really feel that by doing what he had done that I would—as he repeatedly told me—be his forever and go to him any time he decided that he wanted me again?* The anger began to grow stronger deep inside of me. I felt my body shake. I wanted to get up and pace because I was so agitated but I did not want to awaken Shawn. My thoughts turned to Shawn and my anger for Matthew seemed to vanish as I remembered the words Shawn had repeatedly told me over the months. Shawn was so wonderful to me. He had always been there and never expected anything in return. He was genuinely concerned about me and was always there when I needed him the most. I thought back about the first time that Carol had given me his card and told me to call him. I did not think back then that he could really help me. How I had resisted all his help because I was adamant that I could handle it on my own. However, it seemed like Shawn always happened to be there at the right time to help me get through the difficult times. It had been so much easier having him there to stand by me and to hold me when I was upset. His kiss…I unconsciously touched my lips as I remembered how I had felt when he kissed me and how natural it seemed for him to do so. I could feel my anger starting to settle down. I realized that soon I would have the opportunity to have my say to Matthew. My mind and body were exhausted from the events of the day and I eventually fell asleep.

I opened my eyes and slowly looked around my surroundings when I finally awoke. I was not afraid to realize that I had slept overnight in Shawn's bed. I felt comfortable and safe when I was around him and he always made me smile and feel much better. He was an amazing man. He had a way about him and was always in control of the situation. Shawn never seemed to let things bother him. He had a sincere and genuine nature that made him reach out to people and help them. I stretched and then snuggled back down under the covers. It was still very early in the morning. I didn't hear Shawn moving around so I stayed in bed so as not to awaken him. I soon fell back into a peaceful slumber.

Two hours passed and I continued sleeping. Meanwhile Shawn had awoken and made tea but very quietly without awakening me. He wanted me to sleep because he knew that was the best thing for me after the trauma of having remembered the past. The aroma of fresh tea filled my nostrils and I began to stir in bed. There was a knock on the bedroom door and Shawn opened the door and came in. He was carrying a bed tray and came around to the side of the bed and set it down.

"Good morning, Katie," he said cheerfully.

"Good morning, Shawn. What do you have there?" I teasingly asked.

"Fresh brewed herbal tea and some toast for you," he answered smiling.

"I could get used to this," I chuckled.

"Here, let me get you a robe to put on." Shawn walked over to the closet and took out a robe that he brought back and placed on the bed for me.

"Thank you," I mumbled blushing with the realization that I was clad only in my underwear.

"You can put it on while I fetch the rest of your breakfast," Shawn suggested as he turned and went out the door closing it softly behind him.

I got up, slipped into the robe and tied it around me. I climbed back into bed and pulled the covers up around my waist. Reaching over I picked up one of the cups of tea and took a sip. It tasted refreshingly good. I enjoyed the feeling of holding the warm cup in both hands. At the moment I did not want to dwell on the previous day's events. Instead, I merely wanted to relax and drink my tea. I knew that there would be time later to vent my anger but this time it would be directed at the person who deserved it...the person that I had trusted the most...the one who had promised undying love to me but then did the most despicable thing a man could do to any woman. I felt my anger rising again. It was my body and he had no right to take away the most sacred thing that I had…my virginity. It was mine to give and not his to forcefully take away. *What right did he have to think*…my thoughts were interrupted by the knock at the door that brought me back to the present. I watched as the door opened and Shawn returned with a plate of fresh cut-up fruits. He smiled at me as he crossed the floor and sat down on the bed. Shawn held out the plate as he offered me some fruit. I took an orange section and bit on it, breaking the skin as I slowly sucked the juice. It was chilled and tasted very good. He set the plate on my lap so that he could eat some of the fruit. I drank the herbal tea that he had made and it relaxed me. My anger that had resurfaced only moments before was no longer there.

We ate all the fruit and finished drinking our tea. Shawn picked up the plate and set it back down on the tray as he sat on the bed.

"Can we talk before we go?" Shawn asked.

"There is something that I would like you to do for me first, if you don't mind," I requested.

"Sure," he replied.

"There is a bag in your trunk that I didn't take into the merchant's building yesterday. I would really appreciate it if you could please get it for me," I requested as I felt myself blush.

"Sure, I will grab it and be right back. Is that all that you need?" he asked as he stood up and headed towards the door.

"Yes, that is all that I need for now. There are some extra clothes in the bag that I took just in case I needed them but I had never imagined that I would be needing them under these circumstances," I answered.

"You take extra clothes to the fair with you?" he asked as he furrowed his brow and smiled.

"Last year when we were setting up Carol and I ended up getting really dirty. So I thought that this year I would take some extra clothes so that I could change if it happened again," I explained.

"I guess Carol was right. You are ready for everything!" Shawn exclaimed laughing as he rose and went out the door.

I got up and walked around the bedroom before going out to the kitchen to make myself another cup of tea. I gazed through the window while I waited for Shawn to return. The door opened behind me and I knew that it was Shawn so I continued watching the squirrels chasing each other around the yard. I felt very safe with Shawn and I knew that I did not have to worry about anything when I was with him.

"Those two squirrels have been around here for three years now," Shawn chuckled.

"I love watching them scamper around and chattering back and forth," I laughed.

"I will set your bag here on the table," Shawn told me.

"Thank you. Would it be okay if I took a quick shower before going for the face off?" I asked.

"Sure. I will set out towels for you," Shawn told me and went to the bathroom. I could hear him open and close the cabinet. He returned and in a comical gesture bowed slightly and pointed his arm towards the door.

"Thank you, sir," I chuckled as I went past him and through the door.

I slipped out of Shawn's robe and turned the water on as I stepped under the shower head. The warm water felt good. I showered quickly so that I could confront Matthew to get my long-awaited answers. I dried myself off and got dressed. I combed my wet hair and was ready to go. I walked out the door to find Shawn sitting at the kitchen table reading the newspaper. He looked up as I came out and smiled. He had changed his clothes while I was showering and had another cup of tea sitting in front of him and another cup for me.

"Feeling better?" he asked.

"Amazing what a little bit of water will do for you," I replied.

"Whenever you are ready to go just let me know. I just want to talk to you first and tell you some things before you confront him," Shawn stated.

"I think I am ready to go now. I have waited a long time to confront my attacker. Today I will have that chance and maybe finally find out why he had done it," I replied.

"What I have to say won't take long and I think it will help you," Shawn explained.

"Okay. I guess I have waited eight years so a few more minutes aren't going to hurt," I answered.

"Try not to let your anger get the better of you, Katie," Shawn advised.

"I don't know if I will be able to do that," I admitted.

"If you feel yourself losing control take a couple of deep breaths to let yourself calm down a little before going on," Shawn suggested.

"If I can remember to do that I will...but my main concern is that he will tell me he doesn't remember anything because of the accident and I won't really know if he means it or not," I replied.

"Katie, he has remembered everything else. So if he tries hoodwinking you into believing that he does not remember just give him details of the things that you do remember," Shawn explained.

"All I want to know is *why*," I responded.

"I wouldn't count on him giving you too much information, Katie. Look how he faked that he was still in a coma while listening to his mother's continued pleas to open his eyes, talk to her or even just squeeze her finger. That tells you a lot about the kind of man that he is," Shawn explained.

"I wonder just how long he had been awake before talking to me," I replied.

"It shows you how deceitful a man he can be, Katie. So be careful while talking to him," Shawn warned.

"I have now seen him at his worst. After what he did to me there isn't a lot more that he can do," I observed.

"Katie, he will try to turn it around and say that it was your fault. Do not listen to him. You did nothing wrong and it was not something that you wanted or asked for," Shawn reassured me.

"I would like to think that he would not stoop that low but I guess after everything else I should not expect much of him," I replied as I slowly sipped my tea.

"He is not the kind of man that is going to take the blame for anything.

What he did to you is inexcusable and that is why I am warning you to be ready for him to say *You wanted it*," Shawn explained.

"I find it hard to believe that he would even suggest that we get back together knowing that one day I would remember and confront him about it," I admitted.

"He was counting on you never remembering, Katie. He thought that after all this time you would go back to him and that he could somehow convince you that it was only a nightmare and that nothing had ever really happened," Shawn explained.

"But I now know a part of what happened that night and I know there is more because Hank told me that he had come to my rescue in the woods that night," I answered.

"Matthew will give you only the least amount of information he possibly can," Shawn remarked.

"I will just be glad when it is over and I never have to see him again," I admitted.

"You are just going to drop it after you talk to him?" Shawn asked me incredulously.

"I am going to wait until I remember the whole thing. After that I will decide what I am going to do but you can rest assured I will do something," I said confidently.

"I am glad you feel that way and are not going to let him get away with it," Shawn replied.

"No, I am not going to let him get away with anything. I know it has been a long time coming but sooner or later I will remember and that will be my time to get my revenge," I answered.

"You don't think you will have a problem in having Matt charged?" Shawn asked.

"Did he have a problem that night when he decided to do what he did?" I shot back.

"He is a very sneaky, conniving man Katie and you already know what he is capable of doing. I just want you to be prepared for the meeting," Shawn warned me.

"I am sure he is going to do everything he can to talk his way out of it; that is if he talks about it in the first place," I replied.

"Would you like me to be with you while you talk to him?" Shawn asked.

"No, Shawn but thank you for offering," I responded. "Matthew will be defensive if I have you come in with me and he may not talk at all. I want some long-awaited answers," I replied.

"Just remember I won't be far away and if you need me I will be there for you," Shawn reassured.

"I want to thank you for all your help, Shawn. You have been wonderful to me and you have always been there for me even though I fought your help all the way," I replied.

"I am glad that I could help you, Katie," he replied.

"I know that Shawn and I appreciate that very much but I can't always depend on you. I need to stand on my own two feet," I answered.

"There is a difference between dependency and guidance. I just want you to know that I will be there with a listening ear and strong arms to hold you when you need the strength to get through. I guess the main thing I want you to know is that you are not alone," Shawn explained.

"Thank you, Shawn. That means so much to me," I replied.

"Now, if you are ready let's go to the hospital and see if you can get some answers," he suggested.

"I guess I am as ready as I will ever be," I answered.

We drove to the hospital but didn't talk much on the way. I had a lot on my mind and Shawn gave me the leeway I needed to sort things through and decide on how I wanted to confront Matthew. I was not sure what Matthew's reaction was going to be and I did not feel like playing mind games with him. I had questions and I deserved to hear the truth without being put through any more of his lies and meaningless promises. Shawn pulled into the parking space and turned off the engine. I sat looking out through the windshield and didn't even notice that the car had stopped. Shawn didn't say anything but just let me sit there thinking. I am not sure how long we had sat there but I finally noticed that we had stopped and I turned to look at Shawn. He was sitting there looking at me. I felt my face blushing.

"I'm sorry. I didn't realize that we were here already," I answered.

"That's okay. I knew that you had a lot on your mind and I was going to let you think things through. I don't have any plans so I could have sat here all day if you needed that extra time before going in," he replied.

"I'm a little nervous about going in and talking to him. So I was trying to rehearse what I was going to say once I got in there and we were face to face," I explained. "I was trying to anticipate his replies to my questions so that I would be ready with a comeback," I added.

"Take all the time you need. There is no rush," Shawn reassured me.

"A part of me wants to go in and get it over with but another part of me wants to run and hide from the truth because in talking about it I feel used and dirty," I admitted.

"Please don't feel that way, Katie. Remember you did nothing wrong. It was not something you wanted or asked for. It was all Matt's doing because of his own insecurity," Shawn said trying to convince me.

"I only wish I felt that way. Maybe unknowingly I did do something to bring it on," I suggested.

"No, it was nothing that you did. Believe me that is something that he is going to try to tell you but don't believe him. You did nothing to bring this attack on," Shawn replied.

"Okay, I guess you are right. I will just have to work through it and not let him get the upper hand by letting his words intimidate me," I answered with more confidence than I really felt.

"Don't let him try to tell you anything different. You know in your heart that it was his decision and he has let you live on all these years without telling you the truth," Shawn reminded me.

"I know you are right and it is time for me to go in and get some answers," I replied in a determined manner as I put my fingers around the door handle and opened the door.

We got out of the car and slowly walked into the hospital. We chatted as we were walking down the corridor to Matt's room. I could feel my heart begin to pound as we got closer to his door. We walked into his room. Mary was sitting by the bed reading a book. Matt had his eyes closed so I wasn't sure if he was sleeping or just resting with his eyes closed. Either way we were finally going to have the talk that I had been waiting for eight long years.

"Hi, Katie. Hi, Dr. Goodson," Mary greeted us.

"Hi, Mary. Is Matt sleeping?" I asked her.

"Hi, Katie honey. I was just resting," Matt responded as he opened his eyes and looked at me smiling.

"Mary would you like to go down to the cafeteria and let Katie and Matthew talk?" Shawn requested.

"Have you made your decision, Katie?" Matt asked excitedly.

"Oh, Katie! That is wonderful! I hope the two of you can mend the past and get back together," Mary cried as she gave me a hug.

"I have decided what I am going to do but I need to talk to Matt alone right now, if you don't mind," I replied, smiling.

"Sure thing. I will go down the hall with Dr. Goodson and we can have a talk. I want to know what is next on Matthew's treatment," Mary replied.

"We will be right down the hall if you need anything, Katie," Shawn called as he walked out the door with Mary.

Mary and Shawn walked half-way down the hallway and sat down on the chairs that were there. Mary asked Shawn about Matthew's treatment and when she would be able to take him home. Shawn was giving her suggestions on the best treatments that Matt could do.

"Katie, have you made your decision darling?" Matt asked.

"I have made a decision but can we talk first?" I asked.

"Sure, anything you want to know. Just ask me, Katie," Matt replied feeling sure of himself and thinking that he already knew what I had decided.

"I just want to clear up a couple of things before I tell you what I have decided," I replied.

"Come sit here by me so that I can give you a hug and tell me what you have decided. We will have a lifetime to talk about whatever it is you wish to discuss," he remarked.

"No, I want to talk first. It is something that I need to know and you are the only one that can tell me," I responded as my anger began to surface at his smug attitude.

"Sure, Katie. What would you like to know? Go ahead and ask me anything you like," he smiled not knowing what I was about to say.

"*Why?*" I asked, looking at him for an answer.

"Why what?" he responded sounding a little confused.

"Why did you feel the need to rape me that night?" I cried out looking directly at him as I spoke.

"What are you talking about?" he answered quickly but I could see that he was uneasy with the question. After an uneasy pause he added, "I don't know what you are talking about."

"Don't try to pull that dumb, confused act with me. I remember what happened and I want to know *why*?" I demanded.

"I didn't rape you Katie, if you remember correctly," he smirked and looked out the window trying to avoid my stare.

"Don't even try to pull that one on me. You know damn well what you did to me that night and soon everyone else will," I promised.

"Are you going to go around telling everyone that you are a slut?" he asked looking right at me now as he spoke.

"How dare you insinuate that I wanted any part of it when you know better," I shot back furiously.

"You may see it your way but I know the truth. I also know that you wanted it so don't even try to cry 'rape' now. Besides, nobody is going to believe you," he replied.

"Oh, they will believe me when I tell them the whole story because you know very well that was not all that had happened back then. Would you like to explain that to me or are you going to say that that didn't happen either?" I asked trying to trick him into divulging what happened that night.

"Sorry, I am not telling you anything," he replied smugly.

"Fine. I will go ask them and I will tell them that you sent me," I said threateningly, hoping that he would mention a name or say something to help me remember.

"Go do whatever you want but it isn't going to do you any good now is it?" he replied.

"Did it make you feel like a man to overpower me that way?" I asked hoping to get him as upset as I was.

"Whatever," he said speaking in the same tone.

"Whatever!" I retorted as my anger mounted.

"Believe what you want. I don't really care," he answered.

"Did you really think that you would get away with it and that I would never remember any of it?" I asked.

My anger was so profound that I wanted to take my fists and beat him. I remembered what Shawn had told me and I took a deep breath, held it in for a few moments and slowly released it. Matt just lay there looking very nonchalant but I could see in his eyes that he was getting very uncomfortable with my line of questions. We kept glaring at each other without saying a word for what seemed to be forever. When he finally spoke it was in a loud angry voice.

"Don't give me that timid, sweet shy routine. You wanted it and I gave you what you wanted," he yelled at me.

"Do you really think the authorities will believe that when the trauma caused me the loss of my memory for eight years?" I cried out in disbelief as I tried to keep my anger down.

"Look at me, Katie," he said laughing. "They aren't going to do anything to me so you are just wasting your time."

"We will see what the attorney says about it. I am sure that he will think of something. At least this time you won't be able to run away from it," I replied.

The remark that I made was like a slap in the face to Matt. When I said it I had not meant it in the way he took it. I was not ridiculing his paralysis but was referring to eight years ago when he had left town and tried to avoid what had happened. His face contorted with rage. I was finally getting him into the same state that I was in that night eight years ago. When he spoke again he yelled loudly. I returned the same smirk that he had given me earlier. *Two can play at this game* I thought and I was not going to let him win this time. He didn't care eight years ago and I didn't care about his anger now. He was only concerned with what would happen to him and not about what he had done. His angry muffled voice could be heard outside in the hallway. It was Mary this time who stood up with concern but Shawn held her arm. Shawn knew what was going on and therefore he was not going to come rushing in unless Matt's voice grew louder.

"It's okay, Mary. They need to talk," Shawn explained.

"Talk yes, but Matthew is not talking. He is very upset about something and I don't think that is good for him right now," Mary answered with concern in her voice.

"Matthew is a lot stronger than you give him credit for," Shawn reassured her.

"Why is he so upset?" she asked.

"Mary, last night Katie remembered a part of what had happened eight years ago when she was traumatized. She needs to talk to Matthew about it," Shawn informed her.

"But I don't understand what that has to do with Matthew," Mary replied.

"I am sure he will fill you in once Katie is done talking to him unless he decides not to talk again," Shawn replied.

Mary sat nervously wringing her fingers waiting for Katie to come out. Shawn calmed her down by reassuring her that it would soon be over and that she could find out from Matthew what was going on. Mary could not understand why Matthew was so upset and yelling. She wondered if Katie had refused to get back together with him and whether that was troubling him.

"Do you think your threats upset me, Katie?" Matt asked.

"Is that how you see it, Matt?" I responded.

"I won't have to worry once I tell them what really happened that night," Matt smirked.

"I wouldn't count on that Matt. You'll see…I will bring charges against you," I promised.

"Do I look concerned about it, Katie?" he asked.

"Well, I guess you are either not concerned or you just don't want to admit it to me. However, with your refusal to tell me I will get satisfaction knowing that you will constantly have to watch out for the police to see if they are coming to get you," I replied with a smile trying not to let my escalating anger show.

"Let's just say it caught me off the hook back then. I am not going to worry about it now, not after all this time. Don't forget the statutes of limitations. You are a few years too late to do anything about it now," he said laughing.

"We will just see about that," I told him. I could feel the tears burning in my eyes and I knew he was not going to tell me what I wanted to know. I just wanted to get out of the room before he could see how much he had hurt me by his words.

"Whatever!" he replied.

"Strangely enough I had once thought that I could not live without you but looking at you now and listening to the words you are saying I wonder how I could have ever loved you," I remarked.

"Once a fool always a fool," he answered and turned his head to look out the window.

I had had enough of his words and lies so I turned and walked to the door. I put my hand on the doorknob but stopped and turned around to face him. He had turned his head and was looking at me as I slowly spoke trying to maintain my composure. I did not want him to know just how upset and angry I was.

"Before I forget I have an answer for you, Matthew," I began. "No, I don't want to go back with you. I could never spend the rest of my life with a cunning, deceitful man like you," I said in a slow controlled voice.

I quickly went through the door before he had had a chance to reply.

Shawn and Mary were still sitting in the chairs but they were no longer talking. Mary looked very concerned as she watched me emerge from the door. They both stood as I walked up to them. Using every ounce of composure that I could muster I stopped and told Mary she could go in now and talk to Matthew. Mary smiled but didn't answer me. She walked past me quickly and went into Matthew's room. I looked at Shawn who smiled reassuringly.

"I need to get out of here now," I told him as I felt myself beginning to shake from the emotional strain that I had just been through.

"The stairway exit is just a few feet away, Katie. Let's take it and we won't run into many people that way," Shawn suggested.

"Okay," I replied.

No other words came to me. My only thought was to get out and away from Matt. Shawn opened the door and I walked through it and descended the flight of stairs. I stopped on the landing, blinded by the tears. Shawn came down the steps and walked around in front of me.

"Katie you are safe and you did a wonderful job of confronting him," Shawn told me.

"He would not answer my question and just like you said he told me that it was my fault and wouldn't tell me what else happened that night," I said choking on my words.

"Don't worry about that right now, Katie. I am with you and he is not going to hurt you anymore," Shawn reassured me.

"Damn him!" I exclaimed.

Shawn took me into his arms and held me close. He put his hand on my head and gently lay my head on his chest. My head was pounding from the stress that I had just experienced from talking to Matt. Shawn held me against him as he spoke to me. His voice was very calm and soothing and I soon stopped trembling.

"Try not to think of his words right now, Katie. He said them to purposely hurt you," Shawn explained.

"But the words still sting and hurt. I am so angry right now," I replied.

"I know you are angry and I want to try something if you trust me and are willing to do as I ask you," Shawn suggested as he held me closer.

"I don't know if I can do it right now," I replied.

"Please look at me, Katie," Shawn requested and I looked up into his eyes.

"You can do this Katie and now is the best time to do it when you are extremely angry and upset," Shawn began. "You trust me don't you, Katie?" he asked after a brief pause.

"Yes, I trust you, Shawn. I will try to do whatever it is you want me to," I responded.

"This will work, Katie. All you have to do is trust me and I can help you," he promised.

For the first time since I was given his business card I looked deep into his eyes and begged, *"Please, help me, Shawn!"*

"I will help you get through this Katie and then you can put the past behind you and begin your life with a fresh start," Shawn pledged as he slowly lowered his face to mine and tenderly kissed me. I felt exhausted but being in Shawn's arms I knew that I had nothing to fear and that nobody could hurt me. I knew that he would protect me and more importantly stand by me and see me through until the end.

We went down the next flight of stairs and walked out the exit door leading to the parking garage. We walked up to Shawn's car and got in. He slowly backed out and he looked at me before putting the car in gear.

"Trust me, Katie, it will work," Shawn said with a sweet smile.

He put the car in gear and we drove down the road. I was uncertain of where he was taking me but I knew that I could trust him and that he genuinely believed he could help me. I didn't care where we went as long as it was far away from Matthew. *What did I have to lose?* I thought to myself as I leaned back in the seat and tried to relax…

Chapter 20

I closed my eyes hoping that the pounding in my head would stop. My thoughts kept racing back and forth between the night of the rape to my confrontation with Matt. How could he be so cruel and heartless? I thought. I could feel the tears stinging my eyes but I told myself that I would not let him get to me again. I would not shed tears for the type of man that he was. I knew now a part of what had happened that night and sooner or later I would remember the rest. What did he mean by 'it got me off the hook'? Was it the rape that he was referring to or was it something that had happened after that? I knew that one or two more people were involved. I just did not know who they were and what really happened other than Hank rescuing me from the woods. I unknowingly shook my head deep in thought trying to sort out what Matt had said to me. I could feel my anger but it was not as strong as it had been when I was talking to Matt.

Until this point Shawn had not said a word to me. He was very quiet as he drove, taking me to some unknown destination. I didn't know where he was taking me or just what his plan was once we got there. He told me he could help me if I trusted him and followed his instructions.

I let out a deep sigh just wanting everything to be over with…to be able to put it completely out of my mind and not think about it ever again. My body had healed from that night but my mind was reeling from the things that I had remembered and I wasn't sure if I wanted to go along with Shawn's new plan. I thought I'd give it a try. If I wasn't comfortable with it I am sure that he would stop and let me wait until I was ready. He had been so patient with me and wanted so much to help me remember that I hated to stop now.

Shawn moved around in the seat and I opened my eyes to see what he was doing. He reached for his cell phone as I closed my eyes again and gently rubbed my right temple to ease the throbbing pain. I heard the beeps as Shawn dialed a number and waited for a response.

"Hi, Hank. It's Shawn and I was wondering if you could do me a favor?" Shawn asked.

"Sure, Shawn. What can I do for you?" Hank replied.

"Katie and I are on our way out. Could you saddle up Lacey for Katie and a horse for me? We are going to go for a ride," Shawn explained.

"When will you be out?" Hank asked.

"We will be there soon," Shawn answered.

"It won't take me long at all to get them ready for you. Is there anything else you need to take with you that I can get ready?" Hank asked.

"A blanket and some water if it isn't too much trouble," Shawn requested.

"Everything will be ready by the time you get here," Hank promised.

"Thanks. We will be there shortly," Shawn replied.

"See you then," Hank responded.

"Okay. Thanks, Hank. Bye," Shawn replied.

"Bye," Hank said as he hung up the phone and stood up to go get the horses ready.

"Are we going for a ride?" I asked in disbelief.

"Yes. I want to take you someplace that you feel safe and comfortable," Shawn replied.

"I'm not sure if I am ready for this," I hesitated.

"This is the best time to do it, Katie. If you want to stop we will but I would like to give it a try right now because you are thinking back on what happened that night and your memory is reliving that night. It will help you go deeper into the past and remember more of what had happened," Shawn explained.

"I am not sure if I want to remember any more of what happened," I replied.

"Would you rather the nightmares and flashbacks continue haunting you?" Shawn queried.

"No. I am tired of the whole episode and want everything to stop and just be able to live my life like any normal person," I answered.

"Trust me, Katie. I am doing this for you and it will help. I know how much you want it to be over with and if you will let me help you it will be over sooner than you think," he promised.

"I wanted to know the truth but after what I already know I am not sure if I want to face anything else," I told him as I turned my head to look outside the window as Shawn continued driving.

"I know how tired you are with all of this but I also know that it will help you and it will soon be over. Katie remember that you are strong and will soon be able to put it behind you and move on with your life," Shawn urged.

"I have spent so many years and countless hours trying to figure out dreams, flashbacks and nightmares that I am tired of going over it again and again in my mind," I admitted.

"We will give it a go and if you want to stop we will but I hope you will give it a chance. I will be there with you so you will have nothing to fear," Shawn reassured me.

I didn't answer him. Instead I continued looking out the window exhausted from my confrontation with Matt and just wanting to go home and forget about everything. I knew that Shawn's persistence would be the only thing that would give me the push that I needed to go through with it.

He slowed the car down and pulled into the driveway leading to

Hank's house. He was going to take that driveway down to the barn. I didn't want to face my parents yet with what I had remembered so I was glad when Shawn took the first driveway. He looked at me and gave me a reassuring smile. I smiled back but did not feel the sincerity in my heart. Shawn pulled up and got out of the car. He walked around the back of the car and came round and opened the door for me. I stepped out of the car and paused. We walked up to the barn just as Hank was coming out to greet us. He gave us a big smile as he walked up to us.

"I have the horses ready and the other things you requested," Hank told us as he shook Shawn's hand.

"Thank you, Hank. I'm sorry I didn't give you much notice," Shawn said apologetically.

"Don't worry about it. I'm just glad that Katie is finally going to give you the opportunity to help her," Hank replied as he looked at me.

"Are you going to rub it in?" I asked sheepishly.

"No, Katie. I am just glad that you are going to let Shawn help you and I will be here for you too if I can be of any help," Hank replied.

"I know you will, Hank. You have always been there for me and I probably wouldn't be standing here now if it wasn't for you," I responded.

"She will do fine, Hank. I think right now is the best time to give it a try," Shawn said confidently.

"Give it a try, Katie," Hank coaxed me, his voice sounding very soothing. He winked at me as he took me in his arms and gave me a reassuring hug.

"Thank you, Hank," I replied as I let the strength of his arms hold me close.

"Are you ready to go, Katie?" Shawn asked.

"If I am not ready, can we call it off?" I teased and laughed.

"No," Shawn chuckled and continued: "How about we just start with a ride and see where it goes from there?"

"It's a beautiful day for a ride," I responded as I looked up at the bright sunny sky.

"It's a gorgeous day and you should take full advantage of it," Hank suggested.

"Okay," I said giggling. "You both are not going to stop until I go, so let's get going and get it over with," I laughed.

"Great idea!" Shawn said excitedly.

We walked over to the horses. Hank clasped his fingers together while I put a foot on his hands and he lifted me up onto Lacey's back. Shawn mounted his horse and was waiting for me to come up to him.

"Have a good ride!" Hank called out to us waving his hand as we turned our horses to go.

We slowly walked the horses through the pasture and on to the meadow. We talked very little at first, which I was glad about. I didn't want to start talking about anything serious right now. I closed my eyes for a moment and let the fragrance of the flowers fill my nostrils. I could pick out the aroma of each of the different flowers that were now in bloom. I opened my eyes again and let them take in the beauty of all the colors that surrounded us. The sight that lay before us was magnificent: the dark blue sky with the backdrop of trees standing with their limbs outstretched as if trying to reach up and touch the sun with the tips of their leaves; the brilliant colored flowers that looked like a rug spread out as far as my eyes could see. A painter would not be able to capture the glorious sight that we were witnessing.

My head was clear and I had no other thoughts except the splendor that I was witnessing. I felt very calm at the moment and decided that even though I did not want to go for the ride I was very glad that Shawn had picked this particular spot. He knew that I would feel safe and would be able to think and remember in an environment that I had spent a lot of time in. Shawn seemed to know me better than I had realized. He was so very different from Matt. *Why would he want to spend all this time working with me to get me to remember?* He was a very kind, caring and compassionate person. I had been taking up a lot of his time and I was beginning to feel very guilty about it. However, I had never asked him for his help or gone to him to talk. I did not want to burden him with my past. Yet Shawn was here again to help me. *But why?* He seemed to have a knack of being there at the right place and time to help me. He is an amazing man…

"Beautiful isn't it?" Shawn was the first to speak and by doing so interrupted my train of thought.

"Yes it is. That is why I love coming out here and going for a ride through the meadow," I replied as I looked at him for the first time since we started our ride.

"I wasn't sure if there was another place you wanted to go so Lacey just brought us to the pond," Shawn said.

"I didn't even notice that the horses had stopped," I said feeling my face blush with embarrassment.

"I didn't want to interrupt your thought processes. You seemed to be so deep in thought and that is what I want you to do right now…think," Shawn told me.

"Actually, I was only thinking about how beautiful it was out here and how you always seem to be at the right place at the right time for me," I replied feeling my face blush again.

"I've always had excellent timing," Shawn replied chuckling.

Shawn dismounted and took the duffle bag from his horse and set it on the ground. He came around and helped me down from Lacey's back. He held his hands on my hips for a few minutes while looking into my eyes. I felt my face blush. After letting go of my hips he grabbed the duffle bag and walked towards the tree. Shawn opened the duffle bag, removed the blanket and spread it out under the tree. I slowly walked around in front of the horses. I watched Shawn as he took his time spreading the blanket and getting out a couple of bottles of chilled water as he set them down on the blanket. While he was doing this the horses began to graze on the grass. My eyes began looking around and before long I was staring at the woods. As I looked at the woods I no longer saw them as a threat. I tried hard to remember something but just as before when I had come to the woods I could only see the woods with the sunlight filtering through them. Nothing else. There was no hint of what had happened that night or what I was running from. I had thought that maybe by coming here and after remembering the rape it might jog my memory again but nothing of that sort had happened so far. I watched as a deer came out of the woods and began to eat. She kept swishing her tail and seemed very nervous as she would quickly nibble at the grass and lift her head again looking around her. She saw me standing there and became very still as she watched what my move was going to be. She twitched her tail a couple of times and then ran off.

"Are you ready to begin, Katie?" Shawn asked. I jumped a little because his voice had startled me.

"I guess as ready as I will ever be," I answered with a sigh.

Shawn gently placed a hand on each of my shoulders and looked deep into my eyes as he spoke to me: "Katie, please don't look at this in a negative way. If you really don't want to do this I will not force you into it but I would really like you to try it now while your anger is strong and the memories are fresh in your mind."

"I know you have your reasons for wanting me to do it now and I should not fight you on it. There has never been a time that you have ever done anything to hurt or harm me and you have always been there for me when I needed you the most," I replied.

"That's the spirit! And if at any time it becomes too overwhelming just let me know and I will stop. But I know that you can do this. Once we are done you will appreciate the fact that it is over and the healing process can begin," Shawn said convincingly.

"Okay. I guess I am ready to begin if you are," I replied.

We walked over to the blanket and we both sat down. Shawn picked up a bottle of water and handed it to me. I smiled and took it from him. I opened the bottle and took a sip. I was beginning to feel nervous and apprehensive about what Shawn wanted me to do. He had not told me what he had planned so I was not sure what I was supposed to do. We just sat there for a few minutes not speaking and my eyes unknowingly went back to the woods. The warm breeze gently blew my hair back from my face which tickled slightly and I unconsciously shivered.

"Would you like to go for a walk in the woods before we begin?" Shawn asked.

I slowly turned my head to look at him and replied, "If that is what you would like to do."

"I would like to sit and talk for a few minutes before I tell you what I would like to do but I see you keep looking towards the woods so I just wondered if you would like to go for a walk," Shawn answered.

"I'm comfortable here," I responded.

"It's very beautiful here. I can understand why you like coming out here to relax," Shawn began.

"I have been coming out here for years. That is why Lacey always comes here without me having to use the reins," I said chuckling.

"Yes. I noticed you were not paying attention while we were riding out here today," Shawn replied.

"I was busy inhaling the aroma of the flowers as well as enjoying the beautiful sunshine and the feel of the warm breeze," I told him as I looked around again. I added with a chuckle, "Besides, Lacey knew where to go."

"Good thing she knew where to go or who knows where we would have ended up?" Shawn replied with a smile.

We sat talking and drinking the water that Hank had sent along with us. I felt comfortable talking to Shawn. He never put any pressure on me and I felt that I could talk to him about anything. He sat with his back leaning against the tree. We had sat talking for over thirty minutes and I had almost forgotten why we had come out here in the first place. Shawn never mentioned the fair, Matthew or the rape. It was amazing the different things that we had in common. We had never really sat down and talked. When we did have a chance to talk it was usually with reference to one of my hair-brained ideas to find out more about my past. He was always patient and never pushed me to do anything that I did not want to do. We always had a good time when we were together and never ran short of things to talk about.

"I would like to begin now Katie, if you are ready," Shawn suggested.

"I am ready but I am not sure what it is that you want me to do," I admitted.

"It is a very simple procedure and the one thing that I need you to do is relax and do what I ask you to do," Shawn explained.

"What if I have trouble and the episode becomes too overwhelming for me?" I asked.

"If at any time you feel uncomfortable and want to stop I will do so. Just relax and remember that I am here and that you are perfectly safe where nobody will harm you," he promised.

"Thanks," I replied gratefully.

"What I need you to do is to lie on your back, put your head on my lap and listen to my voice and the words that I will say to you," Shawn instructed me.

"Is that all I have to do?" I asked.

"That is all you need to do. I will do the rest and also remind you that you are safe throughout the procedure," he replied as he smiled at me.

"And you will stop if I ask you to, right?" I nervously asked him again.

"I will stop the moment you make your request. You don't have to worry, Katie. I am not going to push you any further than you are ready to go," he reassured.

"I will try to give you as much information as I can remember but so far I have not been able to remember much of what had happened that night except for the rape that I remembered last night," I replied.

"Don't worry. You won't have to make much effort to remember if it works like I think it is going to," he answered.

"I will do my best. However, if it has been buried this long and it is something that my mind does not want to handle are you sure that I am going to be able to remember and discuss it freely?" I asked.

"I will slowly go into the events that had happened that night. I am not just going to jump into the past. We will slowly work our way to that," he explained.

"I am ready to begin," I said and slid over towards Shawn. I put my head on his lap as he had requested that I do.

"I am going to take my fingers and rub them across your forehead. As I do this I want you to listen carefully to my voice," Shawn began. "I want you to totally relax your body and clear your mind of any thoughts," Shawn instructed.

"If any questions come to mind do you want me to ask them?" I inquired.

"After we are done you can ask any questions that you have. What I need you to do first is to listen to my voice as I ask you some questions and I also need you to answer the questions," Shawn explained.

"Okay. I think I can do that," I replied.

Shawn began talking to me and as he did so he took his finger and softly and gently ran it across my forehead. He had me close my eyes and instructed me to relax my body completely. As I listened to his soothing, soft-spoken voice I could feel my body relaxing. After my body had relaxed he began to help relax my mind as well. He told me to breathe in deeply through my nose and let the fragrance of the flowers consume my thoughts. As he spoke he continued to gently slide his finger across my forehead. I felt my muscles relax and I thought of nothing but Shawn's calming voice. I felt myself dozing off as Shawn continued talking to me and tenderly stroking my forehead. He paused briefly before continuing. Feeling confident that he had successfully hypnotized me he started the session. Shawn took out a tape-recorder and switched it on. He stated my name and the date. At the moment he was not entirely sure of how the session would unfold and whether he would be able to take me back in time and have me remember. Not knowing how I would react to the events that had happened that night he was unsure if he would have me repress the events or have me remember them when he eventually brought me out of my hypnotic state. He used the tape-recorder so that it could be played back at a later time for me or in court, if needed.

"Katie, I want you to go back and remember for me...but remember you are not alone. I am here with you and nobody is going to hurt you," Shawn spoke softly to me.

"I want you to go back to high school. Do you remember?" Shawn asked.

"Yes, school was over for the day. Matt and I would be going out later that evening. I was with Carol and Mary. We were going shopping so that I could pick up a few things," I told him.

"I want you to go ahead and tell me about your date," Shawn coaxed gently.

"Matt came and picked me up. We were going to Tommy's farewell party," I said smiling.

"How did you feel?" Shawn asked.

"I felt a little awkward because Matt and I had broken up a couple of weeks earlier and I felt that I should have just met him there at the party. We had remained friends and still went places together," I told him.

"You are doing well, Katie," Shawn encouraged me. "Now I want you to think back on where you went after the party," he probed gently.

"I was upset with Matt because he was drinking. I walked into the living room and caught him doing drugs with Scott and Larry," I answered. I could feel my anger mounting and Shawn could hear the anger in the tone of my voice. "Matt had promised me that he would stop doing drugs but since we were not dating anymore he could do as he wished," I added.

"I want you to go ahead now and tell me where you went when you left the party," Shawn urged.

"We were driving along and then stopped at the lake to talk. We sat down on the beach and Matt told me that he had been doing a lot of drugs lately. He said that he was going to stop because he was running into debt buying the drugs. Matt didn't know what he was going to do because he didn't have the money to pay the drug dealer who was pressurizing him to pay his dues." I could feel myself getting very agitated as I spoke.

"You are doing very well, Katie. Do you remember what happened next?" Shawn pressed on.

"Matt wanted to go in the water because it was a very warm night and the water was cool. We stood talking for a bit before he started splashing me and then suddenly grabbed my wrists. I asked him to stop because he was hurting me but he got more aggressive. I turned and tried to get out of the water but he pushed me under water. I was terrified but he wouldn't let go of me so I kicked him and he lost his grip. I turned to run out of the water but he grabbed me again, forcing me under water and holding me down so that I could not escape," I narrated in a high-pitched voice filled with fear.

"Katie, you are safe. I am with you and I am not going to let him hurt you again," Shawn reassured me as he began to gently rub my forehead again.

"I was terrified! Matt had never acted that way before and I just wanted to get away from him," I said as my body began to tremble.

"Take a deep breath, hold it in and slowly exhale," Shawn suggested. "You are doing great, Katie," Shawn reassured me once again.

I did as Shawn had asked me to do. My body was still trembling and it was as though the episode were happening all over again. I could feel the fear that I had felt that night but I also felt something else. I could feel Shawn's fingers tenderly rubbing my forehead as he calmly spoke to me. It helped abate my fears a little as I listened to him speak to me. I could feel my body relaxing a little and my breathing return to its normal pace.

"I was terrified…so very terrified," I replied in a barely audible voice.

"You can do this. Please continue and tell me what happened next," Shawn coaxed.

"I ran but it was hard to do so through the water. I could hear Matt splashing in the water close behind me. I was terrified that he would grab me again but I made it out of the water. I wanted to make a dash for the car, lock myself in it and call for help," I explained.

I was breathing very heavily and had to stop to catch my breath before I could continue.

"Relax, Katie. Breathe in deeply and exhale slowly. Matt is not here and he cannot hurt you. I will keep you safe. You are only thinking about that night. It is not happening to you once again. You are very brave and doing a great job," Shawn encouraged.

Shawn spoke very softly and continued to stroke my forehead. I could feel myself relax and my breathing slow down again. He talked to me for a few moments before urging me to continue.

"I want you to begin at the beach and tell me what happened next," Shawn instructed.

"While running across the beach I suddenly felt Matt grab my thighs. I fell with him landing on top of me. I screamed for him to let go but instead he ripped off my shirt. I struggled frantically as I begged him to stop but he was like an animal. He ripped off my pants and kept telling me that it was what I had wanted. He said that he was going to make me his so that no man would ever want me again and then he…he…raped me." I began to sob uncontrollably as it all came back vividly to me.

"You are fine, Katie. I am with you. Matt is not here and he is not hurting you now. You are safe," Shawn promised as he lifted me and held me in his arms while gently rocking me.

"No, no…please stop!" I screamed still feeling the force of the rape. "Help me, please," I began but my voice trailed off.

After a short pause I continued: "I saw headlights as a car pulled up and I was mortified. It was cruel enough what Matt was doing but to have someone see us was even more horrendous. I begged Matt to stop but he only laughed."

I paused again before continuing: "It was Larry and Scott. After Matt had finally rolled off me I sat up and wrapped my arms around my knees to try and hide my naked body from their drunk and glazed stares. Scott kept passing rude, snide remarks at me while he talked with Matt about the money that he owed him. He reminded Matt that we all were going to go to Larry's house shortly where Matt would need to come up with something to pay off his debt. I grabbed Matt's tee shirt and put it on as they argued. I slowly started to slide backwards trying to get away from them. Once I thought I was at a safe distance I got up to run but I had managed only a few yards before being tackled to the ground…the bright headlights of the car blinding me. I was pinned down and could not move. All I could see were the bright, blinding headlights. I demanded to be let go but they all laughed.

I was forcibly put in a car with Matt and Scott while Larry drove Matt's car. We drove to Larry's house. I had put on my jeans that Matt had thrown me when we got in the car. When the door was opened I tried to run but Matt prevented me by grabbing my wrist. We entered Larry's house where Matt sat in a chair and pulled me down on his lap. Scott and Matt were still arguing about the money. I just wanted to get away but

Matt held on tightly to my wrist. Scott reminded Matt of his one option to clear his debt. All he had to do was agree to it and his debt would be paid in full. Matt looked at Scott, nodded and told him that he agreed." I stopped talking and remained quiet as my mind contemplated the information that I had just revealed. Shawn didn't speak at first. Instead he let me have the time that I needed to mull over what I had just remembered. I remained motionless and Shawn was momentarily concerned that I would not go on. In order for him to help me I had to reveal the rest so he began to urge me to speak again.

"You are doing an excellent job, Katie. Now I want you to remember what happened next. I am with you and you are safe. You are not there...you are here with me and I will not let them hurt you again. I want you to take a deep breath, hold it in and slowly exhale...very good...now do it again and hold it in longer this time. I want you to take a few more deep breaths and then continue telling me what happened," Shawn gently coaxed.

I did as he asked me to do. I felt my body relax again so I slowly resumed speaking.

"Scott walked over to me and grabbed my wrist pulling me off Matt's lap. He was laughing as he dragged me across the floor. I screamed and turned around to look at Matt and ask him what was going on but he just stared at me as though he did not know me. I began struggling against Scott's hold trying to free myself but I couldn't do so. Scott called out to Larry who came over and grabbed me. They started taking me up the stairs. I screamed for Matt to help me but he just sat in the chair as though he didn't hear me. Scott and Larry forced me up the stairs and took me into the bedroom. I fought and screamed for them to let me go but it was to no avail. They were stronger and I was becoming weak from all the struggling. Larry threw me down on the bed. I jumped up and fought them even harder. Scott ripped off my clothes as Larry held me. After they had stripped me I was thrown down on the bed again. Larry then straddled me as he held me down while Scott took out a piece of twine and tied it around my wrists and ankles to restrain me to the bed." I paused again, my mind not wanting to go on. My heart was pounding in terror and I had trouble breathing. Even though I was terrified, my rage was the more dominant at the moment. I knew that I couldn't stop now and that I had to go on and remember…remember all of it, once and for all.

"Katie, you can do this. Listen to my voice and remember that you are safe. You are not alone and you are only remembering the past. It is not really happening to you now," Shawn spoke very softly and his voice was both soothing and reassuring.

Shawn was livid and could not believe what he was hearing. He was filled with contempt at Matt for what he had done but knew that he could not let his voice betray his true feelings. He began to rub my forehead gently as he began to speak to me again. From the details I was giving him Shawn now understood my dreams, nightmares and flashbacks. He had me relax and waited as I calmed down before asking me to continue.

"Larry was still straddling my rib cage and I was afraid that my ribs were going to be crushed by his weight. Scott kept walking around the bed making comments about the things that he wanted to do to me and what he in turn wanted me to do." I was gradually revealing the events of that fateful night and as I spoke my voice was terrified and high-pitched. My body began to tremble. Shawn put his arm around me and held me close. I felt petrified as though I were back in the restraints. I took a deep breath and continued: "I screamed for them to let me go. That only seemed to make Scott more excited. His taunts increased as he kept touching my body while I sought desperately to pull away, repulsed at the thought of his hands on my skin. Scott kept telling me that I had better cooperate with them and do what I was told or he would make it harder on me. When I refused, he reached in the nightstand and pulled out a pistol. *No, no, no* I kept thinking and…and…" I could feel the tears stinging my eyes and could not go on. My body was trembling violently…my head was pounding and I was breathing so hard that I thought my lungs would collapse. I screamed as Shawn hugged me firmly and slowly sat me on his lap as he gently rocked me.

"Katie, it is me. I am Shawn and I am holding you tightly in my arms. Scott is not going to hurt you anymore. You are safe. I am with you. You are only thinking about that night. It is not happening to you right now," Shawn said as he held and comforted me.

Shawn had not foreseen the horrendous events that had happened that night and was not quite prepared for what he was hearing. He had considered stopping the session and releasing me from my hypnotic state. He wanted me to continue revealing what had happened but was not sure whether I would be able to handle it. Shawn then decided to use a different approach that would be easier on me and at the same time allow me to continue without actually reliving the terror of the past events.

"Katie, I want you to relax and listen to my voice. You are safe in my arms. I am holding you close to me where you will not be harmed. I want you to take deep breaths and listen to my voice. You have nothing to worry about. You are sitting on my lap and my arms are holding you close to me where you are safe," Shawn reassured me as he waited for me to slowly calm down and relax again. He continued speaking after he felt my body relax and go limp against his own.

"Katie, what I want you to do for me is to tell me what is happening. I want you to explain to me what is happening but you will not see yourself as the person there. You are going to narrate events as though you are describing a movie that you are watching. You are safe in my arms and we will face this together. You will only tell me what you are seeing. Now please continue and tell me what you are seeing," Shawn gently coaxed.

"She is being taunted by them and they are running their fingers and hands all over her body. She feels anger, anguish and tremendous humiliation because she cannot understand why they are doing this to her. Scott is getting very angry with her because she will not do what he wants her to do. He runs his fingers through her hair and grabs a handful and tells her to cooperate but she pulls her head away from his grip. He takes the gun and presses the tip into her throat as he stares at her with glazed eyes. Scott slowly runs the gun down between her breasts where he stops again and presses the tip deep into her skin. She can feel her heart pounding against the tip. He continues running the tip of the pistol down to her belly button as he glares at her. She tells him that she will never go along with what he wants. Scott then takes her hand in his and starts to toy with her little finger. Scott asks her again if she is going to cooperate and she tells him she never will. He smiles as he looks at her and then suddenly snaps her little finger sideways, breaking it." My voice remained calm and distanced. I did not feel the pain that I had felt that night.

"You are doing great, Katie. Please describe what happens next," Shawn gently coaxed.

"Scott is very angry. He picks up the gun again and this time he flips the chamber making it spin around. When it stops he holds the gun to her temple and asks her again if she is going to cooperate. She tells him that she would rather die. He pulls the trigger but there is only a click. Larry is frightened because of the way Scott is behaving and he tells Scott to just leave her alone and let her go. Scott points the pistol at Larry and laughs. He again spins the chamber and holds the pistol to her head. *Click*...the hammer hits the empty chamber...the noise resounding throughout the room. Scott would ask again and each time Katie's answer *"NO"* got louder. Larry suggested that they have a drink while they wait and maybe she would get in the mood while she had time to think it over. When they left the room Katie fought and struggled against the restraints but could not get free. She heard them in the other room laughing as she heard cans being opened. Katie just lay there staring at the ceiling...praying for her escape. After about half an hour she heard the sound of approaching footsteps and hoped that it was Matt coming to her rescue. She closed her eyes, unable to face anyone who might come through the door." I could see it happening in my mind's eye but I did not feel the pain or terror that I had felt all those years ago. It did not seem to bother me as much watching it happen instead of reliving those experiences. I took a breath and continued.

"She looked at the doorway...it was Larry. She began to struggle against the restraints. The twine was cutting into her skin and she was bleeding. Larry was speaking to her but she did not hear him because she was screaming and begging him to let her go without hurting her anymore. Larry sits on the bed but she struggles unsuccessfully to free herself. He covers her mouth with his hand so that she could not scream. Larry tells her to relax but she did not know what he was going to do. He straddles her hips and holds her arms down so that she cannot fight against the restraints. When he speaks this time she listens. He tells her that Scott has passed out and that he was going to untie her but she needed to stop screaming or she would wake him up. Larry tells her that he was sorry as he had no idea that Scott was going to do those things to her. He was afraid of what Scott was going to do but would not allow him to do anything else to me. As Larry cut the twine he kept looking at the door because Scott still had the pistol and he wasn't sure what he would do with it. Katie was finally untied. Larry threw her a tee shirt and jeans which she quickly put on. He offered to drive her home or any place that she wanted to go but she was terrified and just wanted to get away where she would be safe. *Run, run as fast as you can…get out…get out now before he gets you* was all that she could think of. Katie runs for the bedroom door, down the stairs and towards the main door. As she reaches the main door Scott opens his eyes and glares at her in hatred. She opens the door quickly and runs out without closing it behind her. *Run, run…and just don't stop.* That was the only thing going through her mind. She ran as fast as she could down the road and into the woods."

As I was speaking I could see myself running but I did not relive the terror that I had experienced that night. I could see it all happening but it was as though I were watching it on a movie screen with no feelings going through my body. I took another breath and continued.

"There is a bad thunderstorm and the lightning is flashing across the sky. The brightness hurts her eyes. The trees seem to come alive and the thorns were cutting her bare feet but she did not feel the pain. She keeps running and yelling for help. She continues running until she recognizes the woods. She then screams for help as she runs out of the woods. She yells for Hank. She can see a horse and tries to run towards it. Suddenly everything goes blank as she falls to the ground." I finished speaking and just lay back exhausted in Shawn's arms. Shawn held me in his arms for a few moments to let me absorb everything that I had just revealed.

"Okay, Katie. You have done an excellent job. Now I want you to listen to my voice. At the count of three I am going to snap my fingers and you are going to awaken. You will remember everything that you have told me but you will not feel the terror of that night. You will not feel the embarrassment or guilt about what had happened to you. One…two…three…Shawn snapped his fingers after which I slowly blinked my eyes and opened them.

"Are you okay, Katie?" Shawn asked.

"Yes, I am okay. I now remember everything that happened that night and who it was that did it to me but more importantly I know the *why*," I replied.

"You didn't do anything wrong, Katie. You did not want or entice the events that happened," Shawn reassured me.

"I know now that I didn't but what really hurt me was the fact that Matt intended to use me as a pawn to erase his drug debt. How could he be that callous after everything that we had been through together? How could he tell me that he loved me and offer me to his friends as payment? What about all the promises that we had made to each other? Did they mean nothing to him? Were they just meaningless words to him?" I wondered.

I looked deep into Shawn's eyes hoping to see the answers there but I knew in my heart that I had never really known the type of man that Matt was and what he was capable of doing until that night…that fateful night that had changed me forever…

Chapter 21

Shawn held me tightly in his arms as I cried. He didn't speak…only cuddled me tenderly and slowly rocked me. I now knew everything that had happened that night but I didn't feel the relief that I had hoped to feel. I only felt mentally and physically drained. The questions that I had once had were now finally answered. My tears had dried and I let out a heavy sigh. I was just glad that it was finally over and as promised Shawn had stood by me and helped me to get through it.

I don't know how long we sat there and I wasn't sure if I ever wanted to leave. I felt safe and comfortable in Shawn's arms but I knew that I had to go and face Matt once again to let him know that I knew everything that had happened that night. I would also have to visit a lawyer to have charges filed against all three of them. *But was it already too late?* I wondered. Matt had brought to my attention that he was now paralyzed and that they would not be able to do much with him. Scott and Larry, on the other hand, were not above the law and they would have to face whatever charges I brought against them. I now understood why Scott had always given me such a hard time. *Did they figure the trauma from that night would lead me to forget the past forever? Was there a statute of limitations on charges that I could file?* I guess I would find out soon enough.

I moved slightly, opened my eyes and lifted my face to look at Shawn. He smiled at me but still did not speak. I felt sure that he had questions but I was not sure if I was ready to answer them or not. I smiled back and I could feel myself blush as I did so. I could tell by the sun that it was late afternoon and that we needed to head back. Shawn was being very patient and didn't push me to talk or to leave. He was such a wonderful man. I was the first to speak because I felt that I had taken up enough of his time.

"I am sorry, Shawn. Would you like me to move? You must be very sore from sitting for so long in the same position," I remarked.

"I am fine and you can take all the time that you need," he replied.

"Actually, I am very comfortable," I chuckled.

"Is there anything that you would like to discuss?" he asked.

"I guess I know everything that happened now but I don't feel the relief that I had hoped I would feel. Instead I just feel numb and detached in a way," I explained. "I had thought that once I knew everything I would be able to get on with my life but I hadn't planned on it being such a horrendous attack," I added.

"It is a lot to take in. It will take some time for it all to sink in and for you to get through the anger," Shawn responded.

"The anger that I thought would be there is not for some strange reason," I answered.

"The anger will come but it will also pass. You will get through it and be able to move on with your life without the void that you once had. As each day passes the pain and anger will lessen and soon it will be only a faded memory that you and you alone can bring back. It won't be in flashbacks, dreams or nightmares any longer," Shawn explained.

"I am just not sure where to go from here," I replied.

"What would you like to see happen from this?" he asked.

"I do want to see Matt and let him know that I remember everything but he will once again blame you for dragging it out of me," I admitted.

"Does he blame me?" Shawn asked chuckling.

"Yes. He said that if you had not kept bugging me to remember the past it never would have surfaced," I responded.

"What part did he feel the nightmares, dreams and flashbacks played in your remembering?" Shawn asked laughing.

"I don't think he was concerned about me remembering until he found out that you had tried talking to me about it," I replied.

"Well, you were beginning to remember on your own and I didn't play any part in the things that you were starting to remember," Shawn remarked.

"You know what..." I began but hesitated a moment before continuing: "I am not going to waste my time going back to see Matt."

"Good for you!" Shawn exclaimed.

"The last time I had tried talking to him he put the blame on me. I don't want to listen to any more of his lies and I am not interested in what excuses he tries to give me," I replied.

"Oh Katie, I am so proud of you," Shawn responded smiling at me. He added, "You did a wonderful job and you got through it."

"I feel better and I am glad that it is over. Well, I still want to file charges against all of them for what they did to me," I replied.

"When we get back to the barn you can use the phone to call and set up an appointment with your lawyer. I will gladly go with you if you would like me to," he offered.

"Are you sure you don't mind?" I asked.

"I have been with you up to this point so I will gladly see you through until the end," Shawn replied.

"I seem to be taking up so much of your time, Shawn. Are you sure you don't mind helping me?" I asked.

"I had told you Katie that I would see you through this and I meant it. I don't mind the time that we spend together," Shawn admitted blushing.

"I enjoy the time that we spend together too but I hope that I am not becoming a burden to you," I replied sheepishly.

"Don't give it another thought, Katie. If I didn't want to be with you I would not keep offering to be here," Shawn confessed.

"I would like to talk to Hank when we get back. There are a few things after he found me that I would like to ask him about," I informed Shawn.

"Yes, he can fill in the last of what happened and you will know everything that happened down to the last detail. I taped our session so we will have that for your lawyer and it can also be used in court if need be," Shawn explained.

"I am surprised. I thought I would feel much worse about it when I found out but for some reason it doesn't seem to bother me like I thought it would," I admitted.

"There is a reason for that. I will now tell you why but first I want to tell you that I did it for your own good," Shawn responded.

"What did you do?" I asked.

"When I had you hypnotized I repressed the feeling part of your memory," he answered.

"What does that mean?" I queried.

"It means that you will be able to remember everything that happened but you won't feel the fear, terror and all the other emotions that you felt that night," he replied.

"Is that why it doesn't seem to bother me now when I think about what happened?" I asked.

"Yes, that is the reason that you are able to think and talk about it so freely without any feelings regarding what happened. I thought it was the best way to handle it from your reaction when you first started telling me what happened and I hope you don't mind," he responded.

"No, I am glad you told me. I thought there was something wrong with me because I didn't seem to care about what had happened," I admitted.

"You will eventually begin to feel the emotions so that you can go through them and get past the event but for right now, for your own well-being, I did it this way for you," Shawn explained.

"I know now what happened and I remember the fear and terror I was feeling back then. I think this is better for me but will it one day come back all at once and will I then feel all the emotions that I had felt that night?" I asked.

"You will remember but the feelings won't be as severe and you will be able to put them into perspective," Shawn replied.

"If you are ready, I think I would like to go back and talk to Hank so that I can find out the rest of what he knows," I stated.

"I think that is a good idea," Shawn remarked.

I was still lying in Shawn's arms. I rose so that he could stand up. I gathered the water bottles and put them in the duffle bag. While Shawn was folding the blanket to put in the bag I went and fetched the horses. I brought them over to where Shawn was standing. He threw the duffle bag up on the horse's back and walked over to me. He cupped his fingers together and lifted me up on to Lacey's back. Shawn mounted his horse and we turned them around and headed back towards the barn. We walked the horses for a short while before deciding to run. It felt good having the wind blowing against me. I finally felt some relief having discovered the events that had happened that night. I now had a better understanding of why Matt had left town and why Scott had taken every opportunity to antagonize me. He had tried to keep my mind focused on the present to prevent me from remembering what he had done to me all those years ago. Now it was time to attend to the unfinished business that needed to be taken care of.

Hank was in the office when we rode back. He walked over and helped me down from my horse as Shawn dismounted his own. Hank then gave me a long comforting hug while Shawn placed the horses in the coral. Shawn then brought in the duffle bag, took out the bottles and threw them in the trash. After zipping the bag he placed it back in the corner where it had been before.

"How did it go?" Hank asked cautiously as he looked at me.

"I remembered everything that had happened and now I have some questions that I hope you will be able to answer for me," I responded.

"Sure, I will try to tell you everything that I am aware of," Hank replied.

Hank sat down at the desk while Shawn and I pulled up chairs. I narrated to Hank what had happened that night. He sat and listened very intently and didn't interrupt me while I spoke. Shawn stood up and got each of us another bottle of water before quietly resuming his seat. As I narrated the events that had happened that night Hank became very agitated and began to fidget in his chair. His face became very red with anger. I felt no emotions as I narrated the events to Hank. A couple of times tears welled up in Hank's eyes but he quickly brushed them aside. He listened to me and didn't say a word until I had finished. I could see the anger and contempt in his eyes. I told him that everything was okay and that now the law would take over. I was going to file charges against all of them for what they had done. At this point Shawn replaced the tape in the tape recorder so that he could continue taping my conversation with Hank to obtain the complete story.

"Katie, I am so sorry for what they did to you," Hank commiserated when I completed my story.

"I am okay Hank but I need some information now. I know from what you have told me before that you can provide details of what happened when you found me," I responded.

"What would you like to know, Katie?" Hank asked.

"First, I would like to know for sure if you were in the woods that night," I began.

"Yes, it was me," Hank replied. He added, "Lacey was very agitated that night and kept pawing the floor and banging against the door of her stall. You weren't here and I knew that something was bothering her, so I took her out for a run to see if I could get her to settle down."

"Did she head to the woods herself or did you ride her that way?" I asked.

"She headed to the woods for some odd reason but the closer we got to the woods the clearer I could see a figure running out," Hank replied.

"When you got to me did you bring me here to the office?" I asked.

"I brought you to the office and put Lacey back in the barn. When I saw your condition I carried you up to the house. Your Mom was awake and she told me to carry you up the stairs and put you in bed," Hank replied.

"What happened then?" I asked.

"Your wrists, feet and ankles were all cut up and bleeding. Your Mom washed your cuts and I put antiseptic on them so that they would heal," Hank explained.

"What happened after that because I don't seem to remember anything that happened that night?" I inquired.

"You were unconscious. Your Mom called the doctor who came and checked you over. He told us that you had been raped but we had no idea what had caused the rest of your injuries with your wrists, ankles and feet," Hank answered.

"Why don't I remember anything?" I asked.

"When you awoke you were in a frenzied state. The doctor was still here so he quickly gave you medication to calm you down. You were in terrible shock so the doctor instructed us not to refer to any of the events when you had awakened. He told us to keep quiet about it and instead let you talk about the incident when you were ready to speak about it," Hank explained. "That is why when you had asked me for details I had refrained from saying anything. The doctor had warned that it could cause you more trauma if we tried to talk to you about it. So he suggested that we wait until you would remember and tell us in your own time."

"How long did it take for me to come out of shock?" I asked.

"You were heavily sedated for two months. When they stopped the medicine you did not remember anything that had happened to you. Your cuts and bruises had healed but you became timid and shy and very reclusive. You spent a lot of time alone or out at the pond," Hank replied.

"Okay, thanks, Hank. I guess those are the only questions that I have and I appreciate you answering them," I responded.

"Katie, I would have told you back then when it had happened but the doctor warned us against saying anything to you about it," Hank said apologetically.

"The doctor was right in doing what he did and telling you that because if she would have been forced to remember it at that time she might not have been able to handle it," Shawn interjected.

"I am glad that it is finally over and that I now remember that part of my past," I said with a sigh.

"What are you going to do now?" Hank asked.

"I am going to use your phone and call my lawyer to set up an appointment. I want to press charges against my attackers," I replied.

Shawn stopped the tape recorder, removed the cassette and placed it carefully in his pocket. I went over to the desk, picked up the phone and dialed. Meanwhile, Hank went over and sat down beside Shawn. The two of them talked as I made an appointment with the lawyer over the phone. I hung up and informed them that I had an appointment for the following morning at 9:00am. I stood up and stretched. I was tired and ready to go. Shawn must have known what I felt because he asked me if I was ready to leave.

"Thank you Hank for filling in the blank spaces and I will let you know how it goes tomorrow," I informed him.

Hank gave me another hug before accompanying Shawn and me to the car. We got in as Shawn and Hank continued to speak to each other. Presently, Shawn started up the car, backed up and drove off. Hank waved goodbye to us as we drove off.

Shawn took me to my house because my car was still at the hospital. He offered to pick me up in the morning to take me to the lawyer's office and I accepted his kind offer.

"I want to thank you again, Shawn, for all your help," I said gratefully.

"I am glad that I could help, Katie," he replied.

"See you in the morning," I said as I opened the car door.

"If you need anything just give me a call," Shawn reminded me.

"I should be fine until morning," I replied as I got out of the car.

Shawn waited for me to get indoors before he pulled out of the driveway and drove down the road. I heated some water for a cup of tea and sat down with my thoughts. After I had drunk my tea I went into the bedroom and lay on the bed to rest but the exhaustion of the day caught up with me and I quickly fell asleep.

The ringing of the phone awoke me. I reached over to the nightstand and picked up the receiver. It was Shawn calling to tell me that he would be over at 8:00am to get me. He said he also had something to show me. I told him that I would be ready and we hung up. I sat up in bed and thought about the past…the past that I now knew about. I knew what I had to do and my only wish was that it was not too late to do something about it. I got up and made some tea before going in to take my shower and get dressed. After I was ready I went in and poured myself some more tea. I then lit a candle on the table and sat down to put on my shoes. Slowly sipping my tea I watched the candle flame dance. I tried to make my mind a blank. I would be going over it all again later this morning and I did not want to think about it now. I had been haunted with enough flashbacks to last a lifetime. At the present time I merely wanted to sit and enjoy the peace and tranquility that I felt. I had been through a mixture of emotions during the past twenty-four hours and now was the time to just sit and relax before I was forced to once again relive and discuss my painful past. Only this time I would know everything and parts would not be blocked from my memory.

I heard Shawn drive up. I rose and went to the door to let him in. I walked back to the cupboard, grabbed him a cup and poured him some tea. We went to the table and sat down.

"I want to show you something, Katie," Shawn told me as he reached in his briefcase and pulled out some papers.

"What do you have there?" I asked as I looked at the papers.

"When I got home last night I went through and transcribed from the tapes what you had narrated yesterday," he said. "I also recorded another tape for the lawyer so that he could listen to the emotions that you went through as you were remembering," Shawn explained.

"Does that mean that I will not have to tell him everything in detail?" I queried.

"Yes, that means you will only have to provide some basic information and he will be able to listen to the tape and get the rest of it," Shawn replied.

"Oh that would be wonderful not having to go over the whole thing again!" I exclaimed in relief.

"I did it so that it would prevent you from having to go over it. So all you need to do is to discuss with the lawyer the charges to be filed," Shawn stated.

"Thank you for taking the time to do this for me," I replied in gratitude.

"I told you that I would try and help you as much as I could. It didn't take long and it will save so much time," he answered.

"I am glad that most of it is over now. Soon it will all be over and I won't have to talk about it any more," I admitted.

"It is time to go. Are you ready?" Shawn asked.

"As ready as I will ever be," I chuckled.

"You can do this, Katie," Shawn reassured me.

"Thank you so much for all your help. I just hope that someday I will be able to do something to repay you for your kindness," I remarked.

"Hmmm, I will think of something," Shawn said with a smile.

We drove to the lawyer's office and pulled up into a parking spot right in front of the door. I sat and looked at the door for a moment before turning to look at Shawn. He was sitting there looking at me but did not speak. He gave me an encouraging smile that I returned but I did not feel as confident as he did. He took my hand in his and slowly brought it up to his lips as he tenderly kissed the back of it.

"You can do this, Katie. I am going to be with you," Shawn reassured me.

"I know and believe me I am very glad that you are here for me. I only wish I had promptly acted upon the advice of everyone and come to see you all those months ago. Had I done that this would all have been over with by now," I said sheepishly.

"You are doing it now and that is all that counts. It will be over with soon," Shawn promised.

"I hope so. I am ready to get past it and not have to worry about it any more," I admitted.

Shawn put my hand back down and opened the door as I got out. We walked into the lawyer's office together. As he opened the office door for me I took a deep breath. I knew that it was time now for those to pay for what they had done to me.

The lawyer opened the door to his office and escorted us inside. After the usual introductions, handshakes, and small talk we got down to the business at hand. I narrated my story of the events that had happened that night. He sat with his hands folded in front of him as he listened intently. He didn't interrupt but waited until I had finished.

After I was done Shawn spoke and explained to him how he had recorded the session and transcribed it so that the lawyer would be able to go over it once we had left. Shawn took out the folder with the transcribed pages and the tapes. The lawyer thanked him for being so efficient and said that the tapes would come in handy for court. He went over some of the charges that were going to be filed and said that after he had listened to the tape he would be able to give us more information. The lawyer did tell me that even though some of the charges were past the time limit he would still be able to file them because of the trauma caused and the loss of my memory that had occurred. He explained that due to my memory loss I wasn't in a position to file charges until I had remembered events clearly.

I finally felt an overwhelming sense of relief that I had not felt earlier. I realized that I would finally be able to get past it by facing and triumphing over my attackers…something that for a long time I thought was impossible. We all stood up. My lawyer promised that he would get in touch within the next couple of days to let me know what was going to happen next. He told me not to worry about it as it would soon be over and that I would be able to get on with my life. We walked out of the office and got in the car. Shawn looked at me and smiled.

"Well, I guess this is the beginning of the end," I remarked.

"It is the beginning, Katie. It is the beginning of a new 'you' and the opportunity for a new start once the past is buried," Shawn replied.

"I'm eager to start afresh," I answered.

"Well, let's go!" Shawn exclaimed.

"Where are we going?" I asked chuckling.

"To have some fun!" Shawn laughed as he backed out and we sped off…

Chapter 22

The next two months went by very quickly. The charges had been filed and we would be going to court soon.

Hank and Mom would be testifying to what they had witnessed that night and the doctor had also said that he would come in and give them the medical information on my behalf. Shawn and I had been spending a lot of time together. He continued counseling me. On sunny days we would ride the horses out to the pond where I felt the most comfortable. He stood by me through the whole process just like he had promised he would. The closer it got to the court date the more nervous I felt about going to court. Scott and Larry had been arrested and were awaiting trial. Matt was still going through physical therapy but he would also be facing charges at the same time as the other two. Matt had called me the day that the police had gone to the hospital to formally charge him. He was very upset with me and tried to tell me how I was ruining his life. He asked me how I could do such a thing. Shawn was at the house and when he heard me say Matt's name he walked over and put the receiver down.

"Don't listen to him, Katie. He is only trying to get you to drop the charges," Shawn explained.

"He was telling me that I was trying to ruin his life. Can you imagine the gall of him to say that after everything that he has done to me?" I asked irritably.

"If he calls again just hang up on him. Don't bother listening to anything that he has to say," Shawn advised.

"He has nothing to say that I want to hear," I told Shawn. "He had his chance all these years but would not talk about it so I don't really want to hear what he has to say now," I added.

"Good. I am glad that you are strong enough now to listen to your own feelings. It will be over soon and you won't have to think about it any more," Shawn said confidently.

"But will it be that easy to forget?" I asked.

"In time you will not think about it. The only reason that it is bothering you now is because the trial is tomorrow," he informed me.

"I know and it doesn't help having Scott's and Larry's families calling me and harassing me either," I confessed.

"I didn't know they were calling you," Shawn replied.

"Not so much now, but right after they were arrested they had called quite often," I admitted.

"You should have told me about it. I would have taken care of it for you sooner," Shawn remarked.

"You have done so much for me already. I feel guilty coming to you for help every time," I replied.

"I told you Katie…I am here for you and that if there is anything I can do for you to let me know. I think this falls under that category," Shawn said with a scowl.

"I can't depend on you for everything. There are some things that I need to do on my own. Besides, once the trial is over we will be getting back to our lives and going our separate ways," I replied.

"I guess that is a bridge that we will cross when we get to it," Shawn said with a smile.

The trial was to begin in the morning. It was going to be a trial by judge. Scott, Larry and Matt did not want the case to go in front of a jury. They wanted to keep it quiet and because of the circumstances it was closed to the public. Shawn had stayed late to keep me company and try to keep my mind off the trial. It was getting late but I didn't want him to leave. I felt so much better when we were together but I also had to be realistic and remember that he was only helping me and that there would never be anything between us. It was nice knowing that he was such a good friend and that we would always be there for each other. Shawn stood up to leave and I walked him to the door.

"I want you to get to bed early. Sleep well and don't let the thought of going to court upset you," Shawn instructed firmly.

"I will try. I know I will feel a lot better once this is over with so that I can get on with my life," I answered.

"You will be fine tomorrow, Katie. Remember that I will be right there with you and you don't have to worry about anything," he replied.

"Thank you, Shawn. You don't realize how good your support makes me feel. I want you to know that I appreciate everything that you have done for me," I replied thankfully.

"Anytime, Katie. Haven't I always told you that I am only a phone call away," Shawn reminded me as he took my hand and gently pulled me to him. He took me into his arms and held me close. I wrapped my arms around his neck and pressed my body against his. I did not want this moment to end but I knew that he had to go and I also knew that he had no real feelings for me. Shawn cupped my chin with his hand and slowly lifted my face up to his. He paused for a moment before kissing me softly on my lips. After he kissed me he looked into my eyes. I wanted so much to ask him to stay but I knew that he would only stay because I had asked him to, so I said nothing. He told me that he would be there in the morning at 8:00am. With that Shawn turned and walked to his car. He climbed in, started it up and waved goodbye as I watched him leave.

The ringing of the phone startled me. I let it ring. I was afraid that it might be Matt or a family member of Scott's or Larry's and I was not in the mood to talk to any of them. *Why couldn't they understand that I was the victim here and it was not my doing that got them into this?* They were the ones that had decided to do what they had done that night. It would be over soon and I would not have to worry about any of them calling me any more. The phone disconnected and then rang again. This time I walked over and picked it up.

"Hello," I ventured hesitantly.

"Hello, Katie. How are you?" Hank asked.

"Hi, Hank. I am doing fine; a little nervous, but otherwise I'm okay," I answered, relieved to hear his voice.

"It will be over soon," Hank reassured me. "Is Shawn still there?" he asked.

"No, he has just left and I think that I am going to go to bed," I replied.

"I think that is a good idea. You have a big day ahead of you tomorrow. I was just calling to see if you needed anything or if you wanted to talk. Everything is going to be fine," Hank reassured me.

"I know. I guess I just have a case of the jitters," I said chuckling.

"Is Shawn coming over in the morning?" Hank inquired.

"Yes, he is coming at 8:00am," I replied.

"He is a very good man, Katie. I am glad that you finally opened up to him," Hank remarked.

"I know Hank and I am glad that he stuck it out even though I fought talking to him all that time," I admitted.

"He cares a lot for you, Katie," Hank noted.

"Hank, he cares about everybody, not just me," I replied.

"You can see it in his eyes, Katie," Hank confided.

"I think you are just seeing things," I chuckled.

"Well, I will let you get to bed now. I will see you in the morning at court," Hank said.

"Thanks for calling, Hank...and thanks for being there for me," I replied.

"I will always be there for you, Katie. I hope you know that," Hank reminded me.

"Yes, I know that and I hope you know how much it means to me," I responded.

"Scoot to bed now sweetie and sleep well. I love you and I will see you in the morning," Hank ended.

"Good night, Hank. See you in the morning," I replied.

I hung up the phone and turned off the ringer so that if the phone rang it would take a message. I didn't feel like talking to anyone else tonight. I simply wanted to relax so that I would be fresh and ready for court. I went over to the sink, filled the tea kettle and put it on the stove. The tea would relax me and help me sleep better. Shawn had given me some herbal tea to help me relax and this was definitely a time that I needed it. I turned off the lights and only had the candles lit around the room to exude a soft, relaxing atmosphere. I grabbed my tea and went over to sit on the sofa. I wrapped the quilt around myself and sipped my tea slowly. Setting the tea cup down I snuggled inside the quilt and closed my eyes as the fragrance of the candles filled my nostrils. I slowly drank some more tea. I could feel my body gradually relaxing as I began to feel very drowsy. I got up and blew out all the candles—except the one on the coffee table in front of the sofa—and snuggled back into the quilt. I felt warm, cozy and very relaxed. I had thought about going into the bedroom but changed my mind. I wanted to stay on the sofa. I could still smell Shawn's cologne in the room and it made me feel safe. I wanted to stay in the comfort zone that I was in. I thought about calling Shawn so that I could hear his voice again but decided against it. I had to get used to the idea of not depending on him as much as I had been. He was only helping me get through a tough time and soon he too would be a part of my past and would not be spending the time with me that he had been. The one thing that I was very grateful about was that I didn't have to worry about the flashbacks, nightmares or dreams any more. I had not had any since the day that Shawn had hypnotized me. I was very relaxed and I soon fell into a deep restful sleep.

I awoke early the next morning. I rose, folded the quilt and went in to boil some water for tea. I walked to the bathroom to fill the tub. The tea kettle began to whistle so I went to the kitchen to turn off the burner. I felt relaxed and was not anxious as I had thought I would be. My lawyer told me that I had nothing to worry about and that he had all the evidence that he needed for a conviction. I stepped into the tub and let the water envelope me. I felt a great sense of relief that it would soon be over. I was ready to face my past and get through the events that had happened that night so that I could put them behind me. Shawn had been working with me and discussing the things that had happened. I had successfully worked my way through the anger. I had never really believed that I would ever remember what had happened that night. Shawn had kept telling me to trust him, believe in him and do the things that he had asked me to so that he could help me get through it. Now in just a few hours it would be over once and for all.

I got out of the tub, dried off and went into the bedroom to get dressed. I still had time before Shawn was due to arrive. I sat down on the bed and let my thoughts drift back to the past. I could not help feeling sorry for Matt. I thought about how insecure he must have been back when it had happened. I thought I knew him so well but now I realized otherwise. He was a facade that I had fallen in love with and I did not see him for what he really was. I also knew that in time I would have to forgive them all in order to finally get past it and be able to move on with my life. *Time heals all pain* was a phrase that Mom had kept reminding me of. I had heard it countless times while growing up but until the present it had never really meant anything to me. Over the last couple of months Shawn had not only helped me remember what had happened that night but had also helped me get through the fear and terror of it all. He had helped me to face my traumatic past with dignity. Shawn had continued to stand by me as I learned to accept the things that I had gone through. His constant reassurance was that it was not my fault and that it was not something that I had wanted. He had stood by me and had held me as I cried because I didn't think I could do it. He infused a renewed confidence in myself and had promised that he was only a phone call away. He told me that I needed to go through the next two phases on my own. He would be there for me if I needed him though. Shawn explained that the next phase dealt with forgiveness. I would need to forgive my wrongdoers in order to be able to go on to the final phase which would be to forget and move on with my life. At first when he suggested it I thought that he had gone completely mad but I realized that he was right. *What kind of person would I be if I could not forgive and forget a wrongful act or deed?* That was not how I was raised and it also went against what I myself believed in. Turn the other cheek, do unto others as you would have them do unto you…forgive and forget…*But how could I look any of my attackers in the eye and actually forgive them for what they had done to me?* I wondered.

I got dressed and went in to clean up the bathroom. A final look in the mirror and I was ready to face the day. I went to the kitchen to heat some water for tea. Shawn would be here soon and we could have a cup of tea before leaving for court. I heard Shawn's car drive in, I heard him turn off the engine and shut the door. I walked over to the door to unlock it and let him in.

"Good Morning," Shawn said with a smile as he walked past me into the kitchen.

"Good Morning," I replied. Looking at the clock I added, "You are always on time. You are the most punctual person that I know."

"I always like to be on time," he chuckled.

"I could set my clock by your punctuality," I replied with a giggle.

"I tried calling earlier but there was no answer," Shawn told me with some concern in his voice.

"I'm sorry. Hank had called last night after you had left. He wanted to see if I was okay. After I had hung up I turned off the ringer so that I would not be disturbed," I explained.

"Nobody else called?" he asked.

"No, only Hank," I reassured him.

"Okay, I am glad to hear that," he replied with a smile.

"I just heated some water. Would you like some tea before we go?" I asked.

"Yes, please. That sounds wonderful," he replied.

Shawn went over to the table and sat down. I went to the stove and filled the cups, then walked over to the table and sat Shawn's cup down in front of him.

"Thank you," Shawn responded.

"You're welcome," I replied.

"I hope you are not nervous about going to court," he began.

"I am not nervous at all for once," I admitted.

"Good! You have nothing to be nervous about and it will be over soon. The lawyer has already told you that it was an 'open and shut case', so it will not take long," Shawn reminded me.

"I will just be glad when it is over and I can get on with other things," I admitted.

"After this is over I would like to invite you to a nice home-cooked 'congratulatory/glad-it's-over' meal at my house," Shawn offered.

"When would you like to do that?" I asked.

"How about tonight? It will be an ending to your painful past today and this will be a befitting way to celebrate it with a delicious meal. And just think...you won't have to clean up after," he said chuckling.

"I would like that very much. It will give me a chance to unwind from court and a way for me to forget about it," I replied.

"Good. I was hoping that you would agree. I have everything at the house so all I have to do is cook it when we get back from court," Shawn said as he smiled at me.

"This doesn't sound like a spur of the moment plan to me," I chuckled.

"No it isn't. I have been planning it now for a few weeks," he replied and blushed.

We finished our tea and decided that it was time to go to the courthouse. We were to meet with the lawyer before going into court. We went out and got in the car. Shawn started it up and we drove off. We chatted on the way to the courthouse. I was still not feeling nervous but was only a little anxious to get it over with.

We arrived at the courthouse. From the car I had spotted Matt's parents walking in the doorway. I looked at Shawn and gave him a weak smile. He teasingly waved his index finger at me in a mock 'no' and I laughed. We got out of the car and walked up the steps to enter the building. Before we had walked in the door I paused to look at Shawn and smile. I then sighed heavily before we walked in together. The lawyer was waiting for us. We went into one of the rooms so that he could talk to us. He confirmed what he had told me before about it being an easy, simple case and for me not to worry about anything. He then told me that it was time to go into the courtroom. Suddenly unsure of myself, I looked at Shawn who sensed my hesitation. He stood up and took my hand and we walked into the courtroom together…

Chapter 23

We walked into the courtroom and went and sat down at the table with my lawyer. I had already requested that Shawn be allowed to sit up there with me. Hank, Mom and Dad were sitting on the bench behind us and smiled at me reassuringly when I saw them. I looked at the seats on the other side of the room. Scott's and Larry's parents were sitting there, talking quietly between themselves. The door opened and Matt's parents entered. They seated themselves next to the other parents. Mary sat down and glared at me when she saw that I was looking in their direction. This was the first time that I had seen her since filing the police report. She had called me a few times and while crying had told me how I was making Matt's life a living hell. She said that I had no right to put him through any more pain after all that he had gone through. She urged me to drop all the charges because the incident had happened several years ago and I had got through unscathed. I could not believe that she could be so cold-hearted. I had slammed the receiver down and had not spoken to her since. I looked back at my family who gave me encouraging smiles.

We were waiting for the guys to be brought in. Meanwhile, Shawn and my lawyer—Amos—were chatting to each other. I was beginning to feel a little nervous and poured a glass of water from the pitcher that was on the table.

The side door finally opened and the other three lawyers came walking in and sat down at the table that was alongside ours. Right behind them Scott and Larry (with two police officers on either side of them) were escorted in. Scott was in handcuffs and also had leg irons around his ankles to prevent him from running. Larry walked in behind him and was only in handcuffs. They both had to walk in front of me in order to get to their lawyer's table. Scott walked very slowly as he passed by and he glared at me but did not utter a word. Larry walked by without looking at me. I held my breath as they walked past not knowing what to expect from them. Shawn softly placed his hand over mine and smiled reassuringly as I looked at him. We waited a few more minutes and the door opened again. This time it was Matt being pushed in by an officer. He, too, was handcuffed and did not look at me as he went past. Finally, everyone was there and we could begin.

The bailiff walked in and ordered everyone to rise. We all stood up as the judge walked in and went to his chair to sit down. We were then told to seat ourselves. The bailiff announced our case and handed the judge the folders containing the paperwork. The judge opened the folder and looked it over before speaking.

"I have read the papers, listened to the tape and read the transcripts from it," the judge declared. He continued, "If there is any additional paperwork I need to have it brought to me."

"Nothing new your honor," Amos responded.

"We have nothing new your honor," responded the other two lawyers.

"If both sides are ready to proceed please begin," Judge Hall announced.

"Your Honor, we have submitted to the court all the necessary papers, a tape and transcript regarding the night in question and we have three witnesses that I would like to bring in at this time," Amos told the judge.

"Please call your first witness, Mr. Randolph," Judge Hall summoned.

"I would like to call Hank Roberts to the stand, Your Honor," Amos responded.

Hank got up and walked over to the witness stand and was sworn in before sitting down. Amos questioned Hank on the events that had happened that night. Once he felt he had covered everything he announced that he had no more questions. The other lawyers waited until he had finished speaking. Scott's lawyer was the first to stand to counter with his line of questions. Hank answered all his questions. Matt's lawyer was the next to cross-examine Hank who did a great job at keeping his anger down when Matt's lawyer tried to get him to admit that it was partially my fault. After Matt's lawyer finished with his cross-examination Larry's lawyer took over and began to ask his questions. Hank was on the witness stand for almost two hours answering all of their questions. The lawyer finally announced that he was done with the witness and Judge Hall told Hank that he could step down. Hank walked back to his seat and smiled at me as he passed by.

Amos stood again and announced, "Your Honor, I would like to call Marge Stevens to the stand."

Mom stood up and walked over to the witness stand and was sworn in. She sat down and waited for the questions to begin. Amos started and asked her all the questions that he had about that fateful night. She answered all his questions and sometimes added a little too much unsolicited information that caused the other lawyers to object and remind the judge that she was only to answer the question. Amos asked her questions about what had happened once I was brought into the house and about the doctor's arrival. With that Amos was done with his questions and announced to the judge that he had no more questions for Mom. The other lawyers then went in the same order starting with Scott's lawyer, followed by Matt's and finishing with Larry's lawyer. Each of the lawyers tried their best to find something wrong with Mom's testimony but could not. She repeated the same story that she had told before. Finally, Larry's lawyer announced that he was done cross-examining her and Judge Hall told her that she could step down from the witness stand. It was late morning and the judge called for an hour's recess so that we could go and eat. The prisoners were taken to a locked room to be kept until court resumed after lunch. Amos came with us and we all went to a nearby restaurant to eat: the same restaurant that Shawn, Carol and I had gone to the day we were switching over the files for Shawn when he transferred.

As we ate we discussed the proceedings that had occurred so far. Amos told us that after the doctor's testimony he also had Officer Kendall that would be going on the stand to give evidence that the police had confiscated from both Scott's and Larry's homes. Amos did not go into detail about the evidence but said that once it was presented the case would be over and the other lawyers would not be able to do much once the officer was done testifying.

We finished our meal and had a cup of tea as we relaxed a little before returning to the court. Amos answered all the questions that we had and explained to us the things that we were not sure of. After tea we returned to the courthouse. As we pulled in we could see Matt's and Scott's parents standing at the entrance. When they saw us pull up they turned and walked into the building. We got out of the car and walked into the building. Taking our seats we once again waited for the prisoners to be brought in. Once they were brought in the courtroom the bailiff walked in and summoned everyone to stand. We stood as the judge walked in and sat down after which we were instructed to take our seats.

Amos announced to the judge that he would like to call Dr. Richard Fellows to the stand who was sworn in before taking his seat. Amos began his line of questioning and Judge Hall listened intently to what the doctor said. Amos told the judge that he was done with the witness and walked over and sat back down at our table. Again the other lawyers went in the same order as before—starting with Scott's lawyer followed by Matt's lawyer and concluding with Larry's. They tried to find discrepancies and a way to discredit his testimony but were not successful. In defeat, each announced to the judge that he had no more questions for the witness. The judge ordered Dr. Fellows to step down from the witness stand.

Amos stood once again and announced to the judge that he had one final witness (Officer Kendall) that he would like to call to the stand.

Officer Kendall stood and walked down to the witness stand where he was sworn in before sitting down. Before beginning his questioning Amos announced to the judge that he would like to submit into evidence items found when a search of Scott's and Larry's homes was conducted. Amos walked over to the evidence table and handed the judge two ledgers, a bag of drug paraphernalia, money and guns that were confiscated at the time of the search. Amos began his questions and none of the lawyers objected or interrupted. As Amos questioned Officer Kendall the judge looked over the ledger and the quotations that were in it. He paid close attention to the notation made the night it happened. Next to Matt's name was the notation '*paid in full*'. Amos asked his last question and announced to the judge that he had no more questions for Officer Kendall.

Judge Hall told the other lawyers that they could begin their cross-examination of Officer Kendall. They quietly talked among themselves briefly. Scott's lawyer stood and began his cross-examination but he only had a few questions for Officer Kendall. The other two lawyers did not have any questions and with that they announced to the judge that they too rested their cases.

Judge Hall announced a thirty-minute recess. We all stood as he left the room. We went out in the corridor to stand and talk. The prisoners were taken back into the locked room to wait.

"When the judge comes back he will ask if you have anything to say to any of the defendants before the sentencing and I will tell him that you have nothing to say to them," Amos informed me.

"I wish to speak," I requested as everyone turned to look at me.

"Are you sure you want to speak?" Amos asked.

"Yes. There is something that I need to say to each of them and now it would be easier for me instead of having to go to each of them individually," I explained.

"I will let the judge know so that you can be given the opportunity to say what you wish," Amos replied.

"Do you want to talk to them?" Shawn was the next to ask.

"Yes, I need to say something to each of them and I don't want to have to go to them later. I will do it here and it will be done with," I answered.

"If you are sure that is what you want to do; but I can't imagine what you have to say to any of them," Shawn replied.

The bailiff came to inform us that Judge Hall was ready to return with his decision and that he would follow that with the sentencing. We all walked in and took our seats and waited for the prisoners to once again be brought in. Once everyone was back in, the bailiff told us to stand. We all stood again until the judge seated himself. After that we sat back down in our seats and waited.

"I have carefully gone over the evidence and in the context of that I have made my decision. Before I pronounce that decision, Miss Stevens, is there anything you would like to say?" Judge Hall asked as he waited for my reply.

I stood and answered, "Yes, Your Honor. I would like to say something, if I may."

"Please come up to the podium and when you are ready, please speak," Judge Hall replied.

I slowly walked over to the podium and wondered if I was doing the right thing. I stood a few minutes looking at the prisoners before speaking. I knew in my heart that that was something that I needed to do if I was to completely get past the episode. I cleared my throat and addressed the prisoners.

"After all these years I never thought it possible that I would ever remember what had happened that night, much less stand before you and address you. These past few months I have been doing a lot of soul-searching. In order for me to come to terms with what happened and move on with my life I know that I need to speak to each of you," I began. I took a deep breath and continued, "Matthew, I shall address you first. After everything we had been through, all the promises that we made to each other and the undying love you professed I find it very hard to believe that you could do such a thing to me. I realize now how insecure you were back then and how even though you could speak of love you know nothing at all about it. You were only concerned about your own self gratification and did not care how you got it or who you hurt along the way. You showed me just how uncaring and callous you could be that night. The fact that we were no longer dating never even entered your mind...you had already made your decision and no matter how much I begged, you went on and brutally raped me. Then, if that wasn't bad enough, you took me to a place I did not know and offered me to your friends to pay off a drug debt like I was some worthless possession even though I screamed and begged for your help. Looking back now I find it so hard to believe that I could have ever loved you. I see you now for the real person that you are and I feel nothing for you except sadness and sorrow. I could spend the rest of my life with the deep hatred that I felt when I remembered what had happened but I am not that kind of person. I will not allow myself to be lowered to your level. So I want you to know that after everything you have done I forgive you and hope that one day you will be able to find it in your own heart to forgive yourself."

I looked at Shawn and he gave me a reassuring smile knowing that I was going to use this opportunity to get through the next phase of my recovery. I could tell by looking at him that he now understood why I needed to speak to them. I wasn't sure if I would be able to do it so that is why I did not mention the reason behind it. I poured a glass of water and took a few sips before proceeding.

"I will address Scott next," I slowly began and took a deep breath hoping that I could make it through. "You are the worst of my demons from the past because you not only did despicable things to me but also felt no remorse for what you did and took great pleasure in the torture that you subjected me through. Even after you broke my finger and despite my continued refusal to go along with your plan you took out your gun thinking that I would change my mind."

I paused because I began to shake with refreshed memories and the anger that I could feel rising inside me. I glanced at Shawn and he slowly nodded, giving me the strength that I needed to go on. I took another deep breath and continued, "Instead of going against my morals I told you to go ahead and kill me because I would rather have died than be treated that way and have to endure the things that you were going to do to me. I lay there praying for a quick end as you spun the chamber and held the gun to my temple as you laughed. Your actions that night were deplorable and it shows the kind of sick and twisted man that you are. You were not happy with torturing me that night and letting it go but spent all these years harassing me and every chance you got you said and did things to purposely hurt me. I could never understand why until I remembered everything that had happened that night. So as I think about the kind of person you are and the sickness and hate you harbor within yourself I can search my own soul and find it in my heart to forgive you."

Scott looked at me for a minute and laughed at me for the words I had just spoken to him.

I took another drink of water and stepped back from the podium. I needed a moment to collect myself before I could go on. This time I did not look at Shawn but continued looking at Scott who only glared at me in return. I stepped back up to the podium thinking that I now only had one more to go. I urged myself to go on. I knew it would soon be over and that I would not have to face the demons again.

"Larry, I left you for last for a reason. Even though you started out as one of the willing participants that night I know that if it was not for you I would probably not be standing here today. I also know that part of what you did was because you worked for Scott and felt obligated to do what he told you to do. But the fact remains that you did risk your own safety to release me and did offer to take me away. I chose my own way of escape after you apologized to me telling me that you had no idea regarding the events that had happened that night. I also know that you took a chance because you did not know what Scott's reaction was going to be for letting me go. You showed me the true remorse that you were feeling and I can, without hesitation, find it in my heart to forgive you." I spoke slowly and sighed softly to myself as I finished.

"May I please speak Your Honor?" Larry asked the judge as he stood up.

"Normally I would not have allowed it but nothing about this case is normal so go ahead and say what you have to say," Judge Hall responded.

"Katie, I just want you to know that I am very sorry about what happened that night and I am glad that I could get you out before something worse happened," Larry said as he looked directly at me. He then added, "I appreciate the fact that you can forgive me. I just hope that someday I can find it in my own heart to forgive myself."

Larry sat back down and I turned to the judge and told him that I had nothing else to say. I walked back to my seat and sat down. Shawn gave me a reassuring smile and I was glad that I could get through it and would not have to face any of them again.

The judge spoke next asking if there was anyone else that wanted to speak but the courtroom was silent. The judge then had each of the accused prisoners stand up as he read their sentences. He started with Matt first. Larry wheeled Matt towards the front of the lawyer's table so that he could face the judge. The judge read the verdict and Mary let out a gasp as it was read. Matt received ten years in prison for the combined charges of kidnapping, life endangerment and rape. Scott was asked to stand and the judge read the verdict for him. He received forty years for assault, kidnapping, attempted rape and attempted murder. Scott's mother began to sob uncontrollably as the verdict was read. Larry was asked to stand to receive his sentence. Larry stood up and the judge read the verdict. He received two years. He was given leniency because he did not partake in the rape, assault or kidnapping and did help me to escape but the judge was harsh on him for not coming forward on his own to resolve the matter sooner and added probation and eighty hours of community service.

I breathed a sigh of relief once all the verdicts were read and was satisfied with what they had all received. Shawn reached over and gently touched my hand. I turned to look at him and he smiled. The judge went on to talk about appeals, how to apply for them and when the deadline was. When he had finished speaking the bailiff stepped forward and asked us to rise. We all stood and the judge stood up and walked into his chambers. When the judge closed the door the police officers walked over to the prisoners to escort them to the facility that they were to report to.

Amos shook my hand and congratulated me on the verdicts. As I turned to look at Hank, Mom and Dad I could see that Mary was still crying. I felt sad for her not because of the sentence that Matt had just received but for her having to sit and listen to everything that had happened that night and for her believing that Matt had gone through enough and should not have to endure any more. I had never thought of her as a shallow person prior to that.

Mom, Dad and Hank all gave me a hug and told me how proud they were that I could find it in my heart to forgive them. Amos bid us all farewell; he had other clients he needed to see, so he had to return to his office. We walked out of the courtroom doors and I stopped when I reached the top step. I took in a deep breath and exhaled slowly before descending the steps.

"Would you two like to come out for some tea and cake?" Mom asked us.

"Katie has a date tonight and can't make it," Shawn replied.

"A date, Katie?" Mom asked surprised. "Who is this mystery man?"

"Her date is with me," Shawn interjected before I could speak.

"That is wonderful, Katie!" Mom exclaimed.

"Oh Mom, it is not a real date!" I replied as I felt my face grow hot with embarrassment.

"You two go on and have a great time," Mom told us.

"It is about time," Hank said smiling.

"I will call you in the morning," Mom smiled as she turned and walked over to their car.

"You didn't need to tell her that we were going on a date, Shawn. I will never hear the end of it," I told him laughing.

We walked over to the car, got in and Shawn drove off. It was almost 6:00pm. Shawn had everything that he needed at his house, so he drove home without stopping. Once we pulled in the driveway and Shawn turned the car off he turned to look at me and gave me a warm smile. We got out and walked up to his house. Shawn asked me to sit at the kitchen table while he made me some tea. Once it was done, Shawn grabbed his cup, came over and sat down at the table with me.

"Things went very well today, Katie. How do you feel about the verdicts?" he asked.

"I am fine with what they all got, especially Larry, and I am sure that sounds ridiculous after everything that happened," I replied.

"No, actually I can understand your feelings about it," Shawn admitted.

"I mean I realize he was there but I honestly think that if it had not been for him I would not be here today," I explained.

"Chances are that you are correct with that assumption. He took a chance but wanted you safe and was willing to take the risk," Shawn replied.

"I could not believe Mary's reaction." I paused and continued: "I mean she was there and heard everything that Matt did to me and how he traded me like some worthless trinket."

"All she was thinking about was her son…her baby…her world and she did not comprehend the cowardly act he committed," Shawn emphasized.

"I guess you're right and who knows maybe in time she will learn to accept that it was something that I had to do for my own sanity. After all, eight years was a long time for me to try to learn and come to terms with it," I confessed.

"You are on the right track and from now on things will only get better," Shawn promised.

We continued chatting while Shawn got up and started getting things ready. He had bought steaks for our meal and we went out on the back patio while he grilled them. I sat and watched the birds as he grilled. I was in a serene mood because I knew that the worst was now behind me. I knew now that I could face the past and move on with renewed confidence. Shawn announced that the steaks were 'grilled to perfection' and we went back into the house to eat. We talked about the events at court and Shawn convinced me that it would not be long before the memories would fade. We finished our meal and Shawn handed me a cup of tea while he cleaned up. He reminded me that he had promised he was going to do everything. When he was done he escorted me into the living room and I sat down on the sofa while he started a fire. He had candles lit around the room and it felt very cozy. I sat watching the flames of the fire while Shawn had excused himself and left the room. He came back a few minutes later with a bottle of champagne and two glasses.

"I want to make a toast," Shawn announced.

"Ok, what are we celebrating?" I giggled.

"Well, I am not sure yet if we are celebrating," Shawn laughed and set the bottle and glasses down on the coffee table.

"I am listening but you better hurry. You know I don't stay quiet for very long," I chuckled.

"First, Katie I want to tell you how proud I am of you for facing your demons and also for what you did in court today. I know it took a lot of courage to forgive them for what they had done to you," Shawn remarked.

"You had told me that it was something that one day I would have to do and I knew you were right. I have done everything so far that you have asked me to do. I figured today would be the best time to do it so that I would not have to worry about facing them again one day," I replied.

"It will take some time for the fresh memories to fade but just remember that they will and you will not be troubled by them anymore. So now you have gone through the different stages you need to for healing except for the last one," Shawn told me.

"And here I thought that I had completed every step that I needed to finally be done with this," I said chuckling.

"No, Katie. The last stage is probably the most complicated stage that you will have to face but I am sure that you can do it," Shawn replied.

"You are being serious aren't you?" I asked.

"I am being very serious, Katie. Would you like to know what it is?" he asked looking very solemn.

"I'm not sure if I am ready to face anything else," I admitted.

"You don't have to worry, Katie. I will be there with you and you will never be alone," he assured me.

"That is something that I do have to acknowledge. You stood by me through all of this even though I fought you so hard at the beginning," I replied.

"Katie, over the months that we have been together I have got to know you and I admire so many things about you. But now it is over and you no longer need me as your counselor," Shawn explained.

"So do you want to toast to our ending?" I asked.

"I told you Katie that you have one more stage that you need to go through but it is a stage that only you can control," Shawn replied.

"I guess you are right. I have been very demanding and I am sure that you are just as happy as I am about it being over," I replied.

"Aren't you going to ask me what the next stage is?" Shawn asked in astonishment.

"What is the last stage that I have to go through?" I asked wearily.

"The last stage that you have to go through Katie is moving forward and that is why I must ask you something," Shawn requested.

"What would you like to know?" I asked.

"I am not sure in which direction you are thinking of going," Shawn began as he got down on one knee in front of the sofa and continued, "but I am hoping that you will go in the same direction as I will."

"Shawn..." I began speaking but he put his finger to my lips and stopped me.

He reached in his pocket and asked, "I cannot imagine my life without you in it and I would be very honored if you would be my wife...Katie will you marry me?"

He extended his hand and he had a small box that he was holding. He opened the box to reveal a beautiful diamond wedding ring. I was speechless. I thought that he was telling me that we were done and that we would be going our separate ways; instead he surprised me and asked me to be his wife. I just looked at him but did not speak at first. I could feel the tears welling up in my eyes as I looked at him.

"From the way you were talking I thought that you were telling me that I was ready to go and face the world alone," I mumbled.

"You will never be alone, Katie. I want to spend every day of the rest of my life with you," he said as he picked my hand up, brought it to his lips and gently kissed the back of my hand.

"Is this really what you want?" I asked.

"I cannot imagine one day without you. I wanted to wait until today after court when you were ready to start your new beginning. I could not think of a better beginning than starting a new life together." Shawn paused a moment before adding, "So tell me, Katie, shall I break the seal of the champagne…I still need your answer."

"I would be both honored and privileged to be your wife, Shawn. Yes, I will marry you," I replied.

Shawn leaned forward and ran his fingers through my hair as he gently pulled me forward and kissed me softly. He took the engagement ring out of the box and slid it on my finger. Shawn popped the cork of the champagne bottle and poured us each a glass. He handed me a glass and held his glass up to mine.

"To the best beginning we could have. I pledge you a lifetime of love, understanding, caring and compassion. I love you, Katie Stevens," Shawn announced and we gently clicked our glasses together and drank to our future.

"I love you too Dr. Shawn Goodson and I couldn't think of a better beginning," I replied.

We finished our glasses and Shawn set them down on the table. He sat back on the sofa and put his arm around me pulling me close to him. I cuddled up close to him and we started making plans for our future.

We talked for over an hour after which Shawn stood up. He reached down to take my hand and gently pulled me up. He put his arms around my waist and held me close. I wrapped my arms around his neck and pressed my body against his. He reached down and in one swift move picked me up in his arms and walked into the bedroom where he gently laid me down on the bed.

"Just what do you think you are doing Dr. Goodson?" I asked teasingly.

"We are going to start making our own happy memories, Katie Stevens. Right here, right now," Shawn said laughing.

Shawn carefully lay down beside me as he held me in his arms. I looked deeply into his eyes while he gently lowered his face and brushed his lips to mine.

"A new beginning that you will never forget…I love you, Katie," he whispered softly…

Printed in the United States
51487LVS00006B/46-84